A poodle leaped from the darkness between two pallets. I rolled to the side, putting a bullet into it and ruining a leather recliner. Liam always wanted one of those. Another poodle snarled and yipped as it leaped for my ankle. I sidestepped and kicked as it landed, dodging razor-sharp teeth and snapping its spine.

The crippled poodle shrieked in pain and feral rage, desperate to tear our throats out. Ari walked over and crushed its bouffant head under her heel. "I don't get why these things are so dangerous."

Another bout of screaming killed my reply. I took off at a run toward the sound with Ari close behind. At the edge of the loading bay stood a fort of recliners, turned on their sides to make a wall. A few desperate workers were making a last stand inside, armed with broken recliner levers.

A hedge's worth of poodles ringed the fort, occasionally leaping at the edges. Then I realized that in the corner, a strike team of poodles had begun to gnaw their way through the back of a recliner.

"There're too many to take on. Get out of here," I whispered to Ari. The thump of an approaching helicopter made the loading doors shake as Grimm's mercenaries circled, but these folks wouldn't last another two minutes.

Every single poodle in the flock turned as one to look at us, growling like a hundred miniature wood chippers. I shuddered clean down to my toes and glanced back at Ari, who held a silver whistle in her lips. "What did you do?"

She spat out the whistle. "Called for help."

I fired six rounds, killing a couple of poodles with each, while beside me Ari's Desert Eagle roared, plowing through a row of them with every bullet, but still they came for us, a fluffy white cloud of doom.

Armageddon Rules

J. C. NELSON

ACE BOOKS, NEW YORK

THE BERKLEY PUBLISHING GROUP
Published by the Penguin Group
Penguin Group (USA) LLC
375 Hudson Street, New York, New York 10014

USA • Canada • UK • Ireland • Australia • New Zealand • India • South Africa • China

penguin.com

A Penguin Random House Company

ARMAGEDDON RULES

An Ace Book / published by arrangement with the author

Ace Books are published by The Berkley Publishing Group.
ACE and the "A" design are trademarks of Penguin Group (USA) LLC.

For information, address: The Berkley Publishing Group,
a division of Penguin Group (USA) LLC,
375 Hudson Street, New York, New York 10014.

ISBN: 978-0-425-27290-9

PUBLISHING HISTORY
Ace mass-market edition / March 2015

PRINTED IN THE UNITED STATES OF AMERICA

10 9 8 7 6 5 4 3 2 1

Cover art by Tony Mauro.
Cover design by Danielle Abbiate.
Interior text design by Kelly Lipovich.

For Abigail, who will one day make a wonderful lawyer

Acknowledgments

While the other pages of this book will be largely dedicated to the story (with a few exceptions for the title, dedication, and an about-the-author page people don't generally read), this page is the space for me to thank the people who helped me shape this book.

First off, to my friends at critiquecircle.com—Laurel, Leslie, John, Jim, and Andy—thank you as always. Your insights and gentle reminders helped me sharpen the story.

My agent, Pam van Hylckama Vlieg, remains awesome. Not that there was ever any question as to that.

Leis Pederson, my editor, gave me critical eyes and feedback where I needed them the most. As always, it's a better story thanks to her.

My family gave me patience when I spent long nights reading and writing, and early mornings editing. More than anything, their gift of time to pursue this story made this book a possibility.

And, as always, thank you to the readers. What began with *Free Agent* continues now. My modern-day fairy tale . . .

One

IN MY DEFENSE, I didn't mean to start the apocalypse. It wasn't just my personal aversion to oblivion; I had a clear financial motive: The end of the world is bad for business.

Speaking of business, that Monday began the same way almost every Monday had for the past three weeks: with a plague. Last week it was frogs.

I rolled into the office at about nine forty-five, and, as usual, the Agency was pure chaos. Rosa—our receptionist—was opening a fresh container of Taser darts and we'd only been open for forty-five minutes.

"Miss Locks, you gotta help." A man in an orange jumpsuit with "Corrections Department" stamped in block letters down the side grabbed my shoulder as I walked past, spinning me around. "I gotta get me a wish."

Strike one: escaping from a garbage-pickup crew. Strike two: putting grubby fingers on my brand-new top. Strike three: calling me "Miss" instead of "Ms." Locks. Far as I was concerned, Miss Locks left the building the day I turned eighteen and hadn't been seen around here since.

"I'll make a few calls." To the police, if possible. To the morgue, if necessary.

He nodded gratefully and sat down on a bench.

I slipped through the "Staff Only" door, made it to the kitchen, and almost poured a cup of coffee before the screaming started. One should never face disaster without caffeine. So I got my coffee and headed back out to the lobby, strolling through the door to see exactly what we'd been struck with.

Rats ran everywhere. They scrabbled on the walls, gnawed on the furniture, and covered the floor like a shag carpet from 1973. In the middle of the lobby stood a teenage girl, six feet tall, rail thin with platinum blonde hair. Her clothes hung in tatters from bony white arms, and red blotches surrounded each of her many, many piercings. Her extravagant collection of tattoos spoke of poor impulse control and even worse decision-making skills. She looked up at me with baleful eyes. "Please. I need help."

I glanced around the room. The couple nearest the door held a cage with an amphibian I could only loosely call a frog. In the corner waited a group of kobolds. Roughly five feet tall, and with humanoid features except for their scaled skin and forked tongues, these Germanic lizard-men came every Monday to demand and be refused Grimm's help in forming a professional soccer team. That left the homeless guy by the door, a man we called Payday George. He still hadn't figured out this wasn't a payday-loan joint, probably because most days I felt sorry for him and just gave him a twenty. I opened the staff door and waved to the girl. "Come on."

Rosa glowered at me, mumbling curses in Spanish. She hated when I picked clients, and if she had her way, we'd take them one at a time, from number one to number six hundred in exactly that order. Even if fifty-three was a starving fungal giant and sixty-two was a samurai with a serious shiitake addiction. To her credit, Rosa kept her mouth shut. One does not argue with the boss.

We headed down the hall to a conference room, me, the girl, and enough rats to supply a hot dog factory running three shifts, seven days a week. I took a seat on one side of the table, she took a seat on the other, and the rats took seats everywhere. Flicking one off my knee, I began the interview. "So what exactly do you want me to do for you?"

Tears smudged the sludge of makeup she wore, and she waved her arms around. "Duh. Isn't it obvious?"

Absolutely. Obvious that she needed help. Figuring out which kind first, that was the hard part. I walked over and ran my fingers through her tangled, crispy hair, took a good look at all sixteen rings in her ear and the tasteful depiction on her shoulder of what was either Bob Dylan in "Man in the Long Black Coat" or a velociraptor playing acoustic guitar. "We can help. First, let's take out those piercings. I'll get you some alcohol and a prescription for some antibiotics. Your hair is crunchy from whatever you used to bleach it, and the tattoos are going to take years to remove."

A rat jumped into my coffee and poked its head out. The girl stared as I fished it out by the tail, set it on the table, and handed it a sugar cube.

"What about the rats?"

I took another sip of coffee, which tasted Parisian with a hint of rat. "What about them?"

"The only thing I need is for you to get rid of the rats." She shivered.

I pushed a box of tissues across to her. "What's your name?"

She scratched out a tissue and wiped her eyes. The tissue caught in her makeup and left shreds clinging to her cheeks. "Elizabeth. I like Beth."

I brushed the rats out of the way and sat down on the table, my mind already made up. "Well, Beth, I have good news and bad news. Good news is I can help with the hair, the piercings, and I've got a lady in my wardrobe department who can teach you how to use less than a pound of cosmetics a day. The bad news, I'm not going to do a thing about the rats."

She stared at me as her brain tried to process what I said. I leaned across and patted her hand. "You look hungry." Truth was, she could have starred in one of those commercials for starving kids. I used to watch TV, and every once in a while I'd see commercials where you could mail order a kid for fifty dollars a month. Always wanted to try, but given my track record with pets, I'd signed an agreement with animal control saying that anything more than a goldfish required daily home visitation. Anyway, Beth reminded me of those kids.

"I can't eat. Every time I try to eat, the rats take it from me."

I should've asked about her credit. I should've asked Rosa if her application was complete, but one look at her said I'd found my charity case for the week. "I'm going to order a pizza or two. I'll have one of my employees bring a barrel of garbage up from the Dumpster to distract your companions. I need you to sit tight for a bit, okay?"

She nodded and put her head down on the table. Walking out the door, on the way to my office, I made a mental note to have the table cleaned, or burned, or both.

MY OFFICE, INCIDENTALLY, was almost the biggest in the Agency. That was only right, since for most things, most days, I was in charge. I was a partner, the junior partner, but definitely not a silent one. On my desk sat a vase with yellow flowers. Daffodils, my favorite. The attached card read, *"La fille du majordome est mon amant.* Love, Liam." His attempts to learn French from the foreign film festival went about as well as my Spanish-by-mail lessons, because the butler's daughter was not his lover. My dad was an accountant, and Liam and I didn't even have a butler.

I pulled a towel off the full-length mirror in the corner and made a call. "Grimm, how's it going?"

Grimm snapped into view in the mirror, looking more like an English butler than a sentient manifestation of magic. Grimm was the Fairy Godfather, founder of the Agency, once my boss, and sometimes my friend. He could grant wishes if he wanted to, but most people didn't need wishes. They needed solutions to their problems.

Just so we're clear, I had no magic. I wasn't a princess, witch, half blood, or anything like that. The only magic I could work was performed with bullets, bacon, or boobs. Anything that couldn't be handled with the big three, I called in Grimm. I didn't call often.

He smiled, making the wrinkles in his face crease together. "Marissa, my dear, it is only Monday. Do you require my assistance already?" His voice always reminded me of some nature documentary narrator.

I shook my head. "Nah. Nothing we can't handle yet. Got a new piper though. She can't be more than seventeen."

Grimm slid his glasses forward to look at me over the thick, black edges. "What, may I ask, is she piping?"

I shrugged. "The usual for newbies." New pipers, particularly girls, always started with brainless, easy-to-influence creatures like rats or teenage boys. "If we can get her trained, this year's Poodling will go a lot easier."

He raised one eyebrow and pursed his lips. "And if you can't, my dear?"

Grimm had never appreciated my term for our yearly pest-control operations. Every year, like clockwork, infernal energy welled to the surface. Instead of manifesting as something reasonable, like a six-headed hydra or a flaming squid, it tended to take the form of small, white, dog-shaped creatures with a taste for murder. "If I can't, she can supply Kingdom with organic, free-range rats. Can you tell me where Ari is?"

Arianna, my right-hand woman, my best friend, my girl Friday, or at least girl Thursday. At her name, Grimm's lips turned down. "I already checked. She slept through her alarm, missed her bus to the Agency, and failed her civics test. On top of Arianna's Department of Licensing disaster, she's planning to call in sick."

Ari had spent the last two years in college. Grimm and I had running bets on what she planned on majoring in. Grimm always said, "Do what you are best at." From what I could tell, Ari was going to major in failing the driver's license test. "She failed this weekend? Couldn't you intervene?"

"Marissa, I *did* intervene. She mistook the accelerator for the volume control and drove three blocks through the market at full speed. Again. It took every bit of magic I could pull off to make certain no one got more than a little run over."

"I'll go fetch her." Ari usually rose with the sun, and by now, she could have walked into the Agency. And Grimm hadn't said she was sick. Only that she planned on calling in sick. The more I thought about it, the more I figured there had to be another reason. "Did she fail one of your magic tests too?"

Grimm's expression said it all. He wouldn't meet my eyes, his face turned down. "Not exactly. She failed my pretest. I asked her to summon a dog with eyes the size of cup saucers. What she summoned hasn't tread the earth since the Jurassic Period."

Grimm had spent the last few years training Ari in magic. He traded passing tests in college for new lessons on how not to kill herself with magic. I remained unconvinced it was a fair trade. Grimm said he was taking his time because he didn't want her exposed to evil. If that were true, he wouldn't have made her take calculus.

I picked up my purse and took my jacket. "I'll be back soon. The piper's in 2A; I suggest nobody opens the door. The kobolds need to be turned down, Rosa will send away Payday George, and there's a frog prince waiting in the lobby."

Grimm sighed and faded out of view. I wonder at times what he ever did without me.

ARI LIVED IN a brownstone about twenty minutes from the Agency. Technically she lived alone. I knocked, and she answered without bothering to check the peephole. Her yellow sundress with matching hat made her pale complexion look a lot better, and she kept her red hair pulled back so that it didn't fall into her face.

I pulled my nine millimeter from my purse and pointed it at her. "What have I told you about answering the door without looking first?"

Ari ignored me and shuffled back inside. "I can see through the door, M, and Yeller would take care of anyone who bothered me." At the sound of his name, a dog the size of a Shetland pony padded forward. Only Ari would keep a hellhound as a pet. He looked like Cujo crossed with an alligator and a zombie. None of those crosses improved his disposition.

He stared at me, the gun in my hand, and began to growl, long and low. I put the gun away, since I'd grown somewhat attached to my hands. "Hey, Yeller. I have a poodle for you in the trunk of my car." Yeller bared his teeth at me.

Ari left the door open and walked down the hall. "Come on in, M. I'm making tea."

I hated Ari's apartment. She lived there because it was the only thing she could afford. She could afford it because it was haunted, and I don't mean "things that go bump in the night" haunted. I mean "things that devour your spirit."

Inside, the apartment still looked as if the previous owner lived there (which he didn't) and like he was still around (he was). Ari brought out a tea kettle and poured three cups, then sat back on a couch, the cover of which looked like woven hair. She clinked her spoon against the cup, like ringing a dinner bell. "Larry, I'm having tea with Marissa. Are you going to join us?"

The basement door blew open, and a ghastly form made of shadows flowed out.

I nodded to him. "Larry."

He looked at me with those dull red orbs that passed for eyes, a look that said he would rather be devouring my spirit than sipping tea. "Marissa."

That one word took five syllables. I didn't have the patience to talk with liches. I was supposed to have evicted this one a few years ago. Evictions were cheaper than exorcisms and worked about as often, but the day I went to court to close it, I made a nasty discovery.

I still remember standing there in my business suit with my property attorney at my side, while we waited for the lich to fail to make an appearance. They never showed—being bound to the place of one's death limited mobility options. Right as the judge was getting ready to approve it, the courtroom door swung open.

In lurched a postman, his mailbag still hanging from his side. He moved in awkward, jerky movements like a teenager at his first dance. The postman staggered to the bench and handed a scrawled paper to the judge. A few minutes later, when I should have been filing the new deed, I was sitting outside asking our lawyer how we got beat by a possessed postman.

I spent the better part of the next year fighting him. Well, technically him. Whether it was the grandma in her walker, or the hipster on his single-speed bike, they all developed an unholy knowledge of property law when possessed by Larry the Lich. I think the low point was getting hit with attorney's fees by an eight-year-old boy.

At that point we actually did research and discovered that

before death, Larry the Lich had been Larry Gulberson, Attorney at Law. That was before he took up a more respectable profession, committing unspeakable acts of evil.

So we negotiated a new contract. Technically, Grimm and Larry did, and Ari sublet the top three floors from an undead spirit of wrath. He wasn't a terrible landlord for someone bound to this plane only by the sheer weight of his hatred and malice. Ari claimed he wasn't that bad, once you got past the glowing eyes, spectral form, and tendency to devour the meter man. She always did find the positive things.

So Ari went with me when we needed to hunt uglies. She helped me out when I needed to tame something nasty. Even if she was part princess and part sorceress, I trusted her.

I stood at the coffee table. "You're late. Work started hours ago."

"I didn't feel like coming in today. Summer semester tests are next week and I need to study more." Ari made a terrible liar, her cheeks bright red, her hand over her mouth.

"I need your help with a new piper. She's a mess. Got so many piercings she looks like a tackle box, and more tattoos than the Detroit Lions cheerleading squad. I could use a hand." I took my tea and sat down beside her. As I did, I winced where the fabric of my pants rubbed fresh burns.

Ari looked at me and nodded. "Liam singed you again?"

"Yeah." My boyfriend, Liam, burned with more than desire.

Ari stood up. "I'll get you some ice. Where'd he get you this time?"

I gave her the look.

She stopped for a moment, then opened her mouth. "Oh. You want burn cream?"

"No. Remind me to ask Grimm for help when we get back to the Agency."

Ari nodded. "How was the film festival?"

"Wonderful. I watched this movie—all in French—you've got to see it." I stopped, since Ari's eyes glazed over like I'd wrapped her in a plastic bag again. Liam stayed by my side through three days of foreign-language films. I think he spent more time watching me than the movies.

"You're thinking about him. You get that smile when you

do." Ari blushed, happy for me that at least I'd found my happy, if not the ever after.

"We've got work to do. I'm sorry about the driving test. I'm sorry about the magic test, and I'm sorry about the civics exam. I've got a lobby full of potential clients, and I'm missing my right-hand woman."

Ari stared at me for a moment. "We don't get the results of the civics test until tonight."

"Well, in that case I have a feeling you'll be doing the makeup exam. Now go get dressed for business, and we'll try doing something you're good at." She left me with the lich, and as she walked out the mood in the room changed.

I knew Grimm negotiated safety for folks who stayed out of the basement. As the lights flickered and black smoke began to ooze out from the lich like tendrils, I kept my cool. "Larry, you hear about her driver's test?"

The tendrils paused for a moment and stopped snaking toward me. Larry nodded.

"When it comes to driver's tests, that girl is cursed."

The lich shook his head, managing to keep it attached. Not bad for someone who'd been dead a few decades.

"Sorry," I said, "I don't mean actually cursed. She just has really bad luck."

Again the lich shook his head. Then he drifted over toward one of the towering bookcases and began to point one-by-one at black bound tomes as if counting. He stretched out a skeletal hand toward one and beckoned to me with the other.

If it were anyone other than Grimm who laid out the contract Ari signed before moving in, I'd have worried. Your normal rental agreement detailed due dates and damage waivers. Grimm's covered every conceivable way an evil spirit might want to harm a person in the house. We rented a truck to move the paper version of the contract after Grimm drafted it. I took out the book the lich pointed to and gave it a glance, trying to make sense of triangle-based hieroglyphics.

"I don't read anything but English." I went to put the book back, but he held out a hand, stopping me. One claw touched the book and a vapor-like mist seeped out from what remained of the finger bones. Through the mist, the letters crawled like maggots, rearranging themselves into words I could read. Also, I wasn't hungry anymore. *Celestial Law, Volume Three Hundred*, read the title.

I opened the book, and a wind began to whip through the room, blowing Ari's mail into the air and flipping the pages until at last it died down. Again the lich did the maggot words thing. I read the chapter title: "The Exchange Principle."

I struggled through the first paragraph, then followed a bone finger to a single sentence. "For everything given, something must be taken. For every blessing, a curse."

At the words *blessing* and *curse* I shivered for reasons of my own. Blessings, curses, no real difference. I've had a curse do great things for me and a blessing do awful things. I had one of each. "This isn't about me. I was talking about Ari."

He shook his head again and pointed up the stairs. That got my mind to work. Ari, through no fault of her own, was a princess. Born to a royal family, though the royal families these days had long since traded throne rooms for boardrooms. My point being, as part of their contract with the universe, members of the royal families had what could only be described as ridiculous luck.

Reality itself bent over backwards to make things work out for them. Vicious creatures like hellhounds loved them, evil creatures like wraiths tolerated them, and hungry creatures like wolves would rather eat gym-sock soup than a single bite of princess. But maybe, I thought, all this came at a cost. If the only cost was not being able to drive, that was quite a bargain.

"Larry, are you trying to devour Marissa again?" Ari stood on the stairs dressed in a standard black business suit with white shirt. She looked almost professional, but still cute.

The lich shook his skull and held up his hands in mock surrender.

"Larry was explaining something to me. On his best behavior, I promise." I exchanged a glance with the lich and returned the book to its place. Then I took Ari and got the hell out of the haunted house she called home.

Two

BACK AT THE Agency, the kobolds were gone, the frog folks were presumably in with Grimm, and Payday George was still pinning down a chair in the lobby. Ari and I slipped past him and down the hall toward the room where I'd left our new piper.

Standing at the doorway, hand on knob, I looked to Ari. "Ever seen a new piper before?"

She shook her head.

I believed in trial by fire, so I threw the door open. "Beth, I'd like you to meet the agent who will be helping me with your case, Princess Arianna Thromson."

At her title, Ari blushed and narrowed her eyes. She stomped into the room, kicking a rat so it sailed through the air and hit the wall with a thud. "My name is *Ari*. It's what you'll call me if you want help."

"I asked Ari to help because princesses have a way with creatures. I figure she can tame your friends here until you learn to control them." The threadbare, ragged state of Beth's clothes said she'd been living on the street. "I'm going to set you up at a motel on the south side. It's such a dump, the rats are a step up from their usual clientele."

Beth wiped a smear of pizza sauce from her cheek and nodded. "When do I get rid of them?"

I gave her a hug, ignoring the fact that her bra squirmed. "You'll need to complete your paperwork. It's going to take a bit for me to find what we need, but you can come back tomorrow and get started." I had a contractor take her down to a taxi and headed back to my office, Ari in tow.

I tapped on the mirror, just because the Fairy Godfather hated being treated like an aquarium fish. "Grimm, you got a moment?"

He swirled into view and gave Ari a glance that made me sorry for her. "Of course. I'm ordering a frog potion. Ari, I'll need you to head over to Kingdom and acquire it from the Isyle Witch this afternoon."

Ari stared at the floor. Neither of us could stand the Isyle Witch, for good reason. I glanced at the scars on my left hand and shivered. "Grimm, shouldn't that be an anti-frog potion?"

Grimm shook his head. "They waited over a month to contact me about their son, so I'm afraid that's out of the question. After some counseling, the family has accepted a relocation package to a swamp in Louisiana. The cost of living is much lower, there's a lovely bog waiting, and I think the mother will definitely look good in green."

Ari looked up at Grimm. "Marissa told me about the civics test."

Grimm nodded. "There's a retake on Thursday. I'm certain you'll do better this time. And I'll schedule you another appointment at the DMV, young lady."

I sat up in my chair. "I'm not so sure that's a good idea. You ever heard of the Exchange Principle?"

Grimm looked surprised. "Marissa, have you been dabbling in celestial law? A degree in English in no way qualifies you to negotiate with demons."

"No. Just learned something new about blessings and curses."

Grimm rolled his eyes. "Really, Marissa, I thought you had made your peace with them."

"I'm fine. But I think the principle applies to princesses as well."

Grimm thought about it a moment and nodded. "Well then, perhaps we'll wait on the driver's test."

"While you are here, I need help. Something to control Liam's wilder side." We'd been working for the last two years on lifting Liam's curse, which at times left him scaly, with morning breath that could smelt copper. The cost in toothbrushes alone made finding a cure a necessity.

Grimm rubbed his palms together, avoiding my gaze entirely. "My dear, I was thinking quite the opposite. When Liam finally gets in, the three of us need to talk. I take it from his tardiness he played poker again this weekend?"

The mention of poker set my teeth on edge. A year ago I'd introduced Liam to the dwarves. They started a Friday-night poker game that stretched into Saturday. The last few months, Saturday stretched into Sunday, and last night, I think Liam came home after three in the morning. "Yes."

Grimm was smart enough not to inquire further.

"Would you mind doing me a favor? I need to know something about the future. I could take a test, but I trust you more." My nerves made sitting still impossible.

"Of course. Now, let me see, I believe you are wondering if you contracted hepatitis from eating at that foul Italian restaurant. The answer is no." Grimm smiled and nodded.

I forced myself to look at him. "I wanted to know if I was pregnant."

Ari made a squeak that sounded like she was trying to communicate with the rats. Her eyes went wide with excitement, and her lips with a grin she could only have because it wasn't her.

Grimm didn't leave the mirror for even a second. "Ah, a different form of infection. No, you are not. Really, if you were worried, you could have asked sooner."

Relief, mixed with a sadness I couldn't pinpoint swept through me, making my arms weak and my hands shaky. "I'm sorry. The pill isn't one hundred percent, and I worry about passing on Liam's curse."

"I thought you wanted a baby." Ari found her tongue when I'd rather she held it.

"I do," I said. "One day, I'll have a family of my own, but it has to be when I'm ready. When both of us are ready."

"I'll have Rosa make an appointment with your doctor. Perhaps an implant would suit you better." Grimm started to fade out.

"No. I need to be certain." Grimm's obsession with skimping on magic drove me crazy.

Grimm looked at the floor. "I think the pill will do fine. Are you taking the ones I gave you faithfully?"

"Like clockwork, but you aren't listening." I stood at my desk, trying to stay calm. "No offense, but you aren't human, you aren't a woman, and you've never been pregnant. I *need* your help until we are ready. Once we figure out that curse, we can talk." I pointed my finger at him the same way I ordered our contractors around. "I want you to put that brain of yours to work. Find a foolproof way to keep me from having a cursed baby that doesn't involve separate beds."

Grimm looked past me, at Ari. "Marissa, we will talk about this later, in private."

"Now. She lived in our apartment for three weeks. She knows."

Ari rolled her eyes. "I know. The neighbors know. Passengers on overhead jets know."

I'd been practicing my "I'm the boss, keep your mouth shut" stare for more than two years. It worked. Ari covered her mouth and looked at the floor.

I turned back to Grimm. "Why won't you help me?"

Grimm threw up his hands. "I'll make an appointment with a specialist in Kingdom. Even I can't get you in for a few days, but I assure you, the auguries say you will not get pregnant before then." I let him go this time.

"Sorry, M." Ari gave me a pat on the shoulder, knowing how much I wanted a family of my own. Then she left me alone in my office, where I dove into a pile of paperwork that threatened to ruin my happily ever after, or at least my evening.

THE ALARM CUT into my paperwork, a wailing screech like someone making howler monkey sausage using a live monkey.

Grimm popped up in my mirror, something he didn't usually do without permission. "Marissa, I'm detecting a buildup of infernal energy across the river. It's early, but I'm afraid it might manifest as poodles."

I slid the desk drawer open and flipped through the custom ammunition for my nine millimeter. Balrog, klingon, ogre, there it was: poodle. I stuffed all three clips into my purse and ran for the door. Ari waited in the hallway, a shopping bag big enough to hold a pair of boots on her arm.

"We're heading out," I said, and we ran for the stairs to our parking garage.

Grimm popped into view in the rearview mirror the moment I slid into the driver's seat. "Cross the bridge, take the expressway south, and then go west. You'll find them in a warehouse for recliners."

We raced as fast as the speed limit would let us, flying down the expressway and making right-hand turns from the far left lane. It felt like ages before we pulled up at the warehouse, a vast metal building with layers of peeling yellow paint laced with rust. I cut straight across the parking lot and skidded to a stop on the gravel at the warehouse office. If there was any hope of survivors, it would be there.

I trotted through the office door, smelling nothing but leather. No blood. No screams. Behind the counter, a teenage girl bopped to the grind of something that sounded like country-western heavy metal.

"Pickups are in the rear!" she said to us, continuing to dance in a way that bore absolutely no relationship to a beat so loud it threatened to shake my fillings out.

I walked over to the counter and hit the power to her stereo. "Have you seen anything small, furry, or deadly?"

She wrinkled her nose like my words stank and started to give a retort. I'm sure it was going to be something sassy. Something that said "I'm eighteen and you're twenty-seven and I'm so much cooler than you." But her eyes grew wide and her mouth dropped open. I turned as a blast like a cannon roared beside me.

Ari held her choice in weaponry, a Desert Eagle pistol with extended magazine. The gun dwarfed her tiny hands, and the stench of sulfur from it filled the air. In the doorway to the warehouse, the tattered remains of a toy poodle lay torn to bloody shreds.

I'd always favored the nine millimeter. Compact, quick change on the clip, and accurate enough that I'm the limiting factor. Back when I first started training Ari, I tried to get her to use something reasonable. Something you could fit in a purse. Something you wouldn't find mounted on a tank. Ari said if she shot something, she wanted it to stay dead.

Another poodle bounded through the doorway, slobbering and growling like the bite of hell it was. Ari had used the momentary pause to put a pair of stylish white ear protectors on. Her second bullet almost tore the dog in half.

Did I say dog? Did I mention the glowing red eyes? The bloody teeth and claws? The fact that it was choking down a man's hand? These weren't dogs. These were poodles. Toy poodles, to be precise, though they were toys in the same way that razor blades and hornets were. I ran to the office door and slammed it.

Ari walked to the counter and set the Desert Eagle down. She pulled off her earmuffs and looked the girl in the eye. "How many people are in there?"

Ari's gaze drew the girl out of shock. Ari, as I've mentioned, was a princess. I tried not to hold that against her. Princesses have this natural *geis* where people feel the urge to be nice to them. To listen to them. The girl started to breathe easier. "Ten. No, wait. Mom came in today. Eleven."

I flipped open my pocket compact. I'd thrown the makeup in it away a few years ago; always made me itch. I kept it for the mirror. "Grimm, we've got poodles, and there were ten people in there."

"Mom!" said the teen girl, jumping over the counter and running for the door to the warehouse. Ari held out her hand, and my skin felt like it lit on fire as she drew in the magic. A bolt of purple light hit the girl and she slumped to the floor. Did I mention Ari could perform magic?

I nudged the girl with my foot. "Sleep?"

Ari shrugged. "Can't do sleep yet."

The girl moaned and rolled over, then puked on the carpet.

I rolled her over with my foot, noting her breathing. "Looks like sleep."

"She's drunk. Completely wasted. I'm still working on sleep."

"Ahem," said Grimm, watching from the compact.

"Did I do good?"

Grimm shrugged. "Did you give her ethanol poisoning?"

Ari took a penlight from her bag and flashed it in the girl's eyes. "I don't think so. I haven't done that to anyone in days."

"Then you did fine. I have a SWAT team en route. My closest team of mercenaries is twenty minutes out, but I have a mobile grooming service less than five minutes out." Grimm sighed.

"What exactly is a mobile groomer going to do against flesh-eating monsters?" Ari could be so naïve at times.

I put my hand on her shoulder. "Bows. All you have to do is stick a bow on one; it'll die of shame."

A woman's scream from the warehouse, along with the sound of many small dogs yipping. My gaze snapped to the door and I took off for it at a run.

"Marissa, don't go in there. I'm detecting a full-blown outbreak now, and that was probably the last of the survivors. Wait for the SWAT team." Grimm spoke with all the authority that living through several eternities gave him.

I flipped the compact shut and looked to Ari. "Stay with her."

Ari dropped the girl's head with a thud and picked up her gun from the counter. "Two barrels are better than one."

Grimm would be ticked about me going through the door. He'd be even more ticked about me taking Ari. But I had this thing about families. I still missed mine, and I wasn't going to stand around if I could save someone else's.

Ari grabbed the warehouse door and looked over her shoulder. "Ready?"

"Let's do this," I said, and she flung open the door.

Three

~∞~

A BLAST OF hot, humid air hit me as we stepped inside. Overhead, the lights flickered and buzzed like a giant bug zapper. The skittering of pedicured claws on concrete and the clink of bone-shaped name tags against rhinestone collars echoed in the warehouse.

Ari kicked the remains of a poodle out of the way. "What do you think caused them to break out here?"

"They're attracted to places where atrocities were committed." I peeked around the corner of one pallet. A bloody, mangled body lay on the floor.

"Some sort of gang shooting in the past?"

I took my flashlight out and shone it into the shadows, looking for hellish eyes. "Could be almost anything. Maybe one of them picked out the gold carpet in their office. The music that girl was listening to. You see the bumper stickers out front? Mets fans. Their pitching's worth a poodle all by itself."

A poodle leaped from the darkness between two pallets. I rolled to the side, putting a bullet into it and ruining a leather recliner. Liam always wanted one of those. Another poodle snarled and yipped as it leaped for my ankle. I sidestepped and kicked as it landed, dodging razor-sharp teeth and snapping its spine.

The crippled poodle shrieked in pain and feral rage, desperate to tear our throats out. Ari walked over and crushed its bouffant head under her heel. "I don't get why these things are so dangerous."

Another bout of screaming killed my reply. I took off at a run toward the sound with Ari close behind. At the edge of the loading bay stood a fort of recliners, turned on their sides to make a wall. A few desperate workers were making a last stand inside, armed with broken recliner levers.

A hedge's worth of poodles ringed the fort, occasionally leaping at the edges. Then I realized that in the corner, a strike team of poodles had begun to gnaw their way through the back of a recliner.

"There're too many to take on. Get out of here," I whispered to Ari. The thump of an approaching helicopter made the loading doors shake as Grimm's mercenaries circled, but these folks wouldn't last another two minutes.

Every single poodle in the flock turned as one to look at us, growling like a hundred miniature wood chippers. I shuddered clean down to my toes and glanced back at Ari, who held a silver whistle in her lips. "What did you do?"

She spat out the whistle. "Called for help."

I fired six rounds, killing a couple of poodles with each, while beside me Ari's Desert Eagle roared, plowing through a row of them with every bullet, but still they came for us, a fluffy white cloud of doom.

"Run," I yelled. We took off at a sprint, tiny terrors with bloody muzzles nipping at our heels.

I made it to a tall metal shelf four steps behind Ari, who could outsprint me any day. I liked to think of myself as being built for distance rather than just slow. She began to climb, and I followed behind her, shaking a poodle from my pant leg. Beneath us, poodles howled in frustration.

At the top of her shelf, Ari leaned over and blew a raspberry at them. "I've seen Chihuahuas that were deadlier. And cuter."

"Don't mock them." My throat constricted with fear. From below came the sound of rasping metal as the beasts gnawed raw steel. For one moment, the warehouse stood silent, then the shelf groaned, shuddered, and folded over. I could only watch as Ari slipped off the edge of her shelf and fell into a churning mass of curly white dogs.

She screamed as they bit at her, and I lunged into the fray, crushing dogs underfoot and hurling them away as fast as I could grab them. Teeth gnawed my ankles, and a poodle hung from my jacket sleeve. I glanced behind me. Wall to wall poodles filled the warehouse. Then someone grabbed me from the side and threw me to the floor.

"Hold still," said Ari, her face bleeding from a dozen nips. Every poodle that bit her did so exactly once, then fell over, vomiting. Half-digested chunks of flesh covered the floor around us.

That's about when the wall exploded. Debris stung my eyes, but the only sounds were the terrified screams of poodles, and the wet noises of tearing flesh and snapping bones.

Then the room went silent.

A shadowy form with four-inch claws padded up and began to lick Ari. She rolled off me and put her arms around Yeller, now the size of a subcompact car. "Good dog. Someone's earned a lawyer for dinner." Yeller wagged his tail, walked into the shadows, and faded away.

I stood up, wincing from every single bite. "What took him so long?"

"Do you have any idea how many fire hydrants there are between here and my apartment?" Ari wiped blood from her eyes.

"We've got to train him to hail a cab." I ran my fingers down my arms, grateful I wasn't missing large chunks of flesh. "What was with trying to protect me?"

Ari reached out and touched her tongue to the back of her wrist, then spat. "Remember?"

Of course. From all accounts, princesses tasted like gym socks boiled in iodine, then soaked in pus.

A team of mercenaries wearing night-vision goggles smashed in the loading bay door, training laser sights on anything and everything. Yeller's rampage left only a single poodle, lying on its side, gasping its final breaths. The strike team commander swaggered over and put a bullet through it.

He flipped up his visor and triggered the radio. "It was rough, but we managed to secure the place. Threat neutralized."

Behind him, his team led out the survivors, who would most definitely be cat people for the rest of their lives.

"Ma'am," said the commander, "you need to leave. We're going to level the place."

I took Ari's hand, and we headed out into the sunlight. Grimm watched us from the silver lettering in the door, then in the chrome on my bumper, and finally in my rearview mirror.

He stared at me until I finally looked him in the eye. "Marissa, I believe I told you to wait for the mercenaries."

"So fire me."

Grimm shook his head. "I tried that once. It's not a mistake I'll repeat. Take Ari to the emergency room and have those bites cleaned out. Tell them she hid pepperoni in her pockets and tried to run through a dog show."

Ari leaned back in her seat as I drove us away, adding yet another layer of bloodstains on my car's upholstery. Two o'clock on a Monday, and we were already heading in for sutures and shots. Just another day in the Agency business.

THE AGENCY, IN case you were wondering, was a normal business. We paid normal rent and normal taxes. We had normal janitors and a somewhat normal receptionist. I say somewhat normal because Rosa was downright awful. She had a look that could turn Medusa to stone and was equally handy with a sawed-off shotgun or a credit card machine.

As you might expect, the Agency also had agents. We worked for Grimm, handling problems too sensitive to contract out or tasks that had to be done right. In theory, Liam was an agent as well, but since he was a man, we used him for what men were best at. He broke toys, played with fire, and beat the living daylights out of the occasional hard case. Also, I loved him more than anyone I'd ever known. For him, I'd kill any of the things that go bump in the night.

That's why I drove to my apartment instead of the hospital. I wanted to see Liam, maybe offer him a ride to work. Mind you, I also planned on fixing up Ari. I kept a full suture kit and bought antibiotic ointment in five-gallon buckets. Came in handy in the Agency business.

I kicked open the apartment door and yelled, "Honey, I'm home," at the top of my lungs. The only answer was a slight shimmer in the room. Ari walked past me, looking like a stunt double for a bag of dog chow, and into my guest bathroom. For the better part of a year, Ari lived in my apartment. When Liam moved in, she moved out, saying we never slept, and she couldn't either.

While Ari showered, I went to my bathroom mirror to pick blood out of my hair. "Hey, Grimm, Liam out on assignment?"

He appeared almost immediately. "Your boyfriend is making the usual Monday rounds, now that he's awake. Didn't I say to go to the emergency room?"

"I'll take care of Ari."

Grimm shook his head. "You were a lot easier to deal with as a slave."

I studied the golden band I wore on my wrist. These days, it was my choice. "Was I?"

Grimm thought about it a moment. "No, not really." Then he faded out of view, off to grant someone else an answer to their problems.

I picked up one of Liam's flannel shirts and sniffed it. It smelled like wood smoke and man, a scent I'd grown to know and love. Liam was a blacksmith. When he wasn't breaking people's toys or teeth for Grimm, he made iron art at a studio on the south edge of the city.

The shower cut off, and a few minutes later Ari emerged, dressed in one of the only outfits she'd left at my house when she moved. She wore the frilly tracksuit like a cone of shame. I glanced up at her. "Who's a pretty princess in pink?"

Ari tensed like a spring, scrunching her eyes and face. "I wish you'd stop saying things like that. Stop introducing me as 'princess.' Stop buying pink bandages. There are other colors, you know. I like blue. Or green." Ari was so cute when she was ticked.

"You've got to learn to be who you are." I poured Ari a consolation cup of stale coffee, adding sugar and cream until it congealed into pudding. "Here. Just the way you like it."

She slid into a chair at my table, her head in her hands. "I'm not a princess anymore." This was technically true and false at the same time. Ari's stepmother threw her out of the house, and in fact cast her out of Kingdom entirely a couple years ago.

"Grimm says different. Being a princess is like a soul tattoo. Can't be undone." Personally, I bet it was a huge, ugly tattoo of Bob Marley's face. "So what's going on with school? You breezed through the first two years. You got good grades. Your teachers love you." Admittedly it probably wasn't their fault. Princesses had that effect on everything.

Ari sighed in frustration and put her head down on the table. "I met someone."

"As in 'I ran into or over the postman again' or I *met someone* met someone?"

Ari's groan gave me the answer I expected. "I wasn't studying for the civics exam on Thursday. I was out with him."

"I had to exorcise the Hukkkuti brothers by myself so you could play kissy-face with some guy? The least you could do would be to introduce me. I'm your best friend; I should get to make sure he's good enough for you."

Ari looked up, her eyes wide with fear. "No! He doesn't know where I work."

"You mean he doesn't know what you are." I put my hand on hers. "He'll find out. People love princesses. They can't help it. And you're a seal bearer. That's got to count for something." Though the royal families pretended otherwise, their true purpose was to make sure the realm seals remained intact, and in order to do that, one woman from each generation per family would be bound to a realm seal.

Ari rocked back in her chair, her mouth crumpled into a frown. "I don't want someone to love me for what I am. I want them to love me for *who* I am."

I understood that. "You've at least got to tell me his name."

"Wyatt." Her eyes got this distant haze in them, and a smile crept across her face in spite of the bite marks.

"What are you going to tell him when he sees you bitten like that?" I went to the cupboard and took out a box of adhesive bandages, sticking them to her until she looked like a mummy.

Ari grinned. "I'm going to say I volunteer at a shelter for dogs with neurotic biting tendencies, and I tried to take six of them for a walk at once." The only dog walking Ari did was when she'd take Yeller out for a walk at night, when people could mistake him for a Clydesdale.

"All right. But you have to tell him the truth at some point. Now we need to get going. Grimm's going to be upset as it is. I need to feed blessing and curse." I kept a pet cat once. We won't go into exactly what happened to Mr. Sniffers, but let's just say after that I kept things I didn't have to feed or water, and planted an azalea bush in the courtyard in Mr. Sniffers's memory.

My current pets were a mix of spells and creature, called harakathin. You can think of them as a combination ghost and cat. I'd say psychotic cat, but that would be redundant. In theory, these two were charged with giving me good fortune. Unfortunately, they rarely took my personal safety into account.

When Liam moved in, my jealous harakathin turned from silver-eyed monsters to green-eyed monsters. They spent the first few weeks tripping him in the dark, setting his clothes on fire, or turning the boiler up to 300 degrees while he was showering. The usual stuff.

So we bought two cat beds, one for each of them, and most days I dumped a can of cat food on a plate. Harakathin fed on attention. My daily routine mollified them, and I considered it practicing for a real cat. I opened two cans and put them near the cat beds.

Ari wrinkled her nose at the smell of cat food. "You've been making offerings to them?"

"Works even better than naming them. Call it community service. Feed my blessings, feed the hungry." I left the plates sitting for a minute while I waited. The lights dimmed and flickered, but at least the pipes didn't break and the drywall didn't crack. "Can you see them?"

Being a seal bearer, Ari had spirit sight. That meant she could see all the things that went bump in the night, whether they wanted her to or not, whether she wanted to or not. Being relatively normal, I relied on her to tell me where my pets were. Ari glanced around. "No. They're here, but I can't see them."

I'd never seen them even take a bite of cat food, but just offering it to them made all the difference. Most days, they simply stayed at home unless called. I opened the window and picked up a wrought-iron triangle Liam made for me.

When I clanged it, a man's head popped up out of the Dumpster. "Rapunzel?"

"How many times do I have to tell you that's not my name?" I went to my kitchen and pulled the steak and potatoes left over from Liam's birthday dinner out of the fridge, then lowered them down in a basket tied to a rope made of hair. "You can have steak. The cat food goes to—"

"Rapunzel." He handed the paper plate to a mangy tabby, who rubbed up against him. "She's my good girl."

I shut the window, grabbed Ari, and headed back to the Agency. Definitely a Monday.

Four

~

THE MOMENT I passed the staff door, I heard Liam's deep laugh coming from Grimm's office. I ran to meet him, not bothering to knock. Liam stood nearly six feet tall, with a barrel chest and arms that could tear your own off. Being a blacksmith will do that to you (give you arms, not tear them off).

"M!" He crushed me in a hug, picking me up off the ground. "Sorry about this weekend."

I was still angry, but it was hard to be held and angry at the same time, so I put my head on his shoulder and relaxed. Then my eyes snapped open. I pushed back and looked at him again as he set me down. Bruises covered both of his cheeks, and bloody patches clung to his knuckles.

I ran a finger along his eyebrow, wiping blood from it. "What have you been doing?"

He took my hand in his and put the other on my cheek. "The usual Monday things."

Translation: making weekly rounds, reminding a few people that whatever else they had planned, this week was a bad week to get revenge on me. I'd made a lot of enemies. At least two queens wanted me killed on sight. An entire army of wolves wanted me dead for shooting their leader, and at one point the entire postal service wanted to see me returned to sender. For a while, I had assassins showing up every couple of days. All that changed when Liam moved in. My enemies probably still wanted to kill me but valued their intestines too much to try.

Grimm cleared his throat. "Now that you are finally here, I'd like to talk to both of you about an opportunity."

"He's not going to pose nude for the art college. We already had that discussion."

Liam blushed and looked at the floor. I didn't care how many times he did that before, I had my rules, and one of them was my boyfriend kept his boy bits between us.

"Tell me you've found a way to dull the curse. I've reached my yearly limit of burn cream. Any more and I have to register as a wholesale dealer."

Liam snorted and a bit of smoke curled out of his nostrils.

Grimm crossed his arms. "Actually, I had quite the opposite in mind. I've been researching ways to trigger the curse and keep it active even when he goes to sleep."

"You've been doing what?" My face flushed, and I put my hands on my hips. "Why?"

Liam looked to Grimm in a panic that I found completely appropriate.

Grimm disappeared for a moment, and flowing script filled the mirror, though in no language or alphabet I'd ever seen. His voice came from the mirror, though I couldn't see him. "See for yourself, my dear."

"Neither of us read hieroglyphics. Translation?"

Grimm reappeared in the mirror. "I will arrange to have you taught Vampirese at some other time. For now, let us simply say that the time has come for the oldest undead family to take their once-a-century dirt nap."

I glared at Grimm, waiting for him to get to the part that involved Liam and me.

"Now, in the old days, this would be when peasants would descend on castles, coffins would be overturned, steaks driven through vampires' mouths, and then garlic salt sprinkled on them."

I nodded. "Sounds like a plan. Put me on a plane to Europe and I'll get it done."

"The vampires of today are not bloodthirsty monsters,

Marissa. Sunlight won't kill them, holy water only upsets them because their clothes have to be dry-cleaned. And I don't want them killed. I want them protected for two weeks while they sleep."

"But I never got to put a stake through a vampire's heart before." I'd accomplished most of the things on my bucket list in the first six years I worked for Grimm. I'd been buried alive in a coffin three times before I turned twenty-one. Found love with a man who loved me back. Heck, I scratched off "Get in a fistfight with a mime" my first week in the city. But vampire slaying remained on my to-do list.

Grimm sighed. "Marissa, sit down. A vampire's heart does not beat, so I can't believe you actually fell for such a simple ruse. It was the steak in the mouth that killed them. Today's vampires are more enlightened. More evolved. They are vegans. If they consume meat products, the fire of their own hypocrisy burns them to a crisp."

"What about drinking blood?"

"Honestly, my dear, do you believe everything you read? If it weren't for vampire families celebrating Thanksgiving, tofurkey would have failed long ago."

I always figured Vampire Thanksgiving involved carving up a redhead or something. We ate goose every year, because Grimm said it was more traditional. Also, every couple of months I had to find and kill another gold-egg-laying goose before it upset the markets. I could only fit so many of them in my freezer.

My frustration with the hours spent learning useless facts mounted. Particularly as Grimm must have known that it wasn't right. "And crosses? I bet they can't hurt them either."

Grimm creased his brow, thinking. "No, I believe that a cross could in fact harm one."

"How?"

"Well, if the cross weighed several tons and fell on them. Or if it were mounted on wheels and moving at, say, thirty-five miles per hour and ran into one. Or if one sharpened the edges and swung it at a vampire." Grimm nodded, more to himself than me.

"If they don't drink blood, they don't hide from the sun, and crosses don't hurt them, they aren't vampires. They sound more Californian than Transylvanian. Where, exactly, do we come into this?"

Liam took my hand. "The old vampire families are obsessed with the best guards money or magic can buy. They wanted a family of dragons to guard their keep, but ever since the treaty put dragons on the endangered species list, they aren't available."

The light went on in my head. See, agents were usually magical. Princesses. Half djinns. Liam accidentally got cursed a few years ago. He wasn't half djinn, and if he ever wound up with even a trace of princess on him, I planned to take my knife and carve it out. He was, however, a were-dragon, doing time-share in his body with a curse older than the Roman Empire. A curse I accidentally put on him.

That's why my enemies decided every week that this week they'd take up knitting or lean on the local grocer. Liam belched hellfire when he *wasn't* angry. When he got upset, it was like the Incredible Hulk had a child with a Komodo dragon and a napalm factory. "No. I'm not letting you turn him into a dragon. You have any idea how many princes would love to add 'slew the dragon' to their list of accomplishments?"

"Tell her about the pay." Liam looked at Grimm.

"I'd rather be dirt-poor than rich and alone," I said, unwilling to look at either of them.

"Marissa, I give you my word I didn't take this offer at face value. Indeed, I believed it some form of mistake until clarified. The senior royal family of the undead court has had thousands of years to accumulate money, and hundreds of years where they have collected magic." Grimm stopped and waited for me to look up, where the page waited, the glowing script pulsing.

The number on the page looked like an international phone number or two. The second number had to be the amount of Glitter they offered. Since I'm completely nonmagical, the metric system never made sense. Grimm tried to teach me once. He gave up when I told him Pedo-liters were how many creepy old men fit in a jar.

The numbers were big. Really big. So big, in fact, they stank of something rotten. "Fake," I said, holding my hand over my nose to emphasize that Grimm got taken.

"I assure you, my dear, this is no mistake nor a fake. I have an escrow agency who assures me that they have in fact taken delivery of the payments, pending our agreement."

I shook my head. "Still doesn't make sense. Why would they need me?" I waited in the silence as the two of them looked at each other.

Liam turned toward me. "I need you. Need you to let me go. Need you to keep yourself safe for a few weeks. Not go challenging anyone to duels, or opening cursed sarcophagi, or running into poodle-filled warehouses."

My stomach turned cold like I'd drunk a gallon of ice water. The last two years had been the happiest years of my life. I finally found someone who loved me, really loved me. I had friends and respect. "You really want to leave me?"

Liam got down on one knee like he was about to propose, and my heart skipped several beats. "No. Truth is, I'd rather die than leave you. But I want to be able to *be* with you. I'm tired of worrying about setting the house on fire, or having to swallow my steak tartare in order for it to arrive in my stomach well-done. I want to have a life with you. I want to have children."

Grimm cleared his throat again. "Marissa, with that much magic, I could do almost anything."

He meant he could finally cure Liam's curse.

"No one has that much Glitter." I ransacked my mind for reasons this couldn't happen. "Even if they did, they'd use it, not give it away for two weeks of protection."

Liam leaned in to speak to me face-to-face. "You've said Glitter is basically magic, right? And magic is basically hope, right?"

I nodded.

Grimm cut in. "My dear, you have to consider that hope would be poisonous to an undead creature. Of course they'd be willing to pay with it. It's like when I pay the kobolds in nuclear waste. They believe they are getting a fantastic deal."

I sat back in the chair with my eyes closed. Two weeks for enough magic to un-work the worst curse Grimm had ever seen.

Ever.

The deal still stank. "No. He'll get killed by a prince. Or a team of princes. Or a nuclear strike."

Grimm disappeared again and the mirror scrolled for

minutes, page after page of mind-numbing legal jargon. "I've been drafting this contract for more than six months, Marissa. I assure you the vampires will take every precaution. The penalties against them if Liam were even wounded would cost them their castles, their bank accounts. He would be the final line of defense in an arsenal of traps designed to maim all-comers. Assuming one survives the labyrinth, then one of six teams of assassins would kill them."

"And if they survived?"

Liam put his hands on my cheeks so I would look at him. His eyes began to glow with fire, and when he spoke, the curse spoke as well, in a second voice. "Then I will unleash the fires of hell on them. Two weeks, M."

"How are you going to keep Liam a dragon?"

Grimm nodded toward Liam, who leaned his head back like he was going to take a nap. "I've had Mr. Stone take a few naps in the Agency. When he's asleep I can talk to the curse directly."

Curses were like blessings—alive, and intelligent. From what I knew, this one had been ancient when the Romans were wearing diapers and Rome was a fishmonger's hut on a hill. "So you asked it how you could keep it active? Why didn't you ask how to get rid of it?"

"Really, my dear. It was the first thing we discussed, and I have to say the subject was poorly received. It would be simpler to make a list of people the curse did not threaten to disembowel, devour, or disembowel and then devour."

"I get it. The big bad curse wants to eat me."

Grimm raised his eyebrows. "No, my dear. You were to receive a burst of hellfire, blown directly into—"

"I get it. Didn't want to negotiate." I turned toward Grimm's mirror and leaned forward. "Are you sure you can do this?"

He frowned and narrowed his eyes at me. "Of course I can."

One look at the set of Liam's jaw told me he'd already made up his mind. He had known about the offer. Two weeks of work for a thousand years' worth of Glitter. I'd have to be crazy to tell him not to take it. That seemed okay to me, but I closed my eyes and wrapped my arms around him and held him for a while.

Five

∿

WITH THREE DAYS until Liam's flight to eastern Europe, I booked Liam's tickets myself, first-class. Grimm had a tendency to try to ship his agents as cargo, to save a few bucks, but took one look at my face and chose to pick a fight with the kobolds instead. With the only thing I could do done, I resolved to bury myself in work rather than dread each hour.

In the meantime, I had a piper to deal with and a Poodling to get ready for. Ari had managed to listen to her alarm that day, and when I passed the rental truck in the Agency loading bay, my day started looking up. We met almost-Piper Beth at the elevator to avoid the usual round of hysteria and screaming.

The elevator door slid open and rats gushed out into the hall. Beth followed them, stumbling, nearly collapsing. Sweat beaded on her like she had a fever, and red splotches traveled out like spiderwebs from the skin under her nose ring. Ari took one arm, I took the other, and we headed down the hall, through the service entrance, and straight into a conference room.

Inside, a golden glow of reflected light lit the tables. Beth squinted and then, as her eyes adjusted, they grew wide. "Is this all for me?"

On the table sat a huge assortment of instruments. Coronets and trumpets, saxophones and recorders, and of course a few flutes in case she was an old-school piper. I gestured to the instruments. "You tell me. One of these is going to really light you up. You take piano lessons as a kid?"

She shook her head.

Ari handed her a flute. "How about this?"

Again, no. I patted the girl on the back, where her shoulder rings sported fiery red welts. "Ari, would you mind helping her check out a few of these while I grab something?" It wasn't really a question, and even if Ari did mind, she could whine about it later.

I went to the kitchen and took an insulated box from the fridge. "Human organs," read the label. I dumped the contents into the trash—the "use or freeze by" date passed the Friday before, so it wasn't like anyone was going to eat them.

Box in hand, I marched back to the conference room and set it in front of Beth. "Every piercing, chain, and ring goes in the box, now."

She snarled at me, showing enough teeth to make a wolf proud. "I have every right to look how I want."

I'd been snarled at by things that would eat my organs without putting them in a lunch box first. "You have an infection. Probably subcutaneous, possibly staph. Chains, safety pins, and rings in the box, please. I don't care if you make yourself into a human pot rack once we are done, but I'm not letting you die on my watch." I tapped the box for emphasis. "Did you fill the prescription I got you?"

Her eyes said no, what little I could see of them under the half ton of makeup she was wearing. Ari stood up and started for the door. "I'll be back. I'm going to head down to the pharmacy and pick it up. Are you hungry, Beth?"

It was only nine thirty in the morning, but the girl's bony ribs gave me an answer before she could.

Ari looked over her shoulder. "Do you want Chinese? Pizza? Subs? What do you like to eat?"

Beth looked up, and her eyes brimmed with tears. "Food." A rat nibbled at the chain that went from her nose to her left ear as she pulled it out. "I don't understand why you want to change me."

"If looking like a circus clown crossed with a heavy-metal drummer suits you, fine. Go to it. Just don't die in my office, in my Agency." I grabbed my purse and stood up.

"Do I have to leave?" Beth's eyes widened, still brimming with tears.

I opened the door. "This room, yes. The Agency, no. Come on, we're going to get you cleaned up and find some clothes that don't look like rats gnawed on them." I turned and acted on pure instinct, the only thing that saved me so many times.

I pulled the gun out of my purse without thinking and fired two bullets right into the chest of the young man in the hall. I followed them with another bullet through his left leg, and one in his right, then lined up to put one through his head.

He looked up at me and smiled, flecks of blood on his teeth. "Morning, Marissa."

I think that's about when Beth started screaming, and that brought Grimm. Well, that and the gunshots, though in this building, this office, neither were rare.

"Marissa, how many times have I told you *not to shoot the intern*?" Grimm yelled at me.

Beth grabbed a prepaid phone from one tattered pocket and attempted to dial 911. I took the phone from her and closed it. She went back to screaming.

The young man slowly stood up, leaving a smear of blood on the wall behind him. Then he walked into the room and began to cough until he spat something out in his hand—my spent bullet. "Nice blossom on this one. Think your rifling is getting worn though."

I took the bullet from him. "Sorry, Mikey." He was right. I'd make an appointment with my gunsmith. I went every few months. Think of it like a dental cleaning, only not as scary.

Grimm spoke from behind me. "That's the fifth time, my dear. Even Mr. Stone has figured out that there's no need to kill my employees. I expect this will be the last time. Correct?"

I nodded. "Got it. Sorry again, Mikey."

Mikey bent over and pulled a bullet out of his leg and handed it to me, then repeated the process with the other leg.

"I am so calling the cops," Beth said. "You shot him."

Mikey tossed Beth a bullet, then lifted up his shirt to show smooth skin, with no trace of a gunshot wound. "And what are you going to tell them?"

I walked over to put a hand on her shoulder, but she flinched. Some people, you shoot even one person in front of them, and their entire opinion changes. I patted Mikey on the back. "Mikey here is different. Like you, in some ways. He's a . . ." I tried to make my mouth say it, but all it did was make me want to shoot him again.

Mikey grinned at me, showing those pearly white teeth that grew back in every time I knocked them out. "Go on, say it and we'll call it even."

I swallowed the lump in my throat. "Mikey's a wolf."

"That wasn't so hard, was it?" Mikey smoothed out his T-shirt, ignoring the bloodstains.

I never wanted Grimm to take a wolf as an intern. I might have mentioned that I killed the leader of the wolves. I might have mentioned that they'd made a few attempts on my life. At one point it was "Wake up and shoot the wolf outside the door. Make breakfast, shoot the wolf outside the door. Go to work, and shoot the wolf in the elevator, the two in the garage, and the one that shredded my backseat." Old habits, like wolves, died hard.

"I'll try not to do it again. Mikey, meet Beth. Beth's going to be a piper."

Mikey looked down at the cloud of rats and picked one up by the tail. "You mind?"

I shrugged. "Be my guest."

He bit the rat in two and chewed thoughtfully. "Tastes like Dumpster. Much better than sewer rats. Those taste like ass."

Beth watched as he swallowed the tail, slurping it down like a piece of spaghetti, then fainted.

"I'm really sorry about the shirt. Give me a hand and I'll buy you a scone. Or a dog biscuit." I made myself look him in the eyes, and he rewarded me with a grin that made me glad I wasn't a pig. So I took one foot and Mikey took the other and we dragged her down the hall to the shower.

We didn't always have showers. After I made partner, I had them installed. The number of times I'd come in covered in blood (my own or someone else's) or crap (definitely someone else's) made it necessity, not luxury. We dumped her in the shower, turned on the water, and let it run.

When Beth woke up, it was clearly an "exactly where am I?" moment. She looked around at drenched rats and then to Mikey and me. "I had this dream. I dreamed you shot him."

Mikey winked at me, his lips pulled back in a grin. I took my gun out and shot him at point-blank, right in the stomach. Beth's eyes rolled back in her head, and she slumped over again.

"Marissa!" yelled Grimm, reflecting from the chrome shower doors. "What in Kingdom is going on?"

Mikey sat up and started laughing with me. "Grimms, you gotta see her face when Marissa does that. Priceless."

Grimm glowered at Mikey until he stopped laughing, though Mikey still chuckled under his breath. "That is enough. Marissa, act your age. Mikey, you are needed in cargo. Really, I don't have employees. I have children. I should have opened a day care instead of an Agency."

A few minutes later, Beth roused again. Her clothes were completely soaked, and it was just as well that she sat up, since rats had clogged the drain and she was in mild danger of drowning. She looked at me, then the empty space on the bench next to me.

"It was all a dream," I said, getting a towel from the rack. "There's soap in there, and shampoo. I'll put your piercing box here, since I'm betting that you have more metal than a cyborg. When you're done, grab a robe from the closet and I'll take you to our wardrobe department."

Then I went down and got myself some coffee, because in most respects Tuesday is no better than Monday.

ARI CAME BACK with enough Chinese food for all of China-town. I'm not certain who she thought she was feeding, because one skinny girl couldn't eat two pounds of chow mein and three large pizzas. On the other hand, all the rats needed to go to a diet support group. Ari came in with Mikey trailing, carrying the boxes.

"Didn't Grimm say they needed you in cargo?" I took a box from him.

Ari blew hair out of her eyes. "I needed help carrying the

food." She sniffed for a moment and then looked at Mikey. "Do I smell gunpowder?"

I pushed open the conference room door, where a washed, dressed, and much nicer-looking Beth sat, putting antibiotic ointment on her various piercing points. The organ box had several more pounds of "jewelry," most of which resembled surgical implements.

"What do you want now?" asked Beth, glaring at me. Then she smelled the food. I waited, blocking the doorway until I could see her mouth water.

"I want to feed you, and maybe figure out where your talent lies." I set my pizza in the middle of the table and smashed a rat with a xylophone. "It works like this. You pick up an instrument, you play a few tunes on it."

Beth ignored the chow mein, took a foot-long sub, and began to digest it the way a python swallows a rabbit—whole.

"Slow down," said Ari. "You're going to make yourself sick."

Beth continued to swallow chunks of sub like she was trying out for an eating contest. "Mmmmffmmmammf mmmm."

I glanced at Ari. "Neither of us speak dwarf. Mikey, you speak dwarf?"

Mikey dry swallowed a piece of sub. "I barely speak English."

"I said, 'You shot him.'" Beth wiped her mouth with a napkin.

I kept my poker face on. "Nope. I think you're starting to hallucinate from silver poisoning. Or maybe that infection has gone to your brain."

Ari reached into her shopping bag. "I *knew* that was gunpowder. If you think it's funny to play nasty jokes on customers, let's try with my gun."

Mike scooted away. "No shooting me with that. Last time you did, I spent a week growing my leg back."

Ari shook her head and set down her bag, then brushed a rat off Beth's shoulder. "I'm so sorry. Yes, Marissa has problems with wolves. Yes, Mikey's a wolf. Now, when you're done with your sandwich, we should start. You look like you might play the saxophone."

So I took my sandwich and left my understudy to do the hard work. Seniority had its privileges.

Six

WEDNESDAY SUCKED. I referred three cases to the police department, armed two people who wished to find missing keys with metal detectors, and personally dispatched the kobold soccer team before Ari even showed up. Even then, she wasn't going to help around the office, not that day. I picked up Beth from the waiting room and headed straight to the back of the Agency to see Ari off.

Wednesdays were Ari's magic-training days, and she spent most of the day trapped in another dimension, in another universe. At least, that's as close as I got to understanding Grimm's explanation of where exactly it was. I didn't go, because I'd visited once. I almost died there, and it killed my enthusiasm for a return tour.

The only real advantage was that there, Ari could practice magic. That was, she could practice without killing everyone in the building (nearly happened three times), transforming every man for three blocks into a goat (twice), or giving everyone in a six-mile radius flatulence (I swear she did that on purpose).

Grimm waited in the back room of the Agency, which

housed a portal we used when no combination of frequent-flier miles could get us somewhere.

Ari stood at the mirror, taking deep breaths to calm her nerves.

"Young lady, I am ready when you are." Grimm faded out of the mirror, clearing it for her use.

"I'm not," said Ari. "I'd rather go home and study for the civics exam."

When Ari first came to work for Grimm, she couldn't wait to learn more magic. Then she learned how hard it was, and suddenly college seemed like a fantastic idea.

Grimm spoke from a half-buried stainless steel oven. "I'm sorry, but you really don't have a choice. You must continue to exercise Seal Magic or you will lose all the progress we have made. I promise I will have you home in time to study."

Ari should have learned Seal Magic from her mother, but her mother died of cancer before Ari even bonded with a seal, let alone had time to train. Grimm had taken over Ari's education himself.

I took her hand. "You want me to go with you? I'll run grab a set of pom-poms from the morgue and be your personal cheerleader." The closest I ever got to casting a spell was Liam saying that when I walked into a room, I made the other women disappear.

"Marissa, I need you to run the Agency while I attend to Ari's training," said Grimm. He'd always offered to let me go before. Then again, it was my fault Ari had to go at all.

"I'll be fine." From the tremble in her fingertips, I figured Ari spoke as much to herself as me. Normally, being a seal bearer took years of formal training, which began with touching a seal and ended with the right to access its full power. The seal changed its bearer, allowing them to unleash spells other casters could only dream of.

"Arianna, I know you are afraid, but I must insist. Your healing is not complete until your training is complete." Grimm faded from the mirror, leaving it open for Ari.

I helped Ari learn magic on her own, casting spells she shouldn't have been able to. It left her wounded, according to Grimm, by Wild Magic. Only witches used pure Wild Magic,

magic unfiltered by seals and nearly limitless in power. Witches paid for it. The witch mark gave them Spirit Sight but took their eyes, removing the cornea and pupil so that anyone who saw a witch knew what they were.

The way Grimm told it, with enough practice and training, the damage to Ari's soul from the Wild Magic would be healed. Ari would be a normal magic-wielding, seal-bearing princess and no longer at risk of losing her eyes to the witch mark. So she did have to go, and I would take care of things here.

Ari touched the mirror, and the surface rippled like a pond. I began to shiver, remembering traveling through the mirror. How it felt like glass taffy, sticking to my skin as I sank into it. She stepped forward into the mirror, and it closed around her, wrapping and bubbling until it settled to absolute calm.

Only the back room showed in the mirror. Ari was a million light-years away, maybe farther, in a realm where time had no meaning and distance did not exist. I forced my trembling hand to the glass, proving to myself that it was solid.

Beth pointed to a trash can. "You look like you're gonna puke. That was awesome."

"Only because you've never been through. Now tell me, what did Ari and you decide on for your instrument?"

"We didn't exactly find anything. But I hate the tuba." That only proved that Beth wasn't insane. So I walked her back to the conference room, filled with dozens of different types of instruments I was renting by the day, and got her back to trying. I left her in the room, where she continued her audio torture session.

BETH CAME TO my office late that afternoon, so excited she could barely hold still. "Miss Locks, you have to see what I can do." I bristled at the "miss" but let it go, hoping for something great.

I followed her into the conference room, where she picked up a saxophone and began to blow on it. What came out sounded like a camel being eaten by a pack of kindergartners, one bite at a time. As Beth played, the rats scampered to the far end of the room, where they huddled in a writhing mess.

"See? I think it's because of my power." Beth held up the saxophone with pride.

"Not so fast. I think it's because they have ears. They're disease-bearing pests, but they aren't deaf." I opened the door and a flood of rats rushed past my feet, eager to get out of earshot. "Follow me." We went to the waiting room, where the usual throng of wishers waited. "Play."

She began, blasting out squeaky notes that didn't resemble a tune as much as an audio-torture session. The rats began to flee, along with the customers. Honestly, I didn't mind seeing either leave; we had plenty of business. When the lobby stood empty, I put a hand over the saxophone mouth. "That will do."

Beth held the saxophone in awe. "Is this my instrument?"

"No. I could do that too if I played that badly. Come on, we've got fifty more to try." The crowds in the waiting room had left so quickly they'd dropped magazines, at least one purse, and a plastic bag I'm nearly certain contained a kidney. I figured I'd put the kidney in the fridge; if nothing else Mikey could use it to make kidney bean soup.

As I grabbed the bag, my hand brushed something plastic, a kid's toy of some sort. A kazoo. A cheap, plastic, and wax paper kazoo. I picked it up and flicked it to Beth. "Consider this number fifty-one."

The rats began to return, chewing under the door and scampering from behind Rosa's counter. As I opened the door, Beth put the kazoo in her mouth and blew on it. I made a mental note to teach her not to put things in her mouth without washing them first.

"Hum," I said. "It's not a reed. You hum into it."

She began to hum "Happy Birthday" and then stopped and giggled like a six-year-old. I wasn't paying attention to her though. I was watching the army of rats who stood in orderly ranks, staring at her in rapt attention.

"Rosa, call the instrument rental place and have them pick up everything. Grimm's not going to believe this."

Rosa did the politest thing she'd done all day. She ignored me. So I took my piper (well, sort of) and we went back to my office to have a chat.

"Normally it's something we can work with." I sat at my

desk, alternating picking at my cuticles with stabbing rats who came too close. "Normally it's an instrument that magnifies your volume and projects your power out."

Beth began to hum "Auld Lang Syne," and the rats got down off my desk. Fast learner, that one.

"Do you know anything about poodles?"

Beth hummed a "No," causing a wave of rats to jump into the air.

"Let's do the litmus test." I reached into my desk and took out pictures from a recent infestation. I found the one I wanted, a toy poodle. Big one, maybe two or three pounds, perched on the back of the man he'd killed, growling. "Cute or not?"

Her lips curled upward in a smile, when what I really needed was a snarl. I put my head down on my desk. "Fairy Godfather will never let me live this down." I shoved the picture toward her, but instead Beth took my hand.

"You hypocrite. You lecture about me having tattoos, you've got a little ink yourself. Got a tramp stamp too?" She held on to my left hand as though she'd found the murder weapon in a Sherlock Holmes mystery. Beth wasn't the first person to make that mistake. The morning I woke up and found the scars had turned inky black, I nearly had a breakdown.

"That's not a tattoo." I pointed at the raised edges. Together, they formed a picture of a rose in a ring of woven thorns. "That's a mark. The handmaiden's mark."

"It looks a lot like a tattoo."

"It's the symbol of the Black Queen. If and when you start having to deal with Kingdom folks, I wouldn't mention her. She's been dead for more than four hundred years, and folks are still terrified." I leaned back in my chair, rubbing my fingers over the scars.

Beth was no idiot. The look she gave me clearly said she was calling bull on my claim. "If she's been dead that long, how'd you get her mark?"

"Dead doesn't mean gone. A few years ago I went through a mirror, picked a fight with a fairy, and killed her using the Black Queen's own hand. That's like killing a black hole with a garden rake, in case you are wondering."

I have to admit, the look of fear on Beth's face made me quite pleased. I expected people to treat me with a little respect, and to accept that around here I knew what I was doing. If I hadn't been a teenager so recently, I don't think I could have stood being in the same room with one. "Any more questions?"

She kept her eyes off me, but finally she spoke up. "What's Kingdom?"

I smiled, went to the door to grab my jacket, and opened my office door. "You look hungry. Grab that kazoo and let's go get some lunch."

Beth stood, but to her credit, I could see the defiance still in her. She reminded me of myself in that way. "What is Kingdom?"

I had to get her on board with helping me with this year's Poodling. It wasn't about the money, or the magic. It was about the fact that everything pointed to this being the worst year for poodles in a decade at least. I gestured to the door. "I think you need to see it for yourself."

Seven

~

WE DROVE DOWN to the Gates of Kingdom, at the far edge of the city, and sat there, watching people turn up the Avenue. Beth was an East Side girl, according to her application.

She watched the crowds move back and forth, humming on her kazoo to pass the time. "You want to tell me what we're doing here?" Every time she hummed, the pigeons around us began Irish line dancing a version of *Gutterdance*.

"You ever drive up that street?"

She looked over at me. "I don't have my license."

That wasn't a bad thing in my book. "You'll never be able to turn that corner again as a passenger unless the driver's got magic too. If you pass through the gates and he doesn't, you'll hit the concrete at full speed."

The look she gave me said I was more than a little crazy. Given what she'd lived through since she first started attracting rats, it was likely she'd be spending money on therapy for the rest of her life.

"Let's go. We're here to eat lunch, and we're here to see Liam. I don't actually care if we eat lunch or not, but I'm not going to get to see him by sitting here." I got out and walked to the corner of the Avenue. I couldn't actually see the Gates of Kingdom, but I knew they were there.

Beth came along behind me, still wondering what we were doing on the wrong end of the city, at a street corner that looked like every other. I pulled her toward me. "Each time I take a step, you do." Again I got the "Holy crap she's crazy" look. I got it a lot.

One step forward down the Avenue. Nothing changed. I glanced over to Beth as the crowds shuffled past and gave her a smile. Crazy, said her face. Two steps in, nothing different, and she looked like she was deciding if I was off my meds or on too many. Three steps farther and the magic kicked in. The hair on the back of my neck stood up and I got goose bumps all over my arms. The smug look ran off Beth's face like a hot dog vendor slapped with a health inspection.

"Get ready." I took one more step, and as I did the crowd around me faded like ghosts while a new set emerged, becoming more solid. To the normal folks, I'd look like I stepped in front of someone, or someone pushed their way in front of me. I glanced around. "Beth? Beth Crowley, you there?"

Her voice sounded like it came from a thousand yards away. "Marissa? I can't see you."

"Don't move at all!" I yelled. I shivered as I realized what had happened, fear, not excitement, this time. So you might have figured out that the Gates of Kingdom acted as a kind of exit or overpass for the Avenue. Folks with magic passed through them, and instead of walking down the Avenue they took the bridge to High Kingdom, which overlapped the city like a ghost dimension.

Another possibility lurked here as well.

An underpass of sorts, a tunnel a person could accidentally fall into if they had enough sorrow, despair, or evil to make the trip. The gates could take you to *Low* Kingdom, where trolls played "Bad Cop, Bad Cop" with unfortunate passersby, and the streetlamps were lit with pixies being burned to death.

"Beth, I want you to step backwards very slowly." If she had gone too far, she wouldn't be able to. There was a day when I chose to walk into Low Kingdom. A day when I had enough pain and sadness to hide any hope or happiness. These days, I couldn't enter if I wanted to. Having a boyfriend, a best friend, and a boss who actually respected me made getting into Low Kingdom damn near impossible.

I stepped backwards, and Beth flickered back into view right beside me. Grabbing her hand, I dragged her one step forward. My contact with her would force her to come with me into High Kingdom. The air exploded with color as we passed the barrier and the gates activated, tearing the real world away. I took a few more steps to be sure.

"I saw . . ." She fixed me with a look of horror, but the words wouldn't come. I knew what she saw. I'd been there. Then her eyes caught the glint of gold on the streets, and the shimmering facade of magical store fronts. Trumpets blared as a procession of ogres marched past, displaying Kingdom's military and magical might.

A squirrel ran up to us, ignoring me and tugging at Beth's leg. "Please? Take me with you. I'll be your lifelong friend."

"Go away." Once it latched on to her, it would never leave Beth alone.

Beth knelt, tickling the squirrel's chin. "You're a cute little guy."

"Leave her alone and find someone else to pester." I let my tone imply that I'd eaten squirrel dumplings before and would probably do so again.

"You're my friend!" The squirrel began to dance around Beth, the bonding ritual.

I snagged it by the tail and shoved it headfirst into the post-office box on the corner. With any luck, the postal gnomes would ship it to Cambodia.

Beth stared at me like I'd crushed it.

"What? I warned him. Welcome to Kingdom."

BETH ALTERNATED BETWEEN crying over a talking squirrel and staring at the wyverns, trolls, and princesses for the better part of the next ten minutes. Finally, I led her to a cart where dozens more talking squirrels waited. "I have to make a phone call. You stay here and talk to these little guys, and if you still want one, when I get back, I'll buy it for you." I left her there, cooing and giggling as she traded greetings, and went to call Liam.

Grimm usually acted as a sort of telephone operator for calls between his agents. He soon tired of the sorts of conversations Liam and I had, and set up our own private "chat" line. All I had to do was put my hand on my bracelet and think of Liam.

"Liam?" I was used to looking in mirrors or anything that can reflect when I called by bracelet, but since neither of us were fairies, Grimm said we didn't have a data plan, just voice.

After a moment he answered. "Kind of busy, M. Call you back?" In the background, someone screamed, someone else growled, and then came a crunching sound like chicken bones snapping.

"What are you doing?" Then I remembered what day it was. "Are you fighting with the bridge troll again? What did I tell you about that? Let it go."

"Maybe."

Maybe, my ass. "You either are or you aren't."

"I'm not."

I so wished I could scowl at him, so I made certain he could hear it in my tone. "Are you telling me there isn't a bridge troll within ten feet of you?"

He panted as he ran. "No. Definitely not even within twenty feet. I'm trying to get a few loose ends tied up before I leave."

Grimm had spent the last couple weeks trying to persuade a certain troll to stop devouring bicyclists. I don't actually think Grimm cared about the cyclists, but the troll showed signs of spandex poisoning, and trolls weren't known for listening to their dieticians.

"Listen, I'm taking our new piper to lunch at the Mile High Club. Meet me there?" From Liam's end, the drone of cars passing overhead confirmed what I already suspected.

"Give me forty-five minutes," said Liam. I didn't like it. He could've walked there in twenty, which meant he wanted to have another go at the troll before he left. Boyfriend, I reminded myself. Not slave (at least, not all the time), so I let it go.

Back at the cart, Beth had her kazoo to her mouth and was humming "It's a Small World" as loud as one could on a plastic kazoo, which wasn't very loud. In the cages, animals rocked back and forth, enthralled. As I walked up, a look of relief swept through her. She took the kazoo out and dropped her shoulders.

I smiled. Maybe this year's Poodling would go better after all. "Looks like someone is figuring out how to control their power."

She glared at the stack of cages. "They don't ever shut up." Another lesson learned, but I had another to teach, and doing that required a visit to my third least favorite place in the world. Number two was the Kingdom Post Office. Inferno ranked at Four, in case you are wondering. Yeah, I'd rather go to hell than visit the post office. The Department of Licensing was a special case. I hated it worse than the others combined, but as far as I'm concerned the DOL *is* a province of Inferno.

We walked down streets, taking our time. Gradually Beth learned to close her mouth, and to look out for wyvern droppings, and not to talk to strange clowns in weird masks. That's not a Kingdom-specific lesson, but obviously no one ever taught it to her. "Here." I pointed across the street to a shop. Not the Mile High Club, yet.

The outside of the shop was your standard Kingdom magical facade. Pink, shimmery, and glittered in the sun. The gold lettering on the door said "Isyle Witch" in large block letters.

"Does that mean 'witch' like warts and cauldrons and spells?" asked Beth. She was actually taking most of this well.

"Yup. We're here on business though. Just making a pit stop. This place is like a hardware store. You ever need something magical, you get it here. We use her because her bindings are the strongest of all the witches." I pointed to an eight-page contract framed in the window.

"There are more?" Her voice had a tremor this time.

"In Low Kingdom, yes. You don't go to Low Kingdom. Ever. You need something magical, you come here." I'd get her a map of Kingdom before we left and mark out all the bad places to eat.

Beth stood rock-still, staring at the ground. "Is that where I was going, back where the world went away?"

I leaned against a newspaper machine. "Yeah. Out of curiosity, how many times have you eaten human flesh in the last

year? The limit's once if you want to enter High Kingdom."
Her stare told me she hadn't eaten at any hot dog vendors for
quite a while. "Okay, no human flesh. So you've had it pretty
rough. You can be evil, or you can be sad. Either will open the
underpass to Low Kingdom."

I took her hand and led her inside. Her look said she didn't
really want to go. Even I didn't really want to go, but business
was business. I opened the door to the witch's shop and
motioned her in. Inside, the humidity was at least one hundred percent, and at the temperature inside, I could bake a
chicken in my pocket while I browsed.

"Who enters my home?" asked the witch. The counter
wasn't visible from the doorway, so I took Beth and led her
over to the corner where a huge crystal vat held dozens of frogs.

The witch saw me, Beth saw the witch, and that's about
when the screaming started. I walked over to the counter and
nodded. "How's business?"

"Is your pet going to do this the entire time?" The witch
pointed to an engraved plaque that read "No Screaming." The
one below it read "No Shoes, No Shirt, No Soul, No Service."

The witch leaned across the counter. "I'll make an excep-
tion in your case."

"Nah, she's got to get over this. Beth, come here." Beth
didn't move, so I went and moved her. Also, I might have
clamped my hand over her mouth, you know, to move her.
And she might have bitten me twice. "Beth, this is the Isyle
Witch. Witch, this is Beth. Beth's going to be a piper."

Beth took a break from screaming to stutter, "Her eyes."

The witch grinned, wrinkled lips pulling back across
toothless gums. "I see as well as you do, child. Better, when it
comes to the spirit world." The witch stared at her, showing
sickly yellow eyes, like someone had removed her pupil and
iris, leaving only diseased white in their place.

"It's the witch mark. She's got the witch mark. I've got the
handmaiden's mark." I held up my hand to show my rose scar.
I looked at the witch. "Is there a piper mark?"

The Isyle Witch shook her head.

I looked back at Beth, trying to make sure my face said "I
care about your problems" more than "gut up and deal with it."

"Well, you've still got a lovely tattoo of a dinosaur on your shoulder. So we're all friends with weird tattoos on our eyes, or hands, or shoulders. Now, will you *please* stop screaming?"

Beth shut her mouth but did her best to hide behind me.

Which gave me the chance to actually do some business. "Got any new frogs since Ari was in? I'll take them if you do."

The witch reached behind the counter and brought out a trident.

"Alive."

She sighed and handed me a net and a plastic bag. I took Beth (who maintained a death grip on my shoulder) over and fumbled in my purse until I found a cracker in a plastic wrapper. I pointed to the frogs. "See, some of these are *amphibious normalcus*. That's your garden-variety frog. Some of them, however, are most likely royalty."

Beth stopped giving me a bruise on my shoulder to look at the hordes of frogs swimming back and forth. "How do you know which is which?"

"I'm glad you asked." I unwrapped the cracker and held it over the tank. Most of the frogs dove for the bottom in fear, but four of them floated near the top, beady little eyes fixed on me. I held my hand closer and all but one opened its mouth.

Beth clapped her hands. "I get it! Frogs eat flies, but those are willing to eat crackers, so you know they were once human!"

"Hardly." I scooped the four up and dumped them into the bag in one motion. "There are two key things that tell you I've got three princes and probably a businessman who was in the wrong place at the wrong time. First off, they weren't afraid when I came up to the tank. That means they're too stupid to have lived in the wild. Secondly, three of them opened their mouths when I offered them food, meaning they're so lazy they can't even be bothered to flick a tongue. They feel entitled to be fed by hand. Lastly, they're dumb enough to eat something that would kill them. Stupid, lazy, and entitled. That's how you recognize a prince."

I walked over to the counter where the witch waited and took out my company card. I wanted Beth to see this. "Time to pay." I tapped the card and it changed into a glass vial filled with glowing gold dust. "This is Glitter. It's the currency of magic, and while you'll need plenty of green in the real world, you'll need this to buy anything in Kingdom."

I tapped the vial, and a swirl of Glitter ran from it onto the witch's scales, exactly paying my bill. Not one speck more or less. Beth looked at the pile of dust with awe and wonder. "I don't have any of that."

"Exactly." I nodded to the witch. "Thanks again, and have a good one."

"Handmaiden," said the witch, "have you used my gift to you?"

A few years ago she gave me a potion. A love potion, which I almost used and almost made a horrible mess of everything. I still had it, locked in a safe-deposit box in Grimm's office. "I found love on my own, thanks."

The witch nodded and smiled at me. "Then you are truly ready for our queen's return."

I took Beth and dragged her from the shop as fast as I could, running down the street outside so fast, I almost ran over a group of senior citizens tap-dancing with canes and walkers.

Beth came running after me. "What was that about?"

"She's crazy. Obsessed with the idea that the Black Queen is going to come back." I looked at my bag of shaken and stirred frogs. "I only go in there on business. Speaking of which, let's head on over to the restaurant and talk money."

WITH A STREAM of rats behind us, we entered the base of the building that led to the Mile High Club and waited for the elevator. Places like that were posh enough to afford separate up and down elevators. The up ones only go up, the down ones, well, you get the idea. While we waited, I began my pitch.

"You're going to need to make a living. In time you'll get enough control over your power that you won't accidentally attract rats or teenagers. Then you're going to need to decide how you are going to make money."

"I need to eat," said Beth. This was a somewhat obvious statement, since Beth was both skeleton thin and not likely to stop eating anytime soon.

"You do indeed. Ever been to a concert where it seemed like only one of the band members could play, and everyone else had taken music lessons by mail? Yet their concerts sold out and people lined up to hear them?"

Her eyes lit up with understanding.

"So I have to ask, Beth. How interested are you in being beheaded?"

It took her a moment to be sure she heard me right, and a moment longer to figure out how to answer that question. She narrowed her eyes. "Not at all."

"Well, in that case, I need to give you a few ground rules. Pipe teenage boys to music concerts? No problem. Authorities will smile, people will love you. Pipe adult men to follow you to war or elect you to office?" I drew my hand across my neck. "We'll get to see how you look with about ten inches off the top."

"So I can control more than animals?" A dangerous smile spread across her face. One that made me hope she had a good neckline, and no plans for an open-casket funeral.

I looked her in the eye. "Men are just another species of animal."

"Are you talking about me again?" asked Liam, joining me in line. He picked me up off the ground in a huge hug and then kissed me twice.

Beth looked at him like she'd encountered an ogre.

"Beth, this is Liam. Liam, this is Beth, our newest piper."

"Pleased to meet you, Beth." Liam gave her that goofy grin of his and took her hand. "What instrument do you play?"

Beth spent a moment looking guilty, then took her kazoo out of her pocket and waved it at him.

"No, really. What do you play?" Liam asked.

I gave his shin a vicious kick.

"You know," he said, "I hear that Marissa is looking for help with poodles this year." I'd make sure he understood his mistake later.

"I'm still not sure how I'm going to help," said Beth, giving my boyfriend far too friendly a smile for my tastes.

If she tried her "follow me" trick with him, I'd introduce her to the business end of a bus in short order. "Beth wants a job where she can earn a little green and a little gold. I was about to tell her that I might have a position opening up."

Liam raised his eyebrows at me, but kept his mouth shut, even giving me a hand kicking rats out of the elevator. I figured we'd have plenty of time to eat while the rats figured out a way up, and whenever they arrived, well, that would be our signal that the lunch special just ended.

Once we were seated, Beth alternated between inhaling platefuls of pasta and staring at the view. I'd brought her to this place on purpose. I needed to impress her, needed her commitment to help with the Poodling, and I figured the view from a restaurant over a mile in the sky would be just the thing.

It was.

The longer she stared out the window, the less she ate. When she finally came back she looked completely dazed. "I never thought I'd see something like this."

"You never thought you'd be followed by hordes of rats. You never thought you'd need to keep them away with a kazoo, and you also never thought there were at least two additional layers to the city that you'd never known existed." I figured that if she was going to deal with stuff, I might as well make her deal with it all.

"I'm a piper." She turned the kazoo over in her fingers, like it was magic instead of a few cents' worth of plastic.

"Yes. So tell me, Beth. Will you help me with my poodle problem? I'll train you to control your power. I'll teach you to stop calling waves of rats. You will help me send about a thousand tiny monsters to their death before they kill half the people in the city." I stared at her, knowing what I needed her answer to be.

"These 'poodles.' They're dangerous?"

I nodded. "We lose people every year to 'Oh, what a cute little dog. Does it want a treat?' What they want is your liver, preferably torn straight out of your chest. You'd be saving people."

"Then you've got yourself a deal," she said. A grin spread across her face like I hadn't seen before. "But I want my piercings back. At least a few of them."

"Long as you don't die of lead poisoning, you can va-jazzle yourself to your heart's content." At last I could relax. Beth would learn to control the poodles enough for us to run them off into the ocean. Grimm would once again get to say "Marissa, you were right," my favorite phrase to hear from all the men in my life.

Beth got up from her chair and looked around. "I, umm, need to use the restroom."

"The restroom? Or the restrooms?" Liam pointed over his shoulder at a set of doors. "Those are the restrooms. If you actually need to go to the bathroom, you want that one over there." He pointed to a much smaller set of doors.

Beth looked at him like now the third eye had attached to his head.

"Beth, with a name like 'The Mile High Club,' didn't it occur to you that there might be people having sex almost anyplace private?" I smiled as a look of shock spread over her face. "Small restrooms are for using the bathroom."

She shuffled off to the small bathrooms, eyeing everyone else at the tables she passed with suspicion.

Liam caught my hand, and smiled at me. "Remember the scene in that one film where the lady in brown meets her cousin's husband? What did she tell him? *Il ya un gopher dans mon pantalon.* It means 'Things are going to be fine.'"

Despite his claim of having a gopher in his pants, I almost believed him.

Eight

FRIDAY CAME TOO soon. The truth was, if Friday had come next year, it would have come too soon. I'm not a controlling, possessive woman. Okay, I am possessive. I'm terribly jealous, and impossibly in love, but it wasn't just that. I missed Liam already, and he wasn't even gone.

We drove to the airport, and Ari came along to give me company on the way back. I had hoped for trouble getting through security. Or a long baggage line, or a problem with Liam's passport. Anything to give us more time. Airport security selected me for the random mammogram and anal probe and let Liam breeze through.

We sat in the terminal, lines of passengers rushing past us and announcers blaring out warnings in every language on earth. I leaned up against him, and he put his arm around me.

"It's only two weeks, M. Then we'll have enough Glitter to end this curse. Enough money to retire on, if you want. We can raise our kids and work when we want to, if we want to." His chin prickled the top of my head as I looked up at him.

"Kids?" We'd talked about one. I wanted a daughter of my own. Liam wanted a son. The thought of being responsible for another life scared me worse than a platoon of gremlins in an espresso bar, but it would give me the chance to love someone the way I wished I had been.

Liam misread the look on my face. "We don't have to have a whole litter."

"How 'bout one, to start? We can add on later." I didn't bother trying to hide the tears that came to my eyes.

Liam wrapped me in his arms and held me. All my adult life I'd always been the strong woman. The one who could walk into a room full of goblins knowing I'd be shooting someone. The one who climbed a beanstalk in spite of my fear of heights and did a low oxygen jump to escape. With Liam, I didn't have to be that person.

"Don't go," I said, holding on to his shirt with both hands.

He put his hands over mine, rough and warm, and smiled. "I'll be back before you know it. Like that guy said in the third film, *Si seulement il y avait un moyen de sauver les canards.* It means 'I couldn't ever forget you.'"

He'd actually lamented not being able to save the ducks, but I didn't feel like pointing that out. Liam was leaving. No matter what I told him, no matter what I said, he was going to get on that plane and fly to Europe. I'd spend the rest of the month alone while he worked a job that only mattered to him because of our future.

Then it was time for him to board. We kissed. I said I loved him more times than I could count, and he walked away to security. I stood, isolated in a throng of passing people, alone in a crowd.

ARI WAITED FOR me back at the car, lost in her own thoughts. As we drove back, I finally spoke. "How'd training go?" I hadn't seen Ari the rest of Wednesday but heard she didn't get back until well after three in the morning.

Ari rubbed her fingers together, generating surges of lightning as she worried.

"You failed the retake in civics?" I privately resolved to make it clear to Grimm that if he cut into her study time, he was footing the bill for her retaking the class.

"The damage from the Wild Magic isn't healing as fast as Grimm thought it would."

I had to write a five-paragraph paper on each of the sources of magic during training, then had to rewrite when an off-leash hellhound ate not only the paper but the courier carrying it back to the Agency for me. The way I understood it, a seal bearer's magic came from three sources: first off, the realm seal itself. Secondly, from inside the seal bearer herself. Those two were limited. The magic in the environment, around us, that was Wild Magic. It could be safely used as long as it was mixed with a little of the other two.

"Grimm will think of something. I'll make him." I silently worried as I drove back. Magic couldn't directly oppose magic. Damage from one type of magic couldn't be undone with another type, normally. Then again, nothing about magic-wielding, seal-bearing princesses was remotely normal. So maybe the same rules didn't apply. Maybe.

BACK AT THE Agency, I sank into a normal workday. I convinced the kobolds to leave by telling them I'd seen a dead deer in the alley on my way in. I sent Payday George away with a twenty-dollar bill and received a promise not to come back. A promise that would last at least until Monday. I returned another call from the owner of a shoe factory in west Pennsylvania who couldn't figure out why his factory machines turned themselves on at night. That one I'd have to deal with. If you think child labor laws are restrictive, elf labor laws are about a dozen times worse.

Then I put my head down on my desk and wished for the day to be over.

You'd think that having worked the last eight years for the Fairy Godfather, I'd get at least one wish. No such luck. Rosa poked her head in the door.

"Someone I need to take care of?"

"Yes." In eight years, I'd come to believe that if Rosa spoke more than six words at a time, she'd explode. Single syllables, a glare that could turn your blood to ice, and a sawed-off shotgun kept our lobby in order.

"Send them in."

A moment later, a soft knock on the door preceded a trio of dwarves entering my office. Three feet tall, nasty beards, and every last one of them had a beer bottle in one hand. And I recognized these three. "You're too late. Liam's flight was this morning. Didn't he tell you he was going to Europe on business?"

The tallest of the three (by about an inch) took the red cap off his head and walked forward. "Magnus Mage, ma'am. Ms. Locks, we were hoping that you could help us. It ain't about yer man." He shuffled forward and dropped a jewelry box on my desk. "And we were 'posed to have this ready Monday, but Yiffy there bet me he could go on a longer bender."

I picked up the box, black metal with invisible hinges, and snapped it open. Inside lay a single gold band with a diamond inset. A ridiculously large diamond inset. I know my gems, and there was no way this wasn't real. "You made this for Liam?"

"Aye. Though I think 'twer for you. He been giving us the fire to forge it for the last few months."

Gaze locked on the ring, I lifted it, slipping it on. "He wasn't playing cards." Right then I knew I'd never take it off. "So tell me what you need."

The second dwarf stepped forward, hat in hand. "No authorities, miss. We were hoping you could handle this without their involvement. It'd be best if you saw for yourself."

"Few ground rules: If you've killed someone, I'm calling the cops. If you are dealing drugs, I'm calling the cops. If you are wanting me to buy Girl Scout cookies, I'm calling the cops. Anything else, I'll help you with." I grabbed my purse, put on my jacket, and headed for the door.

"Rosa, tell Grimm I'm doing some field investigation," I said as I left. She gave me the stink eye like always. Then I took three wee little men down to my car and we went for a drive.

It took almost forty-five minutes to get there, mostly because the dwarves couldn't see over the dashboard to give me direction, and wouldn't sit in the booster seat I kept for exactly that purpose. When we finally pulled up in front of a tired strip mall at the edge of Chinatown, I was so glad to be there I almost forgave their constant bickering.

"Small Wonders Jewelry," read the sign outside the shop. The dwarves piled out of the car and into the shop, opening bars and grates and finally opening six different locks. Once we were inside, they locked the whole thing behind us.

"I thought you guys were forbidden to have shops anywhere outside of Kingdom." Generally speaking, you don't find anything but humans roaming the city, and definitely not setting up businesses. Dwarves, however, could pretend to be little people.

"That's practically an Americans with Disabilities violation, right there," said Magnus. I followed them into a back room, into a vault, and there Magnus unlocked a door a toddler would have trouble fitting through. I recognized the room inside as an elevator. "You'll have to go down by yerself first, on account of your hideous size and smell," said Magnus. "We'll be along after you. Don't touch nothing."

So I crammed myself into the box, pulling my knees up to my chest, and panicked as the elevator plunged downward. The ride went on for what felt like two or three eternities. I really can't say how far it went down, traveling so fast my stomach caught in my throat, but when the elevator finally slowed and the door opened, my legs were stiff.

I stumbled and rolled out of the elevator, surrounded by a fog of smoke and the roar of flames. It was your typical dwarven forge. I'd spent a lot of time in Liam's studio where he did his ironwork, so I knew the basics. Get things hot, use pure muscle to bend them. Pretty much the same approach men use for everything.

Clouds of coal smoke floated above me. Then the elevator rattled. It was near impossible for it to be back that fast. To move like that it must have plummeted at terminal velocity or faster. A trio of dwarves stumbled out, their hair twisted wildly, looking like they'd skydived down the chute.

"This is where Liam's been coming?"

Magnus nodded. "Been working with us for a year. And all he wanted was a few trinkets."

"How exactly did he pay you?" I didn't keep secrets from Liam, and I was more than a little surprised he'd managed to keep this one from me. He wasn't usually good at that sort of thing.

"Fool. Paid us in pure cubic zirconia and hellfire. Anyone

can come up with diamonds or rubies. Zirconia, on the other hand is worth its weight in gold."

Magnus walked over and took my hand. "Let me see that."

I grudgingly removed the ring and handed it to him. He held it in the forge until the gold glowed. "We put your name and his inside the ring. That and the sculpting ain't visible till it gets hot." He removed the band from the fire and revealed the hidden script. Only dwarves had the skill to do that kind of writing. And the outside of the ring was no longer plain gold—it had a pattern on it, like scales. In fact, the whole ring looked changed. It was a dragon clasping the diamond in his mouth.

"That's amazing. And if it weren't for the third-degree burns it would take to see it, I'd admire it more often. Seriously, what is it with dwarves and engravings you can only see when you are being burned to death or baked in a casserole?"

Magnus snorted and dropped the glowing ring into his hand. Dwarves were flame resistant, sure, but this seemed extreme. Then he grabbed my hand and slipped the ring on. It was cool to the touch, despite the fact that I could still see the scales fading into the gold. "Put yer hand in the fire."

I held my hand closer and closer to the fire, then passed my hand briefly over the flame. I felt a warm draft, but it didn't even singe my sleeve. The next pass I reached into the flame. The flame flickered over me like warm running water.

"We didn't need no hellfire fer the forging. But fer the enchantment, that took all he could give."

I closed my hand into a fist, resolved that I would never take that ring off again willingly. Protection from hellfire. The ability to be close to him and not worry about whether a burp would leave me with blisters. An engagement ring. It was everything I could ask for.

My determination forged as firmly as the ring on my hand, I looked up at them. "Show me what's wrong."

The trio walked away, down paths through heaps of swords and armor, kicking aside a pile of what I'm dead certain were rubies. Magnus pointed down into a hole, a pit of darkness. "We were looking for more zirconia. Too many worthless diamonds, and stupid gold blocking our way. Then Yiffy gets the idea to dig *under* the blasted stuff.

"Wait." That last phrase had triggered an image in my mind. A certain memory of a disaster from a few years ago. "Tell me you didn't dig out of bounds. Tell me you didn't dig beyond the surveyor's limits."

Three very small men all avoided looking at me.

"Did you dig into a freaking balrog? Again? I don't care what I said, if you dug up a balrog, say so now so that I can go get the army. I know you all want magic solutions, but nothing says 'You shall not pass' like a howitzer." I crossed my arms and tapped my foot while I waited.

"Ain't no balrog," said Magnus. "Truth be, I don't know what it is."

"Anything going to eat me or otherwise kill me if I go in there and take a look?" I watched their faces for signs of a lie. Dwarves aren't known for being big on betrayal, but I'd rather catch Judas now than later.

"No, ma'am," said Magnus.

So I took out my flashlight and headed into the tunnel. True to form, it went deeper and deeper, arcing down so steeply that at times I almost slipped. Also, because they'd dug it for themselves, I was reduced to crawling. I'd bill them for the dress slacks later.

Then the tunnel stopped up short. Dwarves leave smooth rock behind as they go, perfectly round with a nice rough patch underfoot to keep you from slipping, or to shred the knees in two-hundred-dollar dress slacks. The wall broke off into rough rock. I stepped in and one glance told me whatever the dwarves had tunneled into, it was old.

Old as in high-arched ceilings, tall enough that I could easily stand up. Old as in "not built by humans." The floor underneath was carved rock, carved in a pattern like scales that I had seen before from a curse. As I stood there, the tunnel lit up.

In movies, the explorers always find lit torches. Torches require fuel, and they tend to dry out. The wall sconces held flames, but not torches. So this tunnel might be forgotten, but it wasn't abandoned. The lighting still worked, coming on when needed.

A heavy oak door hung on iron hinges in the wall, with an intricate lock and cast metal handle in the shape of a gargoyle.

It stood slightly open, and from behind it came a warm breeze with the scent of sulfur. I shone my light at the edge of the door and noticed a ring of white crystal just inside the room.

Definitely time to call for help.

I took my compact out of my purse and opened it. "Grimm? I could really use some of your expertise."

He snapped into view, a smile on his face. "Liam's flight left New York without incident a few minutes ago. Where exactly are you, my dear?"

I held up the compact and showed it around. "Dwarves found it by accident."

"Do I need to call the army? I'd like to remind you that you are not a wizard. Being able to pull a card from a deck does not even qualify you as a magician, Marissa."

I held the compact up to show him the door. "Not a balrog. Whatever it is, it's old. You three, was that door open when you found it?" I spun to look at the dwarves, who'd followed me down. Again they studied their feet. "You *do not* open doors. Especially not ancient ones in collapsed tunnels where you aren't supposed to be in the first place. Grimm, there's like half a dozen workplace safety violations here, but I don't see anything for me to do. Any idea what this place is?"

Grimm thought for a moment. "I think if there were anything hungry behind it, you would already be eaten. Open the door, but don't go in. Let's see what lies beyond."

I swung the door open, and in response, the sconces in the room lit up, throwing orange light across it. From edge to edge, it had to be at least thirty yards across, and the walls were the same crystal that ringed the door. It glowed orange, pulsing with a light like lava. In the center of the room stood a huge table, tall enough that it would come to my chin, and off to the side was a circle of runes I recognized as a summoning circle.

The circle pulsed red and the occasional burst of flame ringed the edges. "They left it open," said Grimm, almost to himself. "That explains the additional poodles. Marissa, shut the door." I swung the door shut, and as I did a gust of wind and a foul odor of sulfur came gusting out, buffeting me. I threw myself against it.

"Who has the key?" said Grimm, yelling at the dwarves.

Magnus rushed forward and handed me a cast-iron key, long and slender with a single tooth at the end of it. I thrust it into the lock and turned it. At that moment, claws scraped across the wood on the other side. I stood rooted to the spot as something snuffled on the other side, letting out bellows. A sour stench worked its way into my nose.

I yanked the key from the lock, backed away up the tunnel, then crawled as fast as I could through the darkness. At any moment, I expected I'd hear the screams of dwarves being taken by something, and then it would be after me. Back at the forge, I ran straight for the elevator, slipping in a pile of diamonds and getting quite a bruise from where I landed on a helmet.

It wasn't until after the elevator ride, which seemed to go on for hours, that I finally stopped gasping and shaking. I considered myself good at my job. But part of being good at my job was understanding which battles I was able to fight and which ones were a job for hired spell slingers, priests, or lawyers.

In the closed-up jeweler's shop, I stopped running and found a mirror where I could have a proper conversation with Grimm.

"What was that?" I still hadn't caught my breath.

Grimm waited for me to stop panting, then spoke. "The room is most certainly a dealing room. Contracts, not cards. It's like a visitor's forum several hundred miles above the surface of Inferno, where someone foolish enough to make deals with demons could do so. Whoever last accessed the room left the summoning gate unlocked, and then our half-sized friends opened the door. Now that it's shut, we shouldn't have worse than normal poodle issues, though I'd prefer to close that portal."

"So whatever that was could get out?"

"No, my dear. That's Celestial Crystal forming the boundary. While I'm certain it would have been quite frightening, demons *cannot* cross into a realm unless called by one under contract. If you'd like to go back down there and open the door, I'll have a word with it." Grimm said it like I was going to the grocery store.

"That doesn't sound like a good idea, Grimm." I had this mortal fear of death that kept me from doing certain things.

Grimm shrugged. "All right then. I'll send a team of clerks down to check it out later."

"You mean clerics, right?" I looked over as the elevator began to rattle, signaling what I hoped was the arrival of my dwarven clients.

"Clerics are expensive. Clerks work for minimum wage and don't have health benefits. It's cheaper to hire a team of them than a single cleric."

As the elevator opened and the dwarves came stumbling out, Grimm faded away. "Fairy Godfather will send a threat assessment team of experts soon. I'll be keeping this," I said, pocketing the key, "so that it doesn't accidentally get opened. Again."

The dwarves were careful not to meet my stare. When I finally left the jewelry shop above hell I drove back to the Agency and spent the rest of the day doing normal stuff, like torching the lost-and-found pile with a flamethrower.

Nine

AT FOUR O'CLOCK, I called everyone into my office. I liked to make assignments on Fridays so that when Monday morning came around, we could jump right into work. We didn't work weekends anymore unless it was an emergency. Which it often was. I gathered Ari, myself, Rosa, and, against my better judgment, Mikey. Grimm kept telling me how important it was to include the intern.

I shuffled through the list of new clients, sorted out a few that looked important. "Ari, you'll handle a grocery store on 11th. Based on the smell, it either has a yeti living in it or a pack of homeless people. Either way, going to be hard to re-open with them there."

"One charm job, check." Ari could soothe almost any sort of savage beast. Except dragons. That was my realm of expertise. She looked at me. "What exactly will you be doing?"

"I'm going back to school." I waited for her dubious stare. Cheerful? Absolutely. Optimistic? Unfortunately, one thing Ari wasn't was gullible. "I'm kidding. Grimm's magic monitors detected a spike in a college theater dressing room. I'm guessing a minor hex put there by some understudy."

Rosa whispered to Mikey more words than I'd seen her

say in a month. He got that stupid grin like he'd eaten another ten pounds of bacon. "According to the monitors, it might be a magic mirror. At your college."

Ari sat up straight. The blood drained from her face and her eyes went wide. "Grimm doesn't do student consultations, and I'm certain he wasn't checking in on me. M, you think there's another fairy in town?"

I still remembered the last time a fairy came to town. They're normally pretty territorial, but that didn't stop Odette from offering me a few wishes. People always said, "Be careful what you wish for." Odette, Fairy Godmother, wished for me, and gave me what I always wanted. The experience almost killed me.

"Grimm?" I waited for him to appear in the mirror. "Odds on it actually being a magic mirror at Ari's college?"

Grimm looked at me like I'd asked him the odds on winning the lottery. "A billion to one. At least. Make that six billion. If you insist on my input, I'd suspect an acne-causing spell."

I gave Ari my "what did I tell you" smile. "But, let's say it was another fairy. This time around, I'd play nice. No throwing onyx at mirrors. No insults or Peter Pan references. I'd talk to them, turn down their offer of employment, and try to feel out what exactly they thought they were doing in Grimm's town."

"What about me?" Mikey would've wagged his tail if he had one at the moment. "I'm practically an agent. I could be both halves of a K-9 unit."

"Mikey, if I promoted you twice you might be on the same level as the plants in the waiting room. Monday we're getting a huge shipment of laxatives that need to get into Kingdom on time, or you'll be making enemas for ogres for a week."

Mikey bit his bottom lip, but not before it could quiver.

"Cheer up. We all have to play our part. Hey, you want me to make reservations for your date tonight?" I figured I could toss the kid a bone.

"Got it covered. Liam gave me directions to a killer Italian joint before he left. I'm taking Steph there."

I was so glad I'd already swallowed my coffee. I knew exactly where Liam had recommended they go. My best theory was that some form of magic prevented the health inspector from finding the place. Reaching into my desk drawer, I pulled out a pair of wrapped plastic forks. "Take these with you."

When Rosa and Mikey left me alone with Ari, I finally leaned back and relaxed. "You want to come over and watch a movie?"

Ari blushed. "I'm so sorry, M. Wyatt is taking me out on a date tonight. Someplace romantic."

Ari's idea of romantic would be the vegetable section of the grocery store, because she'd never quite managed to nail down normal princess behavior. Normal meaning "flail helplessly while waiting for a man." I completely approved, and had trained her so that anyone who laid a finger on her would either get punched, spelled, or ventilated with a gun that could punch holes in concrete.

"So when do I get to meet Mr. Right?"

Ari's smile fell away and she looked afraid. "When you can be Marissa, my friend who owns a bookstore, or Marissa, my accountant. Not Marissa, my boss at The Agency, partner of the Fairy Godfather. People understand Godfather. They think *mafia*. Fairies, they think Elton John. You put the two together and people don't understand."

"He's going to find out," I said. "Better he find out from you than discover it the hard way. Like if you bring him home after a date and he meets Yeller. Think the fact that you have a hellhound as a pet might not be a tipoff?"

Ari glared at me. "We've already had that discussion. He's an Aleutian hairless with chronic mange."

"You shouldn't lie to him." I worried a little bit about the fact that she'd obviously given her story some thought. Truth is like a jury summons. It has a nasty way of showing up when you least expect it.

Ari swung her purse onto her arm and headed out at a run. Up front, the security system chimed as Rosa armed it, meaning that the lobby now contained several hundred live asps. Grimm had them brought in from Egypt, along with his monthly shipment of cursed artifacts.

I went to grab a stack of expense reports from our enchanter, figuring I'd get some of the paperwork done. Most of them looked normal. Frogs transformed back into princes, a few hexes laid on a parking spot. I wasn't looking, and when I noticed Grimm watching from the mirror, I almost screamed.

"Evening, Marissa. Friday night, and here you are working. It almost feels like old times."

I have a silver bell on my desk, and he was supposed to ring it to let me know he wanted to talk. "Just trying to get some paperwork done. New enchantress is overcharging us for frogs, and judging from these spell reports, there's a parking spot at Macy's that's like the ninth circle of hell."

"Leave the paperwork for Monday, my dear. It will still be here, and you can keep yourself busy as Liam requested. Doing safe things." Grimm's words reminded me of my promise.

I closed the file. "I'll take some time off when you do." Fairies don't sleep. They don't eat, really. They work night and day at whatever their goals are. Grimm's goals were the collection of magic made solid (Glitter) and preventing the kobolds from forming a professional soccer team. The second was really a hobby.

"Why don't you do an errand for me, then? I have a package that didn't get out in time for the post. It needs to go to Middle Kingdom. You could have dinner there. Watch a parade. Generally speaking, enjoy yourself." Grimm gave me the same stern look he used back when he could order me around.

"Fine." Kingdom on a Friday night was going to be like a rock concert, street parade, and monster mash all in one. Not normally my cup of tea, but package delivery for Grimm almost always involved bullets. "What kind of ammo should I pack?"

Grimm frowned. "I thought I made it clear I want you doing safe things. Leave the gun here. You won't be needing it. In fact, not carrying a weapon will make you more cautious. I gave Liam my word I'd steer you toward less dangerous activities."

I slipped the nine millimeter out of my purse. Leaving my gun behind was like putting one of my kidneys into the drawer instead of a hunk of steel meant to spew death. "What are you going to do?"

Grimm's eyes lit up. "I'm going to reverse the transformation on a few frogs and give them the directional test." The directional test didn't involve up or down. It involved being able to follow the signs saying "Service Exit." Those who walked through the normal exit to the front lobby would be allowed to test their asp resistance.

"Night, Grimm." I picked up a box from outside his office, snuck out the service entrance, and headed out into the city.

By the time I finally *got* to Kingdom, the party was already under way. There were princes drinking champagne, a parade of impromptu floats making its way down the main street, and since it was Friday, even the no-human types were allowed to come out and live a little in Upper Kingdom.

No one powerful, like the fae, thank goodness. The fae were about one step down from fairies in terms of pure power, and thank Kingdom, they mostly stayed to themselves. One of them took an interest in my life, once, and the result put me in the hospital for three days.

If you were mostly human, you could mostly come out in Upper Kingdom, particularly on Friday. I waited for the parade to pass so I could head down to Middle Kingdom, where Grimm's package belonged. Middle Kingdom doesn't even come close to touching our reality. It was where almost everything that couldn't pass for human lived.

The parade went on for blocks. Princes in sports cars. Princesses throwing out bead necklaces. The moment I saw those, I waded into the crowd and elbowed an old lady to get a spot. By the time the car passed me, I was the only person who hadn't mysteriously fallen or gotten pushed over. I caught three of the necklaces.

Think of it like Mardi Gras, except the beads actually had a purpose. I touched my tongue to one and immediately puckered my lips. Yep, these were hangover beads. I was busy adjusting my necklaces when I realized the cheering crowds had grown silent. With that much alcohol in the crowd, there was only one thing that could cause it: The queens had joined the parade.

As best I could tell, all the kings in the royal families did was negotiate treaties, decide who went to war with who, and run the businesses. All the real power belonged to the queens. Every last one of the seven original royal families has a queen, and all but one of them loved to exercise their authority.

The crowds would cheer for the High King, but they'd bow

before the High Queen. Incidentally, there's no matrimonial relationship between High King and High Queen. It'd been tried a couple of times, and that much power concentrated in one relationship made everyone nervous. So the kings negotiated High King however they did it. Queens negotiated High Queen however they did it, and everyone stayed out of the queen's way.

Sure enough, a fleet of convertibles came rolling down the street. The first was empty. That one was reserved for the queen of the First Royal Family, who never took part in festivities. In fact, I don't think anyone had seen her in the last twenty years. It was okay. There was enough bitchiness in the other six to make up for it.

I spent so much time watching the first one go by that I almost missed the second. I wish I had, in fact. I looked out at the next convertible knowing damn well who I was going to see. She stood in the passenger seat, a single hand raised to the crowd. As she passed, they bowed. While I'm not one to grovel, in this particular case, I hit my knees faster than a priest who just found an issue of *Playboy*.

From the corner of my eye I watched her. Tall, sleek black hair, a complexion that was only possible with a ton of makeup, and eyes like black pits. Her thin face and slight build reminded me more of a straight razor than a person. I could break her in half in a fistfight, but it would never come to that. This was Queen Mihail, of the Second Royal Family. The backseat of her convertible was empty. Normally her sons and daughters would ride with her. Of course, I'd sort of made sure that wasn't possible.

See, her son took up with an older woman. Sort of a Mrs. Robinson situation. The son was thoroughly repulsive, completely disgusting, and completely typical for a prince. Incidentally, Ari was supposed to have married him. That didn't exactly work out. Prince Mihail got the bad end of a magic apple, and when last I saw him, he looked like the thing from the black lagoon.

I chanced a look up at the queen as she passed, and froze. It wasn't possible. In a crowd of thousands, her eyes couldn't possibly be fixed on me. But they were. She kept that icy stare fixed on me until the procession carried her out of view. I let out a sigh and realized that somewhere in the process I'd clenched my fists until my nails left marks in my palm.

Queen Mihail had promised me wrath, if anything happened to her son. Not only had something happened, I was directly responsible for that something. So keeping clear of her was on my to-do list.

The third car came into view, and I immediately stood up, a lone figure in a crowd of kneeling drunks. I had a hunch who was in the third car, and I wanted to make something clear: I had no respect for her. The third car belonged to Queen Thromson, queen of the Third Royal Family. Ari's stepmother. The Mrs. Robinson who Prince Mihail had taken up with.

Queen Thromson has also tried to kill me. In fact, the list of people who have tried to kill me was disturbingly long. Some days, it seemed like every new face I met was either going to be my new best friend or my new best enemy. I had enough enemies.

Queen Thromson had gray hair where it wasn't white (courtesy of me), wrinkles like an old leather bag (courtesy of me), and a clutch of red-haired princesses in the car with her. For the record, I had nothing to do with the princesses.

The wrinkles and the hair were because when she tried to kill me, she used magic, and at some point it starts taking quite the toll on you. Also, I might have fired a spell shaped like a bullet at her. Twice.

Unlike Queen Mihail, Queen Thromson found everyone else interesting to look at. She avoided me like I had eye chicken pox. I spent the better part of a year trying to get her arrested for taking up with an evil fairy and nearly killing Ari and myself. Too late I found I'd filed charges in the wrong court.

After four more convertibles passed, the rest of the parade contained nothing but princesses and lesser royal families. Like cockroaches, princesses tended to show up everywhere and proved impossible to get rid of.

I made my way out of Upper Kingdom, delighted to finally be free of the crowds. Middle Kingdom looked like something from a storybook. Thatched roofs, quaint stone chimneys, and the smell of open sewers. Every once in a while I'd get a call from some parent desperate for help with their son or daughter.

It was always the same story. An obsession with role-playing. A closet full of costumes that would look silly on a superhero. Attempting to play the lute. Renaissance fair attendance constituted the final step in this addiction. The idea that somehow, if we went back eight hundred years, everything would be better.

I had a cottage down here for such cases. Drop them in Middle Kingdom for a week and let the wee lad or lass discover that kinder, gentler times didn't have running water. Or toilet paper. Or grocery stores. "I'm sorry. You've failed your saving throw against lice," was usually the point at which they came home, bought smartphones, dressed in denim, and never looked back.

I finally found the place I was looking for, on a narrow cobblestone road way down in Middle Kingdom. The building looked odd for Middle Kingdom. Huge arched roofs, and what I'd almost have sworn was a steel roof. I knocked on the door, walked in, and nearly killed someone. Someone small. Someone about two feet tall, to be exact. A gnome. The building was packed with gnomes.

Gnomes ran the Kingdom Postal Service during the week, and during the weekends, well, I'd never actually thought about what they did. It appeared they gathered in large buildings, in orderly lines, and waited for instructions.

I stepped over and around gnomes, making my way up to the front desk. "I have a delivery here, from the Fairy Godfather."

The counter gnome looked at the box. He looked at me. Then his eyes went wide. "Death Bringer Marissa? Is that really you?"

Ten

〜

"SIGN FOR THE package, please." I dropped the package on the counter and fished in my purse for a pen, painfully aware of the murmurs going on around me. Back when I was first learning to drive, I ran over a gnome. It wasn't my fault; he was sleeping in a pothole.

Afterward, the gnomes made sure I didn't get a single piece of mail from Kingdom for the next four years. They even jiggered up my regular mail, threatened to saw me into pieces, and once nearly got me bitten by asps.

The murmuring nearly reached a roar, then one of the gnomes pounded on the counter bell until the crowd quieted. "Marissa. It really *is* you." He looked at my blank stare for a moment, then added. "Petri? From the Kingdom Postal Service?" Then he dropped his pants and mooned me.

There, on his left cheek, was my signature. Exactly how my John Hancock got on the rear end of a postal gnome is a story I'd rather not go into. "Hi, Petri. I have to get going. Lots of important things to do." I turned to face a solid wall of gnomes.

Petri tapped me on the shoulder using a back scratcher. "We're honored that you chose to attend." Then he turned to the crowd. "Tonight, we race for Marissa herself!"

The crowd surged forward, a wave of gnomes rushing toward the back of the building. Each stopped at the entrance turnstile to have their hand stamped in seven different places. Petri perched on the top of one of the entrance booths and waved. "Aren't you coming?"

I waited for the crowd to thin, and approached. "Coming where?"

"The race! It's Friday night, and thanks to you, we race every Friday night." He began to hop up and down in anticipation. Gnomes were weird to start with. I mean, honestly, they ran the entire postal service, but this was beyond gnormal.

"You can't blame this on me," I said, hands on my hips. I gave him my very best "Boss" stare.

It was like kicking a poodle, only less fun. The little gnome's purple hat sagged down on his head. "We don't blame you, Marissa. You taught us the meaning of living!"

"How exactly did I do that?" I began to suspect Petri had spent the day licking stamps and now suffered from glue poisoning. It was about the only way his scenario made sense. "I ran over one of your cousins. You guys were furious."

"Yes!" He pumped a walnut-sized fist. "We were. We were afraid. Then we realized, fear is what makes us know we are alive! So we work our day jobs and live for the weekend." That actually sounded like everyone else.

I turned to leave. "Okay, well—"

Petri leaped from the counter and grabbed my hand. "Hooray! Come on, the races are starting soon."

I raised my hand, leaving him dangling a few feet off the ground. "What exactly are you racing? Shopping carts? Golf carts? Go-karts?" About that time a roar like the voice of God shook the building. On instinct, I ran for the back exits where the other gnomes had gone, dragging Petri along with me.

I threw open the door, and my mouth flew open just as wide. Monster trucks stood lined up, revving their engines so loud the sound hit me like a punch to the chest.

"Monster trucks are more fun than go-karts." Petri dropped to his feet and dusted himself off. "Come on. You can have the seat of honor." I stumbled down steps about three inches wide to a booth that would have been perfect for sitting under if I were the size of a miniature Chihuahua.

Petri bowed, sweeping his hand. "This is where the race judges sit."

I took a seat. Actually, I took three, because gnomes are somewhat thinner than people. Petri tapped on a microphone to gather the crowd's attention. "Brothers and sisters. We gather to feel alive! And tonight, we honor the presence of Marissa, Bringer of Death!"

The crowd rose to its feet and saluted me with raised fists. And that is where things got strange. The drivers in their monster trucks began to gun the engines. A gnome stepped out into the roadway, a napkin in his hand, and waved it. In a cloud of exhaust and a roar of thunder, the trucks exploded from the starting line.

They tore down the street toward the end, rubbing fenders and slamming into each other like rockers in a mosh pit. They rounded the corner, still knocking bumpers together and losing that beautiful black paint job. "How many times do they go around?"

Petri watched them hit the far straightaway and smiled. "That depends on the road hazards." As they came barreling around to our side, I watched in horror as a group of gnomes clad in white wandered aimlessly onto the track, arranging themselves like traffic cones. Petri pointed with his flag. "See? Hazards."

Each gnome knelt in the raceway, curling into a ball.

"Get them off the track," I shouted. There couldn't possibly be time. The monster trucks made it back to the near corner and flames gushed from one's wheel well. The leaders swerved, weaving among the track gnomes so close the monster tires seemed to almost kiss them. About then I noticed the loser. The front wheel had blown out, and it careened straight for the stands, leaving a trail of sparks and flames.

I threw myself behind the railing as the monster truck slammed into the wall and went sailing. It missed my head by a foot and buried itself in the wall behind the stands.

"You're going to get someone killed!" I yelled.

"Several someones. It's audience participation night." Petri reached under his seat and brought out a box. "Normally these only come with a paid admission."

Around me gnomes were opening their boxes and taking

out small, evil-looking bits of metal, sticks that looked suspiciously like disposable wands, and what I'm certain were illegal bear traps. The three remaining trucks slowed as the drivers exchanged gunfire, then came flying around the track like smoking hell beasts.

I opened my box and took out what looked like a flute. A flute with a trigger.

"Awesome!" said Petri, giving me a grin. "Point and click." Then he looked down, a little disappointed. "I never get a magic missile launcher."

Around me, gnomes tossed wicked bits of metal onto the track, while others attempted to hex anything that moved. The drivers, in turn, ceased to race with one another, and came full on toward the stands.

I stood, aimed, and then swung the muzzle down.

"Shoot!" screamed Petri.

I squeezed the trigger and nearly had my arm ripped off as it threw out a trail of smoke, blowing a huge crater in the track. The trucks hit it and dropped nose first into the pit, yielding a heartwarming combination of breaking glass and crushed metal.

The crowd cheered, despite the fact that no one won the race. Then they poured out of the stands, wielding spiked clubs and razor whips.

I plopped down in my seat, taking deep breaths. "What are they doing?"

"Sudden death overtime," said Petri.

And right about then, a fresh wave of screaming burst across the stadium.

Not the screaming of a gnome on fire (there were several of those). Or of a gnome hit by small arms fire (several more of those), or of a gnome smashed by a monster truck tire (unfortunately, only one of those). This was fear. And if the gnomes thought feeling fear was being alive, they were really, really alive. A green hand the size of a beer keg reached up out of the pit, digging into the track.

"Petri, what were you using to power the trucks? Tell me that's not an ogre," I said. "Oh, please."

He bounced up and down at the railing. "I told you they were monster trucks."

I dashed for the exit, cursing myself for leaving the pistol back at the office. Petri clung to my back, evading my attempts to elbow him, scrambling away each time I reached for him.

I swiped at him again, and missed. "Tell me you have control collars for them. Tell me that."

"Yep. They're in the box you delivered." Petri leaped onto my shoulder. "Don't you feel alive?"

I ran through the door into the building, hopped the ticket turnstile, and sprinted for the exit. "If I survive, I'm going to make you feel more alive than you've ever felt." I swear he was smiling. I didn't pay much attention, because right about then the back of the building blew out, and an ogre came tromping through the hole.

I threw the front door open and swiped Petri from my shoulder. Then I hit the ground and rolled into the gutter. Right behind me, the front door exploded outward, showering me with wood and steel. With one hand, I grabbed a piece of sheet metal and pulled it over us. As it took one thunderous step closer and then another, I held my breath and attempted to squeeze Petri into pulp.

The stench of the ogre smelled like overcooked broccoli combined with sewer and rotten fish. Then it slowly thudded away, stopping only to smash a wagon that got in its way. I sat up. My hands were bleeding where the cobblestones scraped them. I had splinters in my hair and holes in my pants.

Petri rolled on the ground, laughing, even though his face still looked blue. "Aren't you going after that thing? It's headed into Upper Kingdom."

I briefly considered it. Then I remembered a promise I'd made. No opening tombs. No dragging ghouls to dental appointments. No ogres. "Let animal control handle him. I need a drink."

Petri hopped onto the sidewalk and toddled back toward the smashed building. "Come on. We've got a full service bar and field hospital."

I followed him to what was now an open-seating bar, where another gnome skipped along the bar, taking orders. "Burn ward's full, but we have draft beer on the house tonight."

"Something sweet. Red wine?" I slid onto a bar stool, thankful that at least it was normal size.

Petri whispered to the bartender, and he came back with a shot glass of something that looked like brake fluid and smelled about the same. I downed it without hesitation, and to my shock found it tasted just like cherry soda. "Fantastic. I'll have another. You know, you guys are absolutely insane."

Petri sat next to me, drinking from a thimble filled with black ichor. "I haven't felt so alive since last weekend. You know, Marissa, you did us gnomes a huge favor. We learned the meaning of death, and we learned to appreciate life."

I knocked back another shot, letting liquid calm burn its way through me. My hands no longer shook, and I could easily walk home, as soon as I figured out where I left my feet. "What's in this stuff?"

Petri looked at it and shrugged. "Dwarven liquor. It's like, ten thousand proof. Wait, I can't remember. You don't have a liver, do you?"

I poured a drop from the bottom of the glass and watched as it burned a hole into the bar top. For the record, I stood absolutely still as the world suddenly decided to spin around me like a top. Fortunately the earth was nearby, and it gave me a nice, hard hug upside the head when it rose up and hit me.

WHEN I WOKE up, my stomach and my bladder were competing to see which could make me evacuate it first. The building was empty. My purse was empty, and it looked like someone had drawn tattoos all over me with permanent marker. I took one of my bead necklaces off and tentatively took a bite. It tasted like ground-up aspirin, which made me want to puke, but my head throbbed and I could hear every noise in the street like it was being screamed in my ear, so I kept chewing.

I left the gnomes a present in their trophy cup, then found an empty bottle with a silver label and put in an emergency call. "Grimm, I could use a little help."

He tried to flash into the bottle, but it wouldn't hold his reflection. Then I heard him from behind me. One of the chairs had metal legs, and he was able to form a stable image there. "Marissa, what happened to you?"

He doesn't actually *speak*. That is, you couldn't record him on tape, and yet for some reason it still sounded like he was shouting. I put my hands over my ears. "Gnome races. Ogres. Dwarven liquor."

Grimm sighed. "This simply won't do. Do you have any idea what day it is? Liam's flight touched down yesterday. Even with an eighteen-hour layover in Moscow and the drive into the mountains, he's been on the ground for nearly a day. It's time for him to begin guarding, and he's refused to do it until he can talk to you."

A pang of guilt and fear hit me. What if he had already taken the potion? What if I hadn't gotten to talk to him, all because I went on some stupid errand into Middle Kingdom? "Put me through to him," I said.

"No. We've got to get you cleaned up. He's already a nervous wreck and seeing you like that would have him on a plane back in minutes. Can you see yourself?" Grimm faded out. Sure enough, marker tattoos covered most of my face.

"Would he really come home?" I can't say that the thought filled me with horror.

"Without a moment's notice, absolutely. And I assure you he would start a new war with the vampires by breaching our deal. Try to keep your tongue in check, my dear. I'm going to tell him you can't get video reception."

A moment later, a different presence entered the connection. One I knew. I could almost smell him through the link, and even in my hungover state I smiled. "Hey. How was your flight?"

"M, I've been worried sick about you," said Liam. His voice almost quavered, and I couldn't tell if he was angry or afraid.

"I'm sorry. I had a rough Friday, and I sort of passed out. I'm not feeling well." I picked my words carefully. I didn't want to lie. I also didn't want to tell the truth.

When he spoke his voice was warm again, that kind, soft baritone that I hear in my dreams every night. "It's time. These guys are really jumpy, and I'm going to take the potion and get to work. Two weeks, M. Be careful. *Je t'aime*."

My voice choked up on me, and what came out was a squeak with a croak combined, but I meant "I love you too."

The connection broke, and he was gone. Changed. Probably huge, red, and scaly. I loved him like that too.

I dusted myself off and began the long walk back to the gates. Ari met me in Upper Kingdom, along with Mikey, and to my relief, my car. Mikey rolled down the window. "Ari said I could drive."

"You did good, but there's no need to shout." I slipped into the front seat, shivered at the cold rush of magic as Ari began to chant under her breath. "What are you doing?"

Her cold fingertips brushed my temple, then an electric shock like a tingle ran through me. My eyes still refused to completely focus, but the splitting headache and the noise sensitivity were gone.

"There," said Ari. "I can't fix it all, but that should let you function."

"Can you do anything about the marker?"

She handed me a package of wet wipes from her purse. "Sorry. Haven't learned how to remove marker yet. In fact, healing in general is hard."

I had an awful thought, and grabbed my bracelet. "Grimm, Ari did magic on me. Is she going to be okay?"

He popped into the passenger-side mirror. "Relax, Marissa. Healing magic is on Ari's approved list. We'll dial back her training exercises. Fantastic work, princess." He faded away, leaving Ari with a grimace.

"Did it hurt to do that?"

She shook her head and threw up her hands in exasperation. "I can't get him to stop calling me 'princess.'"

"You have to be what you are," I said.

"I could give you that hangover back, you know." Ari couldn't quite hide the smile at the edge of her lips.

"Mikey, drop me off at the college and take Ari on over to the supermarket. I'll catch a cab back later." Mikey started the car, but before he could pull out, Ari spoke.

"You shouldn't be looking into mirrors. And I need to sweet-talk a professor about my lab assignments, M. You go kick out the bums, and I'll look at all the mirrors on campus and call it done."

I'd have argued with Ari, but honestly, even after her spell,

I still felt woozy, weak, and dizzy. "Fine. The women's dressing room in the second theater is probably hexed to Inferno and back. Do your squinty spirit-sight thing and then we'll call in a shaman to dispel it. And stay away from the mirror. Just in case." Then I put my head over on the seat and tried to sleep.

Eleven

‿❧‿

I HAD MIKEY drop me off at a convenience store a couple of blocks away. Inside, I bought enough wipes and rubbing alcohol to make it look like I was only mildly crazy. After forty minutes of heavy scrubbing, I came out looking red and pink, with only traces of black.

Then I walked to the supermarket to see what I was up against. It was on the bottom floor of a redbrick building, apartments on top, and, underneath, what I guess was a Sell-A-Lot grocery store. Gray dust coated the windows so thickly I couldn't see in.

Mikey had been kind enough to bring my nine millimeter from the Agency. I'd seen parents of missing children who weren't as happy to see their kids returned as I was to have my gun back. For that matter, I'd seen parents who would've been happier if their kids stayed missing.

I checked the front doors, and sure enough, some moron left them unlocked. That was probably how the homeless people started sleeping there in the first place. I know, I'd told Ari it might be a yeti, but honestly, there was a better chance of me being the death goddess of a gnome cult than of there actually being a yeti. If it were, I'd back away, come back armed with a chain saw and a dog-grooming kit and take care of business.

Sell-A-Lot tried to combine small department store and small grocery store. Unlike the "medical supply/fast-food restaurant" places, it quickly went out of business. The "Final Sale" signs still in the window advertised blenders and toasters for ten bucks. I slipped the door open, listened for sounds of trouble, and walked inside.

The door locking behind me was the giveaway. Self-locking doors never do so with the monster on the other side, but for the moment I refused to panic. Don't get me wrong. Panic is a perfectly good reaction when there's nothing else useful to do, but I wasn't certain of that yet.

The place looked wrong. Rows and rows of empty shelves, the occasional ancient cereal box. Then I realized what was bothering me: A thick layer of gray dust covered everything. There wasn't a single mirror or reflective surface anywhere.

"Grimm?" I put my hand on my bracelet. "Grimm, you there?" Of course he wasn't. There wasn't going to be any calling for help.

Like the whisper of rat's feet, a voice answered, from everywhere and nowhere, all at once. "Princess."

And it ticked me off. It wasn't that I was pretty sure this was an ambush. It also wasn't that I was almost certainly locked in with something nasty. It was that once again some idiot had mistaken me for a princess.

"Princess," said the voice again, coming louder.

I walked along the rows, careful to keep my back to a shelf, and my gun ready.

"I don't know who you are, but you picked a really bad day to start a fight." I hoped my voice didn't waver. Truth is, there were lots of fights I'd won, but very few I won without getting hurt in the process.

"I am dust," said the voice. I'd never really understood why they couldn't ever have normal names. I found the place I was looking for, once part of home electronics. I chose it because it had a nice U-shaped inlet, perfect for backing up to. I backed myself up to the wall and waited.

"Princess," it said again.

"Someone failed their vocabulary test. It's going to be hard to have a conversation if that's all you can say." From the shadows all around me it laughed. "Blessing? Curse? I could use some help." In answer the lights began to flicker and shake. My harakathin were coming, and no power on earth would persuade them to stop.

Lights flickered from the front of the store to the back, then back and forth, in mesmerizing patterns. With a crash, a shape punched up from the ground, and I shot at it twice. Then it sagged back down into the ground. With a sinking feeling it finally hit me: The thing that had risen was the dust itself, forming a blanket. No, a barrier.

I ran to where it had risen and tried to brush the dust away, but no matter how much I scraped, the layer never changed, sifting like water back onto the ground. I tried the same thing on the polished counter top, trying to get enough reflection to contact Grimm. He could at least call the cops.

"That won't work, princess." This time the voice came from a few feet away. I ran to the wall and backed up to it, gun out, ready. Three times more the ash erupted in explosions as my harakathin tried to break through.

Then the dust began to gather, running together into a mound, and the mound took form. A man rose from the pile, like he was climbing a staircase, until he stood a few feet away. "Do you know who I am, princess?"

And to my horror, I did. Kingdom may be what you think of when you think of fairy tales, but the folks in Kingdom have their own legends. Their own myths, and ghost stories, and boogeymen. The actual boogeymen were nice, assuming you didn't get all violent with a flashlight. On the other hand, I knew exactly who I was looking at. Kingdom's own boogeyman, the name royals threatened their kids with if they wouldn't polish their crown. "You're the Gray Man."

He wore coveralls, like a farmer, with a plaid flannel shirt that I think was red where it wasn't covered in dust. It covered him like he'd rolled in a fireplace, white ash over pale skin. He took a few steps toward me. "You know what I'm called, but not my name. I am Rip Van Winkle." He held out his palm and blew at me, a cloud of white and gray that billowed out and enveloped me.

I clamped my hand over my mouth a second too late. Like a fist in my face, the cloud forced my jaws open. With each breath, I sucked in more and more of that infernal gray. It moved inside me like he'd shoved a hand down my throat and started tearing out my lungs. I collapsed on the floor, unable to breathe as he advanced.

Then he stood over me and took a small notebook from his coveralls. "I make an effort to keep track of who I dispose of. Princess, what is your title? Princess of Wind? Earth? I know you are special. She could have bought a dozen assassins for what she paid me."

The dust in my throat let loose, and with a wheezing cough I choked it out, looking less like a person and more like Liam the one time he tried smoking a pipe. Van Winkle grabbed me by the shirt and slung me to my feet. "Now. What exactly is your title? Tell me and I'll make it quick."

I sagged against a shelf and knocked over a box of toasters. "Mfffammmmfammham," I said. Again the magic drew back, allowing me to spit out another clump of dust.

"I'm sorry. I couldn't quite make that out."

"I said small kitchen appliances."

"Sad." He noted it in his book, clicked the pen, and put it away. "You royals have got to stop breeding so much."

That is the point at which I clocked him with a blender. And again, and again until the pitcher smashed over his head. I'm no idiot. I hit him with every single thing I found on the shelves, up to and including a fondue set. Then I went for my gun.

When I turned, he was already on his feet. I shot him three times, dead center of the torso. Perfect for perforating intestines, severing arteries, and generally making it hard to breathe. And still he stood. He ran his hand along his stomach and picked something off. "Now, little lady, that's not polite."

"How in Kingdom did you . . . ?" I trailed off as he dropped a spent bullet to the ground.

The dust swirled around him, covering him and making him look almost muddy.

"I reckon you'll find out soon enough, miss. See, from dust you came, and to dust you shall return. So when you're dead, I'll take your bones and grind them up and add them to my collection."

I looked around at the layers that covered everything in the store. More dust than a single body could supply.

He watched my gaze with a toothless grin. "I been killing royalty for centuries."

I ran.

Down the aisles, straight for the front of the store I ran, leaving a cloud of bone dust in my wake. A layer of dust so thick it looked like volcanic ash covered the front, jamming the door. I slammed into it, kicked at the glass, and hurled a stool from a checkout stand.

Over and over, mountains of ash burst up in the dust as my harakathin tried to break through, but the shield of bone held them away.

"Now, princess, that's enough," said Rip Van Winkle as he approached. "I hear the fairy's been training you. Not half-bad job." He limped toward me, dragging one foot.

"You have the wrong girl," I said, looking for something to use against him. The dust grew thick in the air as I searched. At any moment he could bring it back to choke me to death.

"Nope. Heard that one a few times before." He fished a knife from one pocket and clicked the blade open. He held one hand to his head where I'd hit him. Ash clumped on the wound, but sloughed away where the blood ran. "Normally, I'd make this easy on y'all. But seein' as you want to play rough, I can do that too."

I advanced on him, shoving my gun into a side pocket and trying to relax as I moved toward a legend's legend and a nightmare's nightmare. Grimm had other agents who were deadly in hand-to-hand combat before me. Some could move into a crowd of attackers and break and bend, and others used knives. I'd never been quite that type, but knife defense I'd had drilled into me for over eight years.

He nodded as I approached. "Good girl. Come here and die."

I'm only five foot eight. He stood a good five inches taller than me, looking like a farmer dumped in bone-meal flour. That certainly explained the legends about him. How ashes fell like snow, and the ghost of the Gray Man came for you. How the only thing left would be a pile of meat and a pool of blood.

From my hands, which almost shook, to my shoulder muscles knotted like iron, it took all my training to keep my body under control. I'd get one shot at this, since I couldn't defend against the dust thing. Oxygen was my weakness, along with most other creatures on the planet. So I went to him.

"Night-night, princess." Rip Van Winkle flipped the knife over so that the simple lock blade pointed downward, and held out his arms like he wanted to give me a great big hug. One that would end with a knife blade driven into my spine.

I waited until the last possible moment, let those dusty white arms come within an inch of me, and as his muscles tensed for the strike I spun. Just like I'd trained. The blade came down like a streak of silver, and I let it.

I turned as it did, using my forearm to force his to the side. I didn't try to stop the swing. He was too strong. I *changed* it. Enough to miss me. Then I grabbed his wrist and threw myself against him, driving the knife right into his thigh.

He fell backwards, a short cry of pain escaping him along with all the air in his lungs, and I didn't give him a chance to get up. I'd learned a lot about fighting. One of the key rules was never fight fair. Always kick a man when he's down. So I did, driving that knife farther into his leg and then stomping his head as he rolled, trying to keep his arms in front of him.

As I swung my foot at his temple the dust covering him bunched together, solidifying. I might as well have kicked a statue. Something cracked in my foot and I fell, pain like bursts of lightning up my leg. I rolled away from him as fast as I could, but he grabbed my leg with an iron grip, squeezing the foot I'd broken like a vice.

I screamed into the dust.

"Now you done made me angry." He rose, a specter of gray and white, his face contorted with rage. Blood ran from his thigh, causing clumps of ash to thicken and drop from him. When Ari does magic, there's this moment when you feel like you are standing in a stream with water running over your skin. Rip Van Winkle did the total opposite.

No, this was more like Rip Van Winkle set off a bomb targeting only magic. A fine layer of frost covered me as magic rushed away from him. I had no control over magic, but that didn't mean I couldn't sense it. Feel it. Every bit of light and warmth fled before him. The force pushed me like a blow, throwing me backwards. In the silence, my ears rang.

"Long 'fore I did bone magic, I was killing," said Rip Van Winkle. Now he shuffled with both feet when he walked. "How's it feel, princess? To be stripped of any magic at all? If you can't breathe, that ain't the dust. Big ol' princes. Feisty princesses. Even killed myself a king or two at times. Just can't quite function without magic."

About then the ground under his feet exploded. Strictly speaking, the ash under his feet leaped upward as my hara-kathin attempted once more to punch a way through the layer of bones, but this time they'd grown smarter. The eruption threw Rip Van Winkle off to the side, straight into a cash register.

Then as he slumped toward the ground, it exploded up-ward again, bashing him in the head. I struggled to my feet, unable to put any weight on my broken foot, but as I approached him I took the gun out.

He rolled over and started to laugh. "You done tried that already."

I pointed with the gun, and shot him twice. "You made a clean spot." Right where his own blood had washed away the dust, I put two bullets.

He rolled over, clutching his thigh in an attempt to quell the rush of red. And he laughed. Not just giggled. Deep-throated laughter that bent him over so that he curled up in a ball, even as he convulsed in pain. "You ain't no princess."

I knelt, putting my knee on his chest and shoving my gun in his face. "No. Who paid you to kill Ari?" I pressed down on him, driving the air that kept him laughing out. Instead, his body shook and a wild grin spread across his face.

"What's so funny?"

"You best be calling the police. Taking me to jail or somet'n."

I stopped for a moment, thinking about how Ari would have reacted to a void spot in the magic. Wondered if she could even breathe. Wondered if she'd die from the lack of it. "You aren't going to jail."

He nodded in acceptance. He'd killed so many people, I suppose death was natural for him. Maybe even normal. "I didn't figure you for a killer."

"Some gnomes stole my cell phone, and I can't call Grimm

with your bone dust in the way. Not that it would matter. There are a couple of furious harakathin who will come through the first crack in your spell. I don't know what they can or will do, but I know I won't be able to stop them."

I put the gun to his head. "Then there's Ari. I don't believe a jail cell would hold you for a minute, and she'd spend the rest of her life wondering when you would show up. I'm not normally a killer, but I do have my limits."

He stared at the gun, then his eyes got wider, and I realized he wasn't looking at it anymore. He was staring at my hand, where the Black Queen's emblem darkened my skin. "Handmaiden. You think I'm evil 'cause I kill girls and grind up their bones. You got the mark of real evil."

"How do you know?" I took his face in my hands and made him look at me.

He gasped for breath, the blood loss killing him. "I been sleeping and killing for centuries, but I do it honest, with my own two hands. The Black Queen, she killed her handmaidens by killing others. When you die inside, you'll do whatever she wants." He closed his eyes. "I was jes' wonderin', handmaiden. Wondering what got sent after you." Then he shuddered and the dust exploded in a cloud as it fell from the ceilings and walls.

Bursts of ash signaled the final arrival of my harakathin. The hair on my skin stood up as they passed by. "Blessing, curse, you did good. Extra treats tonight."

Rip Van Winkle was dead.

I took his head with me in a box. Not because I like heads in boxes. It's very rare that you get in a situation where you'll say, "You know what I need? A severed head in a box." I took it because I figured that people wouldn't believe me otherwise. Also, if he'd really been killing that long, there might be a reward on his head. In Kingdom, people tended to be literal. I packed it in bone dust and sealed it in the largest salad-fresh container I could find. Then I put the container in a Christmas gift bag I got from under a register.

As soon as I was outside, I called Grimm. No answer, though I had enough bone dust on me to cancel almost any form of magic. From my cell phone I ordered a package pickup for the head, having it shipped to myself. Then, as fast as I could limp to a cab, I ordered the driver to take me to the college. I continued to try to call Grimm all the way there, but he still didn't answer. That didn't worry me. Grimm was a big boy, a fairy of near limitless power. Ari, on the other hand, might be in trouble.

Twelve

~∞~

IN THE MIDDLE of a completely average Monday, I arrived at the college. Students packed the front sidewalk, expressing how little they liked being up before noon. Some of them lumbered about like zombies. I'd never understood the fear of zombies. Sure, they're dead. Sure, they're hungry. But the ones I'd seen aren't hungry for brains. Corn chips, on the other hand, can get you killed. Particularly nacho-cheese-flavored ones.

I stopped a zombie/pre-med student and asked him the way to the drama department. He mumbled, pointed, and otherwise provided an answer that was completely unsatisfactory. I shook him a bit and got a much better answer. The drama department was on the fourth floor, east end.

Regardless of what you might have seen in movies, you do not run around with a gun drawn to every door and hallway. In fact, if you have the choice, you don't take out a gun around other people at all. College kids filled the halls, shuffling their way toward algebra, English, and other mundane horrors.

The city's supply of waitresses and burger flippers would be severely damaged if I caused a massacre here. So I carefully climbed the stairs and headed to the drama department.

The sign said "Closed," which didn't bother me a bit, and "No Admittance," which meant "Come Right On In." I wasn't dyslexic. I'd made a career out of ignoring signs.

Right before I opened the door, I had a thought. Grimm still hadn't answered, and normally I'd ask him to call for backup. Today, I needed backup of a different kind. I slipped my nine millimeter out of my purse. Inside the purse, it was hidden from metal detectors and masked by a cheap illusion I bought that made it look like a box of tampons. Aiming with care at the brick wall, I squeezed off three shots.

I'd definitely found the drama department, judging from the screams. I mean, I'd put the bullets into a wall for a reason—I didn't want to hurt anyone. Soon enough, the entire college would be swarming with cops. Then I headed into the theater.

First off, let me say that if you are performing on a stage that small, the only way you will end up on Broadway is by taking a cab. Contrary to what the sign said, the theater wasn't closed. A single stage light lit up one edge, either stage left or stage right. I had a hard enough time with normal left and right.

From the back, an angry woman yelled. Not Ari, but odds were I was going to get the drop on whoever had come after her. I ran down the aisle, vaulted onto the stage, and dashed to the back curtain. Behind it, the dressing rooms split off to the left and the right. The women's dressing room door was shut.

Well, mostly shut. The top half of the door was torn off the hinges. An older woman, dark skin, Haitian jewelry, and a flower-print dress stood in the hall, tossing lightning bolts into the door. She stopped for a moment, and flash of red hair lit up the door as Ari peeked out.

From a display cabinet on the wall, I slipped a trophy out. A cheap imitation of the Golden Globe Award, the figure looked a lot like her left hand was ringing up a cash register and her right hand was offering a box of fries. Either way, the enchantress never saw me coming.

I smashed the trophy right into her kidney, waited until she collapsed, then repeated it on the other kidney. Then I thought about awarding the enchantress her first "bloody red temple," but decided against it. The cops would be here soon enough. "Ari? You okay?"

She stuck her head out the dressing room door. "M!"

I ignored the sweat dripping from her hair, focusing instead on the fact that as I hugged her, she hummed, her skin buzzing like a nest of wasps. "You okay? You don't feel right."

She glanced about, eyes wide, with exhaustion or adrenaline, I couldn't say. "I'll be okay. They were waiting for me when I walked through the doors. The thugs with guns were easy. I just drunked them. The spell slinger, on the other hand . . ." She trailed off, looking at the woman collapsed on the floor. That's when I realized the ground and walls behind the woman were scorched. Ari had returned fire.

"I sort of sent a distress signal before I came in. Cops will be here soon enough. Why didn't you leave after you figured out it was an ambush?" I tried to keep the worry in my heart out of my voice. This was common sense.

"She came in behind me." Ari slumped against the door. "I was barely able to block her first spell, and then I ran. My bag's out in the aisle somewhere, or I'd have shot her through the wall." Ari carried a shopping bag almost everywhere with her Desert Eagle hidden by a similar spell. I believe hers showed up as a vampire romance novel.

"How much magic did you use?" I started to think there might be a good reason for her situation. Grimm had been quite clear about limiting her magic. Ari had run the equivalent of a marathon on bad knees.

She rubbed her fingertips together, and I guessed she could feel it too. "A lot. Mostly shields, but I might have thrown a lightning bolt or two."

Right then I made up my mind. Priority one was getting Ari back to the Agency so I could make Grimm take care of her. "We're going back to the Agency, and we're doing it now. Someone meant to kill both of us. I was supposed to get the enchantress."

Her eyes locked with mine. "What did they send after me?"

I helped her along the hallway backstage, supporting her each time she stumbled. Through the walls, the wail of approaching sirens rose. I'd get the paramedics and tell them that a drama student had collapsed under the pressure of a spelling quiz. "You ever heard of the Gray Man?"

She rolled her eyes, like normal people did if you asked

them about the Easter Bunny. "Dad used to tell me he was under my bed, or in my closet, and if I got one more drink, he'd get me. He's a myth."

"He is now."

Her eyes went wide as she worked out what I meant, and she reached up to rub a trace of bone dust from my forehead.

"Calm," I said, pushing us through the stage curtain. "Once Grimm's cleared you, I'll tell the whole story. Until then, relax. The Royal Boogeyman is now just a boogeyman." My mind clicked on what she'd said before. "You left thugs here?"

Ari nodded. It occurred to me right then how much I couldn't see. How bright the lights were and how dark the theater was. But I'd seen the stage when I walked across it, empty.

"Marissa," said a female voice in the darkness.

My stomach churned as I worked to place her location, but her accent told me who spoke. There was no point in pretending otherwise. "Queen Mihail." I shoved Ari behind me and glanced to the sides.

The sound of metal on metal that echoed through the empty room I recognized as a safety coming off.

"Stay where you are, or I shoot your friend."

"You mean you shoot me." If someone had to be shot, and it couldn't be an intern, I wouldn't let it be my best friend.

"No," said the queen. She moved as she spoke, coming closer until her face emerged from the darkness near the foot of the stage. "I shoot your friend. You, I have something special for."

I thought about the sirens outside. About the dozen police officers checking locked classroom after classroom. All I had to do was delay her. So I asked a question I already knew the answer to. "Why did you send the Gray Man after Ari?"

"Don't feign ignorance with me. My son was destroyed by your hand. Your friend there protected you long enough to allow you to throw the apple. Do you remember my promise to you?" She took one step up the stairs and the stage lights cast her face into shadows.

I did. She'd promised me rewards not even Grimm could provide, and punishments not even he could protect me from. Then I remembered her other promise. That her generosity would fall on everyone who aided me, if I returned her son unharmed.

And so would her wrath.

"You should have left her out of this. Your problem was with me." Queen Mihail wouldn't leave anyone out. It wasn't in her nature, but again, the point was wasting time. I'd stopped counting seconds and started worrying about who else she might have gone after.

"I promised you wrath, Marissa. I always keep my promises. It took me years to find ways to get all of you, but I am patient." What amazed me was how calm her tone was. She spoke the same way I talked about the news over breakfast. Calm, almost cordial. "Even your fairy friend had a weakness."

So that's why Grimm wasn't answering. The traditional way to attack a fairy was to break their original mirror. I'd also managed to do it once the hard way, but I destroyed the only weapon capable of killing a fairy in the process.

"What did you do to him?"

She took another step onto the stairs, rising from the shadows like a cobra. "Your boss? Or your man?"

"You harm a single scale on Liam and I'll make sure you have a family reunion." I spoke before I thought—likely Liam would tear apart almost anything sent after him. If he had a chance. If he saw them coming.

She nodded her head in agreement. "Oh, we already tried. It seems that we might have underestimated what exactly we were dealing with. Your man killed three of my best assassins before we even understood how. But don't worry. I have a strike team of princes on a plane today to take care of him. A lone assassin is one thing. A prince in shining Kevlar is another thing entirely. In a week or so, when they arrive, they'll finish the job."

"The vampires will have something to say about that when they wake up. They'll lose everything but their lives. I mean, their deaths. They'll lose everything if you actually hurt him. Call your strike team off." Queen Mihail had always struck me as a businesswoman. Surely that would make sense to her.

She took another step up, now fully on the stage. I wondered how many gunmen she had aiming at me, and whether or not I could shoot the queen before they shot me. Then I thought of Ari. They'd be certain to hit her, assuming there weren't a couple already aiming at her as well.

"Marissa, I wouldn't call off those princes if I could. I take my promises very seriously. You poisoned my son with an apple, when I promised to reward you for his return." She left out the part where the son had tried to kill me, and intended to rape Ari. Minor details, like that.

"There are police already working their way through the building. You will be arrested and tried and will spend the rest of your life in a little cell with a big woman named Tiny. Let us go, we can work this out."

I could finally see her face in the stage light. She was truly insane. Her eyes were so wide, I could see edges of white around them, and her mouth held a smile that would have looked better on a wolf than a person. "Girl, I am a queen and can only be charged in the Court of Queens. The lawmen of this city will do nothing to me. Now, be a good girl and hold still. If you don't, I'll have one of my guards shoot you, then we do this."

She held up her hand, and in it she held an apple. A single, magical red apple with a candy shell. Don't be fooled—the name might have been "Red Delicious," but the spell wrapped up inside was absolute destruction. Like a hand grenade and a magic spell wrapped into one. Like the one I'd thrown at her son.

"I'm so sorry," said Ari, in my ear.

The queen looked at the apple for a moment, then drew her hand back to throw. It would scatter most of me through the wall, and maybe kill Ari as well.

"Not your fault. I'm the one who ticked her off." If I had to die, I'd have preferred to be at home, surrounded by my friends and family. If I had a second choice, I guess on a stage in a college, blown to bits by an apple would have to do.

"Not for that," said Ari. "For this."

The queen finally threw it, and I tried in that moment to shoot the apple in midair. Then cold fire touched my shoulder. I slumped forward, rolling onto my back. I tried to move, but my hands and feet weighed more than lead. I could only watch as the apple arced cleanly through air where I had been, landing in Ari's outstretched hand.

"NO!" shouted the Queen.

"Murrrfffl," I said.

The doors to the theater flew open as police rushed in. In that one moment, the queen leaped off the stage, into the darkness. I kept my eyes focused as best I could on Ari.

She held the apple, keeping it floating an inch away. It would have killed me, but Ari had one thing going for her that I never would. The girl was a princess, and the normal rules never applied to her. Even through her spell, I recognized what Ari had done—she hit me with her alcohol spell. I would *never* have let her try to catch an apple.

Ari began to glow with spell power as she worked to counter the apple, but it was designed to destroy magic. She wrapped it in a cocoon of light, weaving around her like a blanket, wrapping like a spectral mummy.

In that moment I grasped what she was doing. She wasn't trying to stop it. She was guiding its force away from me. Into her. That feeling of cold water when Ari worked magic, it became a torrent, then a river, then a hurricane of magic that spun through the room.

I didn't have Spirit Sight, but there was so much magic in one place even I could see the beams of light wrapping around her until she glowed like the sun. Then the apple began to crack. To explode, and release its deadly spell. I held my eyes open until an afterimage of Ari remained even with them closed. Or maybe she was so bright I could see her with my eyes shut.

The sound when the apple exploded was a *whoosh*, like air being sucked in, then a thunderclap that left my ears ringing and a flash of light like a nuclear explosion, and a rain of sparks as the theater lights exploded.

In the darkness that followed I heard Ari hit the stage. Voices shouted, and flashlight beams stabbed the darkness. Then faces hovered over me, saying words I didn't understand, and they carried me out to an ambulance. When I fought with them, and tried to get up, to go see what had happened to Ari, they stuck me with a needle, and I finally stopped fighting.

I'D WOKEN MORE times in hospital rooms than I could count. There was, as usual, a police detective waiting to talk to me. I gave him a story that matched what he wanted to hear. About how my friend wanted the lead in a musical, and I helped her practice. About how an enraged gunman had torn through the doors, shooting everywhere.

The electrical explosion, that was his idea, one I didn't bother correcting. And Ari, sure, she had been dieting, if that's what he wanted me to say. As soon as he was gone, I slipped out of bed and went looking for her. I found her in a room on the eighth floor, hooked up to a bunch of machines. She didn't look hurt. That is, I didn't see any wounds or cuts on her.

I took Ari's hand and sat on the bed, trying not to break down in tears. Only the machines made any noise, the steady beep of the heart monitor, the hum of a blood pressure cuff. I would've asked why she did it, but I knew. I made fun of her constantly for being a princess. And a seal bearer. And being almost capable of real magic. This time, there was no denying what Ari accomplished. She'd captured an explosion designed to kill almost anything magical, and trusted in her own innate luck to save us both.

Then the business part of me clicked in. I needed to figure out how far Queen Mihail's madness extended, but I couldn't leave Ari alone in the hospital. Mihail seemed the persistent type, and Ari was one wet pillow away from death if someone so decided.

I picked up the phone and dialed a number. A contract agency Grimm used to hire help from time to time. When the svelte voice on the other end answered, I had my orders ready. "I need a bodyguard. Money is no object." I gave them the hospital room number and sat down to wait.

In the meantime, I tried to raise Grimm again, but I didn't expect him to respond. The last time this happened, I'd panicked. This time around, I knew what to do if someone broke his mirror. Grimm was several thousand years old and had survived all comers. Ari was twenty years old and hadn't managed to pass the driver's exam.

When the knock at the door came, I looked up and immediately panicked. I scrambled for something to throw, something to hit with, anything would do. Then I started thinking logically. In the doorway stood a short Japanese man with speckles of gray in his hair. I'd run into him in the past, and if he were truly here to kill me, there was nearly nothing I could do.

"Shigeru." I bowed to him, trying to show respect for Queen Mihail's personal ninja.

"Ms. Locks," he said, returning the bow.

"Leave Ari out of this, please." His entire order based their lives on honor. At least, as much honor as one could have killing people for a living. I hoped he'd have the decency to keep whatever happened between him and me.

Shigeru bowed slightly and offered me a business card, one that matched the mercenary's guild I'd called.

"I am no longer in the queen's service. I accepted a personal protection contract. This is a happy coincidence."

Much as I wanted to believe that, coincidences in my life tended to range from unpleasant to downright horrific. I kept myself between Ari and Shigeru while I made a second call. "I'd like to verify you sent contractor 12827 in response to my call."

The phone hummed in my fingers, the unmistakable feeling of contact magic. Contact magic didn't require line of sight, only a caster with enough skill and insanity to imbue a regular object with a sliver of the caster's soul. If they had someone with that kind of power, from now on I'd make sure the mercenary guild's bills always got paid up front.

The writing on Shigeru's business card faded, leaving only a silver surface. But instead of my reflection, it showed me Shigeru. First as a young man, with dark black hair and golden yellow skin. The image shifted, and Shigeru grew older. With each change, the image in the card matched the man before me more closely.

The business card turned clear as glass, letting me look at Shigeru's image imposed on top of his face. The slightest movement rippled the image until it refocused. I'd seen this once before, when Grimm suspected one of our applicants of using a glamour. For as long as it lasted, the window would reveal any disguise short of plastic surgery.

At least, that's what I expected. But the clear window shimmered, and my view through it grew fuzzier. Instead of showing me Shigeru's wrinkled face, it showed an azure orb wrapped in golden knots that resembled a cross between Celtic knot work and prison tattoos. "What—" My voice caught in my throat as I identified a familiar pattern in the knots. I whispered into the phone, "You bound your contractor's *soul* to his contracts?"

"If you believe contractor 12827 has failed to fulfill any of his duties, I can promise you his death will be agonizing and inescapable. Your Agency's business is far more valuable to us than the life of one employee, no matter how skilled."

I held my hand over the phone and hissed at Shigeru, "How do you sleep knowing that's hanging over you?"

His lips curled up in a smile. "I take my work seriously."

"I trust I've addressed your concerns?" The dispatcher's smug tone told me it wasn't really a question.

"Trust but verify," I said. "Thanks." I ended the call and handed Shigeru his card back. I don't mind saying the wave of relief almost collapsed me. I might have killed Rip Van Winkle, but he was used to having a magical advantage and was completely unprepared for someone who wasn't rendered helpless by his effect. Shigeru, on the other hand, had served as the queen's bodyguard for years and could have killed me with his pinky.

"If anyone tries to hurt her, you have my permission to do anything it takes."

He nodded and walked over to the seat beside the bed. Then I headed back to my room, stealing a pair of scrubs on the way. They didn't exactly fit, but I needed something to cover my rear long enough for a cab ride home. Then I signed out against medical advice, walked myself to a cab, and headed back to my apartment to rescue the Fairy Godfather. Again.

Thirteen

IF YOU ARE wondering how or why I can deal with these sorts of things and keep going, let's just say this wasn't the first time I'd signed out AMA, called myself a cab, and gone home after getting beaten to a pulp. Don't get me wrong. I had plans for the queen and every intention of fulfilling them in what I hoped was a horribly painful manner, but I also had priorities.

Ari was alive, if barely. Liam survived one attack, which meant the queen's vengeance wasn't impossible to thwart. Though I wanted more than anything to get on the next plane to Europe and ride to Liam's rescue, I knew someone who could make thwarting a whole lot easier.

So rather than chase my heart to Europe, I followed my head home. I stepped into my apartment and locked the door behind me. Then I headed to the bathroom and did the same. Safely barricaded in my bathroom, I opened my medicine cabinet and began to remove pill bottles until I could clearly see the back of it.

Grimm's original mirror had been hidden in Dwarf Town for decades, in a room that didn't even connect to a house in the same part of the world. Once it was discovered there, I decided a more mundane hiding place made sense. So if I ever really wanted to talk to Grimm, all I had to do was go to the bathroom. It didn't hurt that I'd had it encased in bulletproof glass and surrounded by a laminate titanium alloy laminate. If the building collapsed around my apartment, the bathroom mirror and its wall would be the only thing sticking up from the rubble.

His mirror didn't even have a scratch. I collected fleshing silver in case some managed to break it again. Under my sink I kept sixteen types of floor cleaner. I have no idea what Liam actually used to clean the floors, since every single bottle actually held fleshing silver. Grimm stared out at me from his mirror, his face frozen in a look of surprise. Not fear, but definitely apprehension.

Thing is, it shouldn't have been possible to affect him at all.

The mirror might be magic, but the real source of the power was Grimm himself. To hear him tell it, the mirror served to translate for him so that we could understand what he was actually saying. I tapped on the glass a couple of times. Might as well have been a framed print of the Fairy Godfather.

From under my bed I pulled out my spare gun, then changed clothes and headed to the Agency. Queen Mihail had gone after me. She'd gotten to Grimm and nearly killed Ari. She had a team of princes on their way to take out Liam, and Kingdom only knew what she had done to the Agency.

THE AGENCY BUILDING looked like a bomb went off, people gathered around on the sidewalk, the usual "extreme biohazard" and "chemical disaster area" warnings posted on the doors. On second thought, the last time a bomb went off there, it didn't look as bad. We shared the building with twenty, maybe thirty other companies. They had to wonder at times why their building had the most number of days without power, the most incidents of elevator outages, or wack-job terrorist attacks. I went in through the cargo entrance, where I confirmed that we were in full lockdown mode.

"Bill? Big Billy, it's Marissa," I called into the empty cargo bay. Sure enough, a slot opened in one of the steel walls, and a rifle poked out. We got overrun once by some hired uglies, and ever since then, I'd drilled every last one of the staff on plans in case it happened again.

"Ms. Locks? Hold yer hands up where I can see them." I recognized Big Bill's voice. Our union negotiator and professional cargo driver, Bill was cold under fire and willing to do anything to anyone if it paid a living wage.

I held my hands up, knowing he was looking for the handmaiden's mark. While there were lots of things that could shift to look like me, there wasn't anything crazy enough to mimic that. In Kingdom, it was regarded like a swastika, upside-down cross, pentagram, and IRS logo all in one.

Bill opened up the door and our cargo crew emerged. Grimm moved a lot of goods into and out of Kingdom, specializing in interfacing between the races that couldn't or shouldn't leave Kingdom, and the rest of the world. "All our trucks are accounted for. I'm holding deliveries that were out away from the Agency. No contact with the office since the incident, but we don't think anyone's fighting now, on account of the other businesses ain't called the cops."

Keeping our cargo drivers parked in various places rather than letting them come back here made sense. Calling the cops could save us, or expose a bunch of policemen to things they were in no way ready to handle, like, say, a rogue donut baker. The cops were convenient, but not an option. "I'm going up. Come with me."

I headed for the stairs. I chose the stairs for a couple of reasons. First off, when the elevator opens, you're looking down a long hallway with nowhere to hide. I'd rather not have the elevator bell tell them when it was okay to start firing. If it were me, I'd have them shoot anything that happened to stop on our floor.

The other reason is that most mercenaries were lazy. They didn't get paid to carry heavy guns or spell books up stairs, so it was unlikely I'd meet something unpleasant in the stairwell. So I climbed four flights of stairs, finally reached our floor, and got ready to kick some ass.

From the stairwell, I peered down the hallway all the way to the Agency entrance. Two bodies dressed in black lay in the hallway, but there were no other signs of an ambush. "I want you to wait at the front door," I told Bill, "but don't enter until I give the signal." Then I slipped out of the stairwell and tiptoed down the hall as quietly as I could. I passed the service entrance to the Agency, counting steps as I went.

A few years ago, a troll punched a hole in the back corner of the building and took Liam. When we had it repaired I sprang for some magic, and had a safety door installed. From the outside it looked like a nonfunctioning water fountain. In other words, like every other water fountain in the building. I put my hand in the right place, and it clicked, recognizing my print. Then I walked forward, right through the wall.

Two seconds before, it would have been remarkably solid sheet rock. Three seconds later and it would slice me in half as it resolidified. I only needed two seconds until I was safely through, standing in a dark office-supply closet. The door on this room had no knob, and I'd had that done on purpose so it wouldn't make any noise when I opened it. I slid it open a sliver and looked out into the main conference room. Blood covered everything.

From just past the table came a low moan and the sound of labored breathing. I swung the door open and stepped out, ready to shoot anything that moved. Nothing did. Then I discovered where the blood came from. Mikey lay pinned to the wall, shot through with silver crossbow bolts in more places than I could count. He was half wolf, which is to say that he was really, really hairy, and his eyes had changed to those black pits that all wolves have, but I think he recognized me as I approached.

I knelt and whispered, "Hold on, Mikey. I'm going to get you loose." The bolts were obviously huntsman standard, anti-wolf bolts. Each ended in a tri-blade broad head, with hooks on both sides of the blade so that once they entered, you couldn't pull them out. The silver, of course, kept Mikey from healing up the wound.

I took hold of one of the bolts, almost feeling bad for what came next. "You're not going to like this."

He nodded his head, letting it loll back over, his eyes closed in anticipation.

Then I broke the shaft of the bolt off. Kingdom knows it must have hurt, but all Mikey did was whine a little. If there were tears that ran from his muzzle, I'd never say so. With the shaft broken, I pulled his hand free.

We repeated that process five more times, when his arms dangled loose. Then I rolled him onto his stomach and stepped on his back, driving the one in his left lung out. Wolf blood covered my hands, sticky and red. Frankly, I was amazed that Mikey was still breathing. Not all wolves regenerate the same, so Mikey had serious mojo to keep generating blood like that.

I pulled the bolt on through and tried to cover the wound with my hands, but he pushed me away. "Break them," he said, pointing to the bolts that stuck out of his legs. The bolts passed through the thick of his thighs, leaving me nothing to pull at.

I kicked each until they snapped. With each one he let out a muffled whimper, but nothing that would attract attention. When I had the last, he crawled away from the wall.

"Wolf," he gasped. He needed to change to full wolf. He'd heal a lot faster that way. Grimm had a theory that being able to keep themselves human was a side effect of their healing.

"Okay. You wolf out, and I'm going to go see what else is waiting. Anyone else in the office?"

"Grimm—said no wolf." Grimm knew how I felt about them.

"It's okay. You go ahead. If Grimm says anything, I'll handle it."

He ran an inhuman tongue over his muzzle, wiping the froth clear. "The piper. In safe room with Rosa."

I swore under my breath. Beth must have come for training and been in the wrong place at the wrong time. "Baddies?"

He nodded. "Outside Rosa's safe room. Killed all but the huntsman." He was talking a lot better. Even after that much silver. Huntsman bolts were covered in silver dust so that they poisoned the target. The fact that Mikey could heal through that was nothing short of amazing.

So I had a huntsman outside of Rosa's safe room. Huntsmen were assassins that specialized in removing elves, dwarves, and almost anything that wasn't human. The folks in Kingdom thought of them as pest control. The only nonhuman (if you ignored Rosa) had to be Mikey. Queen Mihail had sent a huntsman for him, and Mikey hadn't even been around when I killed her son. I was definitely going to have some words with her when we finally got together.

I left Mikey in the conference room and headed for the lobby. Rosa's safe room, he'd said. I had to laugh. Rosa detested any place in the Agency but the front counter. So her safe room was actually a bulletproof cage that locked down around her. From inside her private rectangle, Rosa could run the entire Agency, and with the cage over her, it was definitely a Mexican Standoff. Rosa, incidentally, came from Guatemala, and would win any standoff, Guatemalan, Mexican, or otherwise. I crept down the hallway to the front office and peeked through the window in the staff door. The man in our lobby was a huntsman, all right.

Six foot six, dressed in enough leather and fur to give every member of PETA a heart attack, and armed to the teeth with knives and a wicked crossbow. It was a crossbow only in name—the old string-driven ones were traded for cartridge-load bolts, meaning that he could fire them as fast as he could pull the trigger. Every clip held six, meaning that the son of a bitch had shot Mikey, pinned him in place, then reloaded and repeated. He wore the traditional gnome-skin hood like huntsmen always did. It was supposed to make him seem mysterious. I considered it cowardice.

In the corner, Rosa glowered at him from behind her bulletproof covering. I was pretty sure that the lump of black cloth and skin hiding behind her was Beth. Rosa held her shotgun, but couldn't shoot the huntsman through the glass any more than he could shoot her.

I took a deep breath, checked my clip and my safety, then kicked the door open and started shooting.

He rolled to the side, taking a couple of shots. Now, since I'd never shot a huntsman before, you can forgive me for not knowing those skins he was wearing were some sort of armor. Who knew badger fur could stop bullets? He fired a bolt at me, barely missing my head. So we weren't going for warning shots.

I put one bullet through the front door, ignoring the fact that it looked like I'd missed. Then I counted. One, two, and as I exhaled on three I shot at the floor.

Not because he was under me. Because I wanted him looking my way. Big Bill kicked open the front door and let loose. Those skins might be armor, but Bill carried a shotgun loaded with slugs. The force slammed the huntsman into the front desk, sending his crossbow flying.

I added a few bullets of my own, just to feel like I'd contributed. I nearly missed the blur of silver when he rolled over, throwing a knife at me. If I'd tried a graceful roll or anything fancy, I might have found out what a silver lobotomy feels like. As it was, blood spurted from my temple where the knife grazed me.

"The hunt's over." The huntsman pulled another blade from his belt.

Big Bill fired again, then shrieked as a silver blade blossomed in his knee, followed by another in his elbow. The huntsman advanced on me, and I weighed my ability to get a head shot in. The movies always made them look easy. Anyone who actually tried it learned better. I tried to push my way back through the door, but it was stuck, so I shot the huntsman a few more times. I might as well have been throwing spit wads.

"I said, the hunt is over." He pulled out a second blade. The trick I'd used on the Gray Man wouldn't play here against a trained knife fighter.

As I prepared to rush him, the wall behind me exploded, throwing both the door and me forward.

Through the dust something roared and leaped over me. Something monstrous and black. I'd never actually seen Mikey change into a wolf. The wolf bloodlines had weakened since the old days, and lots of their descendants were stuck as either fully human or fully wolf. Most in their wolf-man form were the same height as a human. Mikey stood at least eight feet tall, and as wide as a compact car.

With one swipe, Mikey tore the first knife from the huntsman. Then Mikey grabbed him by the leather hood, holding him so his feet dangled. Time and again, the huntsman slashed into Mikey's arms, but as fast as the blade pulled out, Mikey healed.

Then Mikey ripped the knife away, tearing the huntsman's fingers off in the process. Mikey reached up and put a claw into the huntsman's mouth, then stepped on his feet. I winced, knowing what would come, but couldn't cover my ears in time to prevent hearing the wet tearing of flesh as Mikey tore the huntsman's jaw off. Then he snarled, a growling roar that ended with the crunch of teeth on bone.

I can't say what Beth and Rosa were doing. I know I was curled up in a ball, unwilling to look. Not because Mikey had killed the huntsman. The huntsman had definitely tried to kill me. Not because Mikey tore the man's throat out. Wolves do that sometimes. It was because I finally recognized where I'd seen that pattern of fur before. The jagged white stripe of fur down Mikey's back, it was a birthmark of sorts, among wolves.

Mikey began to shift back. Shrinking, becoming paler, less hairy. I understood now why he insisted on pants with elastic bands. When his mouth had changed enough to speak, he came over. "Marissa, are you okay?"

I kept it together enough to ask him. "Why didn't you tell me? Why didn't Grimm tell me?"

His forehead creased and his eyes narrowed. He sniffed the air, like he could read my mind from my scent. "Tell you what?"

"That you came here to kill me."

Fourteen

◈

AFTER A MOMENT of silence in the Agency lobby, Mikey shrugged. "Fairy Godfather said he'd handle explaining to you."

Grimm had definitely left that part out. In fact, when I first found out that he'd hired an intern, and that said intern was a wolf, I think my words were "over my dead body" for good reason. Grimm knew how the wolves felt about me. I'd killed their leader. It was like assassinating the pope, the president, and the guy who runs the local pizza shop all at once. Worse yet, that white-stripe pattern said Mikey was related to Fenris, ex-leader of the wolves, current buffet for compost worms.

"He might have forgotten to mention it."

Rosa canceled the lockdown, and the door to her bullet-proof cage unlocked.

"Marissa, if I wanted you dead, I'd have given the huntsman a couple more seconds." Mikey walked over and slipped the crossbow out from under the chairs. "Can't leave this here. Grimm says if it can't be eaten by a toddler, it doesn't go on the floor."

"So why did you come to work for Grimm?" I ignored Beth's whimpering and stuck with Mikey. Sure, I had a one-track mind, but when it came to people who intended to kill me, it was usually justified. I climbed up off the floor and sat down in a chair, ruining it.

Mikey sat down beside me. "I came here to kill you. Of course, Fairy Godfather already knew. Somehow he knew I didn't have a commercial driver's license, and somehow he knew I was supposed to kill you and bring back your heart."

"And he hired you because?"

Mike wiped his hands on his pants. "Well, I was told that one way to become the greatest leader was to avenge Granddad. Fairy Godfather offered me another way."

Granddad. So that explained the family fur. Also, the serious regeneration. Fenris had been so strong that it took several of Grimm's most powerful weapons to kill him. Even then, it'd been a close thing. "I like the idea of anything that doesn't involve killing me."

"He offered to send me to culinary school. Did you know we've been living in the sixteen hundreds? There's so many great ways to spice and prepare meat that don't involve bacon. For instance, a handful of coriander and peppercorns complements white meat sausage in amazing ways."

"Like pork sausage?"

Mikey studied the carpet for a bit. "Umm, sure. Pork. Coriander and pepper would be great with pork. The point is, we can eat so much better. Grimm sends me to night college, and during the day I work here. When I have my chef's hat I'm going to go back and lead my people by their stomachs. And for once, I won't mean by their entrails."

"You don't happen to go to the same college Ari does, do you?" I suddenly wondered if Grimm hadn't arranged a little protection for Ari while she studied. Even a third-string princess like Ari tended to attract a lot of attention, not all of it positive.

Mikey grinned, waving to Beth as Rosa stood her up. "I walk Ari to campus every night. My building's on the same block."

At the thought of Ari, my stomach turned sour. "We got ambushed."

Rosa led Beth out of the booth and into the back, giving Mikey a thumbs-up. If she ever offered me a thumb, it was in the eye.

"Rosa saved us," said Mikey. "She hit the alarm the moment they came in, pulled the piper girl into her booth, and kept them busy long enough for me to gut the hired help. I'd have gotten the huntsman too, but Fairy Godfather said no changing to full wolf." He traced a scar on his chest where a bolt had pierced him.

"All right." I stood up and locked the front door, turning the "Closed" sign. "Take Big Bill to the hospital. Check on Ari, but don't annoy the ninja, or you might get to regrow a few fingers." Then I went back to the showers, washed the cut on my head clean, and began to worry.

See, we'd had other employees in the past. Previous agents who didn't precisely work for Grimm anymore. Most of the others were dead, but one in particular had me worried. An older woman named Jess Harrison. Half djinn, with the beauty, speed, and incredible emotional imbalances that came with it.

From time to time, Grimm would spring her from the mental hospital, but invariably she'd wind up going off the deep end and hurting some waiter who got her order wrong, or breaking the knees of someone who parked in a handicapped spot without a sticker. I wasn't saying they didn't have it coming. Just that it got harder and harder to justify.

Eventually, we had her committed. On enough Thorazine, she painted beautiful watercolor landscapes without stabbing orderlies in the eye with the paintbrush. As soon as I got out of the shower, I put in a call to the hospital and waited for the automated attendant. A woman with a deep Irish brogue rattled off recorded options:

"You have reached St. Lecter's Home for the Violent. Our menu options have recently changed, so listen closely. If you want to report an escape, press one. If you want to plan an escape, press two. If you are calling to report that a homicidal queen has dispatched an assassin team to cut power to the Home, then get slaughtered by patients while attempting to break in, press three. For all other options, press nine. *Para español, marque ocho.*"

I pressed three, and then hung up. No wonder Grimm liked the place.

I'd barely had time to put my head down on my desk before someone knocked at the door. I looked up to see Rosa.

Our receptionist had never been a people person, unless you counted "Can't Stand Them" as a type of people person. Even after Grimm put me in charge, she still ignored me most days and infuriated me when she wasn't ignoring me.

Under her arm, Rosa carried a metal briefcase. She walked into my office without so much as asking, and slammed it on my desk. "Listen." Then she opened it up. What lay inside looked like a combination DVD player and sixth-grade science project. From the moment she pressed the large button marked "Power," it hummed and shook. Then the whole thing lit up with a laser glow, and a picture of Grimm appeared on the screen.

I looked up at Rosa, who didn't seem the least bit surprised. "If this is one of those 'if you are hearing this, I'm dead' messages, I'm not interested."

Rosa left without a word.

I checked for controls. There weren't any. Not even a volume button. "Isn't this the part where it starts doing something? Some sort of message? Last will and testament?"

"No, my dear," said the image on screen. "This isn't a message. It's a test." Grimm, or something like him, watched me from the screen.

I carefully unhooked my Agency bracelet, noting that his image remained on screen.

Then Rosa came back. She carried her sawed-off shotgun and carefully loaded two slugs into it. Then with a click she closed the chamber and leveled it at me.

"A test?"

"Yes," said the Grimm. "One that I sincerely hope you pass."

A moment ticked by as I watched the screen for some hint of what to do. I looked back at Rosa, wondering if I could make it under my desk faster than she could pull the trigger. "So tell me what kind of test this is. No, wait. Tell me what you are. You aren't him."

"Marissa, I am an echo, captured by intention of Fairy Godfather two years ago, on the twenty-fourth of August. If it makes it easier, you may refer to me as Grimm as well."

"Are you intelligent?" Grimm left a copy of himself. Maybe. An echo? Some form of his power that wasn't affected by whatever had him frozen.

The Echo looked over his glasses at me with a stern look.

"That's no sort of question for me. I'm a complete record of the Fairy Godfather's thoughts while he captured me. In that respect I am smarter than every scientist the human race has ever produced." He definitely had Grimm's arrogance.

"Fine. I'll call you Echo. Grimm's his name, and names mean something to me. Tell me about the test." I glanced over to Rosa, who acted as if she hadn't heard a single word.

Echo cleared his throat and waited for me to look back to him. "It's simple, my dear. Convince me you are not something pretending to be Marissa. I should warn you, the weapon Rosa has is loaded with reaper bullets. You may recall them."

I did. I'd used several of them to kill things that weren't supposed to die. If I got shot by one of those, I hoped it hit me in the head. Otherwise I'd have several agonizing seconds while it devoured me.

So all I had to do was be me. In theory. "Echo, why did Grimm create you?"

He paused for a moment, considering my question. "Surprising. This isn't relevant to your survival, my dear."

"Humor me."

"After his mirror was broken, the Fairy Godfather considered for the first time that there might come an eventuality when he was not available to handle his business. Indeed, until you killed a fairy, we didn't think it was possible." Echo glanced to the handmaiden's mark.

"So are you some sort of will?"

"No, my dear, I am a test." Echo crossed his arms, looking disturbingly like an actual Grimm.

I closed my eyes for a moment, trying to figure out what on earth Grimm was thinking when he came up with this scheme. "So how do I convince you I'm me?"

"Determining that is part of the test."

Echo really was a copy of Grimm, with his annoying "I'm always right" and circular logic loops.

"My name is Marissa Locks. I've been your agent for eight years. You called me Goldy Locks, because I do things *just* right." I stopped and waited.

Echo looked up at Rosa and shook his head.

"My last name was Lambert. My sister's name is Hope. You fixed her heart."

He continued to regard me like a lump of meat. Rosa, on the other hand, had a wicked smile. I hated it when she smiled, because the only thing that really made her happy was ruining someone's day. I figured the only reason Grimm kept her on was she came with the building.

"What does it take to get you to understand that I'm me? I have the handmaiden's mark, for Kingdom's sake." I gave Echo the glare that usually got to Grimm.

Echo rolled his eyes. "If the Black Queen sent someone in your place, she would most certainly bear the mark."

And right there, I stopped worrying about the shotgun pointed at my chest. See, Grimm, the real Grimm, always insisted the Black Queen was dead. That the mark on my hand was some form of minor curse that came around every so often. "Echo, is the Black Queen dead?"

His eyes widened, then the corners of his mouth turned up ever so slightly. "She is not alive. I recommend you don't waste any more of your questions on this line of inquiry. Fairy Godfather suspected Rosa was somewhat inclined to shoot you regardless of the outcome."

"What do you mean?" I sat up and leaned on my desk. "Don't waste my questions?"

"I'll only answer so many of them before I decide that in fact you are a facsimile of Marissa, attempting to determine a way to convince me. That, by the way, was a question."

"So help me out. Tell me what I have to do to convince you." I was careful to avoid phrasing my question in the form of a question. I preferred checkers to sudden-death *Jeopardy!*

Echo folded his arms and waited.

"You don't have to tell me the answer. Let me know if I'm supposed to ask you something, tell you something, or do something."

"Yes," said Echo.

Rosa released the safety on her shotgun and walked to the side to line up a better shot at me.

About then, I realized whatever I was supposed to be doing, I wasn't. I didn't have the slightest idea what Grimm's Echo was looking for to prove myself. I took the briefcase and set it in my lap, weighing my options. Grimm had a set of rules, and all I had to do was figure them out, but I'd never been a "by the rules" girl. So we'd do it my way.

"All right, Echo. One last question. Is this briefcase bulletproof?" In the moment before he could answer, I shot to my feet, briefcase in hand. The metal top collided with Rosa's shotgun right as it went off. I pushed the barrel up and away, charging straight into Rosa, knocking her into the wall.

I'd taken more self-defense courses than I could count, and in the last couple of years I'd had Jess train me on visiting day. Lots of martial arts teach you to use your knees or your fists. I used the briefcase. I smashed it into Rosa's jaw, then her arm, causing her to drop the shotgun. A second blow across her head sent her reeling. I threw down the briefcase and picked up the shotgun.

"Now you listen." I still had one more reaper bullet. The way her gaze flitted to the shotgun told me she knew it too.

To her credit, Rosa dropped the arm she'd held over her face and looked at me. If you had to die, facing it head-on was good in my book.

"You ever aim this thing at me again, I'll have the dwarves grind it up and put it in your feeding tube." I opened the shotgun and removed the remaining reaper bullet, then threw the empty gun at her. "Get back out there, answer the phone, and get ready to open the office. If you even think about reloading and coming back, I'll order Mikey to play with you."

Rosa stood, leaning heavily on the gun. I'd hit her harder than I realized. If it weren't for the fact that she could file a workman's comp claim, I'd have taken a photo for my memory book.

"My dear," said Echo, his voice muffled by the briefcase, "I'd appreciate it if you didn't kill her. She's your notary public, and you'll need her to sign the papers."

Rosa hobbled over and opened the briefcase. With a click, the lower section unsealed. What I thought was only electronics held a thick raft of papers, and one of Grimm's favorite fountain pens. Rosa threw a pen at me, flinching when I caught it. "Start signing."

"I don't sign anything without reading." I turned over the first raft of papers.

"Then we will be here for several weeks," said Echo. "These contracts, to put it simply, give you control of the Agency until the Fairy Godfather returns, or you die."

"So Grimm wanted me to own the Agency?"

Echo nodded. "*Own* is a nebulous word. Fairy Godfather considered you most appropriate to keep the Agency functioning in the event of his demise or incapacitation. His arrangements will put several spell casters on your permanent retainer, and of course, you will have access to all Agency accounts. It was a pleasure not having you killed, Marissa."

Rosa hit the Power button, and Echo disappeared. Then she looked over at me and took out an impossibly large stack of papers. "Sign. Please."

Fifteen

～

IT TOOK NEARLY four hours to finish signing the papers. By that point, writing "Marissa Locks" felt like writing the entirety of a Chinese phone book. I called to arrange backup for Shigeru, selecting an acidic moat monster who could dissolve anything that set foot in the room. How exactly our contractors intended to get it into the hospital was not my problem. Keeping Ari alive was.

Long after Rosa locked the front door, I wandered the halls of the Agency, poking into offices, checking out storage rooms. It wasn't as if I was spying. According to what I'd signed, the lease, the accounts, everything belonged to me. I checked the office fridge for food, and found only the wheel of cheese that'd been there since my first anniversary with the Agency. No one in their right mind touched the thing. Every person who so much as laid a finger on it died bloody deaths within hours.

Then I went into Grimm's office, sat down at his desk, and began to sift through papers. Grimm was never physically at his desk. In fact, we had a scanner that did nothing but slide papers past his mirror. There were the usual receipts. More than a few letters from lawyers threatening to sue, and quite a few thank-you notes. I'm assuming they were thank-you notes, as the writing looked bubbly, and happy, even though I couldn't read the language.

I wanted more than anything to talk to Liam, but Liam was hiding in a castle, hopefully at the end of a long line of traps. Odds were, Grimm's defenses were good. Odds were, the vampire's assassins would kill anyone who survived traveling through the dungeon. But odds were also good Queen Mihail did her homework. That she'd sent a team wearing asbestos underwear. That the man I loved more than anyone else in this world was in serious danger and might die before he could offer me a ring I already wore.

I wouldn't have worried, normally. I could handle anything, with Grimm's knowledge and a little bit of magical assistance. But Grimm was frozen, and the only thing left was an Echo. And right then I began to wonder. I left his office and went back to my own, where I found the briefcase. When I clicked it on, Echo's face appeared.

"Marissa, you have passed the identity test. Thank you for your cooperation, my dear."

"Echo, how much do you know?"

He frowned at me. "We had this conversation. I am a recording of all of Fairy Godfather's thoughts during the recording process."

"Did he think about Ari?" I tapped the pen on my desk nervously, wondering if my idea would work.

Echo nodded. "The sheer number of things he considered during the two point eight milliseconds where I was captured would astound you. He most certainly considered Princess Arianna."

"So if Ari were in a coma, and I needed to keep her safe, how would Grimm do it?" I didn't know how far Echo's limits went, but it couldn't hurt to find out.

"I do not possess his array of knowledge, Marissa. Only a recording of what he thought about during a remarkably brief time. However, I believe we reason along identical lines. This can hardly be the first time a princess has found herself incapacitated. How were they kept safe before?"

"Is the gateway to Grimm's library open?" Grimm had a better selection than the branch library, so long as you didn't want to read romance and you liked memoirs of people dead for five centuries.

Echo stared at me, his eyebrows raised, his lips drawn tight. "The secondary closet across from the teleconference room is the current portal. I realize this is beyond my purpose, but I believe Fairy Godfather would advise you to go home and get some sleep. If Princess Arianna is protected for the moment, then judging from my assessment of your condition, you will deal better with this problem once you have rested. Now kindly turn me off and go home."

AT HOME, I couldn't sleep. It was the knowledge that Liam was in danger. It was the fear of what might happen to Ari. That Grimm might be truly gone. If he were, it was only a matter of time before another Fairy came looking to move in and set up shop. It was unlikely they'd tolerate competition.

I stayed up far into the morning reading about princesses, and their total and complete inability to get hurt like a normal person. Sleeping Beauty, Snow White, that Anesthesia chick in Russia. The clock said I only had a couple hours until my alarm went off when I finally figured I'd put enough of the pieces together. I blinked, and the alarm blared. Not time for work. Time to head into Kingdom for my doctor's appointment.

If—no, *when*—I figured out a way out of this revenge mess, I planned on having a lot of makeup sex and not giving birth to a cursed child. I made it into Kingdom before the doctor's office even opened, and when the elf at the front desk opened for registrations, I marched up and signed my name.

She read it over, wrinkled her nose, and then read it again. "You'll have to come back when you have an appointment."

"I have one. Made by the Fairy Godfather, a couple of days ago." Grimm never slept, never forgot, and never forgave.

The elf sniffed again, wiggling her ears in distress. "I don't have any record of that, Ms. Locks. If you'd like, I can put you on the normal list. We can see you next November." I swore my way out of the office and off to work. When, not if, I managed to get Grimm restored, he was going to answer to me.

Without an appointment to keep, I made it into work early.

Of course, no matter how early I got there, Rosa beat me through the door. I once asked Grimm if Rosa might have actually been some sort of appliance that came with the building. At the front door of the office I nodded to her.

She completely ignored me.

"Morning, Rosa."

She looked over the counter at me like she'd discovered that someone left a bean casserole in the lobby over the weekend. So much for getting more respect. I'd barely made coffee and settled down for the morning paper when the shouting started.

I ignored it.

There was no reason to go running off just because people were upset with each other. In fact, I preferred not to intervene until blood transfusions became necessary. The shouting rose to shrieking, then screaming, then chanting. Screaming, fighting, no problem. When people started casting spells in my lobby, I took issue with it.

I took the paper and my coffee, and went to find out what Rosa wasn't handling. In the lobby stood two people dressed in long robes. Echo said I'd have hired help with the spells, and these looked to be my enchanters. Then I got a better look at them. Those weren't long robes. They were bathrobes. I swore under my breath. Why couldn't Grimm hire real spell slingers?

"Can I help you?" I set down the coffee and rolled up the paper. I'd dealt with enchanters before, and it was like training a puppy.

The woman nodded. She was older, probably nearing fifty, and wore glasses so scratched they were milky white. Her long white hair had pinecones and bits of garbage in it. "We're here to fulfill contract 27-Alpha-323."

I looked at the man standing behind her. He looked curiously familiar, and smelled like a garbage truck and a wine bar combined. "You the enchanters Fairy Godfather hired?"

He kept his eyes on the floor and mumbled something indistinct.

I looked back at the woman.

"Not exactly. We're here to fulfill their contract. See, Grabnar the Great is in jail, and Elinda got bitten by an asp at the post office."

I made a mental note to take a closer look at Grimm's contract to figure out where he'd allowed substitutions. I had an Agency to run, no spell powers of my own, and a couple of enchanters who looked like they'd fallen off the wagon, then been strapped to the wagon wheel and run over repeatedly. "All right. Let me show you to the temp worker's offices."

I waved them on after me.

"Don't you want to know our names?" asked the woman.

"Not really." I treated my temp workers like I treated my potted plants. Until they'd survived several weeks at the Agency, they didn't get names or love. When we got to the temp offices, I put them to work. "We've had four outbreaks of poodles in the last month. That's way too many for this time of year. So put your wands together, draw a few pentagrams, and pull an answer out of your hat for where they're coming from."

"We don't use wands or pentagrams," said the woman, glaring at me.

"Or hats," said the man.

I nodded. "I don't care if you do card tricks. I want to know where the poodles are coming from. Rosa can get you anything you need, as long as you don't need anything. Call me when you have an answer." The office buzzer went off, meaning in the time it'd taken me to park a couple of enchanters, someone else arrived.

I ambled back to the lobby and smiled. Beth sat in a lobby chair, clipboard in hand, filling in her daily application. "Morning, Beth."

She smiled at me, a silver ring flashing in her nose as she did. "I was afraid you wouldn't be here."

I shrugged. "Not the first or last time there'll be a team of assassins dispatched to kill everyone in the office, I expect. It's like that around here. A lot."

Beth blew a single note on the kazoo, and the rat in front of her did cartwheels. "I lived in a crack house for a while, so I'm okay with crazy. I can make rats do anything now!"

I snorted. "Rats. Teenagers. You aren't a real piper until you can control something evil. Something awful."

Beth caught my tone and locked her eyes on me. She put one hand on her hip and cocked an eyebrow. "Such as?"

I waved her on, and she followed me to our back storage room. Inside, a six-foot kennel shook and rattled like something from Inferno raged inside it.

Beth shivered, then clenched her fists and nodded to me.

With a magician's flourish, I yanked the blanket off the kennel, revealing the white terror inside. A single white toy poodle, about two feet long at most, with its tail sculpted in a bob cut.

Its beady eyes focused on Beth as it began to wag its tail, yipping happily and prancing.

Beth knelt by the cage. "Hey, little girl. What's a cute little thing like you doing—"

The poodle rocketed through the air. It slammed into the kennel door, hitting it so hard, the cage lurched forward, smashing Beth in the face.

Beth began cursing like a longshoreman as she rolled onto her knees and stood up. Blood dribbled from her nose, and above her eye she had the makings of a fine bruise. "What the hell is that thing?"

"Poodle." I checked the kennel door to make sure the welds held.

Beth kicked the cage. "My aunt had a poodle. It didn't do that. It didn't look like that."

"That one hadn't fed on hellfire and human flesh. Don't get me wrong, it was still evil, but this, this is a piece of Inferno, come to play games in the city. They get stronger and cuter with every person they kill. So you can lead rats. You can control teenagers. So what? This is what counts."

Beth reached into a pocket and took out her kazoo. A low, mournful hum came from it as she began to play.

The poodle stood its ground, ears flattened back, teeth bared.

Beth played louder, longer, "Mary Had a Little Lamb" with such power it almost compelled me to follow her wherever she would go.

The poodle leaped at the kennel door again, rattling it.

With an exhausted sigh, Beth dropped her kazoo. The brass clinked on the floor as she panted. "I can't do it. It doesn't listen."

"You can. You'll have to practice. Rats want to eat garbage.

Teen boys want to eat and have sex. Poodles have a will of their own, and to be able to run them off into the river, you'll need to match it."

I left her with her fuzzy white nemesis.

WHILE MY TEAM of enchanters worked to figure out where the Poodle leak was, and my new piper worked to control a single weak poodle, I grabbed some lunch. In the kitchen, Mikey sat at the table, his gangly arms propped up as he ate a sandwich of indeterminable origin. He looked like he was about to vomit.

"What's the matter, Mikey? Did you eat the special at Froni's this weekend?"

He slumped over, dejected. "Steph didn't show up for our date. We talked on the phone, I went to meet her at the subway, and she never showed up. I didn't even get spaghetti."

Mikey had never eaten at Froni's, which was the only reason he was upset about not getting to go. The place violated every health ordinance in the city. In fact, I suspected Froni lobbied for new regulations every month so he could break them.

"Sometimes things come up. It'll get better. I need you to take the night shift tonight to give the moat monster and Shigeru a break. Eat anyone who comes near Ari."

He pulled out a phone and dialed a number. After a few moments he slammed the phone down. "She's not answering my calls, and her voice mail is full."

I remembered being so in love with someone I could hardly breathe. "Is she beautiful?" Given Mikey's taste in women, it was possible she looked like a yeti. Heck, it was entirely possible she was a yeti, or the bearded lady at the circus. Wolves were known for their taste in sausage, not women. Also, occasionally for making sausage from women.

Mikey punched a few buttons on his phone. "This is her at the fountain in Kingdom." He handed me the phone.

I looked at her red hair and familiar face, and my stomach turned. "Mikey, what's Steph's last name?"

He caught the tone in my voice and looked up, his forehead creased. "Thromson."

I did my best to keep my voice calm as fear and anger

warred for which emotion would be the first to break through. "Mikey, did Steph ask about your day?"

He nodded.

"Did she ask what you did?" My hands tightened around the phone until I was afraid I'd crush it.

"Yeah. She always asked about my day." Mikey didn't take his eyes off me.

"Did she ask what you were doing Monday?"

He put his head in his hands. "Yes. She asked—she asked what all of us were doing."

I had one more question to ask before I'd know if I needed to go get the reaper bullets and kill Mikey. "What's Ari's last name?"

He didn't as much as flinch. "Locks. It says Locks on all of her packages."

Locks was technically my last name. Ari shared it with me while she lived in my apartment, and since her stepmother disowned her and kicked her out of Kingdom, Ari kept it when she moved out on her own. "Arianna Thromson is her real name, Mikey. You've heard Ari talk about her family, right?"

He dropped his shoulders, and his eyes became unfocused. "But she wouldn't—I mean, Steph didn't—"

"Steph didn't have to do anything. She just had to find out where we were all going to be. Me, at the college. Ari at the department store. You at the Agency."

He jumped to his feet and grabbed the phone, smashing it. A roar came from his throat like a hurricane blast. I thought of the three little pigs and wondered how much of the huffing and puffing was roar.

"You told her where we'd be. You set us up, and it nearly killed all of us."

Mikey seemed to shrink. His face turned white; his hands trembled.

"So now I have to decide what to do with you."

Sixteen

〜

MIKEY PUT HIS hands together in front of him like he was praying. "Please, Marissa. How was I supposed to know my girlfriend was actually the stepdaughter of an evil queen?"

I stood up, walked to my office door, and grabbed my purse. "Follow me."

"I need this job, Miss Locks. I really do." Mikey looked like he was about to choke. He did that one time at lunch, and a pinky finger came out his nose.

I patted my purse. "Come with me willingly, or I'll shoot you and drag you to the elevator."

He came.

We rode down in the elevator, with him staring at the ends of his shoes the whole way. The elevator opened and we walked out into the cargo bay where our workers dispatched shipments. I whistled, and a group of dockworkers gathered.

"Mikey here wants to know how he could have known his girlfriend was actually the stepdaughter of an evil queen."

The men began to chuckle. Then one stepped forward. "Man, I can't remember the last girl I dated who didn't turn out to be the stepdaughter of an evil queen."

"Or the long-lost princess," said another.

"My ex was the evil queen."

The others looked at him a moment.

"Well, she was evil. You've got to give her that."

Mikey sat down on a crate and rubbed his forehead. "So any girl I meet might be working for someone evil, or evil herself?"

The last dockworker came over. "Don't listen to them. Not every girl who wants to marry you is an evil queen or her daughter."

I nodded in agreement. "How's your *sister* doing, Ben?"

He shrugged. "She's good. Still in therapy. We both are, actually."

"I'm so done with this city." Mikey stood up and walked back to the elevator. Interns were only marginally better than princesses, in my book.

A FEW HOURS later, after I hired a team of bakers to dispose of an obese witch, I'd just settled back into paperwork when another knock at my door interrupted. I looked up at one of the enchanters.

He shuffled into my office, sweat pouring down his clammy, olive skin. "We know where the poodles are coming from."

I ran to their office to find an enchantress unfolding a large map of the city on the table. "Where?"

She pointed to the doorway, where an enchanter stood, wheezing. Then they began to hum. Then chant, an eerie, echoing tone. The sound vibrated the bones in my skull, like being too near the speakers at a concert. It rose in pitch, louder, stronger, and she began to sing, a warbling opera note.

The enchanter pitched forward and began to cough violently and shake. Then he reared back his head and coughed. A missile of phlegm shot from his throat to land on the map, and the chanting stopped. "There," he said, pointing to the map.

Magic phlegm rocketed the Enchanters from low on my "detest" list to somewhere in the top five. "Can't you do it the normal way? Like cut open a rabbit, let the guts fall out, and tell things from the patterns?"

The enchantress looked at me with shock. "We're not

fairies or drug companies, so it'd be animal cruelty. Besides, we're not finished."

I looked back to the table, where the map sizzled. The glob of mucus boiled as it sank into the table, then dropped to the floor and burned into the carpet. "Have you been gargling battery acid? Do I need to call 911?"

The enchanter shook his head. "It's below there."

I took a closer look at the map, careful not to touch the moist edges, and swore. The map showed exactly where our poodles came from. "You," I said, pointing to the enchanter, "I'll have Rosa bring you a mask. Don't cough on anyone." I looked to my enchantress. "There's an aquarium of frogs one room over. Start doing the frog prince thing."

I went back to my office and got my purse and jacket, then hit the intercom on my desk. "Rosa, I'm going out to do some fieldwork. Put a muzzle on our enchanters and hold down the fort." I could feel the disdain oozing through the speaker. I meant to get back to visit our dwarves anyway, so now was as good a time as any.

THE SMALL WONDERS jewelry store still stood out as the nicest shop on the block. No dust inside the windows, not a single broken window, and bars that actually looked nice, instead of looking like they'd been forged in the middle ages. I kicked open the door, noting that I left a nice dent, and strode into the shop.

"You're closed." I turned over the door's sign.

"Ms. Locks?" Magnus the dwarf sat on a stool behind the counter, a look of concern on his face.

"I need to see that room you found again."

He rose and locked the door, then led me to the vault. "We ain't been down there since yer strike team went missing."

I shrugged. If I were him, I wouldn't admit to it either. When the elevator opened into the workshop, the first thing I smelled was sulfur, like I'd stepped into the Cabbage and Bean Eating World Championships. Grimm's replacement enchanters might be completely insane, but they were right. I crawled my way down to the tunnel, wondering how much it cost to keep those lights lit just in case someone came crawling down the pipe.

Sure enough, the door stood cracked open, a foul, hot breeze wafting from inside. I threw open the door and looked inside. The dealing room, as Grimm had called it, still glowed with orange light from the walls. I noted the ring of Celestial Crystal at the doorway.

Grimm told me I'd be perfectly safe. He'd even asked me to go back and talk to whatever I'd heard on the other side. At that moment, I wished more than anything I'd said yes. The summoning portal, which should have been sealed, still jetted wisps of flame at intervals, like a miniature geyser.

Throughout the room, statues of six nineteen-year-old slackers in blue jeans and T-shirts stood frozen, looks of horror fixed forever on their faces. Grimm's team of clerks hadn't fared well. With a final look around the room, I stepped over the threshold.

When I did, a shiver crossed my skin, cold pressure pulling me back. Without a doubt, a familiar feeling—the Celestial Crystal had trapped blessing and curse on the other side. The two had a serious case of separation anxiety when forcibly removed, and no doubt they'd spend the rest of the day breaking every bit of glass I came in range of.

I headed for the hellfire portal.

While I couldn't open one of these to save my soul, I'd learned enough about portals to close one. I touched the runes in a pattern I'd practiced over and over, watching them light up under my fingers. When I clicked the last, a single jet of flame popped over the circle, and the orange light in the chamber faded to a dull glow.

Now that I'd sealed the hellfire leak, I took a closer look at my ex-clerks. Normally, I wouldn't bother. Statue transformations were, in essence, permanent. Problem was, the market for fine sculptures of liberal arts majors was quite lean, so if I could do something, I would.

That's when I began to wonder how deep the stone actually was. I knew of two types of statue transformations. One turned you to stone clean through. Gorgoning was pretty much the end of the line. The other covered the victim in a layer of stone, trapping them in statue form.

I glanced around the room, looking for something to chip with. There, on the center table, stood a crystal block, and embedded in it, a long quill worked from quartz. I picked it up, noting how sharp both ends were. Once, someone had used this to sign their soul away.

I knelt by the foot of one of the statues. He'd frozen doing the traditional "beg for mercy" pose. I knelt and swung the quill, aiming for a toe. The quill shattered the stone, showing marble clean through. The population of fast-food workers had gone down permanently by six.

"I didn't like that one either."

Without hesitation, I spun and pulled my gun, squeezing off three shots. A cloud of darkness floated a few feet away, almost taking form, and then turning to mist to let my bullets pass through. It took shape again, forming an impossibly slender man, at least seven feet tall.

I let my gun speak for me, carefully firing a bullet, and noting that it passed through him, leaving barely a vapor disturbed. Then I remembered Grimm's assurance that he would have negotiated with whatever it was. I held my fire, waiting for him to solidify.

"I don't believe we've met," said the man, tipping a bowler hat at me. His translucent purple skin showed the bones underneath, except for his eyes. The eyes were demon eyes, bloodred with black pupils.

"Go to hell," I said. Not exactly the right way to begin negotiations, but Grimm had warned me about demons before.

The man turned and swept his arm toward the portal. "I would, but you've cut off my route home. Quite irresponsible, I think. My name is Malodin. May I have yours?"

Names were power for most things, and I wasn't keen on giving a demon any more power than necessary. "Goldy Locks." Grimm's nickname for me, because I had to get things just right.

"Lie, with a grain of truth," said Malodin. "Your name is Locks. Your first name . . . I'm getting something. Starts with an M."

"Marigold."

"Another lie, Marissa." He took off his hat and bowed low, his knees hinging to the side like a cricket's. "Marissa Locks, I am Malodin, Prince of Inferno."

I ran for the door. When I got back to the office, I'd tell them how I hit him with holy water, or a binding spell, or something that would make a run for the door seem less cowardly and more worthy of the woman in charge of the Agency, but for now, getting out would do fine.

In a flicker of black, he reformed between me and the door.

I steeled myself, remembering Grimm's words. Celestial Crystal meant he couldn't touch me. I took a step forward, eyes closed. Then another. A soft, warm breath of sulfur hit me in the nose, and I opened my eyes. I stood less than a finger length from him.

His mouth hung open in a slack smile, the teeth like shark's teeth inside.

"You can't touch me," I said, as much to myself as him. "That's Celestial Crystal around the edge of the room."

He leaned over and whispered in my ear. "That means I can't touch things outside the room." Then he reached over and patted me on the shoulder.

I rolled backwards, firing four more shots that passed through him, and Malodin began to advance toward me, an idiot grin still plastered to his inhuman face. "Don't panic, little woman. If I wanted you dead, you'd already be dead."

"Then what do you want?" I slipped my gun back into my purse, then flipped the quill over. If it was sharp enough to chip marble, it would make a decent dagger.

"I need someone to do a few odd jobs for me. Prepare the way, as it were."

I swore. Why it was that every time I met someone, they either tried to kill me or hire me, I couldn't say. "I already have a job, thanks. One with great benefits."

Malodin shrugged. "How about a part-time gig? I can offer you anything."

"Sorry, last couple people to offer me anything tried to kill me." Admittedly, one of them was a fairy, and one was a queen, but I figured demons couldn't be much better.

"Let's make a deal," said Malodin, stepping back from me. He leaned up against the doorway, blocking my only exit. "You tell me what you would want if we had an agreement, I let you go."

I ran over his words again and again, considering each way they could be interpreted. No way in hell was I going to make a deal with a demon, but if it would get me out of the room, I'd tell him almost anything. "How do I wake up Ari? How do I bring back Grimm? How do I save Liam? How do I make Queen Mihail pay for what she's done? How do I turn a bunch of clerks back into slackers?"

Malodin cocked his head at each question, his flaming red eyes losing focus. Then he swiveled his head down like some sort of insect, staring at me. "Mihail, you say? I completed a deal with her, not a week ago. To get her, you'll have to bring charges against her at the Court of Queens."

Now the queen's knowledge of how to get at each of us made perfect sense. She'd made a deal with demons for the chance to gain revenge. "She sold you her soul?"

Malodin wrinkled his nose and hissed like a cat sprayed with whip cream. "Not hers. Her soul is so withered it's barely worth taking. She sold us her son."

I can't say if the knowledge that Prince Mihail was still alive or the fact that his mother had sold him to Inferno shocked me more. Last time I saw the prince, he was covered in a corrosive spell and looked more like a B-movie swamp monster than an A-list jerk. "I have to be going."

"Make a deal with me, I'll help you. You can say I tricked you. You can tell everyone that I trapped you. You can lie about it, and no one will ever know." Malodin's words made the chamber vibrate, his voice causing the quill in my hand to resonate.

I glanced over my shoulder. On the drafting table lay a contract the size of a blanket. It draped over the edges.

"I can give you the means to save your friends. A way to revenge. She tried to have your best friend killed. She's landing a strike team to kill your boyfriend right now. And you, you haven't got a prayer against her."

Kingdom help me, but for a moment, I thought about it. About signing the contract and letting him bring down revenge on the queen. Then reality caught up with me. I would *never* agree to his terms.

"No deal. Now let me go."

For a moment, I thought he would leap on me and savage

me with that mouth full of teeth. Instead, he stepped aside with a flourish, and waved to the door. "Then begone, Marissa Locks. I hope your friends survive your decision."

I headed for the door, nearly at a run, when a shadow raced under my feet and popped up, just between me and freedom. Malodin towered over me, a piece of paper in his hand. He'd shrunk the contract to a single page.

"Let me go. We had a deal." I tried to keep the fear out of my voice.

Malodin shook his head slowly. "No, we didn't. I said 'Let's make a deal.' You never agreed to it. All I want is the quill back. You have no idea how hard it is to find a pen when you need one here."

I almost fell for it, handing over the pen. What stopped me was the way he held the contract. If I put it in his hand, the tip of the quill would brush its surface. "Fetch." I threw it over my shoulder.

Malodin flickered, like a video signal glitch, and began to laugh. "Your princess friend needs her prince to wake her. We upgraded your boyfriend's fire. He's about to eat an entire strike team of princes, and though he's going to have a serious stomachache, he'll be fine. Your fairy benefactor isn't dead. He's constrained."

I knew better than to trust anything a demon told me. "Why are you telling me this?"

"We have a deal." He held up the contract. A scratch lay across the surface.

"I didn't sign that." I looked at the paper, and the line rearranged itself like a grave worm crawling into place. A wave of chills washed over me.

"The quill was in your hand. You moved it. It hit the paper."

I shook my head. "That's not fair. You might as well have triggered an earthquake while my hand was near it, or had me sign something else and pulled it away."

Malodin shrank down to look me in the eye. "I had an earthquake ready, but you made it easy. So we have a deal. You're now a contract worker for me. Think I'll call you 'Hell's Handmaiden.'"

I ran to the table and seized the quill, which had reappeared in its holder. "I'm canceling the contract."

Malodin crossed his arms and gave me a doubtful stare. "I would have to sign to cancel, and that's not going to happen. Any demon who canceled his own contract, the adversary would personally punish. Now get to work, handmaiden. The world isn't going to end itself."

I let a moment of anger take over. "I'm nobody's hand-maiden. I used to be an agent for the Fairy Godfather, and I'm not going to bring about the end of the world." I stepped forward, pushing him back.

Malodin's eyes lit up with fire and his skin blistered. "You will. I have waited six thousand years for a decent, by-the-book apocalypse. Summon the harbingers, unleash the plagues, and then you will call down the demon apocalypse on your world."

"And if I don't?"

Malodin smiled and his teeth shifted to pointed ones like a crocodile's. "If you default, I get my apocalypse *now*. I'd rather have a proper one; in fact I'm willing to wait if that's what it takes, but if you don't live up to the terms of our bargain, I guess a garden-variety apocalypse will have to do."

"I'm not going to do anything for you."

"We will see." He caught fire, burning into ashes, and the smoke disappeared, leaving only a shining piece of paper, dense with writing I couldn't even read.

I looked at the paper over and over, but my name still showed at the bottom. Behind me, clerk after clerk tumbled out of stone shells, most of them looking even more bleary than normal.

One of them stumbled up to me. "Dude, am I in hell?"

"Not yet."

THE DWARVES WERE waiting for me when I got out of the elevator. Magnus walked up to me and coughed. "Ma'am, if you don't mind stepping outside."

The other dwarves covered their noses.

"What?"

"You reek of sulfur," said Magnus.

I didn't bother mentioning that I might have accidentally entered into an agreement to end the world. Instead, I thought about the other reason I'd planned on coming down here. "I need you to build something for me."

Magnus pointed to the door, and I walked out. Outside, he stood upwind of me. "What can I do fer ye?"

"I have a princess friend who got herself into a bit of a coma. I can't keep her at the hospital, but I was wondering if you could build me a crystal coffin, like in the fairy tales?"

Magnus scratched his head. "Sure we can, Ms. Locks. I'll need the first million dollars before we can begin work. You can pay the next five million when we finish construction, and I'll take the last twenty-five million upon delivery."

My face grew hot and I narrowed my eyes at him. "Seriously? You want thirty-one million dollars for a crystal casket?"

Magnus nodded like some sort of dashboard ornament. "Celestial Crystal ain't cheap. That's five percent less than I'd charge anyone else, on account of you helping us."

"I'll buy a coffin of my own. How much are the life-support enchantments?"

Magnus went back inside the store and came out with a small gray box. "This here is all you need. You can have it, so long as you go take a bath."

I left him there on the sidewalk, and headed back to the office.

Seventeen

∽

THE FIRST THING Rosa did when I walked in the front door of the Agency was give me an evil stare. Then she wrinkled her nose. I ignored her and headed to my office.

An enchanter came and stuck his head into my office. "We're running searches, but I can't find the source of the poodle leak anymore." He sniffed, first the air, then his armpits. "Did something die in here?"

I looked at his unwashed hair, the bits of garbage clinging to his robe—a very filthy motel robe—and swore under my breath. Smelling worse than an enchanter put the icing on an already bad day. "How's the frog-to-prince bit going?"

He glanced down at his feet in a way that didn't inspire confidence.

I rushed down the hall to the side room where I'd left the enchantress, and from the doorway, raucous laughter echoed out. Inside, naked men lounged on chairs, laughing and toasting each other with wine.

One of them looked up. "Wench, bring me some clothing, or take off yours." Then he looked at me closer. "On second thought, bring me mine." The only thing worse than one prince was a room full of them. The only thing worse than a room full of princes was a room full of naked princes. If there had to be an apocalypse, I hoped these guys died first.

The enchantress sat in the back corner, whispering to a man who kept his head down on the table, occasionally looking wildly around the room.

I marched over to the prince who had ordered me around and knocked the wine glass from his hand. "Get your own clothes." Then I put my foot up in his crotch, resting the heel on a particularly sensitive spot. "And if you ever ask me to take off my clothes again, you'll get to find out what life is like as a hairy, muscular princess."

Silence reigned supreme as I left the room. I had a wardrobe staffer bring up bathrobes, and set a contractor to work filling out the princes' release paperwork. When my room was finally clear, I went back to find the enchantress. She still sat beside the one man. He hadn't put on a robe. He didn't even give me a lecherous stare. Sometimes, life as a frog left princes more tolerable, but not exactly functional.

"He won't talk at all," said the enchantress. She put a hand on his arm, and he flinched, pulling away.

I slid into the seat beside her and smiled at him. "It's going to be okay. You can tell your therapist all about how bad it was. She might even sleep with you if you are charming enough."

He kept his head down. If the chance to bed another unsuspecting woman didn't get a reaction from a prince, nothing would.

"Sometimes it's like this," I told the enchantress. "Might have been a frog for more than a month."

The man's head snapped up, and his head twitched as he followed something. I looked, and at the light, a moth fluttered. That's when I realized what was wrong.

"Might have been a frog his whole life. Did you test them, or did you start transforming frogs into princes?"

The enchantress smacked her head. "Stupid, stupid, stupid."

I thought about yelling at her, but I didn't see any reason to take out my bad day on her. Instead, I hit the intercom. "Rosa, I need you to call down to PetsLoc and order me a gallon-bucket of crickets and the largest heat lamp they've got."

The door to the room swung open, and Mikey stuck his

head in. "Ninja dude is on shift now. I'm going to get some sleep—hey, is that brimstone I smell?"

The enchantress smiled at me. "I think it smells lovely."

"Mikey, could you lead our naked friend down to the shower and put him in it, turn it to about eighty degrees? I don't want his skin drying out while we figure out how to fix this."

Mikey hulked past me, grabbed the frightened man around the waist, and hauled him out of the room. Even though I still blamed him for getting used, the wolf had a decent heart and quite a few livers in his private fridge, if memory served me right.

I checked for Beth in the back room, but she wasn't there. True, if I was forced to end the world in an apocalypse, I might not be too worried about poodles. Then I shut the door to my office, sat down, and tried to make sense of the contract.

I had two immediate problems: The first was that I wasn't a lawyer. The second, more serious one, was that I couldn't even read the writing. It looked strangely familiar though. The longer I thought about it, the more certain I became that I'd seen it before.

When it hit me, I jumped to my feet, ran to the door, and grabbed my jacket. I ran down the hall, took the stairs, and jumped into my car.

WHEN I PULLED up at Ari's brownstone, I received an immediate reminder of why movie night was always at my place. From the dead tree in the front yard to the swing that rocked itself without wind, the place gave me the creeps.

I got out my spare key and was trying to fit it in the lock when the door opened itself. It swung inward, inviting me.

"Close that door and let me unlock it." The key established me as a legitimate friend, therefore under the protection of Ari's lease. With a huff of wind, the door slammed in my face, then swung open and slammed again for good measure. "I get it. You don't like me." It stayed shut long enough for me to unlock the dead bolt, then swung open again.

I walked inside, amazed at how the place looked so dreary without Ari to lighten it up. "Hello?" In the corner, a mass of fur the size of a small horse rose and growled at me. "Not now, Yeller. Ari's in the hospital." Hellhounds weren't known for their intelligence, but he curled back up and whined.

"Creepy dead lawyer, you around here? I need to talk."

A cold trace of dry bone swept across my shoulder. The lich floated behind me, his eyes bottomless pits of darkness. I walked over and sat on the couch.

"Whaaaaaaaaaaeeeerrrr," he wheezed in a spectral voice.

I took out my phone and brought up my apps list. "Hold on. I have a Ouija board app. Should make talking with you bearable." He drifted over and took the phone from my hand, arctic cold seeping out from his bones. Then he clicked the Home button and brought up instant messaging. Letters began to scroll, since spirits had a lot easier time manipulating electronic impulses.

The phone read, "Where is Ari?"

"She's in the hospital."

The lich flared darkness from him like tendrils of visible anger. "Who did it? Please, let it be you."

"Queen Mihail. She tried to kill us with an apple."

The lich typed for a moment, then handed me my phone. He floated over to a recliner, then settled down, approximating, as best he could, sitting down. "I was so worried when she didn't come home," read the phone.

"You? You were worried about her?" Then I began to giggle. "She tamed you." It was hardly the first time Ari had tamed a vicious creature.

The lich's finger bones rasped as he clenched skeletal fists. "Like you have room to talk."

"That's not fair. I was demoted and stuck with Ari. I was lonely. You try not having any friends for six years."

The lich picked up my phone. "I've been dead for sixteen years. Cry me the River Styx and go jump in." Then, after a moment, he added, "Is Ari going to be all right?"

I put my head in my hands. "I don't know. I've got a ninja, a wolf, and an acidic moat monster guarding her, but she's not safe in the hospital. I'm going to build her a coffin and put her in a dungeon on life support. It's supposed to be the traditional way to keep princesses safe. Know of any dungeons for rent?"

The lich rose from the recliner and walked to a door. At his hand, the door opened, leading down into a black well of darkness.

"Sorry, I value my soul." Grimm's contract didn't cover the basement.

"Very funny," said the lich on my phone. "I swear I will not harm you."

"Look, you aren't the first thing to try to trap me today. I already made one contract mistake. I'm not going to make another." I reached into my jacket and pulled out the copy of the contract Malodin had left behind.

The lich drifted over and swiped the contract from me, then spent a minute studying it. The phone beeped again. "You are a damned idiot."

"I know."

"You signed a contract with a demon."

"I know."

The phone beeped once more, and I was afraid to look. "First, we take care of Ari. Follow me."

I stood at the edge of the stairway. "I'm not sure this is a good idea."

"If I kill you, the demons would take it out on me," read my phone. So I put one hand on the stairway and followed an undead sorcerer down into the seat of his power.

I walked down into blackness like the depth of night. When my feet stumbled at the end of the stairway, I looked back at the distant patch of light. Then the door swung closed, burying me in darkness.

"Hello? Can't see."

A pull chain clinked, and a lamp blazed to life in the corner. Then another, and a click as the overhead lights came on. I stood in a basement bedroom. Green shag carpet from the sixties, with dark walnut paneling on the walls. In one corner sat a television the size of a cereal box, and in the other, a recliner.

"I thought this place would be . . . more impressive. Goth-y. Ritualistic."

"Mama did not approve of me painting the walls black," said the lich, speaking through the phone.

"You lived in your mother's basement?" I tried to figure out if he was telling a lie. For regular people, I did pretty well.

The lack of skin made it hard to read the lich. "Not that I have a problem with that. Plenty of men live under their mothers. That way, Mommy can take good care of them."

"Very funny."

"So why didn't you remake it into a den of ritual magic when she passed on?" I sat on the edge of the recliner while the lich looked at a shelf of books.

"Mama didn't die until six years after I did."

I stood up and looked around. "So where's the entrance to the dungeon?"

The lich looked at me and waited in silence.

"This?"

It nodded. "This is where I became undead. It's where I bound my power. Without a contract, I can exercise the full limits of my power here. And I will, if anyone tries to harm Ari."

At least we agreed on that. A pair of chest freezers lined one wall, with more than enough room for a coffin on top. "I tried to get a crystal case for Ari, but Celestial Crystal is expensive. I was thinking of going with something more basic. I have a life-support module from the dwarves that should turn anything from a cardboard box to a bulldozer into a safe place."

The lich drifted over and with a wave of his hand threw a cloud of papers off the chest freezers.

"Yup, I was thinking about putting the coffin on those."

He shook his skull. Then with a wave, one of the freezers opened. I came over and looked inside. It hadn't run in ages. Wasn't cold, and smelled like tuna and dirty laundry.

"No one will think to look in here," said the lich. I took the life-support cube from my jacket pocket and looked at it. "This side toward casket," read the writing on one side. I held it up to the side of the chest freezer, and it leaped from my hand, locking onto the outside. Then metal tentacles grew like vines from it into the chest freezer, and the freezer began to hum. The inside glowed with white light, and a faint scent of roses wafted out.

"Perfect." I borrowed my phone to call the Agency, then Shigeru, and then Mikey. Once I'd given everyone orders, I went back upstairs to wait.

While I paced the floor, the lich continued to watch me.

Everywhere I went, he watched. Finally, I couldn't take it anymore. "Can I help you?"

"You stink. Like brimstone."

"Can I help you with anything else?"

"Why did you sign a contract to end the world?" The lich floated a little closer.

With a sigh of exasperation, I flopped on the disgusting couch and began to explain. By the time I reached the contract, I swear the lich had a knowing grin. Technically, since he was a skeleton, all he ever did was grin, but I felt a smug grin from him.

"Seriously, you fell for that old trick?"

"You aren't helping."

"I'm not the one that agreed to unleash the demon apocalypse. You're going to make Earth into the equivalent of New Jersey. Completely unlivable." The lich brought out a few volumes of celestial law and flipped through the pages while he studied my contract.

"I didn't agree, and I don't want to do it. The way I understand it, so long as I fulfill the bare minimum in the contract, Malodin will wait. Every second I buy gives me time to find a way out." I checked my phone, wondering how long it could take to cart a sleeping princess home from the hospital.

"Here's the simple version. First, you have to unleash the harbingers of the apocalypse."

"I must have missed that class in college. How do I do that?"

The lich handed me back my contract. "You'll figure it out. And you can't do it here. I'm not on good terms with one of them. Calling down three plagues, starting the apocalypse; it's simple enough that even you should be capable of doing it."

The doorbell rang, cutting off any hope I had of a retort, and I rushed to open it. Outside, Mikey stood, with Ari slung over his shoulder like a sack of flour.

"I said to bring her by aid car."

"We had some trouble at the hospital. Got attacked while we were waiting to be discharged." Mikey shouldered past me into the living room.

"Is she hurt?" I rushed over to examine Ari, who hung limp, wrapped in a sheet. The only thing I could tell would be injured was her pride—hospital gowns don't really get the job done when it comes to covering one's rear.

"Best I can tell, she's fine. Then again, I was kinda occupied."

I looked out at the street, where a two-door lowrider sat at an angle to the curb. "That's not an Agency car."

"Nah, some gangbangers dropping off a shooting victim volunteered to let me use it."

I looked at the claw marks, noted the shattered glass, and decided that whatever else Mikey might be, he was a pretty good employee. "You did good. Help me get her downstairs. Got to grab some stuff first." I ran up to Ari's bedroom to get a pillow and a comforter, and then to ransack her kitchen cabinet.

Mikey followed me downstairs without a question, and it was about the time I got down there that I began to wonder where, exactly, our lich landlord was. I opened the chest freezer, arranged the comforter, and helped ease Ari down into it.

The gray life-support block continued to keep the temperature perfect, and as I arranged Ari's hands, it began to spew a white mist that covered her. Then I took two boxes of baking soda and put them in the freezer with her. That way, she wouldn't wake up smelling like roses or tuna. Assuming I could wake her at all.

Mikey, on the other hand, couldn't take his eyes off the freezer. "Are you sure about this?"

"I'm sure. You did good. Go home, get some rest. Tomorrow we're going to figure out how to deal with the woman responsible." I gave Mikey a pat on the back, and he nearly wagged the tail he didn't have in response. He bounded out of the basement, and the front door slammed moments later.

"Exactly why were you hiding?" I said to the empty air.

My phone beeped, and I pulled it out. "I am shy." I looked around the room and found the lich, hovering over his books, carefully reading.

"You're an undead sorcerer."

He did his best to shrug, causing his collarbones to creak as they bent. "With very poor social skills. The ritual requirements don't leave much time for attending parties."

"Thank you. I know how to wake up Ari. The only good thing to come out of that deal is that I know I need to find her boyfriend and get him to kiss her."

The lich's skull whipped 180 degrees, staring at me backwards. Then the lich rushed toward me like a cloud of bitterness. "Did the demon tell you that?"

I nodded.

"Demons never help. If he told you something, it's because he either already made sure you can't get it or—"

"He plans to," I said, staring into the empty bone sockets.

"Anything you receive from one is cursed. Any information you get is wrong, or will lead to worse problems. Demons never help."

I glanced at my watch. Night classes started twenty minutes ago. "Take care of Ari. They tried to get her at the hospital. Odds are they'll try to get her here."

A ripple of power crossed the room, sending the carpet rolling in waves. The lich glowed in a purple-and-green light. "I look forward to it."

I sprinted up the stairs, out the door, and decided that I was temporarily color-blind in regard to lights. I made a single stop at the toy store and a dash into Mary's Cathedral to commit yet another sin in a long list. Then I didn't stop for lights or pedestrians until I squealed to a halt in the loading zone outside the college. I listened for a moment, hoping that what I heard was the sound of a power saw. I knew, however, it was screaming.

Eighteen

～

IF YOU WANT to find a demon, it's simple enough. Find the people running away and swim upstream through the crowd, using fists and feet where necessary. In all my years of community college, the only time anything like this happened was when my lit class threw a surprise retirement party for our professor. He opened his presents to find a nest of live wasps, two angry skunks, and a pistol that was later tied to a double homicide. I learned never to pitch in for gifts.

The people gushing down the stairs quite clearly wanted to get away from something worse than a pop quiz, which meant I most likely wanted to be there. I charged through the crowd at full speed and into a lecture room.

In one corner, a cluster of students huddled, trying to work out what it was their brains were seeing, coming up with anything but a demon. Maybe a rock star or an NBA point guard with wings.

At the front of the pack, a lone priest stood in his black robe. Poor guy probably planned on getting his associate's degree in business, or maybe his mechanic's certification. Instead, he wound up working off the clock.

He held up a crucifix and a rosary, and chanted in Latin.

Really poorly pronounced Latin, on account of his chattering teeth. In fact, I'm fairly sure what he said was "Our Father in Accident." The demon seemed more amused than repelled. I understood. The phrase he wanted was *deliver us from evil*. What came out sounded like "deliver us from postmen." Not that the Postal Service couldn't be evil.

The demon lumbered forward and reached for the priest. That was my cue. I'd bought a high-power water gun and filled it with holy water on the way over. The holy water worked less like acid and more like a laser, slicing into the demon's skin, tearing a hole straight through it so that its intestines spilled out, teeming with maggots. I gave it a few more squirts for good measure, then walked down to the front of the classroom.

"Wyatt? Is there a Wyatt here?"

From behind the podium, a timid voice came. "I'm not interested."

I walked around it and grabbed the cowering young man by the nape of the neck, pulling him to his feet, and then dropped him like a hot coal. It wasn't the waxy, almost white blond hair I was staring at, or the pale blue, almost gray eyes he kept tightly shut, peeking at me every now and then to see if I'd gone away. Why hadn't Ari told me? Of all the things she should have brought up, you'd think it would be that one.

Magic ran from him like a river, the "shine" as it was called, and while Ari had a pretty good snowstorm of magic about her most days, he could certainly keep up. If it weren't for the fact that most royalty were completely blind to the shine, I would have been ticked at Ari for leaving out that detail.

Wyatt did his best to cram himself back into the podium, all of his six feet, bean-pole-thin frame almost fitting.

"You're not safe here." I reached for him again, and he unfolded his legs in a halfhearted kick. "One way or another, you're coming with me."

"I'm not going anywhere until I pick up this week's assignments. My study partner will need them." He slunk to the teacher's desk, which had a nasty spray of demon entrails across one corner, and took a copy of the course work.

"Ari isn't coming back to class anytime soon." When I said it, his eyes locked onto me, and his mouth turned down sharply.

"If you've done something to Arianna, you'll regret it. I'll write a letter to your employer."

I couldn't say if it was "Arianna" or the threat of a strongly worded letter that made me laugh harder. "Come on, prince-boy. Got to get you someplace safe."

He looked at me like I'd called him dead-fish boy. "What did you call me? My name is Wyatt, not Prince, and Mum has given me quite clear instructions. In the event of any sort of danger, I am always to return home immediately."

"Fine. Come on back to my car, and we'll take you home." I looked at the remains of the demon, which still sizzled and twisted.

Wyatt drew himself to his full height, which was only a few inches taller than me. "I take the bus. In order for a city with so many people to work, we need to cooperate, and shared transportation resources are a key element of city life. Come, I'll introduce you to the transit system."

"I know about the buses." I fumed at him, wondering if I could drag him to the car and use a stun gun on him there.

The remains of the demon began to smoke, and the pile of entrails moved, worming its way back into the sliced-open stomach cavity.

"You do not want to be here when that thing gets up and starts walking around."

Wyatt looked at me and swallowed. "Could we call a cab?"

"If it will get you out of here." I headed toward the door, keeping an eye on the corpse. The edges of the wounds flickered with flame, but instead of burning away the flesh, it seemed to heal it. "Come on." I gave the demon a few more squirts, then looked back. "Any day this century would be good."

Wyatt continued to pack his backpack. Then he pulled it on, adjusted his Windbreaker.

We met a second demon in the stairway. The thing looked like a Great Dane mixed with a parrot. Long, lithe dog legs and a beak covered in black blood. Like the first, a few squirts of my ill-gotten holy water left it in a smoldering heap, letting us leave the building.

"This happen to you often?" I kept an eye on Wyatt as he

stepped around the demon remains and then continued to follow me toward the curb.

For most folks, meeting a demon would rank high on their "reasons I'll spend the rest of my life in therapy" list. Wyatt calmly stepped to the curb and whistled for a cab. "No, but Mum has been quite clear that the world at large can be dangerous."

A cab pulled up, and as Wyatt reached for the door, glass shattered above me. I yanked him by the collar, pulling him away as the demon from the classroom smashed onto the roof of the cab. The number of people struggling to find some rational explanation for this went up by about two hundred in the space of a few seconds.

The last of my holy water reduced it again to a pile of gore, and this time I wasn't taking no for an answer. I grabbed Wyatt by the wrist and dragged him after me to my car. "We can make a donation to a home for puppies or something later," I said as I shoved him into the front seat.

I tore two parking tickets from the windshield and peeled out, leaving the area as the first set of police responded. That was the primary reason Grimm let agents carry guns—when seconds mattered, police were minutes away.

"Reach in the back and get one of those water guns," I said, as I ran traffic light after light.

Wyatt fumbled around in the backseat and came up with one. "What am I supposed to do with this?"

"Anything scaly shows up, you shoot it." I swung around a corner, narrowly missing a clot of pedestrians.

"And how would I do that?"

If I could have taken a moment to look at him, I would have. I needed every bit of my attention on the road. "Point and click. Pull the trigger. Like Cowboys and Indians."

"Native American history is not a game."

I finally hit the last corner, and slammed to a halt, blocked by a horde of people making their way up from the waterfront. "Once we're past the gates, we'll be in Kingdom. The police there will be prepared for this sort of problem."

"Where?"

I glanced over to Wyatt, and he looked at me with those pale blue eyes, his eyebrows arched.

"Kingdom?" Nothing. The word meant nothing to him. "Your 'Mum' doesn't live this way, does she?"

He shook his head. "She lives close to the college. You went the wrong direction, but I was worried that if I complained, you might commit a violence against me."

"Violence. Not 'a violence.' "

About then the windshield shattered as another Great-Dane-demon smashed into it. I flicked on the washers and hit the accelerator, leaving a heap of demon meat in the street. Wyatt screamed in pain, flopping back and forth in the seat.

"Did it cut you?"

"My eyes. I can't see." I glanced over; yellow liquid covered him.

"Don't worry. It's mustard, and a little vinegar. Left nozzle is holy water, right one is mustard. Takes care of most of the things that attack me." I handed him a cup from the console. "Rinse your eyes with this."

A moment later I looked over, and despite being stained with stale coffee and doused in mustard, he didn't look wounded. "This way?"

"Right in six blocks, number 113. This is never going to come out of my shirt."

I continued to speed, continued to use the curb as a lane, knowing that at any moment, we could find ourselves faced with more demons. Most of the time, they wouldn't dare attack outside of Kingdom. Inside of Kingdom, the cops carried bullets blessed by almost every religion on earth, up to and including jazz band conductors.

One block from the house, the trunk of my car exploded in a shower of metal. In my rearview mirror, a pair of yellow eyes glowed. I slammed on the brakes, throwing the demon over the car, then hit the accelerator, running it over. Steam shot from my radiator, and the engine sputtered. "We're running from here," I said, and threw open the door.

Wyatt followed my lead, and we took off at a sprint for number 113, a narrow town house tucked into a wall of taller buildings. From the sky above, the swoop of wings gave me a second's warning. I tackled Wyatt just in time to keep a demon-Dane from soaring off with his head.

Behind us, my car flipped over as our assailant from the

college threw it off him like a bag of laundry and began to run, impossibly fast for something that large. I made sure Wyatt got to the gate first, and followed inside, straight to the porch, where I slid to a halt.

Wyatt fumbled with keys, while I looked at the floor of the porch, cloudy-white stone that looked surprisingly familiar. In the yard, the demon crushed the gate and lumbered ever closer, walking with cloven hoofs up the stairs to stand inches from me.

"No soliciting." I tapped my foot.

It thrust a claw up to reach past me, and an orange light like a camera flash exploded in the air. When my eyes cleared, the demon's claw ended in a bloody stump.

Behind me, the door unlocked, and by the time I looked back, Wyatt had disappeared into the house. With a snort, the demon lumbered away into the darkness.

From the doorway, a woman's voice spoke, older, softer. "I always knew one day I'd get a visit from you. Demons or dragons or something. It had to be something."

I got to my feet and looked back to find the speaker, a woman with hair of gray and black. Wrinkles ringed her eyes, her face was thin, and her skin's tone looked pale, but I couldn't mistake the shine of magic that came from her.

When I first came to work for Grimm, I spent months memorizing the government and who's who of Kingdom. Though the woman before me had at least twenty years on the last picture I'd seen of her, I had no doubt. "Yes, Your Majesty."

She looked down at the ground. "I am not High Queen anymore. I am not queen of anything anymore, young lady. Would you like to come inside?"

I dusted myself off and followed her through the door, wondering how on earth the Queen of the First Royal Family had come to live here.

IF SHE'D LEFT an inch of wall without pictures, I couldn't find it. Not that I knew any of the people. Once inside, she waved toward a green-and-orange couch. "Sit. I'll make us tea."

"Wyatt—"

"He's upstairs, bathing. Mustard may be poisonous only to

brownies, but it is harsh on the skin." She disappeared into the kitchen, leaving me to stare at the decorating. In one corner, an ancient upright piano sat, covered in pictures of Wyatt as a young boy.

The windows drew my attention the most. Not glass, but fine lead crystal, engraved in runes that I recognized as protection sigils, despite the fact I couldn't empower one at all. The window frames too held dozens of trinkets, bottles of brick dust and other items. In essence, the house was a fortress of wards.

"Forgive my decoration. I've worked quite hard to keep my son safe," said the queen.

"I'm sorry, Your Majesty. I was trying to keep him safe as well." I bowed, remembering my formal manners.

She frowned and looked at me over her bifocals. "Girl, I'm no longer High Queen. Indeed, I've renounced my throne and Kingdom. You may call me Mrs. Pendlebrook." She brought over a tray with tea and sat across from me. "Now, you have my thanks for protecting my son, but once you've rested a bit, it will be time for you to leave."

"Wyatt is the reason I'm here. I got a tip that demons might be coming after him, and I barely got him out of the college. I need to talk with him." I sat up and sipped the tea, savoring the taste of lavender.

"Out of the question. I know what you are, if not who. The gold bracelet. The holy water and mustard. You work for the Fairy Godfather." She set down her teacup.

"No. I'm his partner. Marissa Locks." The look of surprise on her face brought warmth to my heart. If she had read a copy of the *Kingdom Enquirer* from the last year, she'd know I was his partner. She'd also know that I negotiated with Aliens at Area 51 (true), met Elvis in the sewers (also true), and was personally responsible for burning down a bingo hall (no comment). "I need to speak to Wyatt. My best friend got attacked by a queen, and I think he might be able to wake her."

"I've worked long and hard to shield my son from the realities of Kingdom. The politics, power, and backstabbing. Ms. Locks, I appreciate what you did for him, but I don't want him dragged into a conflict with another queen."

I slammed down the teacup, rattling the table. "I didn't ask your permission. I'm here for your son. He's the only one who can help Ari."

We glowered at each other.

"Something's happened to Arianna?" Wyatt stood at the top of the stairs, dressed in a fuzzy green bathrobe. He walked down the stairs and over to me. "Tell me, is Arianna all right?"

I shot a triumphant glance to his mother, then fixed my eyes on him. "That depends a lot on you."

Nineteen

◊

MRS. PENDLEBROOK GAVE me a look of death, then turned to her son. "Now, Wyatt—"

"Mum, I want to hear what she has to say. Ms. Locks, is it? I believe Arianna mentioned you. The accountant who owns a bookstore, right?" Wyatt sat beside his mother and poured himself a cup of tea. The two of them together made it hard to look that way, with the sheer amount of magic pouring from them.

"Bookstore. Right." I made a mental note to remind Ari to leave me out of her lies, assuming I could convince Prince Charming here to wake her up. "Ari got"—I glanced at Mrs. Pendlebrook—"hurt. She's in a coma, and the doctors think that hearing the voices of people she's in a 'special relationship' with might help."

Mrs. Pendlebrook practically spat on me. "She means she wants you to kiss the girl, son."

Wyatt's face drained of color, a look of sheer terror on it. "Never without Arianna's permission."

"She isn't going to wake up to give you permission if you don't."

He sat back on the couch, then looked over to his mother. "Mum, can you tell me what those things were?"

"Demons."

He nodded, not the least bit shocked or surprised.

"And why exactly would a metaphysical creature have any argument with me, let alone desire to harm me?"

His mother looked at me for a moment, the pain in her eyes unmistakable.

I cut in before she could answer. "Ari. They know you could help Ari, and that's why they were after you. To prevent you from helping her."

He nodded. "So a kiss would possibly help her?"

"It's as good a theory as anything else I've got." I waited in the silence, trying to figure out what his answer would be.

"Son, it's not just a kiss. Generally speaking, the prince— the person who wakes the young lady is committing to a long-term relationship with her." Mrs. Pendlebrook put her hand on Wyatt's, drawing his eyes to her.

He shook his head. "Kissing is a simple courtship or attraction ritual, not related to relationship bonds, legal, or otherwise."

His mother took his other hand, and squeezed them until her knuckles turned white. "Not for princes."

In the moments that passed, I counted the ticks from the grandfather clock in the hallway. When he spoke, I nearly jumped.

"I don't make any decisions in haste, Ms. Locks. I prefer to meditate on matters and consider the long-term consequences of major decisions. Anything beyond breakfast is worthy of contemplation." Wyatt stood, brushing the wrinkles from his robe.

I took a business card from my purse and placed it on the coffee table. "Please. I'll do anything for Ari."

Wyatt nodded. "I believe three days is an appropriate time to consider this. Now, if you'll excuse me, I need to apply my nightly skin mask and record the day in my journal. It was a pleasure being saved from demons by you, Ms. Locks." With that, he kissed his mother good night and climbed the stairs out of view.

The room grew colder in his absence, to the point where I could've stored meat on the tabletop. I rose and brushed myself off, but before I could speak, she interrupted me.

"Tell me about the girl."

"Ari. Five foot three, weighs less than a bag of coffee, red hair. She's one hell of a partner. My best friend. She was doing pretty well in college until she met your son." I stuck with the good bits first.

Mrs. Pendlebrook nodded. "I assume his Friday-night volunteer efforts at the animal shelter were, in fact, dates?"

"Maybe. Ari doesn't exactly tell me where she goes. She's too coy about the whole thing. You know I'm not an accountant, right?"

She rose, walked over, and gave me a hug. "Of course not. I'm going to have to explain everything to my son now. Tell him the truth about myself. About everything."

"Thank Kingdom. That'll make it easier for Ari. She's so afraid of people knowing what she is, she'd rather lie. You know he bought this line about her hellhound having mange?"

She stiffened at my words, stared into my eyes as if I were a crystal ball, then hissed. "She's a *princess*."

Right there, the tension crept back into my shoulders. I looked around, noting where we were. What I could hit her with if she attacked me. "Yes, through no fault of her own. And a seal bearer."

If I'd told her Ari was a stripper with piercings and tattoos, she'd have reacted better. Her eyes narrowed, her fists clenched. "Of what family?"

"Arianna Thromson, of the Third Royal Family."

She let out a breath of air in a long sigh. "It could be worse. Her mother was one of my chief supporters for High Queen, and one of my better friends. How is Janeal?"

"Dead. Cancer. Dad's dead too. Died two years ago. So I suggest you be polite to Ari. And I suggest you consider what you say to your son very carefully. Because if he hurts her, I'll make him wish the demons had caught him."

Mrs. Pendlebrook nodded at me, her face set like steel. "My son owes you his life. Whether or not he owes your friend his love is another question entirely. Now, if you don't mind, it's going to be a long night and day for me."

I walked to the door, then looked back. "If you really want to pay me back, there's something you could do."

"Yes, young lady?"

"Queen Mihail is the one who did this to Ari. She was angry about something that happened to her son. I need to charge her. I need to do it in the Court of Queens." When I spoke, she shuddered.

She walked over and put one hand on the door. "Wyatt is old enough to decide if that world is one he wants to tolerate. I've made my decision. I won't be going back there, for any reason. I'll contact you when Wyatt's made his decision. A decision I hope you'll respect." With that, she opened the door.

I stepped out into the darkness, but before she could close it, a thought occurred to me. "Did you know Fairy Godfather?"

She nodded, and stepped out onto the porch. "He helped me start my new life here. Imported the crystal for my barriers, arranged my wards."

"Queen Mihail did something to him. I have a source who tells me he's *constrained*. Does that mean anything to you?"

She frowned, and closed her eyes. "How much do you actually know about your Fairy Godfather?"

I knew a lot, actually. A lot about the last eight years. Some about the previous ten, and, well, almost nothing about the time before that. I had the contact number for one of Grimm's old agents, but the hospital only allowed calls on Tuesdays.

"Some problems aren't spoken of in polite company, but as High Queen, I had access to secrets long buried. A constraint is a limit on power. Ask yourself a simple question, Ms. Locks: What sin would a fairy commit that the others would agree to place limits on his powers? To be bound?"

I refused to allow the shock inside to show. There'd be hours in the night to pace my kitchen and think about it.

Before Mrs. Pendlebrook shut the door, she looked up at me once more. "And before you think about meddling, answer this: What sin would a fairy commit that he would *agree* to be bound?"

I TRIED TO make my way home. Walking six blocks, not a big deal. Getting a cab to my apartment, not a big deal. Calling the elevator, not a big deal. When the doors closed, and the elevator began to sink, my anxiety shot upward as fast as the elevator went downward.

Then it began to pick up steam, falling faster and faster. Our building had only two basements, so either the building architects had made a serious mistake or things weren't going quite as planned. That and the elevator buttons all glowed bright red. Now the elevator flew so fast I floated, suspended for a moment, then pinned to the ceiling, and still it picked up speed.

I clenched my jaw and tightened my gut, forcing blood up into my head. The elevator began to rattle and shake from side to side, then with a deafening roar, brilliant red light burst from every crevice. A moment later, the elevator slowed, allowing me to stand on the ceiling and grab the handrail. A good thing too, since a moment later it lost enough speed to drop me to the ground. Then it ground to a halt, and the doors opened.

I expected flames. Instead, I got the dim orange lights of the dealing room. In the center, Malodin waited, his hands behind his back.

"Handmaiden, what have you been up to?" His voice made the floor vibrate.

I stepped out of the elevator, wishing I had a squirt gun with some holy water. "Just following up on the information you gave me. Turns out, there were a few demons interested in killing a prince. A prince I need intact to help my friend. You wouldn't have anything to do with that, would you?"

He parted his lips, showing the rows of shark teeth. "Now, that would be downright evil. We have an agreement. Speaking of which, where are my harbingers? Why haven't you unleashed them to wreak havoc on the city, and then the world?" His tongue slithered across his lips, then flicked out to brush the end of his nose.

"Harbingers. Yeah. You know, the apocalypse didn't exactly come with a user manual. How am I supposed to unleash them?" Malodin could've made things a lot easier on himself with good directions.

He held out his hand. "You call to them. They'll present themselves to you. Then you provide their steeds, and they get to work preparing the end." A puddle of hellfire blazed into existence on his palm. "Like that. I called, it came." He flicked his wrist, and I rolled to the side as an arc of fire passed over me.

"What's the matter, Marissa? Afraid of a few little burns?

You know, in case you haven't had time to read your contract, you'll be spared. You'll live out the rest of your life in what we leave." He summoned another puddle of fire and lobbed it at me underhand.

"I'm not going to bring about the apocalypse." I stood my ground as he approached, bringing another palm of fire up in front of me.

"You *will*, or I'll unleash my armies now. You know, for a few eternities, everyone thought that a proper end of the world simply couldn't be done. I knew better. I just needed the right person. Unleash the harbingers. Call down your plagues and finish our deal." He held his hand up under my chin, where the fire leaped and sizzled.

I took a deep breath, running my thumb over Liam's ring, then reached out and scooped the fire out of his hand.

His eyes widened, their vertical, snakelike slits becoming twice their normal size.

It felt like holding a warm sponge, not a primal force of destruction. Then I put my hands together and wrung it out, like I'd watched Liam do so many nights at his forge. "Keep your demons where they are." I turned and walked back to the open elevator.

"If you need any assistance, take an elevator. I've made a few adjustments for you. They all lead to Inferno now, for you."

I punched the floor for my apartment and grabbed onto the handrail. The ride back was worse than the ride down, since I knew what was coming. When the doors finally opened, allowing me to stumble down my hallway, and into my apartment, my stomach continued to do flips.

In the end, I forced myself to go to bed, and spent the night thrashing, entangled in nightmares of demons and destruction.

Twenty

~⌒~

THE NEXT DAY, I went into work. Now, you might be wondering, "Why go to work if the world is ending?" Truth was, I figured the world was always ending. Malodin accidentally gave me hope by admitting that so many attempts at an apocalypse failed before, even demons didn't think it was possible to pull off. So I'd try to avoid triggering his instant apocalypse, and try to figure a way out of the coming one. In the meantime, there was work to be done.

I met Rosa at the front door, proof that she didn't sleep in the Agency at night. "Morning, Rosa."

She gave me the same glare she always did, then made the sign of the cross with her middle finger. I think it was meant to protect her and flip me off at the same time.

"Good seeing you too." By the time we opened for business, I had all the previous day's paperwork organized, reloaded three magazines for my gun, made a fresh pot of coffee, and generally speaking, felt pretty good about the state of my business. I'd at least keep doing what Grimm wanted. Helping people solve their problems, so long as their problem wasn't that the world was ending.

In fact, I was in such a good mood that when Rosa buzzed

me to come to the lobby, I hummed the entire way there. In the lobby, my enchanters wrestled, biting and scratching. I've got to say that whatever was under those fingernails, it would probably leave them both with skin infections.

I looked at Rosa. "Why can't you handle this?"

"Not my problem." She went back to playing solitaire on her computer.

I picked up the nearest fire extinguisher and sprayed them both until they were about ready to pass out from carbon dioxide poisoning. "Step away from each other. You, tell me what started this." I pointed to one of them, I think the woman.

"She called me smelly," he said. Oops.

"You both smell like the ass end of an ogre. If I buy you new bathrobes, will you shower?"

They gave up glaring at each other and glared at me instead.

"We could curse you," said the enchantress.

"Already done."

"Be nice, and we'll grant you a blessing."

"All stocked up. I want you two showered and changed. You can conjure in Agency robes today." I pointed to the staff door, and they shuffled away.

The entrance bell rang, and Beth practically bounced into the lobby.

"Ms. Locks! You won't believe what I can do!" She twirled, and took out her kazoo. Then she began to hum. Behind her, a ball of furry white evil pranced into the room. I took a closer look.

"That's not the test one."

Beth held up her palms. "I found him in an alley, eating the face off a cab driver. I've been practicing all night. Roll over." She hummed, a note that shimmered with power.

The poodle's eyes glowed red as it rolled over. Its jaws quivered, and it drooled and shook with rage as it rose and bared its teeth.

"Sit." She hummed again.

It dropped to its front legs and gnashed its bloody muzzle.

Beth leaned down to the poodle, so close that flecks of blood from its muzzle flew onto her cheeks. "Play dead."

It leaped for her, grabbing her by the hair, clawing at her with its nails as it tried to find a way to tear her throat out.

Beth threw it to one side, and then followed up with a hum that split the glass in the front door. "Down!" The poodle collapsed in a heap.

I walked over and stood Beth up, checking her head. Blood trickled from one ear where the poodle ripped a piercing loose. "You need to be more careful. Those aren't toys. They're terrors, and I'd rather you didn't wind up as a pile of meat."

Beth shook as she rocked back and forth, holding her arms across her chest. "Stop staring at me."

"Sorry. Anytime I see that many hooks, I want to hang a shower curtain from them." I waved her on back to a practice room, where animal control had left four more poodles caged. All of them collected from the scenes of grisly murders.

"I was able to control them, I swear." Beth pulled at her ear where the poodle had nipped her.

"I'm sure you were. It's going to take time and practice. Remember—you let your guard down around these, and they might gnaw your intestines out through your nose." I sat down in a chair and watched her go through the first few notes.

Beth hummed, and they sat. Hummed, and they rolled over. One particularly sharp note kept them from devouring a sausage stuck in through the cage.

Rosa slammed her fist on the practice room door, the closest she ever came to a polite knock, and marched in with a stack of papers. "It can't wait." She smacked them down in front of me, then skittered out like a cockroach under a kitchen light.

I glanced at the top of the pile and resigned myself to necessity.

"She really can't stand you." Beth held her kazoo while she shut the door.

"She really can't stand anyone. You know, as surly as Rosa is, Fairy Godfather told me once she's married and has six kids. She's right, this can't wait." I pulled the top sheet and read it over. "Inspection Report," it read. When I finished it, I clicked my pen and signed my name, authorizing payment.

Then I went on to the next one, and the next. After a few minutes, I realized Beth hadn't played a note in quite a while. She watched me take another form, so I passed one in her direction.

"These are reports. Fairy Godfather funds a chain of drug-recovery houses for women, and orphanage/foster homes. Fail to meet code, or his requirements, and the operators probably don't get a paycheck."

Beth sat down in the chair beside me. "I was in foster care. Bounced from home to home, because of the rats. I wonder if it was one of yours."

"I can find out. Don't recall ever having a rodent-related inspection failure, and I've reviewed these for the last five years. Didn't you say you had a mom and dad?"

Beth looked down at the table. "They adopted me when I was fourteen. Dad never said anything about the rats, and Mom just set traps everywhere. I ran away when they started getting sick from the rats." She frowned as a thought fought off silver poisoning to make it through her brain. "Why do you need orphanages?"

We got that kind of question a lot. "Fairy Godfather is powerful, but one of the most common wishes is one that can't be granted by magic. People want kids. They want a baby and think you can wish one into existence."

"You can't?"

"It takes nine months of hard work, or so I've heard. And you don't need magic. There are plenty of people who don't want their children, and plenty of people who do. We try to hook the two up." A lump formed in my throat as I spoke. I wanted a child to love. One to cherish, more than anything I'd wanted in years. I would be the family I wished I had, and love my son or daughter the way my parents should have loved me.

Beth's voice came out hollow when she spoke. "You don't know what it's like, not knowing where you come from."

"I do." I wasn't much of one for self-pity, or pity of any type. Compassion, I could do, because it came with action. "My first mom and my dad came to Fairy Godfather for a child. Odds are, I was born in one of these, probably this one, based on what I've found." I held up a report paper.

"You ever wonder about who your real mother was?"

"I know who my real mother was. She was the woman who was there when I was sick. When I had six hours of homework. When I got my first period. I never knew my dad's first wife, but his second one raised me." I didn't mention that Mom had traded me for a miracle to Fairy Godfather. Or that we still weren't on speaking terms.

"Do you think I might turn out to be a long-lost princess?"

I spat coffee out in a spray, burning my nose as I laughed. "Listen. Did you ever think that maybe there's a reason the lost princess stays lost? It's because people don't really want to find them. If I lose my car keys, you can bet I'll figure out where they are. Then again, I like my car keys and would feel bad if someone took them."

"What is your problem with princesses? Jealous?" Beth tried giving me a sassy, taunting look. She really needed to work on it because her "sassy" looked a lot like my "ate too much curry" look.

"I'm not jealous. It's just frustrating. Princesses get everything easy. Luck goes their way. Men swoon over them. Cops let them off with a warning, and robbers say please and thank you when they take their wallet. Princes don't work for anything, and they expect you to fall into their arms and onto their bed at the blink of an eye."

"I think it might be fun."

I assembled my papers and rose. "I think I'll get more done in my office. If you get to the point where you can put your hand in the cage without needing stitches, call me."

BY LUNCHTIME, I'D signed every single report, issued only six warnings, and been called out to the lobby to personally deal with a man who insisted he had seven dwarves living in his house. Turns out, he had seven cats, and what he needed wasn't a princess (I was fresh out of those) but animal control. Animal control was an acceptable solution in my mind if it turned out to actually be dwarves as well.

While I ate tuna salad, I wished more than anything that I could talk to Liam. Even after he'd been cursed, his calm and patient nature continued to act as a balance for me. I knew what he'd say. That I'd find a way. That I could buy, borrow, or steal something to put an end to this mess.

He'd say he loved me, and I wanted to hear that more than anything.

The last thing I wanted was for Liam to come home and find out I'd destroyed the world. So it was time to hire some new legal counsel. I checked on my enchanters, found them painting their toenails instead of cursing parking violators, then checked on Beth. She sported several new bite marks to her face and had a look that said if I brought it up, she'd offer me some unconventional piercings on the spot. So I left the Agency and headed out to meet my new lawyer.

When I walked through the door of Ari's apartment, he slithered out, his skeletal form materializing from the black vapor. I opened my purse and took out a present I'd picked up on the way over. A phone with text-to-speech capabilities, which meant I wouldn't have to read his responses. "Larry, I'd like to make a business proposition."

He picked up the phone with one skeletal claw and clipped it to his sternum. "It's a bit late for that. If you asked before you signed the contract, I could have helped."

The only good thing about making a deal with demons was that I had learned to ask about conditions first. "How do I pay you? Check? Card?"

His jaw creaked open in what I hoped was a smile. "Souls. I haven't eaten since Ari moved in."

He wasn't supposed to be eating the garbage or postmen before that, but I didn't feel like arguing the point. "I'll find you someone. Last night I took the express elevator down, and I'm in danger of defaulting on the contract if I don't get started. I'm supposed to be unleashing some harbingers to start. Any idea how?"

The look of contempt he summoned from an empty skull left me envious. "What do they teach in public schools these days?" He drifted over to the coffee table, where my contract sat. "You have to summon the harbingers, provide them with their mounts, and let them go to town on the city. They set the stage for the demons. Think of it like a housewarming, where you set the house on fire."

"These harbingers; Malodin said they'd come when I called."

He spun so quickly the rags on his skeleton flew outward. "Don't do it here."

"I'll wait until I'm back at the office. What exactly are they going to do?"

Larry drifted to a bookcase and levitated out a tome. "I slept through a lot of my History of Fallen Civilizations class, but basically they'll ride around the city twice, then begin the carnage."

"So how do I get out of this?"

Larry moved his hand, and the contract swelled to its full size, becoming several feet across. "If there were an escape clause, I'd have found it by now. They get revised every time someone finds a way to avert the apocalypse. This one looks pretty good."

"There's no way out?" I sat on Ari's couch, sinking into the worn fabric.

"Not if you want to delay the end of the world. You have to do what you are obligated to do. As your counsel, I can't advise you to break the terms of the contract. But don't do anything voluntarily." Dust flew from the corners of the room, and the stench of blood and decay flooded my nose as he began to chant.

A cloud of darkness formed before him, then slowly cleared, leaving a piece of paper. Larry drifted over to me. "Take this." I looked at it. It looked like a normal contract—that is, absolute garbage, but at least it was in English. "Do nothing you don't have to."

"I found Ari's boyfriend."

Larry's eyes lit up with a green glow I hoped meant excitement. "Send him over. I won't eat him until *after* he wakes her."

"He didn't agree to wake her yet. And I think she'd object to you devouring him."

His shoulder blades clattered as he dropped them in disappointment. "What kind of person wouldn't want to help Ari?"

I tucked the contract into my purse and rose. "He's a prince."

"Figures. If he says no, can I still eat him?"

"If he won't help Ari, I'll tie him up and douse him with barbecue sauce, then put him in a chest freezer. Speaking of which, I need to change the baking soda in Ari's, umm, chamber."

Larry waved his hand. "I'll get it later. I've got nothing but time."

So I left Ari in the care of a spirit of evil, and headed back to the office to call down destruction.

Twenty-One

❧

I THINK IF I'd hit one more traffic light on my way back to the Agency, someone would have died. I intended to check on Beth. Instead, I interrupted something that would have constituted a human resources violation even by my limited standards. In the kitchen, Mikey held my enchanter pinned to the wall. The enchanter's feet hung a good six inches off the ground, while Mikey's muscles bulged and the hair on his arms seemed thick and long. He leaned over into the enchanter's face and growled. "Go ahead and say it."

"Not—" the enchanter choked. "Not by the hair on my chinny chin chin."

"Mikey?" I didn't bother going for my gun. If anything, I wanted to make sure I could make an impression on the intern without making a bullet hole.

He looked back like a little boy sent to the principal's office. "He said, I mean, he called me—"

"A big bad wolf?" I kept my tone calm, then motioned to my witless spell slinger. "If you don't mind?"

Mikey dropped him into a heap on the ground and gave a warning growl.

"Come on." Holding open the kitchen door, I waved him

back toward my office. I sat at my desk while Mikey completely dwarfed his chair. "You have to learn to let things go. This is my business. I don't terribly like the Enchanters either; I mean, they're nearly incompetent, they smell—"

"Not as bad as you. You reek of brimstone." Mikey caught himself too late and went back to staring at the floor.

"This isn't about me; it's about you getting along with my other employees. I've said worse than them."

Mikey looked up at me. "Yeah, but Fairy Godfather said not to kill you. It's always the same thing. The big bad wolf. What's wrong with being the big bad wolf? When I was a pup, Dad always said if I ate my meat and got big and strong, I could be like the big bad wolf."

"The big bad wolf got cooked by the pigs. Down a chimney, not Santa, things didn't go well. Though honestly, from what I've seen, if Santa comes down your chimney, you're screwed."

Mikey put his elbows on my desk. His eyes looked off at the ceiling, his mouth turned slightly up. "Maybe in your version. The way I hear it, the pigs never saw him coming. He made bacon for his entire family, two hundred pounds of sausage, six whole hams, and a football for every one of his pups. Then, he rented out the third pig's house and lived off the occasional bad renter." Mikey's eyes gleamed with wild pleasure. "Maybe one day, I can be a landlord too."

I made a mental note to look up my building's ownership and see what exactly my lease allowed them to do. "I need you, Mikey. I'm holding the Agency together until I can find a way to bring back Grimm. I'm sorry that folks don't understand. Wolves aren't exactly popular."

Mikey focused on me for a moment. "How come you smell like demons?"

I sighed. "When I went back to close off a poodle leak, I had a close encounter with one. Now it thinks I've agreed to do something I haven't."

Mikey's eyebrows arched and his eyes widened. "You need anything killed, you come to me first, okay?"

"You got it. If it makes any difference, I'll make our enchanters take sensitivity training. Got any good books on wolf history?"

He practically bounded from the chair. "You bet. Next

time I'm back at the village, I'll bring you something worth reading." Then he loped out of the office, closing my door behind him.

In the empty room, I took out my contract and skimmed it. Harbingers. "The party will summon harbingers and provide them mounts." What had Malodin said? Call, and they would come?

I cleared my throat. "Harbingers of the apocalypse, I call you."

Nothing happened. I slumped back in my chair, wondering what I'd done wrong.

Then the buzzer on my desk went off. I clicked the intercom.

"Visitor," said Rosa.

Before I could get up, my door opened, and in walked a stunning black man. He stood easily six feet, with wide shoulders and long, thin legs. His broad smile showed shining white teeth. "Handmaiden, it's a pleasure to finally meet you. I've been waiting for your call."

I shook his hand, surprised to find a strong, warm grip that matched the smile.

"I'm War, Harbinger of the Apocalypse."

"You're not exactly how I pictured you." In truth, I'd imagined a biker with racist tattoos and a baseball bat.

"Sorry, still wearing my last skin. I was in Nairobi, making sure that people don't forget someone from one side of the river killed someone from the other side of the river two hundred years ago." He sat in my office chair, fitting much better than Mikey had.

"So what now?"

He flashed me those teeth again and laughed, a deep, hearty laugh. "I will wait for the other harbingers to make themselves known. Then, you provide my mount, and I can get to work." His skin began to wrinkle, and turn pale. He shrank, becoming thinner, shorter. His skin became taut, the dark brown of a Latino man. "In the meantime, I'm going to go put on some gang colors and shoot someone. Gang wars are almost as good as tribal feuds." He left my office, whistling a hip-hop tune and adjusting a bandanna.

The buzzer rang again, and I didn't bother getting up. Sure enough, the door opened, and in walked a young man with sandy brown hair and pale skin that his white lab coat made even whiter. He flicked the stethoscope around his neck as he walked.

"Let me guess. Pestilence?"

He nodded and smiled, showing silver caps on each of his teeth. "You're catching on."

I offered my hand, but he kept his folded.

"You have any idea how many germs there are on the average human hand? I'd sooner shake your—"

"I get the point. Seriously though, a doctor? Wouldn't you want to be a biologist, or working on some sort of disease?"

He sprayed down my chair with antibacterial spray and took a seat. "I'm no longer interested in only making people sick. I want to keep them that way. Long-term illness is the new black plague. Though thanks to you, handmaiden, I doubt there'll be a long term for this world."

Some people, you start an apocalypse even once, never let you live it down. "So you shuffle out, someone else shows up, then you go kill people until I get you a horse?" I reached into my drawer and pulled out a surgical mask. Didn't make sense to take risks around him.

"Nah. That's War's gig. I'm going to go volunteer in the emergency room. Maybe leave a sponge, or spread some staph. I'll see you around. Has that ass hat shown up yet?" He looked over his shoulder.

"Fairy Godfather isn't available at the moment." That's all I was going to say on the matter.

"I'm talking about Death. You'll understand." He rose and took a tissue from his pocket, using it to open the door to my office.

When he'd gone, I buzzed Rosa. "When Famine gets here, send him on in."

"Get out here." Rosa sounded worried, and I took that quite seriously. I headed for the door at a run.

In the lobby an obese man sat. His grotesque arms gripped a steel walker, taking turns shoveling corn chips from a messenger bag.

"Famine. I get it. Get the hell out, and send in Death." I shuddered at my own words, but resolved to ignore the manifestation of hunger and starvation. Pestilence came across as reasonable. War was downright friendly. It'd be a cold day in Inferno before I tolerated the mockery of Famine.

"He'll see you when he sees you," said Famine. As he spoke, bits of chip flew from his mouth.

When I approached the door to my office, I swung it open with my foot. No one waited. I walked inside, then hesitated before I sat down, sure there'd be someone waiting in my chair when I looked up. I was still alone. So after a few minutes of looking around, and flinching every time someone misspoke a spell and broke a window, I settled down and finished up another round of paperwork.

When I looked up, it was nearly seven in the evening. I took a bus home, leaving my new Agency car at work rather than fight evening traffic. After walking seven blocks, I finally made it home, and took the stairs to my apartment.

Inside, I opened a can of cat food for blessing, one for curse. As I dumped it out, a chill swept through the apartment, like I'd left the door open. I reached for my purse, and the pistol inside.

"You don't need that, Marissa." The voice cracked like clay in a drought, and rasped like bleached driftwood or dry bones.

"Death?" My fingers trembled, and my stomach churned.

"Yes."

When I finally mustered the courage to look over my shoulder, I met the gaze of a wizened Chinese man. His hair, where he still had hair, was white and thin, and liver spots covered his sallow yellow skin. He sat at my table, his hands folded before him. "You can stop quivering. I'm Death, not Destruction. Come, sit."

I approached the table, wondering if it wouldn't make more sense to run and keep running, anywhere but here.

"I'll show up wherever you go." He folded his hands together. "You know, I've meant to get around to you, ever since you became the handmaiden."

"Agent." I didn't take well to that term. Handmaidens gave manicures and pedicures. I handed out bruises and bullets.

"Not Fairy Godfather. The Black Queen. Normally, she'd mark a whole slew of you, and I'd just wait it out to see who survived. You're the only one this time." He unfolded a single finger to point to the mark on my hand.

"The Black Queen isn't alive. And even if she was, I work for the person who arranged to kill her last time." I met his gaze, empty black eyes staring through me.

"She might be dead. She isn't gone. Like your wraith friend. Dead doesn't mean gone." He spoke without emotion, as if showing a simple math problem.

"Yeah, well, I blame both of them on you. Maybe if you'd done your job, they'd actually be dead and gone." You can only put up with so many supernatural beings in one day, and I was about three past my limit.

Death scratched his head and glanced around my apartment. "That's not what I do. I don't kill people, Marissa. When they are dead, I give them a choice. Move on, or stay. Most of them I can persuade. Some of them, I can force. Sometimes, they aren't ready. Or they're too powerful."

Too powerful for Death? I focused on him now. If Death could be beaten, perhaps demons could be too.

"Not beaten. Delayed. Love, hate. They have something that keeps them pinned here. Love's easy. Lasts until whatever they love dies, then they go along for a group tour. Hate, on the other hand, can pin a soul down. Get enough of it, and it can last forever."

"Like Larry?" I glanced to my purse, wondering if Larry could text.

"Not really. He didn't build up nearly enough hatred. Sooner or later, he'll have to let go, and when he does . . ." Death's voice trailed off without menace or anger.

"You'll punish him?"

"That's not what I do. I'll take him, like I should have sixteen years ago. Like I will everyone that dies in the apocalypse."

I got up and got a bowl of cereal. If I had to tolerate the ramblings of an entity beyond time and space, it might as well be with a full stomach. "Well, I hate to spoil your fun, but I have no intention of completing the apocalypse any sooner than necessary."

"I don't desire for anyone to die. I don't kill people. I'm there when their life ends, waiting. You think I want people to die. You think that I get upset when your Fairy Godfather resurrects someone."

At this I nearly spat out my cereal. Grimm never resurrected people.

Death nodded. "I finally convinced him."

Again with the freaking mind reading. "Convinced him of what?"

"It doesn't change anything. You die now. You die in eighty years. I've seen stars born, Marissa. You could resurrect a thousand times and it would still be like today. Keeping someone alive doesn't change anything, because for them, it's just a phase. Your Fairy Godfather understands that better than most." Death rose from his chair, and picked up the cereal box I'd knocked over.

"You say that you aren't her handmaiden. I'll bet you a year off your life you'll claim that title yourself. And when she finally comes, you'll go to her willingly."

I almost threw up at the smug, calm attitude. I understood now why the other harbingers couldn't stand him. "I'll take your bet. And I'll win."

He ran gnarled fingers across his temples, like he had a migraine the size and age of the universe, and shook his head. "No, Marissa. You won't."

Twenty-Two

~∂~

I BLINKED, AND in that moment, he was gone. While I like to consider myself prepared for almost everything, being visited by the harbinger of death pushed the edges, even for me. I stayed up late reading, wondering what I'd do. When the alarm finally blared, it felt more like mercy than anything else.

There's a reason I don't eat breakfast most mornings. I swung the fridge door open, and a gout of flame burst from the doorway. The interior of my fridge, where I'd meant to snag a hard-boiled egg, belched smoke and sulfur fumes.

Malodin's face took shape in the smoke, looking part hawk, part insect. "Handmaiden."

Demons in my fridge. That's why I don't eat breakfast. I reached through the smoke, disrupting his image, feeling around for the eggs. All I found were stalactites. "I summoned your harbingers."

The gleam in his eyes was like a child tearing open a kitten he found under the Christmas tree. "Now, I demand my first plague. Something horrible. Something to make the people of your city miserable. Make them flee, and lock their doors, afraid to step into the sun. You have until evening, handmaiden."

I slammed the door, opened it to slam it again, and found only the regular interior of my fridge, a yellow monster manufactured a few years before I was. Flies and maggots squirmed on every bit of food, and the interior smelled like I'd set off a stink bomb. Never eat breakfast. It might start the day off right, or open a portal straight to Inferno.

When I got to work, I found Mikey down in the loading bay, sitting with our other cargo workers in a circle.

Mikey stood and waved. "Hey, Ms. Locks. Just attending my support group." He raised a beer to me.

I preferred wine, and I also preferred not to drink until at least eight thirty. I climbed the stairs to the Agency and found Beth sitting outside our door. On either side, a poodle crouched, like tiny, evil Sphinxes.

"Ms. Locks? Look what I can do!" She took out her kazoo and gave it a hum that made the lights flicker. In unison, the poodles rose, turned toward me, and bared red-stained fangs. Beth mumbled something that I think was "Sit." The poodles advanced, growling with the voices of the damned.

"What did you feed them? Did you let them eat someone?" I pulled the pistol from my purse. I could kill one, no problem. The other would take a bite or three out of me with those razor teeth.

Beth hummed again, so strong the lights above us exploded.

The poodles stopped, their hackles raised, their eyes glowing red in the shadows.

"Down," she said, and they circled back to her, tails wagging like nothing had happened. Sweat rolled down Beth's face, and her hands trembled. "I think they ate the housecleaning service at the motel."

"What possessed you to take them home with you?" I opened the door to the Agency and watched with a mixture of fear and amazement as the hell spawn with white fur followed her in.

"I'm getting it. I can do it, most of the time. I need to practice." Beth led her tiny terrors back to the room I'd assigned her, hopefully to lock them in the cage.

Rosa came in the front door.

"Listen up." I walked over to her, blocking her path to the

front desk. "I need to do some research in Grimm's library. You are going to handle the kobolds. You are going to give Payday George money to go away. If either of our enchanters steps out of line, you have my permission to shock them." I stared at her, wishing for the world I had a rolled-up newspaper to swat her on the nose with.

For a moment, I thought Rosa might take a swing at me. Then she lowered her gaze and stepped around me to the desk. I figured that I might not be a piper, but Rosa could at least show me the same amount of respect she did the plastic ferns.

So I headed back to the library. It looked like a book closet, if one combined a library and a janitor's supply room. One that stank of mildew and something unsavory, like a sack lunch left out in the sun for the last century. I stepped in, looking at the row of books that lined each side. With a click, I shut the door behind me, then turned off the light. When I turned it back on, the book closet was gone.

I still can't say exactly where Grimm's library actually existed. Could've been another planet. The room was as wide as a cathedral, fancy arched ceilings disappearing into the darkness where a second and third level of books waited. Vast stained glass windows covered two ends, but I'd never seen a sunrise light them.

I had come here once, in search of a gnomish cookbook Grimm had someone snag at a garage sale. It took me six days wandering through the stacks to find it. When I came back, Grimm was furious. Anger, or worry, I couldn't quite tell.

This time, I'd do things right. I stepped to the center counter and rang a copper bell. Above me, in the darkness, something began to move, to shuffle through stacks. The shelves trembled, and the candles guttered to and fro.

I picked up a candle from the top of a stack, and lit it again. "I command you to show yourself, librarian."

In answer, the carpet rose in a bubble, like something swimming through it. Then the bubble raced toward me.

I rolled out of the way, putting the candle out as I did, and behind me the floor splintered as something crawled up. Fluid dripped in wet splatters as it rose, and chitinous plates clattered. I relit my candle, ready for the image that waited.

The librarian, a monstrous beetle creature, hulked before me. "What does it want?"

"I'm looking for something, and you are going to find it for me." I held the candle between us. In its bulbous eyes, the flame reflected back a thousand times.

When it spoke, its jaws clicked together. "You cannot be my master."

"I own the Agency now. Grimm left everything to me." I stepped forward, and it recoiled from the flame. "I'm looking for a history book. One on the Fairy Godfather himself."

The librarian hissed, and it shook its wings. Above me, the scratch of a thousand legs crawling made my skin itch. "You may not take it from here, pawn."

"I command you to bring me whatever history you have on the Fairy Godfather."

It took one giant step forward, and I retreated. Again and again, until I bumped into a table.

"Stay. You cannot command me, but I will bring the book." It receded into the darkness. With each step, the drag of claws on wood sent shivers down my spine.

At the table, a candelabra held a dozen more candles, and at the edge of their glow, hundreds, thousands more glittering eyes waited. A carpet of beetles covered the floor, waiting beyond the glow of the candles.

Minutes passed, perhaps hours. I'd left my cell phone and my gun back in my office, so telling time was a best-guess kind of thing. The floorboards rattled as the librarian burrowed toward me. When it burst from the floor, it held in its claws a book with dark green binding.

The librarian placed the book on the table before me, then caressed it with one antenna. "Mind the pages. Break a binding and my brood will repair it with your skin."

I forced myself to breath, then nearly gagged at the rotten stench that came from it. Only when it again slipped back into darkness could I sit. In the end, I put a candlestick on each end of the table and sat in the middle, listening to the scuttle of feet on damp wood.

Then I began to read. When I finally found what I was looking for, I cursed into the darkness, a rant that echoed from the walls. At my disruption, the librarian trundled forward, daring approach the candles. "Shhhhhhhhhh. You must not wake the little ones."

Rage and frustration poured through me, anger and betrayal. "I need to take the book."

"Never." The librarian shook its entire body. "It stays here, where the little ones can keep it safe."

I walked up to it, right into its shadow. "I have to take the book. I'm going to take it. My Agency. My library. My book, to do as I see fit." A tear blurred one eye as I kept asking myself what else I didn't know.

"The book will not last without the little ones to care for it."

"Then punch some holes in a mayonnaise bottle and send a few home with me. I'm taking it." I turned back and closed the book, holding it in front of me like a shield.

Something like an earthquake rocked the library, and outside the stained glass windows, a gentle *whoosh* passed. Could Grimm's library be underwater? I wasn't going to stick my head out the door to find out. The librarian bent down, tapping my hair with antennae. It opened its jaws, and I tensed, ready to duck to the side and sprint along the tabletops to the tiny, single lightbulb that marked my return point.

Something wet dropped from its jaws, splattering my hands. Then came the crawling.

I screamed.

Yeah, I did. I stepped away from the librarian, grabbed a candlestick, swinging it wildly.

"Stop," it hissed. "You must not harm them."

In flickering candlelight, I watched as worms the size and length of a bullet crawled off my hands, up the spine of the book, and down into the binding.

"Return it to me, or I will send my brood to find you," said the librarian.

I clutched the book and ran for the lightbulb. When I pulled the chain, darkness enveloped me, and a million spawn chittered.

I swung my hand out to fend them off, and brushed a book. I clicked on the overhead chain, relieved to be back in the book closet. Then the memory of what I read took over, and I sprinted to my office.

"You bastard!" I screamed at Echo the moment he appeared on-screen. "You selfish bastard. Always talking about how careful I needed to be. About how proper I needed to be. About how we'd never even signed my contract."

Echo tilted his head. "Marissa, how may I help you?"

"You said you're a part of him. Why didn't you tell me before?"

"I'll need a bit more context to try to answer. Can you help me understand what has upset you?" Echo folded his hands before him.

I held up my hand, where the handmaiden's mark lay traced. "This." I held up the book. "And this. When was he going to tell me? Ever? Never? Let me guess. It wasn't something he thought about while he recorded you."

Echo froze when he saw the book, and his eyes widened.

As the minutes ticked by, I grew tired of waiting and reached for the Power button.

"Let me explain what I can."

I tossed the briefcase on my desk and sat down. "When did he intend to tell me that the Black Queen was his daughter?"

"I can't say, Marissa, but in the instant in which I was diverted, I assure you he thought of her, and what happened." Echo paused. "Almost as much as he thought of you. I know we regret that she has given you the mark."

"Regret. Do you have any idea how people in Kingdom look at me when they see this? Do you know what kind of stories they tell about her?" I balled a fist, fighting the urge to smash the screen.

"Marissa, I assure you, there is no tale of his daughter the Fairy Godfather has not agonized over. There are few that are untrue. As for her mark, I know what it means to the women who bear it. I assure you, Fairy Godfather would have removed it were it in his power."

That led me to my other point. "His power. Did he ever intend to tell me about that? That he'd been constrained?"

Echo scowled at me, his eyes narrowed. "You do not know what you are talking about, young lady."

"I know he got a princess pregnant. Had a daughter by her, Isolde. That name ring any bells? It took a prince to clean up his mess, and Kingdom only knows how many people died in the process." The fear that swallowed me in the library gave way to pure, hot rage.

"Fairy Godfather granted a wish to a princess, that much is true. She had served as his agent for so long, and he was not as familiar with the nature of women as he is now. So when she wished that he would love her, he was not prepared."

Grimm never granted wishes. Ever. I thought it was a decision, but now I knew better.

"His daughter was the joy of his life for many years. Gifted with power beyond all others, a child born of two magics. His greatest joy and his greatest mistake."

I began to wonder. "What happened to her?"

"When her mother died, Isolde became bitter and angry. She declared herself Queen of Thorns and never came to see Fairy Godfather again. She began to seek to conquer everything, and destroy everything she could not conquer." Echo's voice held a somber note.

"So the other fairies, they constrained him? Because he had a child? Because of what she became?"

Echo nodded. "Fairy Godfather always had an interest in the laws of magic, and how they could be bent and twisted. Dodged. After the destruction wrought by his daughter, he asked the other fairies to constrain him so that he might never endanger an entire realm again."

I thought of all the lewd remarks Grimm made when I first came to work. He'd made innuendos and references to how involved we could be. "He acted like a complete creep."

Echo tilted his head toward me. "You know if he wanted to, Fairy Godfather could have forced you to do anything."

It had all been an act, and one I understood now. Designed to make sure the women that worked for him never considered the Fairy Godfather as anything more than a boss to be escaped. "A demon told me Grimm is constrained right now."

At the word *demon*, Echo winced. "Tell me you didn't get tricked into making a deal with them."

For a brief moment, I almost retreated to that young woman who just acted as his hands. "Did Grimm think about demons or celestial contracts?"

Echo sighed. "I wish he had. I advise you to seek out legal advice."

"Already done. Now, about this constraint. How does it work?"

"Think of it like a faucet. All fairies' power flows through a central nexus, and at that point, it can be obstructed—" Echo's eyes narrowed and he arched his eyebrows. "You must not go there, my dear."

He wasn't fast enough by a long shot. "Why not?"

Echo's image began to flicker and distort. I wondered if I'd run the battery dry. After a moment, the flickering stopped. I swear, if it were possible for a recording to feel pain, that's what I'd say it was. Sweat rolled down skin that didn't exist.

"Marissa, please understand. Certain things, Fairy Godfather chose never to tell you. Those are choices for him. For me, they are the basic foundation of my existence. I cannot change them any more than I can change you. I can tell you that he feared for your safety. That is all I can tell you."

"You can tell me about Isolde, but not why he wouldn't want me to go to the nexus?" I tapped the book nervously, then thought of the worms in the binding and took my hands off it.

"You already know of his shame. I am not breaking any of his decisions by telling you something you already know."

"Why didn't Grimm tell me any of this?" I hoped it wouldn't cause Echo to fritz out again.

Echo hung his head. "Even a fairy may do things they are ashamed of, or make mistakes they wish they could undo. Our memory is perfect. We will never forget decisions made, or their consequences. Until the day the Black Queen marked you, Fairy Godfather believed his daughter gone. I'm sorry, Marissa. The part of me that is him is deeply sorry."

I hit the Power button without waiting to hear more. Then I opened the book to read on. To confirm what Echo told me. To understand what he'd never told me about a subject he *knew* I cared about. Just as I found my place, a knock at the door drew my ire.

"What?" I slammed the book closed, then winced as a squeal, of rage or of pain, came from it.

My office door swung open, and in stepped Beth. Her makeup had runs in it from tears, and fresh gnaw marks covered her hands. "Ms. Locks, I'm so sorry. I was practicing, and when I looked up, everyone was gone."

I glanced at the clock. Eight forty-five in the evening. I had to remember never to go to Grimm's library when my car was parked in a metered spot. I stood up and grabbed my purse, which weighed at least ten pounds more than it ought to. Inside, I found a black leather bag with a drawstring. A parchment fragment hung from the tie. "For summoning of plagues."

"Come on." I took her hand and headed out of my office.

"I tried. The front office is—"

"Filled with poisonous snakes. I know. I signed the bill for our reptile man." I led her down the hall to the service entrance. Grimm had a glamour put on it so that if you weren't staff, it looked more like a broken urinal. I jiggled the handle and watched Beth's face as the door swung open. Then I ran for the stairs and climbed all sixteen flights to the top. I lost Beth about twelve flights down. While she made a pretty good human pincushion, Beth could use some time at the track.

There, I opened the bag. Inside, black sand, like crushed lava, rough to the touch. I took a closer look at the parchment. In silver script, under the large writing, it read "Desire the plague, and cast the dust." Who really desires a plague?

I grabbed a handful of the sand, trying to think of the least harmful plague. There really weren't many good options. Malodin said it had to cause fear. To drive people into their homes. To make them hide from the sun, and not dare to answer the door.

Behind me, the door to the roof swung open, and Beth drooped up against the frame. "What are you doing?"

"Unleashing a plague. The first of three." I made up my mind. Larry said to do only what was required. One plague, and then I'd have time to research more. Time to study and figure out how to end this mess.

"You mean gnats? Flies? Frogs?" Beth looked over the edge and veered away.

"I don't have enough princes for a plague of frogs." I cast the sand from the roof, feeling sick to my stomach as a wind whipped it like a tornado. "It's done." I silently bit my lip and swore I'd make up for this somehow.

Beth limped for the door. "We should get inside before it hits. Hornets? Scorpions?"

"Worse." I followed her down, knowing in my heart I'd crossed a line. Shooting people? On occasion. When they deserved it. Arson? Guilty, fortunately never charged. Bringing about plagues, though, that was a new personal low. "Encyclopedia salesmen. By tomorrow morning, you won't be able to pick up a newspaper without being offered sixty-four volumes for three easy payments."

"What's an encyclopedia?"

"A really heavy set of books. Imagine if someone printed the Internet, then removed all the fun parts. Encyclopedias are a combination exercise and reading program made by cutting down the entire Amazon rain forest."

"Why would anyone want one?"

"They don't, and trust me. The salesmen have this sixth sense for bad timing. Every time you get in the shower—or start eating, or fall asleep—they'll be there to show you all the wonders of the eighties."

Beth cursed, stringing together words like a toddler threading beads on a string.

Her ability to piece the same three words together in different combinations completely failed to impress me. Ari could curse circles around her, thanks to hard work and practice. "See, that's exactly the reaction I was aiming for. On the upside, my lawyer's going to eat well."

Twenty-Three

~~~

MY DOORBELL RANG six times before eight thirty. Not a problem. If it wasn't the SWAT team, I had no intention of answering the door. The SWAT team, incidentally, had keys to my apartment, for reasons I'd rather not go into.

I climbed down the fire escape and ran into a throng of salesmen on the street. All part of my cunning plan. "No, I don't own a smartphone. The Internet is a fad. Why yes, I'd love to sit through an exciting presentation. Could you meet me at home?" I didn't bother mentioning the address I gave them was Ari's house.

Which, incidentally, is exactly where I went, once I'd stopped off for some less wormy breakfast. I opened Ari's front door and stopped, staring at the black haze that drifted over the living room. Smoke. I ran for the basement, determined to get Ari out as soon as possible. Behind me, the door slammed shut. Larry drifted down the stairs, a guttural moan of agony escaping his skull.

"Siiiiiiiick."

For a moment, I didn't understand. Then I looked at the skeletal claw, placed where his abdomen would have been. "You eat breakfast this morning?"

Larry clipped the phone into place on his sternum, then hovered against the wall.

"Yes. I was so hungry."

"I unleashed the first plague last night. Also, there are some harbingers around here. I think I'm supposed to give them steeds, but I figure if they're willing to wait, I am too."

At the mention of the harbingers, Larry's eyes glowed and his teeth chattered like a maraca.

The doorbell rang, and I trotted up the stairs to answer it.

"Please," asked Larry in the robot voice of my phone. "Don't let any more salesmen in. I've been burning encyclopedias all morning, and I'm only through volume N."

I'd promised him payment, and payment he was going to take. I threw open the door. "I don't know, Larry. Where could I possibly find a list of one hundred and sixteen crafts I can make out of milk cartons?"

Four annoyed harbingers of the apocalypse stared back at me. Behind me, the basement door slammed as Larry fled in terror.

"Oh, crap. You guys are here for steeds, right?"

War shouldered past Pestilence. "Handmaiden, it's time. We must ride around the city, then begin the carnage."

I turned to grab my purse, and froze. Death stood next to the basement door. He knocked twice. "Why don't you come with me now? Things are about to get really ugly here anyway. I promise, it won't be any worse where you are going." After a moment of silence, Death stepped away. When he spoke, it was a woman's voice, high and scratchy. "Larry Mathew Gulberson, you come out this instant and go to your eternal judgment. Young man, don't make me tell you twice."

The basement door tore off the hinges, exploding into shards, as Larry rushed like boiling clouds into the room. "I *hated* her. I can't tell you how much I hated her. Even when I was dead, she still ordered me around."

"If you change your mind, I'll be waiting." Death turned and grabbed my purse. "Handmaiden, we're not leaving you until you provide steeds."

I ignored him. "Larry, you and I have business. How can I get a contract canceled if Malodin isn't willing to sign?"

My lawyer stopped emitting wisps of black smoke and

turned his skull toward me. "There's only two ways. You could go to Inferno and try to convince Malodin. That's what I'd do." Larry drifted over to inspect the wreckage of his basement door.

"Or?"

"You could appeal to the angels. Myself, I'd go to Inferno." He picked up a shard of wood, which began to smoke. When Larry handed it to me, an address blackened the wood. "For the angels. Bunch of arrogant bastards."

"Thanks." I headed out to the car, a quartet of destruction in my wake. Incidentally, all the Agency cars seated four. I listened to Pestilence complain about being sandwiched in the middle between War and Famine all the way to the Agency. Did I mention every traffic light in the city was out?

After the longest hour of my life, I finally arrived at the Agency. At the entrance to the service elevator, I turned to face the harbingers. "Ground rules: You are entering my business. No killing people. No cursing them. No exploding or doing whatever it is Harbingers do when they're angry."

War's skin stretched as he rose from a Latino man to a tall, white man in a pinstripe business suit. "Got it." His outfit made sense. Old white men accounted for more atrocities than all the gangbangers in the city put together.

Then we crowded into the elevator and took a ride. The service elevator opened near the staff entrance to the Agency. Down the hall, a line of wishers waited to get into the lobby, as usual. I opened the staff door and led the harbingers down the hall to my office.

A soft strain of music from inside told me my office was already occupied. A woman's voice spoke, followed by Beth's kazoo humming. I opened the door as Beth rose from one of my chairs. "Ms. Locks, I figured out how to control poodles. It's all about chords."

"You can't play a chord on the kazoo."

About that time, the woman in the other chair stood up. Mrs. Pendlebrook, ex–High Queen. "Someone neglected to teach the young lady the basics of harmonic resonance. I have no desire to be torn to shreds by tiny white terrors, so I offered my assistance."

"Can we order breakfast to celebrate?" Beth practically jumped and bounced like a little girl on a sugar high.

Death stepped from behind me and whispered something in her ear. Then he gave her a pat on the back, and she skipped out of the office.

"If you hurt her—"

"Please. I told you that's not what I do. I told her there's a spinach quiche in the fridge that she's welcome to. Also warned her not to touch the wheel of cheese." Death took the now empty seat, leaving the other harbingers to stand.

"That quiche belongs to our lactose-, gluten-, and peanut-allergic accountant. I'm going to spend the next three hours listening to him whine." I took my chair, wondering if I needed a bigger office.

"He won't be complaining anymore. Also, if you were expecting him this morning, you may be waiting awhile." Death gave me a wink.

"Who are these 'gentlemen'?" Mrs. Pendlebrook gave each of them a critical eye.

"They're the harbingers of the apocalypse. The four horsemen."

"I don't see any horses. Therefore, they aren't horsemen. Harbingers. I've seen better manifestations of destruction in middle school." She rose from her chair and glanced at them until they shied away. "You four gentlemen will wait outside while I discuss a personal matter with Ms. Locks." Her tone left no room for argument or confrontation.

I swear, with the two of us in the office, the temperature dropped at least fifty degrees. "Can I help you?"

"My son has twenty-four hours before he can call you, but I fear he might decide to help your friend. I want you to understand something. I can't protect him from this world, but if anything happens to him, I'll hold you personally responsible." She fixed me with that same cold gaze.

If she expected me to falter, she expected wrong. I'd been threatened, attacked, shot at, bitten, and nearly killed in so many ways that half the time, when I took a job, it was to see what else was out there. "I'm not afraid of you. I've been touched by the fae and lived. I've personally killed a fairy, and not too long ago I sent the Gray Man to his grave." At the name of the Gray Man she shuddered but kept her eyes locked on mine. "There's nothing you can do to me that hasn't been done yet, and let me be clear: If your son hurts my friend in any way, I'll make certain he wishes the demons caught him."

A knock at my door turned out to be Rosa, as always, acting like I had a dead fish stuffed in my bra. Then she saw Mrs. Pendlebrook, and Rosa's entire face transformed. Given how often she scowled, I'm sure that smile gave her a charley horse. She knelt. "Your Majesty."

"Rosa Maria Vasquez? How are you?" Mrs. Pendlebrook threw her arms around Rosa and nearly picked her up, despite the fact that Rosa had a figure like a three-hundred-pound pear.

The whole reunion thing was too much for me to handle. I'd seen parking meters with more personality than Rosa, and watching her fawn over an ex-queen was one step too weird for me. "Out. Both of you, out of my office."

When they were gone, I slumped at my desk. The harbingers had to have steeds. They'd circle the city twice, then begin their path of destruction. I flipped open my phone book and began to look through the different businesses where I could rent a few horses for the next couple of days. Security deposit made absolutely no difference to me, since once the world came to an end, a dent in Grimm's bank account wouldn't be as noticeable.

I reached for the phone and froze. The whole time, Mrs. Pendlebrook's words kept rankling in my mind. I reached into my purse and took out my copy of the contract. *Mounts.* The term wasn't *horses.* It was *mounts.* I reread the clause several times. If the world had to end, maybe I could at least buy it a minor reprieve. Then I made a call. A different call than I'd planned, in fact.

Forty-five minutes later, I burst into the conference room where the harbingers sat. "Let's go."

War sprang to his feet, knocking the chair over behind him. Famine took a few tries but eventually made it to his feet. I let them take the elevator and spent some quality time with the stairs. Since the Down button took me way, way down, I figured the stairs and I would have to remain on good terms.

"I don't see any horses," said Pestilence.

"Your mounts aren't here." I gestured to the car, and they once again crammed themselves in. We had cargo vans, but I enjoyed exacting a little bit more torture. We drove through the city, with Death staring at me the entire time. "You can stop staring, you know." At least he had the decency to look at my face instead of my breasts.

"You believe you've accomplished something." Death rolled down his window to wave at an old lady pushing a carriage. "I promise you, whatever trick you think you're going to pull off doesn't change anything."

We pulled up at our destination.

"We do not ride dogs," said War, hitting the palm of one hand with a fist.

"It's called a Greyhound, and you ride in it, not on it."

A bus pulled out, sleek and silver.

"You have to be on one that leaves in thirty-five minutes. It'll take you to your mounts." I started to the door and Death grabbed me by the hand.

"Handmaiden, what do you think you are doing?"

I wanted more than anything to buy him a coffee, help get that rasp out of his throat. "The contract says I have to provide mounts for you to ride. It says nothing about where they have to be, or how you get there. This bus will take you to San Jose, California. There you'll pick up your mounts, and begin your ride."

"We have to ride around the city twice," said War, swearing in between each word.

"That's not my problem." I left them outside and bought tickets for all four, which were considerably cheaper since I didn't have to pay for luggage. Outside, I handed tickets to each of them.

"I'm going to tear this place up when I get back." War flexed his muscles.

"You were going to do that anyway. You should be thankful. I put Death in a row by himself. Also, I bought you a pack of cards and a crossword puzzle." I gave the big man a pat on the back and walked away, feeling the rage seethe out of him.

"Pestilence, have some antiviral drops. Closed-in spaces, and all." I passed over Famine, still ticked he thought being obese while so many starved was appropriate.

"This will take three, four days?" asked Death.

"Three days, assuming nothing goes wrong." I handed Death a copy of a vampire romance. "Some light reading for you."

"This doesn't change anything. Three days is nothing."

I handed Death his ticket and left them standing at the bus terminal. If they missed their bus, the apocalypse would have to wait twelve hours. I had no problem with that.

I ALMOST MADE it back to the office. Almost. The fountain of fire from a manhole cover burned a hole in the truck in front of me and sent the crowds scurrying for cover. I recognized the orange glow of hellfire, and got out of the car as a curtain of ash began to fall on the street.

"Handmaiden." Malodin walked out of the smoke, his legs bending in unnatural places with each long step. "What have you done?"

"What our contract says I have to. You wanted a plague, I gave you one. You wanted harbingers, you got them. They're on their way to get mounts as we speak." I reminded myself to pick up another squirt gun full of holy water.

Malodin swiped at me faster than I could move, grasping me by the shoulders. "Gnat! Insignificant worm!" He shook me so hard the world spun. "You think you can play with my words? I promise you, when the apocalypse begins, it will be your friends who I torture first. You, of course, will be fine. Physically. The next plague had better be something that brings misery and suffering. I want a plague straight out of the book." He dropped me in a heap and stalked back toward the flames.

"Straight out of the book." I noted he hadn't stated which book.

Malodin spun on his heel, a shadowy form of dread. "I dare you to choose another book."

A few minutes later the fountain of flame died down, leaving me to work my way around the crater it left, and back to the office.

There, I opened up the book I'd taken from Grimm's library, and continued reading. Perhaps there I'd find more details on exactly what had been done to Grimm, and how. He owed me answers, and I'd be damned if I didn't collect, and quite possibly even if I did.

Twenty-Four

❧

BY MIDNIGHT, I'D made up my mind that if I ever made it to Inferno, and the author of the book was there, I was going to ask the devil to turn up the heat on him. You don't write a comprehensive history of the Fairy Godfather and write about a "terrible punishment" and leave it at that. You don't.

I flipped the page back and forth, carefully rereading the last words on one side and the first on the other. In my frustration, I flipped a little too hard, and the page ripped, tearing about an inch down. I let it go, swearing softly, and opened my drawer to get out the tape.

The dry scratching noise sent shivers down my spine. Then I watched as two of the worms the librarian sent with me squirmed up out of the binding. They let out squeals as they approached the tear. Then they crawled to either edge, and began to rock back and forth.

Silken threads drifted from their mouths, and they worked their way up and down the tear, laying white thread that sank into the paper, gnawing the edges of the tear to rework it. When at last they stopped, the page looked like new, despite the fact that the book had to be at least three hundred years old. The larva slowly worked their way back into the spine. I decided I'd keep the book locked in a drawer at night. The thought of the brood worming their way into my ear made it hard to sleep.

I SPENT THE night at the Agency, dozing on a couch near the kitchen. Normally, I couldn't sleep there if I had to. At night, all the remnants of Grimm's experiments came out to play. I'd learned long ago to shut my office door and keep my gun loaded. The worst weren't the creatures that devoured everything in the fridge about once a week, up to and occasionally including the container it came in. The worst, hands down, were the things I couldn't see, only feel, watching me. And every once in a while, I'd catch a glimpse of movement from the corner of my eye.

And if I was going to make this agency mine, it started with owning everything. Even the skeletons in the closet. "Hello? Anyone want to come out? Talk? This is my agency. You want to stick around, we need to set some terms. You need something, you write it on the board in my office, if you can't talk face-to-face."

When I woke, a pile of meat lay on the floor next to the couch. Warning? Offering? I couldn't tell. The only thing certain was that I had a severe cramp in my neck and a desire to put an end to this end-of-days thing. From my purse I took the address Larry gave me, and headed over. Technically, leaving Rosa and two half-witted enchanters alone constituted reckless endangerment. I figured the worst that could happen was that they'd kill themselves (hopefully) or everyone in the building (less hopefully).

It turned out the address led me to a solid-waste transfer station. No one called them "dumps" anymore. The place was a dump. Last time I was in a place with that much garbage, it had a crazy cat lady holed up in the bedroom.

A foreman at the gate met me, walking over with stocky stride, his hard hat pulled back at an angle. "You need to clear out, lady. This ain't no place to play."

"I'm here to see someone." I pulled out the burned address Larry gave me, then a copy of my contract.

He glanced it over, scratching a grubby finger on his forehead. "Awww, that ain't good." He waved me on in through the gate, then pointed to a dilapidated trailer off to one side. "You wait in there. I'll get the boss."

I sat in the trailer, which shook and rumbled as trucks came and left, until the door clattered open. In walked a black man, about six feet, about three hundred pounds of muscle, fat, and ugly. The name tag stitched to his uniform read "Eli."

"You the one that started another damned apocalypse?"

"Guilty." I waved the contract.

Eli stalked over to seize it, leaving a grease smear across the page. "Now, this here, it's an old-time apocalypse. Plagues. Harbingers. Speaking of which, where are they? I haven't seen them in a few hundred years."

"They're on a bus to California."

He stared at me with those brown eyes until I squirmed like a schoolgirl at the principal's office. "California."

"Yes. Now could you please help me? My lawyer said you might be able to help."

Eli sat down in a lawn chair that creaked under his weight. "You know what I do, Ms. Locks? Clean up after people. Take care of their garbage. Make it so they can go on living. Every once in a while, I get to maybe save a kid or shoot a kitten out of a tree. But mostly, it's cleaning up after humanity. Same job for the last ten thousand years."

I smacked my hand on the table in frustration. "I get it. I screwed up. I signed a deal, which I'll have you know I didn't actually sign. If I'd come to you first, or something. If I'd asked my lawyer, or something. If I'd not gone there, or something. I get it. Are you going to help me or not?"

"Give me one reason why I should."

"I saved someone from demons the other night. I stopped a war between Kingdom and the fae. I went through a mirror and killed a fairy who was going to wreak havoc on this city." I figured that at least one of those ought to be worth a little help.

Eli laughed, a deep rumble in his belly that shook the chair until I feared it would collapse. "I wouldn't go bragging about that. If I got mugged, I wouldn't run around saying, 'Look at me, someone took my wallet on the subway.' Face it, lady: You got used."

"By who? Grimm?" I'd almost always thought Grimm had my best interests at heart. Given what he'd kept from me, I couldn't be certain.

"That's a nasty mark you got on your hand, lady. Where'd you get something like that? You look like the barbwire bracelet, or Asian character type."

I bit my lip, determined not to let him bait me. "I got it from the Root of Lies, but I'm guessing you already knew that."

He reached out a hand for mine. "May I?" At my nod, he took my hand and traced the pattern of the rose. "You ever known that thing to do something good?"

Before the day I used it as a weapon, we'd kept the Root of Lies to frighten the truth out of uncooperative people. If you lied while holding it, thorns grew straight from it, to your heart, seeking the lies. I'd used that little trick to kill a fairy, though given that it cut straight through me to get to her, I didn't exactly consider it my friend. "I destroyed it killing Fairy Godmother."

"Destroyed? Or changed?"

I'd seen the thorn tree that remained after Fairy Godmother died through the mirror, when Ari went off to train. I'd never been able to look at it, bent and twisted in the shape of a woman, and not feel the thorns tearing through my arm to get at Fairy Godmother. "Why?"

"Lady, I gave up trying to understand humans a few thousand years ago. Why they do anything is a mystery to me. But I wouldn't go around telling folks I helped the Black Queen consume what was left of a fairy. They might not take to it too well."

I stood, understanding why it was that Larry had said not to bother with the angels. "Thanks for your time." I stumbled on the way out, lost, thinking less about how to get home and more about how one of my greatest accomplishments turned out to be "Marissa was someone else's pawn. Again."

Eli grabbed me by the arm, his hand wrapping clear around my wrist. "I'm guessing you came here because you want some sort of magic weapon from me. Some secret way to get out of your deal."

I nodded.

"Get the hell out of my trailer. I'm ready to be done with

this world. You want to keep the world turning, you do it yourself." He turned and pointed to the cabinet behind him. "People always coming round, wanting help. Holy daggers. Unbreakable swords. Hell, check this out."

He took a crystal vial from the cabinet and shook it. "This ain't holy water. It's sweat from the Authority herself. Demons don't heal from what this does to them."

I held out my hand, breathing a sigh of relief. And waited. And waited. "Please?"

"I'm a sort of magician. You want to see me do a magic trick?"

"I guess."

"I call this 'Make my problem disappear.' " He shoved me out the door and locked the trailer behind him. "Have a nice apocalypse, Ms. Locks." With that, he stomped off into the transfer station.

I stood there for several minutes, practically steaming. And made a decision. I was already going to Inferno for starting the apocalypse. I slipped around behind the trailer and bashed out a window. Then, using the chain-link fence, I climbed inside and helped myself to the vial of sweat. A three-foot sword or holy machine gun would be too conspicuous, but this fit in my pocket.

If signing up to bring the apocalypse didn't damn me to hell, stealing from angels had to finish the trick. I exited the trailer and headed where I figured I was going to wind up anyway.

I FOUND THE elevator in the corner of the department store two blocks down and signaled it. The bloom of red light from the shaft when the door opened said I'd found my ride. "This one's full." I pushed a couple of stroller jockey moms back. If they wanted to experience hell, all they had to do was give their kids sugar and go home.

Then I gripped the elevator rail and waited as once more it did an impression of a downward pointed rocket. When the door opened, I looked out, to my surprise, at an office building. The last time I went through a place like this, I was chasing a djinn who abused magic to make a killing on the stock market. Market lost ten percent the day I brought him in.

A line of people in all states of disarray, from purple chok-ing victims to a few soggy divers still gasping for one more breath that would never come. The line led up to a small desk, where a short, balding man waited to hand paperwork to each.

You always read about the wailing of the damned. You never read about the whining, which is about all any of the folks in line did. By the time I reached the desk, I was about ready to pick up a pitchfork and go at it myself.

The clerk kept his head down, handed me a yellow packet of paperwork labled "Welcome to Inferno," and pointed to the right.

"You a Dante or a Faust? Dantes can begin their tour at the terminal on 2B. Fausts, fill out this form, take a number." He looked up for a moment, catching my gaze with black eyes like pits, and then grinned. "Marissa!"

No matter what anyone tells you, being recognized by desk clerks in Inferno is always a bad thing. I turned and headed back to the elevator, but before I could make it there he ran over and grabbed my hand.

"What an honor!" His voice cracked like a teenager's as he said it. "Nick. My name's Nickolas Scratch, and I'll be happy to take you wherever you want to go. Are you here for a tour?"

I shook my head. "I was hoping for a meeting."

"Going straight to the big guy? Wow. You met him?"

I was busy reading the directory posted on the wall. "Nah. Did a delivery once to the North Pole with a friend. Turns out Santa hasn't come out of that survivalist bunker in years. Lives up there in the ice and the cold, wearing reindeer skins and eating elves. I got a stocking full of reindeer guts for three years straight afterward."

Nick wrung his hands. "I meant *our* big guy. Prince of Lies. Lord of Destruction?"

"Definitely not if I can avoid it. I've heard bad things about the Devil." Bad wasn't actually the right term, but I really didn't want to offend the first person I met in hell. After all, he hadn't even threatened me.

"Oh, he's evil, all right. And if you don't get your paper-work done, he'll throw your soul into a fire, for sure. If you ever do meet him, he prefers to be called the Adversary. *Devil* is too generic." Nick dragged me by the hand back to his desk.

"I was wondering if Malodin was available? I need to discuss an alternate deal with him."

Nick swallowed nervously. "You might not want to say that name too loud around here. He's not on good terms with the big guy. Satan. Not Santa. I doubt Santa likes him either, but I'm telling you, since the last time Mal revolted, he's on a short leash. If he doesn't deliver the apocalypse this time, the Adversary's going to personally spend time torturing him."

I found Malodin's name on the directory. "Can you show me where this is?"

Nick grabbed my arm and pulled me. "You want to see him, you have to follow me."

"What about them?" I looked back at the line of damned behind me.

"They'll wait. They've got all the time in eternity." So I followed the desk clerk of hell into the maze of offices. "You might want to watch your step around here. Some of these folks are a little grumpy, on account of the heat. The ones that aren't grumpy because of the heat are unhappy because of the ice."

I followed him down row after row of cracker box offices with names like "Belzior the Defiler" carved in the nameplates. As I read that name, a creeping dread crawled its way through my stomach. I knew that name, and would be better off if I disappeared before the occupant came back. Finally, we rounded a corner and stood before the largest set of double office doors I'd ever seen. A red velvet rope hung between posts, blocking the entrance.

"Here. Malodin's in here." Nick scratched at the bald spot on top of his head and pointed to the doors.

"That's Malodin's office?" I needed an upgrade. Heck, I could take over half the floor and not have an office that size, most likely.

"Oh, no, that's the Adversary's office."

I reached into my pocket for the vial, determined that if I had to go out, I'd go out taking a pile of demons with me.

"Stop!" Nick clung to my arm like a leech. "Malodin's been stuck in there ever since that stunt you pulled with the harbingers. He's not in a very good mood." Then he crept over to the door and unlatched the velvet rope.

"What are you doing? That's probably against the rules."

Time to run. Time to head for the elevator, time to head for the hills. For anywhere but there. As I turned to flee, a group of heavyset demons tromped around the corner, each step sinking their claws into the carpet. I stopped, staring at them.

The largest resembled a walking sore, with blisters on every inch of its gangrenous skin. Black runes covered it from head to toe. Runes I'd seen before, and hoped I'd never see again.

The demon's eyes narrowed, obviously going through the same mechanics.

Nick flung himself in front of me, his scrawny arms outstretched. "Don't you dare touch her. She's here for an appointment with the Adversary."

"What? I am?" I recovered my bearing and cursed my poor lying skills. "I mean, yes. That's exactly what I'm here for. And you better not lay a claw on me, or the Adversary's going to hear about it." I put my hands on my hips and gave them the boss stare.

Belzior the Defiler began to hiss and shake, then roar with laughter, his fangs showing with each howl. Then he turned, and one claw on each of his companions, they walked away.

"That one doesn't like me. We sort of have a history." I'd encountered Belzior when he was still Haniel, Archangel of Grace. I hadn't been able to stop his transformation, but I'd cost him his heavenly power.

"*Hate* would be the word you're looking for. Oh, if I told you how many times Belzior has proclaimed his desire to slay you during company meetings, you'd build a hut out of Celestial Crystal and never leave. The other two, I think you might have shot them with holy water a week ago." Nick flipped open the guest roster beside the door. "Let's just pencil you in."

"That's got to be against the rules. Stop that."

"It's Inferno, Marissa. Following the rules would be a sin. Now, if anyone asks, you were here to see the Adversary by appointment."

I patted him on the back. "You know, clerks will one day rule the world. But I'm getting out of here. Malodin, I'm not afraid of. I'm not going to pick a fight with the Devil."

He gasped and looked up at me. "Your name is on the

calendar. You have to keep the appointment, or he'll be very angry. Besides, he's been looking forward to meeting you."

"How exactly do you know that? And how did you know my name?"

Nick pointed to the wall, where a poster hung. "This year's apocalypse brought to you by:" read the title, and below it was a picture so ugly I swear it came from my driver's license. "Marissa Locks," said Nick, pointing to my name at the bottom. "You shouldn't be so worried. The Adversary's not in his office. You can claim you were here and he wasn't."

Disgusted, I ripped the rope out of the way and barged into Satan's office.

I had a better office than Satan.

I'm guessing the double doors were actually so that the larger, more misshapen of Inferno's citizens could get in. The inside, while large, was closer to one of our conference rooms. I glanced at the cluttered executive desk, the rack of old-style filing cabinets, and the complete lack of Malodin.

"You know, I was expecting some sort of throne room. Where's Malodin?"

Nick walked up to the desk and picked up a mayonnaise jar. Inside, something distinctly insectoid crawled. "Told you he's been in here since that stunt. Malodin's on the Adversary's naughty list. The Adversary spends most of his time out and about in Inferno. He's a hands-on guy." Nick shook the jar until shrieks of rage came from the trapped demon.

I walked over and snatched the jar from him. Sure enough, the tiny, walking-stick-like creature inside was my demonic captor. "I need to talk to you. I want out of our contract, and I'll give you whatever you want."

Malodin stopped skittering around in the jar to stare at me.

"What do you want? Surely there's something you can accept in trade."

Nick tugged at my arm. "Souls. A soul in the hand is worth seven billion in the apocalypse. Do you have any idea how many times we've almost brought the end days? Demons always take the sure thing."

My heart sank as I considered it. My soul. The part of me that made me who and what I was. Versus the end of the world and the death of everyone I loved, and quite a few people I didn't. When I spoke, my voice shook. "Malodin, will you take my soul in exchange?"

The glass muffled the squeaks till they sounded like the chittering of a rat.

"I'm sorry, you'll need to speak up."

Nick walked over and took the jar from me, unscrewed the lid, and dumped the demon out. In an explosion of purple smoke, Malodin rocketed to full size, standing a few heads taller than me.

"Only thing you have that I want is my apocalypse. Now, you owe me another plague." Then he looked over at Nick. "None of you believed I could do it. I'll show you all."

Nick walked around and sat in the chair behind the desk, putting his feet up on it. "Get out of here." I wasn't sure if sitting behind the Devil's desk was the ultimate sin or not, but it seemed like a phenomenally bad idea. Given that Nick just spilled a mug of stale coffee on the papers, I was going with bad idea.

Malodin bent over to whisper. "Straight out of the book. Misery. Suffering." Then he shuffled out.

"What exactly are you doing?" I turned to the desk clerk once the door shut.

"This desk is so much nicer than the one out front. And this chair both leans back and supports my lumbar. I love it." Nick began to spin the chair around, staring at the ceiling.

"We've got to get out of here. Well, I have to. You have a much smaller, but I'm sure quite functional, desk to get back to. This was a waste of time."

"Not really. You couldn't know unless you tried. Plus, not many people get to come in here. Well, at least not many get to leave. How do you like my office, Marissa? It's not as large as yours, but when I need some privacy, it will do."

I stopped, hand on the knob to the door. From the tips of my toenails to the mole on the back of my head, every cell in my body simultaneously screamed to run. To fling the door open and take my chances in the halls of hell. I remembered why it was I came here in the first place, and forced my hand to let go.

"Very nice. I figured at this point you'd be sprinting in the wrong direction for the elevator." Nick still sat at his desk, mopping up spilled coffee.

I couldn't quite bring myself to take a seat in the Adversary's office. "You're in charge of Malodin, right?"

"He's my favorite boy, when he isn't leading an insurrection." Nick set up a photo, him and Malodin.

"Very nice. Fishing?"

"Ice-skating on a rink frozen from the blood of the damned. It's how we celebrated his first contract."

"I want to make a deal with you. My soul, you end Malodin's contract." The moment I said the words, I wished I could take them back. A few weeks ago, I'd sworn I would never make a deal with a demon. Now I stood in the office of the Devil, offering the only thing you ever truly own.

Nick looked up at me, his eyebrows arched. His lips drew back in a tight line, then he stood and walked around the desk. "I admire your courage. Anyone else tried that with me, I'd toss them into a river of fire for the first couple of eternities. Then, I'd do something nasty. You can't buy your way out of this, Marissa, much as I'd like to let you."

"I thought you'd be out, I don't know, making deals yourself."

Nick nodded. "Did that for a while, but people got the craziest ideas about what I wanted. Souls. Is that so hard to understand? Look at this." He turned and pulled another jar from the shelf behind me. "This one dad gave me his daughter's hands. What do I need a girl's hands for?" He held the jar up.

Inside, a pair of woman's hands wiggled back and forth, tapping on the glass.

"What do you do with them?"

"When I've got nothing else to do, I take them out and have a thumb war. Idle hands really are the Devil's plaything. Would you like one to take with you?"

"I'm all good, thanks."

He took a card from his front pocket and handed it to me. Solid red, with gold writing. "It's my work number at job number two. If you want to talk, I'll be happy to. There aren't many people who will willingly step into my office, or stay once they know who I am."

"You want the apocalypse."

Nick shrugged. "Now. Later. It's all the same to me. I'm willing to let the boy take a swing at it. Shows he can think big. Maybe even deliver. That contract, it's a work of art."

I shook his hand from me, ignoring the hurt expression on the prince of destruction's face. "I'm not going to deliver it."

"I'm sure you'll try your best. That's got to count for something, right? Hey, don't go out the main elevator." Nick pointed to a blank wall, and as I watched, a door etched itself into the wall, breaking out the plaster as it grew like some sort of zit. "Belzior might not be too bright, but what he lacks in IQ, he makes up for in stubbornness. I can drop you off at my day job."

I mumbled a form of thanks most appropriate to not being damned and threw the door open. The wall seemed to grow outward, and for a brief moment I sang with panic as the doorway reached out to swallow me.

Then I looked around at the long lines. The drone of constant complaint, and the antiseptic smell that somehow spoke of toilets and sweat.

"Next," called a clerk. I walked out of the Department of Licensing and headed back to the Agency.

When I finally got there, the thought of a long afternoon spent reviewing expense reports seemed like a vacation. The moment I opened the door and saw feet in my office chair, I gave up the vacation dream. Wyatt waited for me in the office.

He pushed the golden hair back out of his eyes and spoke softly, barely audible above the hum of the air conditioner. "I've made my decision."

Twenty-Five

~~~

"I'M GOING TO help Arianna. I knew it was the right thing to do, but it's so easy for emotions to cloud the better part of reason."

Wyatt folded his hands together as if pleased with his speech. I went to hug him, and he shied away.

"If you don't mind, Ms. Locks, I have an 'issue' with other people touching me. Too many germs." He reached into his pocket and pulled out a bottle of hand sanitizer. "Would you like some?"

Of course Ari wouldn't choose a normal boy. A prince, of course, and an obsessive-compulsive one at that. Still, if he'd wake her from the coma, I'd buy the boy a truckload of bleach wipes and pay a crew to spray down the office.

"I'll get my keys; we'll head right over."

"Ms. Locks, I've discussed this with my mum, and I believe there may be another issue." Wyatt really needed to learn to speak up. "You see, I believe it is only love's kiss that cancels out such comas. While I greatly enjoy Arianna's company, and indeed, in time we may develop a true emotional bond, I simply can't say that I love her yet."

I was about to drag Wyatt out the door, and then he has to

go mentioning a detail like that. "You're telling me you don't love Ari?"

Wyatt's face clouded over. "I have deep respect, and I believe attraction, for Arianna. We share so many passions, it's easy to see how we might be compatible. I truly wish I did love her, Ms. Locks. I would do almost anything for her, even hug her if necessary."

Grimm sent us out to help the national guard a few times, and I'd seen natural disasters with less disaster in them. Still, I wasn't one for letting a little detail like love get in my way. I left Wyatt in my office and headed down the hall to Grimm's office.

There, black boxes covered an entire wall, each a safe deposit box. I counted up and over, found the one I wanted, and brought it back to my desk. Inside, a silver flask the size of a wine glass lay cradled in velvet. "You say you wish you loved Ari. I can fix that."

He looked at the potion, then up at me, and nodded. So I took my potion, I took Ari's prince, and we headed over to her house.

OUTSIDE OF ARI'S apartment, I did my prep work. "You need to be aware of a few things. Ari's landlord can be kind of grumpy. You get that way when you've been dead for a few years."

Wyatt nodded, simply accepting what I said. Didn't matter what the boy ran into, nothing disturbed him.

I knocked on the door, then used my key to open it. Inside, the house smelled like cookies. "Larry? Have you been baking?" I walked around the hall to the kitchen, where the lich floated, taking a sheet of cookies out without using pot holders. Having no flesh came in handy from time to time.

"I brought Ari's prince over to wake her up."

"It's about time," said Larry. "I wanted the house to smell nice for her."

"Ms. Locks, where is Arianna?" Wyatt did his best at not staring at the spectral figure baking cookies, though when Larry's bones rubbed together he winced, like hearing fingernails on a chalkboard.

"She's downstairs in the basement, in the chest freezer." I turned back to Larry. "I tried talking to an angel. You could've warned me."

"You wouldn't have believed me." Larry turned off the oven and shut the door.

"Also took a trip to hell. Met the Adversary. Tried to sell him my soul in exchange for canceling the apocalypse."

If it weren't for the fact that he only had eye sockets, I'd have sworn that his eyes got wider. "You shouldn't mock the Devil. If you think things are bad now, they'll only get worse."

About then, Wyatt started screaming. I know because I'd heard Ari scream, and she didn't sound that hysterical. I ran to the basement, the black cloud of mist right behind me. A chest freezer stood with the lid open, a frozen corpse covered in frost inside.

"The other freezer. The one that's not working. Who is that?" I glanced over at Larry.

"Mom."

I opened the lid to Ari's casket appliance, and there she slept, a white fog layered over her. "Hold on. I have to tune the potion to her." I unscrewed the top of the potion, and reached down into the chest freezer, letting an orange vapor leech from the bottle, into Ari's nose. Then I took it out.

"You drink this, you look at her. It's tuned to her now, so even if you see Larry, you won't be getting the hots for someone with an eating disorder." I handed the potion to Wyatt, and he downed it with one gulp.

I'd never actually watched a love potion take effect. When Wyatt opened his eyes, he looked dizzy, like he was about to collapse. He lurched to the side of the freezer and looked down at Ari. The orange vapor that covered him seemed to tint his very skin before subsiding into the shine that covered princes normally.

"How do you feel?" I took his arm, hoping he wasn't going to fall and chip a tooth.

Wyatt looked over at me. "I don't feel different at all."

"Then kiss her, and let's see what happens."

While I waited, Wyatt tried and failed over and over to lean down into the chest freezer. At his height, he should've been able to reach, but the best he could do was reach her heel.

After a while I got up, walked over, and grabbed Ari's feet. Then I began to pull her up out of the freezer until I could grab her hand and flop her over my shoulder. I laid her down on the shag carpet and brushed her red hair out of her face. "Now?"

I looked up at Wyatt. He'd pulled a pocket toothbrush from his jeans, and stood, working his teeth to a shine. Then he took out a mint breath strip, sucked on it, and knelt to wipe Ari's lips clean. "I'm still conflicted over doing this without permission. Perhaps she'll forgive me." Then he kissed her.

I'd felt magic when Ari cast spells. I'd felt it when her stepmother nearly barbecued me once. This was a whirlpool of magic that centered on the two of them. This was love magic, not the power of lips connecting, but of hearts. Grimm always swore that if he could harness it, he could remake the world. Then Ari's hand twitched.

My heart leaped within me, and I wasn't the least bit ashamed of the tears in my eyes.

Ari wrapped her hands around him and kissed him back, much to his surprise. I'd complain about the amount of time she held him, but I figured that after a coma the girl deserved a little slack. Ari deserved happiness, in my book.

Since the first prince I set her up with tried to kill us both, I really hoped her second try would go better.

"I knew you'd come for me." Ari still strangled him like an octopus, and I think that Wyatt was enjoying it.

She let go at last and they faced each other. Ari's long hair obscured her face, but the smile on Wyatt's face could've powered the city for a day. Then the smile failed. His jaw dropped open, his eyes went wide.

Wyatt pushed her away and scrambled on his back, crawling, then leaping to his feet, a wild look of terror on him. As he rushed for the stairs, I tried to stop him, and got an elbow to the head as he flailed at me. The brief beat of feet on the stairs, the slamming of the front door, and silence fell over the house.

Behind me Larry floated wordlessly.

Ari turned and saw me for the first time. "What happened?" I used the same will that held me in the Devil's office to remind myself of who Ari was. I walked toward her and reached out to touch her cheek.

"I don't know." A lie, but I didn't know what else to say.

Ari's face perked at my voice. "Marissa, is that you?" Her eyes were solid yellow, the pupil and iris gone, replaced with the diseased color that marked wielders of Wild Magic. Even Grimm couldn't fix this.

Ari was a witch.

WE SPENT THE first hour or so in the basement. Ari couldn't climb the stairs and remained too proud to let me carry her on my back. She sat, probing her eyes over and over with her fingers.

No tears. Witches don't cry.

"What do you remember?" We sat with our backs against the chest freezer, her hand in mine.

"I remember the apple. Queen Mihail threw it at us."

At me. I knew better. If not for Ari's intervention, I'd be so much applesauce on a college stage. "I'm so sorry. It's my fault."

"I know." Ari's voice stuttered and caught. She had to be thinking about how people in Kingdom treated witches. Barely citizens, practically fair game. Life insurance companies actually had a code for "accidentally rolled down the stairs while tied up in a bag full of forks" just for witches. Witches routinely committed suicide by shooting themselves in the head three to four times, according to the police.

"She got to Grimm too." When I said it, Ari's grip on me tightened until my bones ached. She'd been telling herself Grimm would help.

She leaned her head over against my shoulder, those yellow eyes closed. "Wyatt—" A sob cut into her voice. "What happened?"

"It's a long story."

We both jumped as Larry slammed the freezer door shut. "I'll make some tea." He floated upward through the ceiling, leaving us alone.

"NOT A PRINCE." Ari fixed me with a glare that was worlds more effective without her eyes. "I'd know a prince if I met one. I've kicked four of them in the crotch, sprayed three with pepper spray, and there's one of them missing a finger from trying to push his way into the front door."

"He is. Son of the First Royal Family. Didn't you take Kingdom history in school? The name Pendlebrook didn't ring a bell? He thought I was an accountant, by the way." For a moment, it reminded me of our normal morning bickering. The little exchanges we'd have before I sent her out to charm an ogre, or a banker.

"The name on Wyatt's papers is Ptengdlebhrookz. I guess the T, G, H, and Z are silent." Ari scrunched up her nose, counting the letters, then trailed off. "I'm sorry for lying about everything. I just wanted someone who liked me for who I am, not what I am." Her words pinned me to the chair as well as a broadsword would have. Ari had nothing to apologize for. Would never have anything to apologize for.

Yeller came over and climbed up onto the couch, laying his head in her lap. His head alone weighed nearly thirty pounds. The couch groaned under his weight. Ari ran her fingers over his snout, rubbing that sore spot under his head where his slobber caught fire most days. "If Grimm's gone, are we out of a job?"

"Not exactly." I waited a moment, trying to figure out how to explain this. "There's still an Agency. My Agency, now. Grimm left it to me."

"Did you fire Rosa?"

I could've hugged that girl. "It'd be like firing the toilets."

"I'm not sure I'm up to working right now." Ari glanced around her apartment, though how she could see without eyes was really beginning to bother me.

I gave her hand a squeeze. "It's okay. You need to lay low. Queen Mihail tried to have you killed at the hospital. If it hadn't been for my favorite wolf and my pet ninja, you'd be dead."

"You can't stand wolves."

"Mikey's growing on me. In a few decades I think he'll be able to work with Liam."

Ari's face fell, and she looked at Yeller. "You know who Mikey's related to?" She caught the look of disgust on my face and gave an exasperated sigh. "Grimm didn't tell you. He said he would handle it."

"He didn't tell me a lot of things. When, not if, I manage to restore him, we're going to have some question-and-answer sessions." I thought about telling her about the Black Queen. About the apocalypse. The poor girl'd been through a lot though, and I figured she deserved some time to recoup. When you are ready, I could use your help."

Ari's fingers closed about mine. "Do I look like—" She choked. "Like the Isyle witch?"

"No. She's old. Wrinkly, reminds me of a talking raisin. You're cute."

"Cute?" Ari looked at me, staring with blighted eyes. "Wyatt didn't think so."

I stood up. "You leave him to me. In the meantime, stick close to home, in case Queen Mihail tries something stupider."

The doorbell rang, and Yeller let out a growl that shook the dishes.

"Please," said Larry, "no more."

"Marissa?" Ari arched her eyebrows at me. "What did you do?" She stared at the front door. "Why is there a line of encyclopedia salesmen at my door? Yeller, tell them no soliciting." Yeller shook his hackles and faded into the shadows.

"I'll be in the kitchen. You could use some soup, Ari." Larry drifted out, while screams of agony rose from the porch.

I stood up and grabbed my purse. "I'll handle Wyatt. I'll explain about the door knockers. Give me some time." I started to the door, then swung back and smothered her in a hug. "It's going to be okay. I promise." I didn't normally make promises I couldn't keep. Some promises, however, I'd do my damnedest to keep.

Twenty-Six

❧

I DIDN'T EXPECT my cell phone to ring. I definitely didn't expect to hear the voice of Death on the other end, but once I did, it brought a certain smile to my face. This contract game, I could play it all day.

"Marissa, what do you think you're doing?" asked Death. Muffled shouting made me smile, as one of the harbingers shouted threats.

"Do you like your mounts? I trust you found them at the station?" Smile on your face, smile in your voice, the saying goes.

"Horses, Marissa. We're the horsemen of the apocalypse." A tinge of frustration crept into Death's voice.

"That's not what the contract says. Mounts are what I'm required to get you. You can mount a bicycle and ride it all the way to the city. I got you a nice road bike with a comfy seat and everything. Poor Famine, he's going to have a long, hard trip."

Death muttered something from beyond the receiver, invoking even louder cursing. "We don't sleep, Marissa. We don't eat. We ride, and that's what we'll do. You should have known better than to try something like this."

While I chatted, I walked downstairs to the loading dock and sent my workers on break. "I packed you some spare tubes and gave you each a water bottle. I'll see you in a week or so." Then I hung up on the manifestation of Death, reached into my purse, and got ready.

When a cargo crate burst into flames, and Malodin erupted from the ashes, I was ready. "Malodin. Your harbingers are on their way."

"Horsemen." He nearly screamed, whistling through pointed teeth.

"Not according to this." I took my copy of the contract out and thrust it at him. "I'm required to provide mounts the harbingers can ride. You're lucky I didn't get them pedal carts."

Malodin grew taller, thinner, as he stalked toward me, his claws clicking in agitation. "You know, your clause says you'll be spared. That doesn't mean unharmed. I think I'll take a few fingers to start"—he froze as I drew my other hand out of my purse, clutching the crystal vial of holy sweat—"Where did you . . . ?"

"I'll tell you the same thing I tell every creep in the city. Keep your hands to yourself." I took a step toward him, smiling as he cowered.

Malodin threw his head back as though he were about to howl. "You owe me another plague."

"And I'll deliver. Go back to your hellhole and wait." I stood my ground as flames enveloped Malodin, turning him into a pile of ash. When he was truly gone, I grabbed a walkie-talkie and called the dock men back to work, then headed up to the Agency.

In the lobby, a fish creature with the top half of a tuna and the overweight bottom of a couch potato sat. The unlucky fisherman beside her carried a bucket of water, spritzing her from time to time. Every time one of these mer-maidens showed up, we had to drop everything and dispose of them.

"Rosa, get the enchanters out here to fix this." I ignored her rude gesture and headed back to my office. On the way, the unmistakable sounds of a kazoo caught my attention. In my smallest conference room, Beth and Mikey sat at the table, laughing in a way that sounded a bit too cozy for my tastes.

"What exactly is going on in here?" I slammed the door

open, then had to work at keeping from collapsing in laughter as Mikey turned around.

Piercings and chains hung from every inch of his face. He looked like the jewelry display at the south side flea market, only less respectable. "I can explain, Marissa."

Once I finally caught my breath, I stood up and tried to put on my boss face. "Go on."

After a moment of shifting his eyes around, he looked at the floor, hands in his pockets. "I can't really explain."

"He was helping me." Beth hummed on her kazoo, and a trio of poodles slunk out from under the table to growl at me.

"Where in Inferno did you get those? And why are they not in their cages?" The sight of those white clumps of furry evil drove all the laughter out of me.

"Oh, come on, Ms. Locks. They're friendly." Beth reached over and rubbed one of the poodle's muzzles, where the white fur had clots of blood from the last meal.

"Lock them up. Come with me." I looked at Mikey, who ripped the piercings out, one by one, and put them on the table. "You, get back to work. There's a mer-maiden in the lobby."

Mikey almost drooled on me. "A big one?"

"About two hundred pounds, I'd guess."

Mikey turned to Beth. "Do you like sashimi? Or tuna fish salad?"

"Did you say mermaid?" Beth looked past him, to me.

"All I'm asking for is an open mind and an open mouth. Fresh-cut sashimi is like nothing you've ever had. We can feed the bones to the poodles. Give me twenty minutes, and ignore any screaming you might hear." Mikey practically ran down the hall to the lobby.

When Beth finally got her poodles locked away, I took her with me out to the stairs, where I climbed leisurely to the top of the building. "You worry me. Getting all friendly with those things is a good recipe for winding up poodle-chow." I reached into my purse and found the bag of plague sand.

"I like them. They're cuter than rats, and they keep the salesmen away."

I glowered at her, then tossed a handful of plague sand into the wind. "It's done." I made a mental note to get Larry another soul or two, for good advice, then looked at Beth. "Go back downstairs."

Once I heard the roof-access door close, I called. "Malodin. Your second plague is done." My call echoed, lost in the sound of the city. A soft pattering swept across the city, like rain moving in. Something wet struck my arm. A maggot crawled there as other patters struck my head.

I ran.

Straight for the air-conditioning unit, which I huddled underneath as the sky opened up and it poured maggots. For almost a minute, a gully washer of biblical proportions struck the city. Then it stopped, leaving a moment of strange silence. A layer of maggots thick enough for the sole of my foot to sink into squirmed on top of the building

I'd learned all about omens from Grimm. Some were easy to read. "You are ordered to appear before the court" meant that you had a date with a district attorney in your future. Some were near impossible to divine. If a flock of birds moving south stopped early for the night, Grimm could tell who would win the lottery tomorrow. I could tell it would be a good idea to move my car out from under them. Maggots, however, were a special kind of omen. One that foretold the arrival of demons. And I knew exactly which demon would be coming to gloat.

The maggots began to move, piling together into a mound that rose higher and higher, then compressed inward, taking on the form of something inhuman. With a thunderclap, the mound exploded. Only Malodin remained where it had stood. When I first met him, he resembled an impossibly thin man. Now he looked like a man crossed with a praying mantis. As he walked across the roof toward me, his knees alternated bending forward and backwards, and his shoulders hunched from side to side with each step.

"Handmaiden, what have you graced us with?"

"Blood." I was so glad I didn't wear sandals to work that day.

Malodin nodded, satisfied. "A proper plague, straight out of the book. My father will be pleased. Did you smite their drinking water? Their liquor? Their coffee?"

The thought of the entire city going through caffeine

withdrawal at once gave me shivers worse than a mountain of maggots. "Not exactly. Every woman for one hundred miles just started her period."

Malodin stopped scratching at the open sore on his head to stare at me. "You promised us agony and misery."

I stood my ground. "You've never had cramps or the joys of fourteen straight days on the rag. Every woman in this city is going through a week's worth of PMS in the next ten minutes. The murder rate will double in the next three hours. Enjoy your plague."

"You will not mock me." Malodin's voice took on an eerie resonance, and his chin quivered as he spat each word. "Your final plague must unleash terror and violence, handmaiden." Malodin stalked toward me, then stumbled as a stream of maggots burst from his mouth. "No, Father. Not until my contract is fulfilled." He stared at the ground as he spoke, then took another lurch toward me, covering far too much distance with one step.

"I will have my apocalypse. You will do it for me, and I will be prince among demons once again." As he spoke, maggots squirmed like tears from Malodin's eyes. Then he dissolved, crackling like cellophane, and collapsing into a wet mess.

DOWNSTAIRS IN THE Agency, I found most of the staff gathered in the kitchen, where Mikey spun a pair of blades. He wore a white apron and a chef's hat, and what was left of the largest tuna I'd ever seen graced our counter.

"Marissa, cupcake?" He handed me a tray from the counter, taking one for himself.

A flavor like rich dark chocolate cascaded down my throat, and the candy sprinkles on top perfectly complemented the buttercream frosting. "These are fantastic. You should be a baker."

"I prefer barbecue." Mikey handed me another one. "I took the sprinkles from your desk."

I spewed out cupcake, choking on the bits that I now recognized. "Jar on my desk?"

Mikey swallowed his cupcake whole. "Yup. I ran out of colored ones, but these give it a crunch."

"Those are my birth control pills." Bought in bulk, a container of more than ten thousand of them. Not normally found on cupcakes.

Mikey looked queasy for a moment, then frowned. He reached over on the counter and pulled the container that usually sat in my lower drawer. Taking one from it, he put it on the end of his tongue, then chewed it thoughtfully. "Sugar, iron, and red number five. If that keeps humans from getting pregnant, you'd have gone extinct fifty years ago."

I stood still as a rock, almost ready to scream, cry, or shoot someone. Definitely shoot someone. The problem was, the person I wanted to shoot existed on the other side of the mirror, and the only person I could shoot at the moment, I didn't want to.

I slipped into a chair at the kitchenette, silent, trying to ignore the looks from our staff.

"Here. Try a California roll." Mikey pushed his hat back on top of his head and held out a platter. "I can make it into a Kentucky roll, if you'd like."

I didn't want to eat. In fact, I felt like puking, which sushi almost always did for me. "I'll try a Kentucky roll."

Mikey put one on a plate, then doused it in a bottle of whiskey. "Helps smooth the burn."

After my third or fourth Kentucky roll, I felt better. Better about accidentally starting the end of the world. Better about the plague thing. Every pigeon in the city could barely fly, stuffed from devouring maggots, and I was in no shape to drive. So I went back to my office and had Rosa send in both enchanters.

"Listen." My tongue didn't quite work right, on account of that tuna. "I need you to find something." Something, schomething, I was fairly certain they got my gist. I flipped open the book on Fairy Godfather, browsed past the image of him creating the duck-billed platypus, and found what I was looking for.

My guess is that at the time it was done, the drawing was considered high art. I knew of a day care where I could get kindergartners to produce drawings like this all day for nothing but a bag of marshmallows. It showed a wide beam of light entering a prism and a narrow beam coming out.

I tapped the drawing. "Focus point. Find it." The two of them shuffled out. Bath slippers were hardly business casual, but I was in no mood to complain.

It might have been an hour or two, or maybe a minute before someone woke me. "M?"

I looked up, and in my doorway stood Ari, dressed in a green suit. "How did you get here?" I tried to stand, a little unsteady. That's the point at which I noticed the sunglasses. Ari wore solid black sunglasses. Beside her, Yeller slunk, wearing a guide-dog harness and looking like an extremely embarrassed demonic dog.

"I took the bus. If you wear glasses, people can't tell if you're blind." Ari walked in and gave me a hug.

"You should have a white cane. We'll order you one."

Ari stiffened when I spoke. "How many Kentucky rolls did you eat? I had a cane, I broke it over the head of a man who thought I couldn't see exactly what he was doing. If he tries that again, I'm going to have Yeller play balls."

"I thought you wanted time off." I rummaged through my desk and swallowed a mint breath strip or ten.

"So I can sit at home and stare in the mirror? So I can replay Wyatt running away from me?"

"Can you see? I mean, what can you see?" I didn't really want to pry, but Ari was like my sister. I'd have answered her if our places were reversed.

"I can see. It's like everything's lit by moonlight. And the spirits. You wouldn't believe how many spells, curses, ghosts. They're everywhere. I can even see souls if I look hard enough." For the first time, a smile crossed her face. Trust Ari to find something beautiful regardless.

"I'm going to Wyatt's house. Going to tell him exactly what I think of him running off like that. Then I'm going to go fix whatever happened to Grimm, and tell him what I think of him. That son of a bitch better help you, and then he owes me some answers."

"There's not going to be a fix for this, M." Ari's tone became cold, serious. She stared at me. "The Fae Mother said this would happen. You can't any more remove this than you can your own scars."

"Grimm lied to me. I didn't have an appointment at the

clinic in Kingdom. Mikey says the pills he got me are candy."
A tear found its way down my cheek.

Ari came over and put her arm around me, offering me comfort, when I should have been the one comforting her. "Are you upset because you could have gotten pregnant? Or worried that you haven't?"

"Yes? No? Both? Mostly, I'm *ticked*. Grimm always thinks he knows best, but this is one decision he had no right to make." I forced my head up and ratcheted my tears into anger that would fuel my drive to find Grimm.

"Did you know your piper's playing fetch with a poodle? Seriously." I let Ari's change of subject slide, since it brought a smile to her face and reminded me of her old self. "You think Grimm will still let me work?"

As far as I was concerned, it didn't matter. The Agency was mine. "Let's ask." I opened Echo's case and turned him on.

"I can still confirm you are Marissa, my dear. How may I be of service?"

The words that came out of Ari's mouth weren't remotely appropriate for a princess. I'm not one hundred percent certain they were appropriate for our cargo guys. She picked the case up, looking under and behind it. "What is this?"

"Who. Meet Echo. He's like a sliver of Grimm. Speaking of which, Echo, what exactly are my birth control pills?" I reached out to thump the screen, and he folded his arms.

"I'm certain from the question you know the answer. I'm delighted to tell you that the *why* was not something Fairy Godfather considered during my creation." His eyes flicked to the Power button, expecting me to slam it off. No way was he getting off that easily.

I handed the case to Ari. "Echo will answer your questions. In the meantime, I'm going to go check with those enchanters to see how my project is going."

"Grimm?" Ari's mouth opened as he nodded.

"I am a recording of—"

"Everything Grimm thought of for a couple of seconds," I finished.

Ari slid the briefcase into her lap. "Echo. Will Grimm let a creature of evil work for him?"

"He allows a wolf to work for him. Young lady, consider that the number of homeless in the vicinity of the Agency has only gone down since Michael came to work, and I believe you are fine. Though, may I ask how you came to such a conclusion?" Echo's tone had that same annoying factor Grimm always did.

"I'm a witch. Can't you see what my eyes look like?" Ari gripped the case in frustration.

"I can indeed see. So it seems that Fairy Godfather's suspicions were correct. The wounds on your soul from Wild Magic were in fact too severe to heal." Echo nodded to himself, as if checking off a grocery list.

Ari trembled, making crackling noises as static electricity made her hair stand up.

"Ask him anything you don't need a good answer to." I turned to walk out, then glanced over my shoulder. "Echo, what am I going to find at the focus point?"

He kept it together, almost, nearly. I'd worked with the Fairy Godfather for years, been through wars and massacres and audits. The look on Echo's face, I recognized. Fear.

Twenty-Seven

❧

MY ENCHANTERS. ENCHANTRESSES? Enchanters and enchantresses? My homeless magic workers hunched over a contraption that looked more like a mousetrap combined with a surgical kit than a tool for magic. They'd scrounged desk toys, at least one pacemaker, and it looked like every calculator in the Agency. Also, my enchanters were no longer allowed to play with crayons. The entire room was covered in runes. Badly written runes, primarily because they were written in crayon.

"Tell me something good, and I'll order pizza."

"We know the answer." My enchanter held out a scroll to me. "Next time ask something hard."

I unrolled it, finding a set of seven runes. "Translation?"

He suddenly developed a bad case of lice, itching his head uncontrollably. Okay, truth was he'd probably had them all along, but he chose now to go into an itching fit.

"How do I use this?"

Now I had them both sneezing, itching, or finding any reason not to look me in the eye.

"Do either of you have any idea what this means? Spell? Code word? Reservation code?"

I'm guessing they were both allergic to me, given the

amount of coughing and scratching going on. This was exactly the reason I normally left dealing with enchanters to Ari.

As I approached my office, I could hear Ari's voice from down the hall. The closer I got, the clearer it was that Ari wasn't hysterical. She was furious.

"When was he going to tell me? Every week. Three times a week. I failed civics for magic training, and it wasn't even helping."

Echo's briefcase sat back on the desk, presumably so that Ari wouldn't throw it through the wall.

Ari hunched over, attempting to keep her magic under control. On a normal day, when she got nervous, lightning would leap from her fingertips. I always wondered how she kept her hair from going frizzy with that much static. Today she looked like a plasma ball. I put a hand on her shoulder to comfort her and got a shock that would have done a stun gun proud.

"Marissa?" Ari leaned over me, peering at me through dark sunglasses. "I'm so sorry."

"Not my first time to get struck by lightning. First time indoors." I reluctantly accepted her hand, and sat up. My scroll smoked slightly. I guessed that crispy smell was my hair. "I found the focus point."

I held up the scroll so that Echo could see. "I don't know what this is, exactly, but I asked my enchanters to find the focus point, and they gave me this."

"Marissa, it is important, for your own safety, that you do not go there." Echo's eyes had edges of white.

"Why? Explain to me why, and I'll consider not going. I unleashed another plague on the city." I glanced over at Ari. "I'm sorry."

Echo glared at me. "We've had this discussion. I am incapable of answering that question." I'm guessing I managed to annoy him.

"What about me? I used to be a princess. Does that still get me in the door?" Ari tapped her fingers on the side of the table.

"You are no less a princess now than you were before. Did your stepmother's banishment change that? No. Nor will the state of your eyes change the nature of your soul. But I am afraid that it would be equally dangerous for you. Marissa's presence on the focus point may be tolerated. Yours would certainly attract attention."

Ari glanced over to me with what would have been an envious stare if it hadn't sent shivers down my spine. "Why does she get to go?"

"I made partner. When you make partner, we'll talk about it." I really tried not to sound smug.

"This conversation is over. Neither of you are going anywhere near the focus point. Now, unless you'd like me to verify your identity again, I'll bid you good day."

I thumbed the power switch and snapped the briefcase closed. "I don't know what these mean, but I intend to find out. First, though, I'm going to go over and kick that miserable sack of crap Wyatt in the crotch for running away."

"I want to see him." Ari's voice quavered.

"Then come with me. Yeller, I need you to play nice." As a manifestation of torment, it wasn't normally in his nature to play nice.

On the way out, I checked in with Rosa. "Anything you can't handle here?"

"Him." Rosa pointed to the corner, where Payday George read the news.

"You going to send off the kobolds?"

Rosa reached under her desk and brought out a garden rake. The tines had a yellow crust that looked suspiciously like kobold blood on them. "Yes."

I walked over to George, with Ari in tow. "This isn't a payday-loan place."

He stood, shorter than me, barely taller than Ari. "I just need a little help until Friday, Ms. Locks."

"If I give you a twenty, will you leave?" I already fumbled in my purse, coming up with the contract, my scroll of runes, and a crumpled twenty-dollar bill.

"I'd do almost anything to help you out," said George. Same as he'd said for the last four years.

"Unless you can interpret runes or contracts, you can't help. See you tomorrow, George." I handed him the bill, then nearly broke his nose when he grabbed at my purse. George never attempted to mug me before, which was the only reason

I dealt with him rather than letting Mikey encourage him to go elsewhere.

"Let me see that." He clutched the papers close to him.

"M?" Ari stepped up, ready to try the princess charms on him. "George, why don't you give Marissa her papers back. Please?" Ari took her sunglasses off and gave George a smile that would have defrosted a fridge from a hundred paces.

And Payday George went crazy. He tried to leap backwards, hit the wall, and fell cheek first to the floor, where he scrambled to get as far away from Ari as possible. "Don't let her get me, please, Ms. Locks."

"She's not after you." I resisted punctuating it with my toes to his ribs. "Get up. Give me back my papers, and get the hell out of here."

"I'm so sorry, Ms. Locks." George stumbled to his feet and held out the scroll. "I'm sorry. Them runes, they're coordinates for a portal. I didn't get to finish the contract before she attacked me, but it looks pretty good. I'm guessing you're going to have to call down the apocalypse." Then he ran out, leaving the office door open behind him.

It's safe to say I had several good questions, like, how in hell did Payday George know what runes were? And if he could read celestial writing, why wasn't he making big cash? At the moment though, I had to stuff all those questions and deal with Ari.

I think, somewhere in that Pollyanna mind of hers, things were going to work out. People always loved her. So they always would. The thought that her very face sent people into hysterics probably didn't go too well.

"Everyone out." I didn't carry a shotgun or a garden rake, but I had a buckshot tone in my voice. The kobolds filed out. I stopped a couple with a frog in a plastic bag. "Push the frog through the mail slot there. I'll have him ready for you tomorrow." When the office stood empty, I locked the front door, then sat beside Ari in seats we chose specifically because they weren't comfortable.

After thirty minutes, she finally looked up. No tears to go with the sobs, but I had no doubt how it hurt her. "Look at me. Look me in the eyes." Ari took my hands, her grip crushing my hands.

I did. The edges of the eyes had veins like normal, but where the eye should have been white, Ari had only diseased yellow. The blood vessels looked swollen, irritated. She had no iris, no pupil. Just stretches of yellow, like her eyes rolled back in her head.

And I decided, right then and there. I didn't care. I'd learned to live with Ari when she was a princess. She couldn't help that. I would learn to live with her like this. Witch? Princess? I didn't really care about either of those. It was Ari I cared about.

I made sure to look directly at her when I spoke. "It's going to be okay." I stood, letting her hands slip from mine.

"I can't go see him. I can't take that reaction from him." Ari stayed in her seat.

"Let me take a first pass at him. In the meantime, there's a book in my desk you might want to read. You aren't the only person Grimm wasn't telling the whole truth to. And stay out of the book closet. I think I upset Grimm's librarian last time I was there." I leaned over for one more hug, ignoring the scent of roses she couldn't quite get rid of.

Then I headed down and caught a bus, determined that before the end of the world came, I'd make Ari's prince behave.

WYATT'S HOUSE HAD the curtains drawn on every window. It had a lock on the gate I climbed over. It had four "No Trespassing" signs, two "No Solicitors," and at least one "Keep Out." I liked "Keep Out" signs—they made handy footholds when I had to climb over something.

I walked to the front door and rang the doorbell. Twice. Then I knocked. Knock is a euphemism for pounded, each blow meant to warp the wooden frame. The windows rattled as I worked my way up to kicking in the door.

"I know you are in there," I yelled. A few people stopped on the sidewalk to stare. "Those are your credit cards, Mrs. Pendlebrook. You haven't made your minimum payment." The crowds moved on. At this point, I could lob a Molotov cocktail through the window and people would assume it was a normal debt collection.

"Go away." Her voice came from a second-story window. I backed up off the porch to see her glaring at me.

"Send girly man down to talk to me. Then I'll go away." I stared right back. That woman obviously never had people work for her; I'd met Girl Scouts with better stares.

"He's done enough for you already. He woke your friend, what more do you want?"

"Did he tell you he ran? He ran from her, straight out the front door. Ari's hurt, and she wants to talk to him."

"Keep the witch away from my son, or I will have her dealt with." The tone, cold and calm, left me shaking.

Ari already had one crazy queen trying to kill her. I wasn't going to tolerate a second one. I headed up the stairs, ready to kick in the door.

"I warn you, Ms. Locks. The kind of wards I have on my house won't take nicely to you breaking and entering. For your own sake, leave."

I headed out toward the gate, glanced back to see her giving a satisfied smile to me from her window. "I'm not done. I'll bet dollars to donuts you aren't warded against delivery trucks. Won't be the first time I've driven through someone's front door."

"You'll break the crystal." The tone of fear in her voice was much more to my liking.

"And the china, and pretty much tear the front off the house. You shouldn't have threatened Ari." I hopped over the gate and began to walk up the street. The nearest rental place was at least ten blocks, but she'd given me all the motivation I needed.

"Hold on, Ms. Locks." I was only a couple of blocks from her house, still running on cold fury and determination that there would be one less person threatening Ari very shortly. I swung around on her, wanting more than anything to tackle her.

"You threatened Ari. Let me be clear: There is nothing I won't do to you to protect her. You aren't warded against wrecking balls or back taxes or sewer breaks. You aren't warded against satellite crashes."

The sunlight washed out her skin, revealing liver spots. Her hair seemed so much thinner, so much weaker.

"The wards around my home must remain intact, Ms. Locks. They are not for my protection. They are for my son's." She looked up at me, pleading.

To keep her from charming me, I kept Ari firmly in mind. "You have anyone cut a strand of hair off Ari—"

"I won't. Wyatt told me about the girl. She attempted too much magic at once, didn't she?"

"Ari was trying to protect me." The only person who could really tell me what happened wasn't around. "Are you a seal bearer?"

"No. My sister was the family seal bearer of my generation. She went to visit in Avalon when she was seventeen and never returned. Come back to the house. It isn't safe for me to be out here for long. Even my trip to your Agency was a fool's errand."

"You'll let me speak to Wyatt?" I'd go either way, but I wanted her to be clear.

"No. But I'll explain why he did what he did."

So I followed her back, wondering what else I'd missed out on.

"YOU ARE YOUNG, Ms. Locks. I'm guessing no more than thirty." Mrs. Pendlebrook poured herself a cup of tea without offering me one. Not that I really wanted tea, unless it came with alcohol.

"Twenty-seven. Call me Marissa. I get enough 'Ms. Locks' around the office." Plus, first names were supposed to make people like you better. I waited for her to offer me her first name.

"Do you know why I left Kingdom?"

"I'm guessing mental breakdown. No. Turns out there's a really convenient lack of detail on the subject." At least, according to the intern I paid to read the history book, there was.

"Yes. Your employer. Your partner? Your Fairy Godfather assisted me in that. In April, it will be twenty-four years since my Charles died. Twenty-four years since I gave up the position of High Queen and left Kingdom." She set down the teacup, waiting for a question.

Which one though. That statement left so many to ask. "How did he die?"

"You might say I had him killed."

Twenty-Eight

‿✦‿

GRIMM WOULD NEVER assist someone in disappearing after a murder. Oh, sure, he kept a few assassins on retainer, mainly for government contracts, but your average murderer got an average trip to jail if he showed up asking for help. "I wouldn't say that unless I knew it. How did he die?"

She looked past me, to a painting on the wall. I'm guessing the artist was either poor or love truly was blind. If that was Charles, she must have loved him very much. "All I ever wanted was to be High Queen. To have all those other little snots bow before me and obey my whims. Twenty-three years ago, I went to your Fairy Godfather, and I asked him for a wish. Nothing special. The same as he gave everyone else."

"Grimm doesn't grant wishes. I don't think he has the pow—" I caught myself too late. Some details I didn't exactly mean to share.

"He did. Back then he did. Nowhere near the rate of other fairies, but I assure you, he did. So when I asked him, I expected him to say yes." The bitterness in her tone matched the scent of the tea.

"I've never seen him offer anyone a wish. That's why he keeps agents."

She tilted her head to the side, studying me. "He said no. No matter how I begged. No matter what I offered him, he refused. So I went elsewhere. I found someone else who would make my dream come true."

My voice shook. "A demon?"

Mrs. Pendlebrook narrowed her eyes at me. "Have you not guessed?"

In that moment, it made sense. "You made a deal with a witch."

"High Queen, in exchange for a son I didn't even have. A son who wouldn't be born for a year. Sometimes what you need isn't a wish, Marissa."

Now it all fell into place. The wards. The Celestial Crystal. "You reneged."

"Of course I did. I wasn't going to give my son to that thing. They can't have children of their own, so she wanted mine."

I considered pointing out that only evil witches couldn't have children of their own, but thought better of it. Occasionally I did manage to rein in my tongue.

"For five years I avoided her, and for five years she became more and more enraged. I don't know if it was a fault in the wards, or maybe I was careless about the nighttime rituals, but she came for him. My husband exploded the way one pops a balloon, Marissa." She stared at me, not realizing I'd cleaned up after more massacres than I could keep track of.

"I expected to die the same way, but she ignored me. Went to the nursery. Killed our nanny the same way and tried to take Wyatt from his crib."

"He was still sleeping in a crib at five years old?" I tried not to laugh. Really, I did.

"The crib was warded. She could not touch him within it, no matter how many spells she summoned or how much power she drew. And I too would have died, were it not for one of Fairy Godfather's agents. She came bursting through the door, a brilliant young lady armed with a bag of bone dust."

Grimm had a knack for sending his agents to the right place at the right time. "Bone dust to cancel spells?" I considered my encounter with the Gray Man. Even my hara-kathin had trouble breaking through.

"And a sledgehammer to break the witch's legs. My desire to rule led me to make that deal. It cost me my husband, and my son his father. The only move I could possibly make to atone would be giving it up. I left my position as High Queen. The agent who saved me put me in touch with Fairy Godfather, and he arranged discreet wards, made alterations as necessary to the official records."

"Grimm helped you disappear, and according to our books, Clara Wellington was the agent who handled everything. How did she kill the witch? Sledgehammer?" Clara had been one of Grimm's agents long before me. She made the mistake of getting caught up in Fairy Godmother's plans and paid for it with her life.

Mrs. Pendlebrook looked at me with shock. "The witch wasn't killed. After her trial, she was bound, and forced to serve as a shopkeeper in Kingdom. You want to know why Wyatt is afraid of your friend. The witch's attack is his first memory."

All the curse words in an entire battleship worth of sailors wouldn't have done it for me right then. How was I going to explain this to Ari? I stood, making Mrs. Pendlebrook nervous. Then I got to thinking. Small house. More like a three-level cracker box.

When I spoke, I nearly shouted. "She's still Ari. I don't care what she looks like. Still too optimistic for her own good. Still probably incapable of driving. Still trying to see the best in everything." Any thought of dragging Wyatt back to the Agency was gone. Well, a little thought still remained, but really, it wouldn't work out.

I went to let myself out and couldn't quite shake the detail that still bothered me. "If the witch is bound, how come you have to hide here?"

"She possesses a lock of his hair. She asked for it in his stead, and I did not understand." Finally, it made sense. I always figured Ari would fall in love with a sandwich delivery boy. Instead, she had to pick a promised child with a magical bond on him. It wasn't about the hair. The hair was a promise, an old one with the power of thousands of years of ritual. If the boy left the protection of his wards for more than a day, the witch could pull him straight to her, bound or not.

* * *

ON THE WAY back to the Agency, I passed Beth and Mikey walking in a pack of poodles. The tiny nylon leashes she had clipped to each of them wouldn't have slowed them down for a moment without Beth's power.

"Really? Taking them for a walk? And where do you keep getting them?"

Beth had a chain running from one ear, into one nostril, out the other and out to the other ear. "Mikey found me a police scanner. I go wherever there's been a murder and let out a few bars of 'The Star-Spangled Banner' and they come running."

"How are you going to run them off into the ocean if you're playing catch and rubbing them under the chin?" Business first, murderous toy poodles second.

"These little bumpkins are special-weshal. They're my friends." I liked the rats better, to be honest.

The "Closed" sign still graced the Agency doors, though any of the big hitters, say, the Royal families, would call straight through to Rosa. I went in through the service entrance. Ari's voice drifted from her office down the hall.

"Ari?" I peeked into her office, where I spent six years working. Oh, I recognized the princess hissy right away. Ari's cheeks had a bright red flush to them; her hair clung in little tendrils to her face. She shook her fist at Echo's briefcase.

"M, I swear to you, if I ever see Grimm again, I'm going to break every mirror I see him in for a week. He knew. He knew I wasn't getting better. And he knew about the Black Queen." I always thought Ari looked cute. With witch eyes, her temper tantrums were at least moderately terrifying.

"I'm not the first person to wake up with a hangover, a headache, and a tattoo they don't remember signing up for. I like your attitude. I had some time to think on the way back, and I think Payday George is right. Those runes the enchanters gave me, they're coordinates. You feed them into a portal, they open it to the right place." The more I said it, the more sense it made. Almost always a dangerous sign with magic.

Echo sounded tiny and distant without his case facing me. "Marissa, the only fortunate thing about this situation is that you lack the ability to activate a portal."

"I bet I can do it." Ari nodded to me. "Seal Magic? Wild Magic? According to you, I can do both."

"Fairy Magic. You cannot open that portal or empower it without the power of a fairy. Even you, Arianna, are not capable of doing that." Echo sounded satisfied. "Accept that Fairy Godfather is gone. Take what he's left to you, and do something magnificent with it. Liam will return in a few short days, and you can live your life together."

At Liam's name a wave of joy washed over me. With poodles and apocalypses and murderous queens, I'd lost track of the days that went by. Six days felt more like six years. Then I remembered the reason Liam went in the first place. "And he'll still be cursed. I need Grimm. He owes me a cure and some answers. I promise the cure will be the easy part."

"In my opinion, I doubt that even Fairy Godfather can remove that curse. Call it healthy self-doubt; though at the time I was recorded, he was more optimistic."

"Was he?" That settled it. Lying about my birth control? Lying about being able to remove Liam's curse? Regardless of the cost, I was going to have it out with the Fairy Godfather. "If Ari can't punch our ticket to ride, I'll find a fairy who can."

The look on Echo's face nearly stopped my heart. "Marissa. You must *not* involve another fairy. You are used to the Fairy Godfather. You have no idea what the others are like."

Ari flicked his screen with her fingertips. "Hello. M went three rounds with Fairy Godmother and won."

Eli's words came back to me, leaving me queasy. "I get the impression that's not something to be proud of." I explained Eli's comments, without the arrogant attitude. How he'd implied that I hadn't defeated Fairy Godmother as much as allowed what was left of the Black Queen to consume Fairy Godmother's power.

Ari watched me with narrow eyes, her forehead furrowed in thought. "That thorn tree always did creep me out. Like it was watching me while I practiced. Echo, how could Grimm let something that dangerous stick around?"

Echo sighed. "If Fairy Godfather believed anything there were a threat to you, he would have destroyed it long ago. I'm happy to see some humility on your part, Marissa, but you fail to grasp your situation. You have killed a fairy. What makes you think any of the others would allow you within ten miles?"

"I used the Root of Lies. Or it used me."

"And do you think the other fairies know that? Or do they only know what Fairy Godfather told them? Would he tell them the truth, leaving you open to revenge, or allow them to believe what they wanted, and fear you?" Echo closed his eyes.

If I listened, it was like having Grimm back. Except that Echo wasn't Grimm, at least not all of him. Not enough of him. "I'll ask Grimm once I free him. Now, about that portal. I almost got frostbite the last time I went to Moscow, so it's Portland or bust. I hear the fairy there is grumpy, but I bet if I pay with magic up front, I'll get exactly what I want."

Ari nodded. "I'm with you."

I reached to flip Echo's case shut, and the hinges froze. On-screen, I think Echo was almost in tears, if fairies could cry. "Is there no way I can persuade you to give up this madness?"

"I need answers. I need his help. I need Grimm."

Echo nodded, as if he'd expected my answer. "I have fulfilled my purpose, my dear, verifying your identity. I would, as Fairy Godfather would, prefer that you honor my advice. But I know you better than you imagine. Take my case to the demesne portal, Marissa."

I picked up the case and walked to the back of the Agency, to our storage room. Here, beneath orange-and-green linoleum with a floral pattern, Grimm had a block of onyx set into the concrete. I ran my fingers over the stone circle, tracing the runes that lined the edges. Grimm's demesne portal, capable of transporting me to his home realm, if I dared go.

I set Echo's case down in front of the portal.

"Listen to me, Marissa. Your presence will attract the guardians of the focus point. Negotiate if at all possible, and please, be careful to change as little as possible. The limits on Fairy Godfather's powers are for your protection as much as his punishment." Echo's screen began to glow.

"How exactly does this work?"

Echo stopped concentrating for a moment. "I am a microscopic sliver of the Fairy Godfather, my dear. Split off to serve my purpose. By definition, I am Fairy Magic. It was a pleasure serving you, Marissa. Whatever you find, whatever answers you learn, never doubt that he acted in your best interest."

Echo's screen flashed white, and a beam of power shot from it, illuminating each of the seven runes. The portal activated, tearing into space before us like a rip in my slacks. Echo's screen went dark, and the briefcase smoked at the edges.

I ran to the hallway and yelled. "Rosa. Get your shotgun, get in here."

She waddled down the hallway, looking at me like I was something she'd stepped in.

"This portal goes someplace special. I need you to make sure that nothing comes through it behind me."

Ari stood in front of the portal, staring at it. "M, you won't believe how pretty this is." It never occurred to me that portals might look different to people with Spirit Sight.

"Let's do this." I briefly considered going through my special ammo. I could punch a hole in an ogre, no doubt; kill a werewolf or head cheerleader, no problem. I didn't have anything designed to take down fairies. I did, however, have a couple of aces in the hole. "Blessing? Curse? Bus leaves in thirty seconds."

The foundations of the building shook slightly as my hara-kathin arrived. Most of the time they slept in their cat beds at home, content that I wasn't going to try to escape. Taking portals without them had proven to aggravate a couple of creatures with real anger management issues.

Ari flinched and threw up her hands. "Sweet Kingdom, M. What was that?"

"You're the one with Spirit Sight, and you're asking me?" I took Ari's hand and stepped through, feeling that gut-twisting moment when the world shrank to the size of a pinprick. Then we rocketed out the other side, landing face-first in the dirt.

Before I could even pick myself up, the ground shook. Then a voice like bells and thunder shook me. "Who enters the sacred plane?"

Twenty-Nine

~∽~

I'D BE LYING if I said I didn't consider running back through the portal. Some people will tell you running from things never helps. I'm guessing most of those people have never met a "thing" with more heads than teeth and a sincere desire to devour your spleen. In those cases, running helps a lot.

Problem was, I needed to be here. Why it is that a portal never ended at a nice walkway like in an airport, I couldn't say. This one dropped me off on the top of a stone step pyramid. Once I stopped kissing the pale gray dirt, I couldn't help thinking that the focus point was a real dump.

The entire place looked like a volcanic wasteland, except that instead of regular slag and lava flows, large blocks of quartz, enough diamonds to buy Neiman Marcus, and other gemstones jutted from the ground. On each side of the pyramid, a guard ascended toward us.

One glance at a face with more tattoos than Beth told me the guards were fae. It figured, since I once heard the fae were like children of the fairies. I always thought of it as a metaphysical "children" kind of thing, until I learned about the Black Queen.

Step after step, the guards approached, each holding their

hand out, palm facing me. Each held a pulsing egg of brilliant white light nestled in their hand. When the fae went to war, they didn't go clubbing people with sticks or swords. From those palms, each could summon a beam of white light that would rip your skin off, then smear your soul across the ground.

"Friendly?" I glanced over my shoulder. Somehow, Ari arrived on her feet, dainty as always.

"I'm guessing not, M. Stay close—I'll protect you for as long as I can." Ari clenched her firsts, and for the first time since the apple, she drew in magic. Before, it always felt like standing in a stream, with water running across me. This was more like a pressure washer on my skin, or like I was standing at the bottom of the ocean.

The guards finished their leisurely climb and ringed us on all sides.

"I'm here to fix the Fairy Godfather. Someone has—" My voice died in my throat as the lead guard raised his hand, and the bead of light in it began to glow brighter. Those eyes, cold, boring almost through my skin, told me what would happen. I was so much meat, soon to be spread across the ground like raw hamburger.

The world exploded.

At least, that's what it looked like. The chalk on the ground blossomed into clouds, and the leader of the fae went flying into the darkness, head over heels. To my right, something dragged a guard down the stairs, his head bouncing on each step. I never saw what happened to the one on my left, but the one behind me, I get nightly visits from when I dream.

He hung in the air, arms and legs stretched out, twisted in ways that flesh never should. Then his body slammed into the ground with a sound like a wet rag.

In ten seconds, something had killed four fae guards. I glanced back to Ari, wondering if witch mojo was really this strong. She cowered behind me, her face pale as the dirt. "Marissa, what did you do to them?"

"I didn't touch them."

Ari backed away from me, almost falling down the pyramid steps. "What did you do to your blessings?" She frowned for a moment, then scooped up a handful of dirt. Cupping her hands,

Ari blew into them. A cloud billowed out, past me, and when it settled, I understood.

On one side of me hulked a creature the size of a delivery truck, squat and wide. The dust only gave it general shape, but the sheer size made it clear why Ari feared them. On the other, a thin creature, whose bulbous head looked three times the size it should have, rocked on its heels.

"I think I know why I couldn't see them in their cat bed," said Ari.

"Blessing, curse, don't hurt Ari. Take a break. Extra cat treats for everyone tonight." The clouds on both sides shrank, then lurched toward me, disappearing. I glanced at Ari. "Gone?"

"Inside you."

I'd gotten somewhat used to the idea of foot-long, tiny creatures anchored to my spirit. They used to go everywhere and cause no end of trouble for me. Now that I knew what they looked like, perhaps sleeping in and ordering out was better for everyone.

"Pacci." The word swept over me, lulling me like a full bottle of wine. Ari, on the other hand, brushed it off like someone had once again called her "bitch." I tried to turn, but my arms quivered like jelly, and my body moved in slow motion.

About then, I realized that Ari was kneeling. When I finally completed my slow motion 180-degree turn, I knew who I'd see.

"My blessings were not meant for this." The Fae Mother stood, two steps down on the pyramid, so tall that her head came even with mine. Dressed in a gown that looked like dandelion gossamer spun into fabric, she took another step upward. "You should not be here."

"Please. I'm here to help Fairy Godfather. Someone has altered his power. He's frozen. I came to fix it." The spell she'd spoken slowly wore off, leaving me tired. I once thought the Fae Mother queen of the fae. Once I'd had time to do some research, it turned out I greatly underestimated her position. Separate from the courts and intrigue of the lesser fae, she possessed foreknowledge that rivaled Grimm's own, if you could divine the meaning of her words.

"You are the second to invade this plane. The others paid a

high price for their folly, but the damage to Fairy Godfather was done." She rose to the final step, standing two feet taller than me, looking down.

Ari rose and stepped to my side. "Why didn't you fix whatever they did?"

The Fae Mother tilted her head to one side for a moment, thinking. "Princess, I pay a price for knowing what will come. I cannot interfere."

That was my cue. "Show me what they did. I don't know anything about the future, and interfering is what I do best. Ari's not bad at interfering either." In this case, someone had interfered with Grimm, so I wasn't sure that counter-interference actually counted. If it did, that was fine by me.

"The princess may accompany us to the focus point, but only you may accompany me when we enter it." The Fae Mother fixed her eyes on me, then glanced back to Ari.

"That's not fair." Ari sounded like a grounded teenager.

"When you make partner, we'll see about a field trip to some far-flung world, I promise." I followed the Fae Mother's outstretched hand and hopped down the pyramid, two steps at a time.

Seen from the ground, the landscape looked even more destroyed than I'd thought. Crystals rose in waves from the ground, breaking the barren landscape into a thousand pieces, like a shattered mirror. The Fae Mother glided past me, her feet not quite touching the ground, and we followed.

I THINK I know why the Fae Mother chose to glide. After several hours of walking, my feet hurt. We'd been following the same trail through the nowhere so long that the pyramid where we'd arrived looked like a dot in the distance. Finally, I called for a break, walking off to the side of the path to sit on an outcropping of sapphire. "Can you summon a magic carpet or something?"

Ari shook the dust from her shoes and massaged her feet. "There's no carpet around here. I could probably conjure some thread, then a tiny loom, and then you could weave it into a napkin. That, I could make fly."

"Any sign of my little friends?" I hadn't felt my blessings move since the Fae Mother spoke.

"Nothing. And if that's little, I'd hate to see them when they're all grown up."

For an hour, the only sound was the patter of our own feet and the quiet sigh of wind. When I stopped to dump the rocks from my shoes, something caught my attention. I stood up in the quiet and listened as a chill ran down my spine. "You hear that?"

Ari looked up, and around. "Mmm-hmmm."

I closed my eyes and waited, listening, until I heard it again. A sound like the wind whistling over a pipe. "Hey, any idea what that is?"

The Fae Mother waited, eyes closed, on the path ahead. "Something lost." She didn't open her eyes.

Again the noise came, leaving every hair on my body standing up, in fear or awe, I couldn't say. "Stay here. I'll be back." I wandered into the alien desert, led by my ears. The sound, when it came, reminded me of a child crying and a crystal wind chime at the same time.

The noise set my teeth on edge, drawing me toward it, until I'd circled an outcropping a couple of times. That's when a spark of light drew my gaze to the crystal in the center. There, in the middle of a pillar of quartz, a creature of light danced.

Imagine if a rainbow had a child with a ballet dancer. Or a laser gave birth to a flock of butterflies. It moved in the pillar, bouncing endlessly from edge to edge, at times almost looking like a figure, at other times, a cloud of light, drizzling down the edge of the crystal. It saw me, and called, with that plaintive wail.

It nearly killed me each time. Not physically. Emotionally. The sheer sadness of its lonely cry made me angry and depressed at the same time. I reached out gently, brushing the side of the crystal, and it surged forward, a hairbreadth from my fingertips.

"M?" I turned to see Ari standing, her jaw open.

"You were supposed to stay back on the path. How am I going to find it?" I fought to keep my eyes on Ari as the creature called to me again. Ari too shuddered at the call, but the look on her face was near ecstasy.

"I asked the Fae Mother if it would be okay, and she said it was better that I see now. What is that?" Ari joined me, reaching out without fear to almost touch it.

"No idea. But it's sad, and lonely. Blessing and curse don't think it's a threat." Though my harakathin almost always slept after exerting themselves, I'd know if this thing meant to threaten me.

"Have you never seen a wish?" The Fae Mother's voice sounded like she screamed in my ear, even from a dozen yards away. "Not even in the mirror?"

I shook my head. "Fairy Godfather stopped handing them out a while back. Said what most people needed were solutions, not wishes. I never realized a wish looked like this. That they were alive."

"Your harakathin are alive. Curses are alive. Why would a wish be different?" She gestured with her hand as though it were obvious. "Princess. Look at it with all your sight."

Ari flinched at the word *princess*. I'd have figured it would be the reference to her eyes. She squinted, staring, with her brow furrowed, then hunched shoulders, and glared in determination. A moment later, she opened her eyes, her mouth open like a tiny "o," and gasped. "That's the most beautiful thing I've ever seen."

"What does it look like? Because it looks pretty good from here." I pried my fingers out of her grip—she'd started to crush them.

"I don't know how to describe it, M. It's like all the possibility in the world, rolled together, and it's *all* of those things at once." She turned toward me, her face split by a smile that had to be painful. "M?"

"Yes?"

Ari reached out her fingers to brush my face, as though she'd seen me for the first time.

"Got something on my cheek?" Given the massacre that happened when we arrived, odds were I had fae blood everywhere.

"No. I don't think I ever saw you before. Not like this."

"Will you claim it?" The Fae Mother interrupted our almost sister bonding time, her head nodding toward the wish.

"It doesn't belong to anyone?" Ari stopped staring at me, went back to staring at it.

"It is only a casting off. An accident, trapped here." The Fae Mother set her hands together, and uttered a word, dark like the depths of the ocean. The crystal pillar hummed in response, cracking down the edges. Shards of crystal fell away, leaving the wish glimmering, hovering.

I reached out a hand to it, and it drifted away, like I'd pushed it. A full-on swipe, and it skittered to the side like greased butter.

"You may not claim it." If she'd said that first, I wouldn't have tried.

Ari held out her hand, and it transformed, wrapping and swirling around her like a living light show.

"How come she gets to hold it?"

Ari smiled. "When you make princess, we'll talk about getting you a pet wish, I promise." She looked to the Fae Mother. "What do I do?"

"Desire, and ask, princess. But do not set magic against magic."

The Fae Mother never gave me that much warning, but she had a point. If Ari wished, for instance, to have her eyes back, she'd get them. In a bag. If she wished she wasn't a witch, it might kill her.

I knew what Ari would say before she spoke. What she desired more than anything. "I wish Wyatt still loved me."

The wish began to cry. To wail, and convulse, as strands of it flew outward, like a sweater unraveling. The noise went on for seconds, or an eternity, as the wish tore to pieces. And then it was gone, a fading glow left where once it existed.

"Well done." The Fae Mother turned to go back toward our trail. "You have claimed its power and life for your own. May your wish bring you happiness."

Ari gasped, her hand on her chest like she'd been punched. "I didn't mean—" A sob choked her, and she stumbled forward. "She didn't say that wishing would kill it."

The death wail had done a number on me too. Like I'd run a marathon, followed by a triathlon, followed by getting beat up by an entire team of ogres. In the fairy tales, they never say what wishing does to the wish. You never hear about the thing that dies to give someone their happily ever after.

I took Ari by the hand and stood her up. She stared blankly ahead. I mean, I think she did—I couldn't exactly tell without her eyes, but she took each step only as I pulled her, and she continued to shiver. We made our way back to the path, where the Fae Mother waited, and followed her onward.

FROM A DISTANCE, the focus point looked like a Hollywood opening. Those massive searchlights that beam up into the sky shone up into the darkness, each a slightly different color. When I got closer, I could make out lesser beams of light. Some shone so bright, it hurt to look. Some looked like pale flashlights, barely visible at all.

After a few more hours, the dots on the horizon below the searchlights became pyramids like the ones we arrived on, and with Kingdom only knows how many more steps, we approached a low wall. Only a couple of feet high, it curved into the distance, around the pyramids.

"Princess, you may not enter here. To come into contact with fairy power is death." The Fae Mother drifted over the wall, then beckoned to me.

"I'll be back for you." I hugged Ari.

"I didn't mean to kill it." She sat at the edge, staring off into the distance.

Part of me burned with anger at her. Her words cost the poor wish its existence.

I followed the Fae Mother on. The first pyramids had only weak beams of light arcing into the sky. As we passed others, the light became stronger, brighter. These had channels carved into the ground. Light burst from crystals in the channel, then through prisms that reflected the beams to the top of the pyramid, where they joined into what looked like solid light.

"Beware. Come into contact with another fairy's power, and you too will die." She didn't bother looking back.

At last, we stopped. I'm guessing we'd reached the center of the focus point, and judging from the size of the pyramid, Grimm was once truly powerful, or perhaps truly old, older than I could imagine. The light channels around his pyramid began farther away than I could see, hitting crystal after crystal, joining, rejoining, and finally blasting up toward the top of the pyramid. The beam that came out, however, was pale, barely visible.

I climbed the stairs slowly, to be honest. Not because I wasn't excited about being here after all this time. I could only walk so far. So I took one step at a time, and rested in between. Near the top of the pyramid, the beams gave off a hum that echoed in my bones.

A few steps farther up, the air crackled with power. That's where I could finally see what Grimm had done to himself, and what Queen Mihail had done to him. Fixed in place at the peak of the pyramid stood a crystal buffed until it was nearly opaque. Light entered it full force, but the cloudy crystal reflected only a tiny smidgeon of the light.

This was Grimm's constraint, his punishment for the Black Queen.

If fairies traveled as pure light, this would have reduced his power a thousand-fold. But Queen Mihail had tampered with it, poisoned it. Near the top, spider veins of black spread out, strangling the light. The veins looked like blood vessels at first, but when I finally stood at the top, I saw the truth.

Thorns.

Crystal thorns, grown through his constraint, strangling his power. This was what left him frozen, fading from my bathroom mirror.

The sick feeling in my stomach wasn't fear; it came from the piles of meat cascading down the pyramid steps, chunks of flesh and torn clothing.

Queen Mihail's strike team had delivered their blow and paid for it with their lives.

"Choose." I'd almost forgotten the Fae Mother, lost in my own thoughts, but her word centered me on the now.

"Choose what?" I once accepted a gift from the Fae Mother that turned out to be my blessings. After that, I learned to ask for more details.

"If you free him, you will unleash all his power. The constraint cannot be repaired." I knew that. The spider thorns through it looked somewhat permanent.

"How did Queen Mihail do this to him?"

"The Black Queen has pawns everywhere. Our half sister

is patient and has waited several lifetimes to gain her revenge. Do not help her do this."

"I thought Mihail was the one who attacked Grimm." Having a conversation with the fae taxed my patience at times. Their constant conversational shifts made it possible to say yes and have their next statement be "Thank you for offering me your liver."

"Your foe sought power to harm a fairy. The Black Queen sought a pawn to do her bidding. Your enemies aligned against you."

I approached the constraint, reaching out to touch the edges of it. The smooth rock, cold, and dark, hummed under the force of Grimm's power. With my hand on it, it reminded me of listening through a wall. Grimm's voice came through, muffled.

A sound like ice breaking came from the constraint, and as I watched, the veins of black pushed farther into the constraint, stabbing or eating through it, I couldn't tell. It would continue to grow until all the light was blocked and Grimm was completely sealed away.

I hopped down the pyramid and seized a shattered chunk of crystal from the ground. When I finally made it back to the top, I swung the chunk like a hammer, striking the constraint. It rang like a bell, high and long, and spun in midair, throwing off flashes of Grimm's power.

"Can you give me a hand?" I looked back to the Fae Mother, hoping she could lend a crystal shattering spell or two.

"Your decisions are your own. I cannot act, even to protect you." She bowed her head, looking like a Catholic saint.

"I don't need protection. I need help." I swung again, sending sparks off the constraint, and as it resonated, again the crystal thorns grew thicker. Barely a flicker of light made it through the constraint. I grasped at the edges of the constraint, pulling myself up onto the face of it. Black veins covered it like a crystal tangle.

I began to hammer on it, at the center, the broadest, weakest part. With each blow, the thorns shifted and grew, and the ringing sound the constraint made grew so loud I could hear nothing else. With one final blow I drove my hammer down. The crystal clicked, shivered.

I raised my hand for another blow, then stopped, as the

clicking sounds in the crystal matched a recognition point in my brain. A single shard shot off, allowing a ray of blinding light to lance skyward. I tried half rolling, half jumping, but as I reached the edge of the constraint, it exploded.

A volcano of power blasted me into the sky.

Thirty

~⚬~

THE WORST PART, hands down, was the taste. It tasted like I'd always imagined Grimm smelled. The second worst part was when I flew free of the current, tumbling like a rag doll before gravity grabbed me by the ankle and yanked me toward the ground.

I rolled into a skydiving position, more out of instinct than usefulness, as I'd conveniently forgotten to bring a parachute, let alone wear it. I'd done a HALO jump from a bean stalk once, and fallen from the top of a skyscraper in Kingdom. This, I figured, rated somewhere in the middle—high enough to make breathing difficult and my limbs numb from cold, low enough that I didn't mercifully pass out.

I plummeted toward the ground, watching the pyramids and their light beams pass underneath. And I struck something like iron so hard my teeth rattled. I grasped at the nothingness, the empty air that hit me so hard, and fell again, this time straight down.

Then it smashed me in the face, causing me to see stars. And then in the legs, tumbling me over. The next time, it was right across the breasts, which hurt as bad as my face, if not worse.

Over and over, I'd fall a few feet, then slam into something. One of my teeth slipped down my throat, and a surge of copper filled my mouth as I slammed into the wall again.

"I've got you, M." Ari's voice sounded a thousand feet away. The next time I hit something, it was surprisingly soft, being rocks and dirt. I couldn't move, but Ari rolled me over and looked down at me. The pain from the worst beating of my life made it easy to ignore her eyes. Easy to ignore almost everything.

"Stay with me, M. I almost didn't catch you." She held her hands over me, working that hangover magic. It barely touched the agony in my body.

"That was you?" I'm not sure how she understood me, with my lips swollen like that.

"I had to slow you down. You were moving so fast I could barely see you." She lifted my shirt, looking at my ribs.

"Feels funny." Every inch of me tingled with pins and needles and burned with agony at the same time. It was the same feeling I got that time I rode the escalator for nearly sixteen hours as part of a job. My teeth, my ears, everything about me buzzed.

Ari squinted at me. "This isn't good. You're filled with magic, M. Drowning in it. And I think you have a concussion and at least one broken arm. I'll worry about dragging you back to the portal later. Right now I've got to figure out how to drain off this magic before it chokes you."

She lay a hand on my thigh, and a burst of pain like a trumpet shot through me, coming out as a strangled gasp. "No, that won't work. Did you feel that?"

I gasped, breathing raggedly, and nodded. "Little."

The noise that followed sounded like noon at Grand Central Terminal. Like the roar of the entire baseball stadium when someone hits a grand slam. And every one of those voices belonged to Grimm.

I managed to turn my neck, to where a miniature sun glowed, shining so bright that I couldn't stand to look at him. I once saw Grimm, in his native realm. There, as in the mirror, he looked like a butler. The living sun, that was his true form, stripped of all facade. The Fae Mother stood with him, so close the tendrils of light from him flickered around her, making her look ghostly.

Again, the roar of the crowd came, louder. I recognized my name, maybe Ari's, but the thousands of voices drowned out everything else.

"Princess, my father asks that you create him a mirror to translate for you." The Fae Mother stepped out of Grimm's corona so that we could see her.

Ari ran into the desert, beyond my view.

While she was gone, Grimm began to speak again, this time sounding like the whisper of waves on the beach. A thousand voices trying to comfort me, I think.

Ari came back, lugging a large shard of quartz. Setting it up at an angle, she began to murmur, her hand outstretched toward it. My entire body rippled as she drew in magic. Then a glowing pencil of white-hot light shot from her palm, tracing back and forth. The top gradually cooled to glowing red, then, as the image faded from my eyes, I recognized molten silver.

Ari turned the shard over, yelping as the crystal burned her fingertips.

A beam of light that leaped from Sun-Grimm to the quartz began to glow, and a faint image appeared in the silver.

"Thank you, Arianna." Grimm's voice sounded like a loudspeaker at a football game. "Now, I need your assistance with Marissa."

Ari took her fingers out of her mouth. "I'd rather you handled this. I can't even put people to sleep and you want me to heal her?"

"Young lady, I'm the cause of this. Marissa accidentally absorbed some of my power, and it isn't doing her any good. Also, we must practice your telekinesis. It's not necessary to break every bone in someone's body to catch them."

"I can't take the magic out of her. Every time I try, I tear off a little piece of her." Ari leaned over me, staring into each of my eyes.

"I see the witch's mark on you, Arianna. Though it comes with consequences, it also grants you abilities. Use your sight. Use all of it, and the difference between Marissa and the magic drowning her should be evident. I suggest you use it to heal some of her injuries. Just this once, I won't grade you on efficiency."

"Also thought you could do the healing." Ari's annoyance mirrored my own.

"Young lady, look at me. I can barely hold a stable form. I'm not going to risk working healing magic when there's a perfectly capable spell caster standing right in front of me. Now I'm not going to tell you again. Use your sight, and look into her." I resolved that among the many, many other things I had to say to Grimm, at least one of them would be that his teaching manners could use work.

Ari closed her eyes and then began to look over me. I think it bothered me more that she did it that way than looking with those eyes. After a moment, she reached out and touched my solar plexus, barely brushing it. "I understand."

Ari put one hand on my head, the other on my stomach, and drew her mouth into a tight line with concentration. The hand on my stomach turned ice-cold, the one on my head burned like molten lead. I kept waiting for the piercing agony that hit me last time, but as she moved her gaze from point to point, the humming in my bones began to subside. Also, the double vision that left me seeing at least two of Ari drifted back into one.

"I can't do anything about the tooth." Ari glanced up to Grimm. I moved my neck, and while it was stiff, at least I could move it without aching.

"I'll schedule an implant procedure next week." Grimm almost sounded like his normal self.

"Not going to matter. World won't be around by then." I spoke, my voice raspy, but functional.

"Stop moving, keep quiet." Ari moved her hand from my head to my mouth, smothering my protest, as she continued her work. She glanced up at Grimm. "When I'm done, you and I need to talk." She passed her hand over me, like a silkworm wrapping me up in a cocoon, and the pain faded, bit by bit.

After several minutes, Ari stopped to rest, taking a deep breath.

"You need to rest for a spell?" I reached up to grab her shoulder and pulled myself to a sitting position.

"I don't need to rest. If anything, I need to do more. You

have no idea how much power I'm pulling out. I could work miracles with a fraction of this." Ari snapped her fingers, throwing a bolt of lightning that could have powered a city block. "Maybe I could just wave my hand in the light—"

"Princess—" The Fae Mother raised her hand in alarm, though not because of Ari's pitiful lightning bolt. Fae royalty could swallow a bolt like that and have it tickle.

Grimm glared at Ari. "The sheer power would tear your soul from your body. If you so much as make a move toward those beams, I will send you home faster than you can say 'abracadabra.'" Grimm's anger caused the earth to tremble.

"Whatever." Ari slapped a hand on my chest, pushing me down. "I don't know if you've noticed, but your magic lessons didn't exactly help."

By now, it no longer ached to breathe, and my lips felt more like lips than bratwurst. Where my legs, and frankly, almost every part of me had tingled like I was charged with enough static to kill a cockatrice at twenty paces, now only the tips of my fingers pricked like I'd slept on them. "Can we go?"

"You can. The princess and I have much to discuss." Grimm's sun floated over closer to his mirror, opening the way to the path.

"No way. I didn't travel halfway across the galaxy to find you only to be sent home without answers. I know about the pills. And the appointment." I dusted myself off.

"My dear, you've crossed three singularities and haven't even reached the main transfer point. Exactly which galaxy are you halfway across?" Hug him or kill him, the war within me raged, held only by the fact that I wasn't keen on touching a living sun.

"It's all right, M." Ari wiped her hands down her arms, squeezing lightning from her fingertips with each pass. "I think for once he's right. I really need to talk to Grimm alone."

"I think we figured out why you don't grant wishes anymore." I wasn't sure if I should address the mirror or the fusion ball, so I split my address between them. The seconds ticked by as I waited for his confident, smug response.

"Do you?"

Grimm's tone worried me. I glanced over to Ari, but she looked as confused as I did. "We found a wish trapped, on the way here, and—"

"I didn't know that would happen." Ari's face contorted, and I felt like a heel. Actually, like the fungal growth on a dwarf's heel. Maybe worse.

"Yes." Grimm spoke with confidence now, or maybe acceptance. "To grant a wish, you must take its life and claim the power for your own. I no longer grant wishes because I understand the true cost, as do you, now." He spoke once more as the sea of voices, but this time directed to the Fae Mother.

When she answered, I heard "of course" and "gladly" and "I will be sure," and a dozen others all at once. She turned her gaze on me. "Father asks that I send you home, but you must not arrive before he makes it safe."

She reached for me, and I drew back my hand. Last time she touched me, I spent three days in the hospital, one of them hooked to a ventilator. "Don't fear."

Fear seemed like a reasonable response, to be honest. I forced myself to hold steady, then summoned all my will and reached out toward her.

Our fingertips brushed, maybe didn't quite touch, and the air crackled between us. Then she put her hand down and nodded. "It is done."

I let out my breath. Nearly dying once made me understandably nervous about such things. Beyond the tingling in my fingers, I didn't really feel anything. Then I rubbed my fingertips together, and something clinked.

I glanced at my hands. Each finger had a microscopic diamond on the tip. For one brief moment, I was amazed. Then the diamond divided into two. And four, and then too many to count. I had five karat fingers, which would be amazing if the stones weren't embedded in my skin.

I scraped at the stones, diamond on diamond, then looked up, pleading with Grimm. "Help me. Ari, please." I reached for her, and she stepped back, a look of fear in her eyes.

"Marissa, please try to calm down. You are not being harmed." Grimm's assurance did less than nothing for me. "You didn't complain about this last time."

I pulled up the edge of my shirt to see a wave of tiny diamonds crust over my stomach. My hands grew stiffer, harder to move as the diamonds formed layers. "I don't think I was awake for this last time." Then I felt them on my eyelashes. In my hair. I could no longer turn my head.

"She needs time to recover, princess." Grimm turned his attention from me, unaware that I could still hear and see. "And you and I have much to discuss."

The world looked like a kaleidoscope as my eyes closed to slits. Then I was wrapped in lead, held so tight I couldn't move, couldn't take a breath. And at long last emptiness consumed me. What came next, I can't say.

Thirty-One

~

"MARISSA?" IN MY mind, it was Liam's voice. "Marissa?" Except that Liam was a girl. "Can you hear me?" Definitely a girl, and one I recognized.

I opened my eyes, a crust of diamonds falling from them. With a little work, the casing on my mouth and jaw cracked, and I spat out a tiny chunk of diamond and drool. "Where am I?"

Ari reached down and picked a piece of diamond off my face. "We're back at the Agency."

For a moment, I had this glorious thought. I looked straight into her eyes, which I knew would be blue as always.

Her witch's eyes stared back at me. "It's going to be okay." She gave me a hug, crunching the shell around me as she did. "It's going to be okay, I promise."

"If he told you that, don't believe him." I shook myself and kicked my feet free. Someone had leaned me up against the wall like a crate. I took a few unsteady steps, leaving a glittering trail. "Need to change. I've got diamonds in places I don't even want to talk about."

"Girl's best friend?" Ari gave me the gigawatt smile.

"That would be you. Thanks for not letting me pancake out there."

Ari swept her hand, and the jewels at my feet danced into a pile. "I've got some learning to do about how to catch people, but I'm getting better."

"I'm heading to the showers." I stumbled toward the door and opened it.

"Handmaiden." Malodin leaned in the hallway, waiting. His voice made my skin crawl. "I trust you enjoyed your nap?"

"Get out of my Agency." I spat a diamond at him.

"Marissa, my dear, I've allowed him to stay on his best behavior." Grimm appeared in the hallway mirror, looking sharp as always. If anything, he'd upgraded to a finer silk suit. "When Mr. Malodin first arrived, he was quite rude. Michael helped us reach an understanding of how one behaves around the Fairy Godfather. On the plus side, floor three will be opening for lease soon."

Malodin's sneer turned into a barely controlled mask of rage. "When I destroy the world, I will start with this building. Handmaiden, your third plague is due. The harbingers have almost reached the city."

"Already?" I glanced to Grimm, wondering how long I was asleep.

"Ari, you have a visitor in cargo." Mikey shouldered past Malodin, pushing him out of the way. "Looks like a garbage man, talks like a lawyer." He glanced at the mirror. "You need me to tear demon brat here to pieces again?"

"That won't be necessary, Michael. Please make sure the one o'clock shipments are correct today." Grimm waved him off, and Ari followed.

"You'll get your plague." I leaned against the wall, trying to figure out a way to twist my words.

"A proper plague. Something that causes carnage and suffering. Something that brings fear. When the harbingers arrive, you *will* do your part." Malodin turned without waiting for me to answer and stalked down the hall.

"Marissa, step into my office, please." With those words alone, Grimm sent me back to being an eighteen-year-old recruit, not even trusted to carry a bag from one end of the city to the other. I walked down the hall to his office, figuring my shower would have to wait.

Grimm waited in his desk mirror. I expected anger. All I saw was concern. He kept his eyes closed as he spoke. "My dear, what have you done?"

"It was an accident. I went down to seal off the dealing room, and he was waiting." I sank into a leather chair, rubbing my fingers over the leather till it squeaked.

"Marissa, I only have a few hard rules."

I shook my head, sending diamonds scattering. "I know. No princesses. Speaking of which, where exactly is Ari?"

"She's downstairs fighting with the lich, who wants her to seek safety in his basement when the apocalypse arrives."

"Oh, and let's not forget rule number two: no men. Liam is where? Doing what?"

Grimm opened his eyes and looked over the edge of his glasses. "Those two are special circumstances. When I say No Apocalypse, I mean No Apocalypse. And your boyfriend is preparing to board a flight home as we speak."

My hand whipped to my bracelet as I called his name. "Liam!"

"Marissa, sweetheart." He sounded like always. Just like I remembered him in my dreams. "We're kind of having a problem. G, there were a few issues with the job, and the vampires aren't happy about it." With Grimm's aid, Liam appeared in the full-length mirror before the portal. He sported a beard that would have made Paul Bunyan jealous and fresh scars along his arms and chest.

"Stay calm, sir. I'll negotiate with them shortly. A few issues indeed." Grimm said we'd basically own them skin and bone if anything happened to Liam. The vampires, it seemed, were more attached to their skin and bones than I gave them credit for.

"I love you. I've missed you so much." If tears crept to the edges of my eyes, I didn't mind. Some tears I welcomed. The diamonds, I could live without.

"I'll be home before you know it. My scaly side is ready for a nice long rest, and I feel like I haven't lifted a hammer in ages. I miss the city. This place has great views, but it's a real fixer-upper." Liam yawned and stretched his arms. Behind him, a blond woman with a tan complexion approached and said something in yet another one of those languages I don't speak. Liam nodded and replied with a sound that I'd heard when people had seizures.

"You understand that?"

"It was either 'The masters want to meet downstairs' or something about a school bus and a rabid badger. I'm okay with either. G's going to tell them how it is, then I'm on the first flight out of here. Woke up in a pile of armor."

"Queen Mihail. She tried to kill everyone. Ari, me, Grimm, everyone. She sent a strike team of princes after you." I wanted to hug him. To wrap my arms around him. To do carnal things with him that would scald poor Ari's eyes if she walked into my office without knocking.

He ran a hand along that ferocious beard and growled. "I'll deal with her."

"You'll have to get in line. I think everyone at the Agency is after her, and she's holed up in the Court of Queens. It's going to be like Gwendolyn all over again, except that I can't even bring charges against her."

"M, why don't you have Ari take you on a field trip? She's a princess, right? Isn't that almost as good as a Queen?"

Behind him, the vampire woman spoke again. Their language seemed mostly made up of vowels and biting one's own tongue.

"In a moment," said Liam, then turned back to me. "I'm sorry, M. Negotiations are starting, and I've got to be there." Then his gaze fell to my hand, and he squinted.

I cut the connection out of equal parts fear and frustration. I wanted to call him back. To hear him talk, the sound of his voice, and imagine his callused hands on my cheeks. To ask him exactly what there was to negotiate. The other part of me was near certain that he'd seen the ring. His surprise for me, which I'd carried around the whole time.

"Grimm. What in Kingdom is going on with Liam? Negotiations?"

He snapped into the mirror like I'd turned on the television set. "I trust you feel recovered?"

"I do, though I've got enough gemstones on me to start a jewelry store. What could you possibly have to negotiate?" I walked out, heading toward my office. Might as well sit in a comfy chair while I raked Grimm over the coals.

Grimm followed, looking at me from anything with even a trace of shine. "Our vampire friends are not happy with the terms of their contract and would like to renegotiate."

"You can do that? I mean, once a contract is signed?"

"Marissa, contracts are renegotiated every day. Such as yours. The time frames for each event were very poorly laid out, a fact I've exploited to gain a few days." He disappeared, and the contract scrolled across the mirror, with a few of the squigglies glowing in gold. Not that I could read them any better.

The moment Grimm returned, I locked eyes with him. From the subtle change in his face, he knew what was coming. "Can you fix Ari?"

He waited to answer me. Probably weighing a dozen lies to see if any fit. "I cannot, my dear. Any more than I could heal the handmaiden's mark. Arianna will carry the scars of Wild Magic the rest of her life. My training will ensure that the princes of Kingdom find other, easier targets to kill."

He didn't mention it was my fault. He didn't need to.

"Ask, Marissa. There's no easy way to go about this." He closed his eyes, took a deep breath.

There was a time I'd have fallen for that fatherly look. The kind older gentleman. That time was gone. "You son of a bitch, I don't know where to start. When were you going to let me in on the fact that you didn't have all your power?"

He paused for a moment, gathering his breath, but I didn't give him a chance to answer. "I didn't ever have an appointment with a doctor in Kingdom, did I? Those pills you gave me are iron supplements, not birth control. Did you want me to pass on Liam's curse? And why didn't you tell me the Black Queen was your daughter?"

I think the cursing bothered him more than the questions. As a fairy, curses were no laughing matter, and for the first six years he made me hallucinate about swallowing soap any time I cursed.

"Isolde. Her name was, and will always be, Isolde. It is true. I granted a princess a wish, and she wished that I would love her. Our daughter was my greatest pride. My most shining accomplishment. Skilled in magic beyond any other, gifted with her mother's love and a fairy's power.

"Understand this, Marissa: Everything you've heard about her was true. She took her skills in magic and used them against people, changing them inside and out. She took the power I gave her and used it to crush nations underfoot.

"And I am the one who forged a sword to kill her. I am the one who arranged for a fair prince to wield it. And I knelt by her side as they burned her, holding her power back until the flames consumed her." A single tear of glitter ran from his eye.

"So, yes. The Black Queen was my daughter. Yes, I am responsible for the evil she caused. And I took that responsibility. I ordered the death of my own child, and held her while she burned."

I thought of the Root of Lies. How he'd always kept it in his office. Sweet or creepy, I couldn't quite make up my mind.

"You had limits put on your power. As punishment."

"Protection, for both of us. My daughter's power is derived from my own. While I remained limited, she was but a shadow." Grimm opened his eyes, alert.

That wasn't right. Couldn't be right. I'd seen him. Seen his frozen image, the way the black thorns choked the light from his crystal, sapping his power.

"I saved you. There wasn't any light getting through."

"My dear, I could have burst through that constraint with only the slightest flicker of thought. Indeed, I had grown tired of the bounds on my power and decided to throw them off, when the time was right." I hated it when Grimm used that "as you should well know" tone, but this nagging feeling in my stomach said this is what the Fae Mother tried to tell me.

"When would the time be right?"

"In about eighty years, or so. I think that would have given you long enough to live a natural life, expire of natural causes. Then I could release myself, deal with my daughter, and continue business as usual."

The impact of what I'd done finally reached me. All the anger and righteous offense drained out, leaving me weak. "So where is she? How long do I have?"

Grimm disappeared from the mirror, and the realm where he trained Ari came into view. The thorn tree that loomed over the plain, covered in flowers. "My daughter is no more prescient than I am, my dear. She foolishly anchored her spirit to a tree in another realm. I hope she enjoys an eternity of sunset."

"You could have told me. I trusted you."

Grimm put one hand to his forehead, rubbing his eyebrows. "Have you done nothing you regret? Nothing you are ashamed of, or would take back, if the laws of the universe allowed it?"

Ari. I'd give anything if only I could have known what dropping a spellbook in her lap would cause. A single question to Grimm, and I'd have known. Instead, I pushed her, part of me as excited as she was as her power developed. I dropped my eyes, unable to stare, unwilling to show the tears that welled up in them.

"Arianna's condition is not your fault. Look at me, Marissa."

"I don't appreciate you reading my mind."

His laughter caused the mirror to vibrate, a deep, rolling laugh that turned his face red. "I know you. I've watched you more closely than you could possibly realize. If the wind blows wrong, part of you wonders if it was your fault. If the cab pulls away, you blame yourself for not running faster. Some things are beyond your control."

"Why didn't you make an appointment for me?" After the shock of learning about the Black Queen, a ball of fear rumbled in my stomach as I ran over the possible reasons.

"You didn't need it. I'm sorry for the deception with your pills. I wanted to avoid this conversation for as long as possible, and your red blood cell count is always low. I wanted to spare you this pain for as long as possible." He waited for a moment, long enough for my hands to go numb from the grip I had on the chair. "Marissa, you can't have children."

Thirty-Two

∼⌒∼

ALL THE MAGIC in the world couldn't soften that crushing blow. I sagged onto the bed, refusing to accept it. The sane part of me remembered the only thing Grimm valued more than magic was knowledge. "How long have you known?"

"Two years, my dear. I needed to be able to plan your maternity leave."

"Was it something that happened on the job? Something I was exposed to?" The number of things I'd gotten into that might be considered hazardous to my health would fill an encyclopedia. I held my breath while I waited for his answer.

"No. I believe you have always been this way. It isn't something you did, or something done to you. It is no one's fault."

I caught a hitching sob in my throat, trying to turn it to anger. Trying to turn it back on him. The only thing that came out was a squeak. "Don't tell Liam. I don't want him to hear it from you."

Grimm bowed his head in acceptance, then faded away in the silence. Alone, with only the muffled sounds of Ari's voice through the walls, I lay my head down on the desk, covered my head with my jacket, and wept for children I would never have.

* * *

I SPENT SEVERAL hours alone, until the rational side of me kept nagging. If the world ended, not being able to have children wouldn't make a difference. I put my hand on my wrist and called Grimm. He snapped into view, his face scrunched up in a scowl. "Do you know what that piper you found is doing? She leads an entire flock of poodles around. Bought them collars. I caught her and Michael playing Frisbee in the park."

"I've got bigger problems. End of the world. Apocalypse, remember?" I liked to face my problems head-on.

"My dear, I am well aware of that. And I think there's an answer you'll enjoy greatly." The smug grin on his face made me wonder exactly what crackpot idea he'd settled on.

"Kill Malodin?"

"No. Settle a score with Queen Mihail. I have no qualms about having someone killed, when necessary, but I want that meddlesome woman alive. She's the key to getting out of your contract. You see, Malodin made a deal with her before you. Demons are only allowed one active contract, so Malodin is in breach of his until his terms are fulfilled."

"I want in on this." Ari stood at my office door, once again eavesdropping. For a princess, she did that a lot.

"Come in, Arianna. I'm glad to hear that, since you are a key component in my plan." Grimm nodded toward one of my chairs.

Ari slipped into a seat. "I'd like to throw a spell or two Mihail's direction."

"I was thinking something more mundane, yet effective. She tried to have Arianna killed, and so can be charged in the Court of Queens. Indeed, it is the only place where you will gain the upper hand."

"Not a queen. Not even a princess. In case you can't see from that mirror, I'm a witch." Ari spat the word *princess* out as if she'd said "dead toad."

"You are hardly the first princess scarred by Wild Magic, and no power on earth can change the mark on your soul. I've checked your soul quite carefully, and you bear no darkness.

You can enter the Court of Queens to seek redress from Queen Mihail." Grimm's tone allowed no question.

"If it gets me within hair-pulling distance of her, I'm up for it. I haven't been there in years." Ari sat up.

I made a fist and pointed it at her. "No pulling hair. Thumbs in the eye socket, smash the nose into your knee. I want a full account when you get back."

Grimm cleared his throat. "You'll be going as well, Marissa."

"Not a princess. I mean, for real, not a princess. You need those glasses adjusted." My jealousy of princesses' natural luck faded the longer I watched what Ari went through.

"No. But no queen brings a charge directly against another. They have their handmaiden do it."

"No." I sat up and slammed my hand on the desk.

Ari giggled. "If Marissa is my handmaiden, does she have to do what I tell her?"

"No." I glared at her, which only caused her to laugh harder. "She's not a queen, can't pick handmaidens, and I'm betting her stepmother ain't going to designate me one. Good plan, bad execution."

Grimm shook his head. "Marissa, surely you expect I have a way for you to enter the Court of Queens." Grimm had a sly smile on his face. He had something up his sleeves. If he had sleeves, real ones, that is.

"About time you made me a princess."

He sighed in exasperation. "I will do no such thing. Let us say you went by proxy, for another queen. It was not uncommon for a queen to send her handmaiden instead."

"I prefer the term *agent*. You know someone who would let me do that?"

He nodded toward the door. "Go to my office."

We slipped out, passing the temporary offices where my enchanters were loading into cardboard boxes anything not nailed down.

Grimm waited in his mirror. "I have a signet ring, from someone who died."

"And they'd let me in with it?" I walked over to the wall, looking at the hundreds of tiny containers and bottles, souvenirs from several thousand years of wish granting.

"A handmaiden is considered queen while she wears it." He appeared in the stainless steel plating at the far end, and I followed.

"Don't they take them back when queens die?"

"My dear, the authorities were otherwise occupied."

I shook my head. "If she's dead, they'll throw me out again."

Grimm pointed to a tiny metal case on the lowest shelf. "Ah yes, but first they'd need to convene and prove it. And with the other queens present . . ."

"I could charge Mihail for attacking Ari." I opened the case to find a dozen different rings. Some dazzled with diamonds, some that shimmered and moved. One was solid back with serpents engraved on it and a purple sheen to the metal. I spent minutes looking at each, trying to pick out the right one.

The ring I kept coming back to was a simple silver ring. No decoration, and it didn't feel like magic. I slipped it onto my finger next to the engagement ring, contemplating the look. "What do you think?"

Grimm hadn't spoken the entire time I looked at the case. "I think I expected you to choose that one. You are correct. They'll throw you out, but with charges leveled, the damage will already be done. Then we negotiate. She holds Malodin in breach of contract in return for us not demanding retribution." He watched me fidget with my hands. "You do know you are supposed to wait until Liam asks to accept his ring."

I smiled at Grimm. "I already know what my answer is. Keep an eye on the piper. Let me grab something from my office, then we're going into Kingdom."

"Keep it hidden in your pocket; don't put it on until you reach the Court of Queens." Grimm's tone took on the same deathly chill he used to inform people their son would be remaining toadish.

"Am I going to become a ringwraith?"

"Hardly, but the queens have prying eyes everywhere, and it wouldn't do to give your enemies any warning. And regarding your potential engagement, I suppose I should offer you congratulations in advance, Marissa," said Grimm.

I smiled all the way to the car.

* * *

THE ENTRANCE TO the Court of Queens moves. I have no idea where the court actually is. Not sure anyone really does, but the entrance is what counts. We drove down into Kingdom, then walked to the old castle.

"You'd make better time if you weren't carrying a package." Grimm watched us from a storefront window. I slipped my Bluetooth earpiece off. With it on, in the city, folks figured I was on my cell or insane.

"Ask yourself a question. What has Marissa got in the box?" I handed it off to Ari to carry for a moment, letting my aching arms rest.

Grimm disappeared, off to slaughter some bunnies and check the auguries. We made it two more blocks before he reappeared, coming from every single reflective surface in sight.

The look of horror on his face shocked me. He practically shouted. "Marissa! You said nothing about the Gray Man."

"Nothing to say. She sent him after Ari. He won't be harming her." I took my box back. "I figure there's a reward on his head."

Grimm whistled, long and low. "You have no idea how many young ladies that monster killed. Once he discovered bone magic, even I couldn't take action against him."

"Dad used to say that he'd creep into my room and take me if I didn't go to sleep. I never dreamed he was real." Ari switched sides with me, as if the head in the box might bite her.

"Never should've called me princess. Anyway, like I said, might be good for a dime."

"Marissa, Rip Van Winkle is the subject of one of the earliest bounties. Nearly a pound of Glitter offered by the Sixteenth Royal Family." Grimm beckoned up the street, no longer on every surface.

"Seven. There are seven royal families. All of whom are assholes." I glanced over at Ari. "Except you."

"And Wyatt. And his mother."

"Jury's still out."

"There were thirty families at one point, but most of them were slaughtered. The men were slaughtered, the women married to the sons of the survivors. The Sixteenth Royal Family was devoured by, let us see . . ." Grimm faded out again.

We finally reached the entrance to the Court of Queens. The old castle. The castle the government used to operate from, so long ago.

"Ready?" I glanced over at Ari. Beads of sweat lined her forehead.

"No. I hate this place almost as much as you hate the post office." Ari took my hand and marched toward the castle door. She knocked, and the massive doors slid open.

I'd never quite gotten used to moving entrances. The room that the doors revealed looked like the waiting area for a posh restaurant. A short man, more reminiscent of a barrel with arms and legs than a human, stood beside a short podium.

Ari jerked me close by the elbow. "Watch your mouth with the doorman."

"Who claims entrance to the Court of Queens?" He stepped around, blocking the arched doorway beyond.

Ari dropped my hand and stepped forward. "I do. I am Princess Arianna Thromson."

The Court doorman looked at Ari and smiled. He knew without checking. Then his gaze turned to me, and something like a cold spotlight swept over me. "You don't belong here."

"We didn't walk all the way through Kingdom to get turned away. Next time, I'll make reservations, I promise."

He looked over at Ari. "My lady, does your closet door no longer work? I'll send someone to repair it."

Ari let out a tiny squeak, and the tips of her ears flushed red. "I don't use that way anymore."

"We'll talk about this later," I said, assuring myself that I'd take plenty of time to discuss with Ari what else she might have failed to mention. I turned back to the doorman and slipped the ring from my pocket. "I have this."

His eyes widened and the corners of his mouth turned down in a frown. "If you dare, put it on."

I slipped it on over the engagement ring. Grimm had me prepared for I don't know what. Turning invisible? Being able to fly? I had mood rings that did more. The doorman stepped out of the way, and Ari and I entered.

The Court of Queens resembled sixteenth-century palace meets modern-day spa and movie theater. A wide amphitheater opened before us, and at the back women lounged, having their hair done, feet up, and drinking what I hoped were margaritas.

"The Princess Arianna, Princess of Clouds," said the doorman in a voice that echoed through the hall.

I'd never heard Ari's title before. "Clouds? You never mentioned that. Fluffy white clouds. Awwww."

Ari elbowed me.

The doorman looked to me and took a deep breath. "Present by proxy, Isolde Faron, Queen of Thorns."

Thirty-Three

SILENCE LAY LIKE a heavy quilt across the Court of Queens for moments. Then whispers began to filter through it, until it sounded like a windstorm. From one of the side halls at the back of the court, a woman emerged, followed by a group of handmaidens.

I recognized the Dian-Xi, Queen of the Fifth Royal Family, current High Queen. She approached and bowed, bending at the waist until her head dipped low, but not too low. Her gray hair, pulled back in a bun, and tan skin made me think of Death. Her gaze, sharp as knives, swept over us, as she decided what sort of trouble we represented.

"Princess, it has been too long since I last saw you." The Dian-Xi's voice cracked when she spoke.

Ari curtsied. "Thank you, Your Highness."

"Well, what do we have here?" I recognized the voice the moment I heard it. A high-pitched woman's voice, like finger-nails on a chalkboard mixed with a cheerleader chant.

Ari shuddered. "Gwendolyn." That one word had more venom than all the asps at the Kingdom Post Office combined. Ari's stepmother ranked pretty high on people I'd like to harm. In my defense, she tried to kill us both.

"Arianna, you will call me Mother."

I'd been in deep freezers with more warmth than the two of them.

"And you will call me Ari." Ari looked at her stepmother, and she saw Ari's eyes for the first time.

"Witch!" Gwendolyn shrieked, causing an even louder stir. "I knew you played with Wild Magic, girl. Someone should have killed you when they had the chance. You have no place here. Go to the Witch's gallery, and never let me see you again." With each word, her voice rose in pitch, until the last was almost a scream.

"Patience." The Dian-Xi walked over, her shoulders stooped, and took Ari's hands. "The doorman would not have let you in, child, if you were a creature of darkness." She glanced upward, into the cavernous reaches of the court.

A second level, like an opera house, stood above the amphitheater. There, shadowy forms moved back and forth, covered in cloaks. "If you take evil into your heart, you will join them there. For now, you are welcome here."

She turned to me. "Why are you here? Why do you bring the name of suffering into our refuge?"

"I'm here to settle with Queen Mihail. She tried to have Ari killed."

"Those are serious charges, handmaiden. You will give me an hour to convene the full court. In the interest of peace, you two will spend it in your private lounges. Come out, and I will have you both removed. The court is a place of peace." The Dian-Xi stared at me as she spoke the last words, then took the arms of her handmaidens and shuffled away.

Ari grabbed me, towing me down around the edge of the amphitheater, to one of the three halls that split off. "You heard her."

"You have a private lounge? And you crashed in my apartment?" Ari owed me quite a few explanations at this point.

"My last birthday gift from Mom. I don't like going there. All it does is remind me of what I've lost." Ari halted.

The guards before us did not move an inch. "Princess, you may pass. Handmaiden, by order of the High Queen, you will go to your queen's lounge." One of them pointed, across, to the other side.

I dropped Ari's hand, ignoring the stares from around the room.

"Call me," Ari said, then slipped past the guards. She practically skipped down the hallway, then disappeared into a room.

"Can I visit her?"

The guard pointed again, and I shifted my box to the other arm and walked around the back edge. One thing I hadn't realized was how large this place was. At the back of the amphitheater, down marble stairs, a full spa stood. The women inside looked at me with fear or confusion as I passed.

The next section had full-service restaurants, and the next clothes. The Court of Queens had what amounted to a miniature mall built in. When finally I reached the far edge, I turned into the last hallway, passing the guards without a word.

Dust blanketed the floor a few feet in. With each step, I sent up tiny clouds. The most striking thing about the hallway was that it ended in a single door, heavy oak carved with figures on horseback. I reached for the door, and my hand tingled where the ring touched it. The door swung open ahead of my hand.

Now, normally rules are that you never go through a door that opens itself. Particularly not when the door leads to the one-time private hangout of an evil queen. Thing was, the High Queen had been quite clear about this being a place of peace. So I pushed the door wider and stepped in.

I don't know what I expected. Something black. Something draped in cobwebs, like the hallway, or with bones on every table. Maybe pentagrams on the floor, or tapered candles. Instead, it looked almost pleasant. From the full couch, to the massive bed, it looked more like an ancient hotel room than the lair of evil.

Carrying a box with the head of a serial killer halfway through Kingdom had my arm aching, so I dropped it at the door. I ran my fingers on the black marble that formed a hot-tub-sized bath. The towels on the side felt soft, almost fluffy, instead of stale. Like the Black Queen had stepped out for a few minutes, but would return at any moment.

A knock on the door had me grabbing for my gun, which of course, I left back at the office. The door swung open, and the doorman entered.

"I have missed her presence these last four hundred years." He looked around, as if expecting the Black Queen to appear.

"If you are four hundred years old, there are women who will kill for your skin-care secrets."

He almost smiled at my joke. Almost. "I am an expression of the magic here. Judge before the court, bouncer at the door, waiter at the restaurant. I bestowed the first crowns. I record the titles of each when she is born, and when she ascends to the throne. I come to warn you, handmaiden. Dress for court appropriately, and make yourself presentable." He pointed to the wardrobe on the right.

"I didn't bring any clothes."

"Your queen's clothes will fit you, though they may be too loose in the chest and a bit tight in the hips."

I looked at the dressing mirror, full of odd bottles of makeup, containers, combs, and pins. A white gauze hung over the mirror. It came off with a simple pull, showing a mirror like soapy water.

"Your queen has never liked mirrors. Rub it with your hand."

I did, and it became clear. Then slowly, the milky white returned, like someone showered right next to it. When I looked back, the doorman was gone.

For a queen of evil, Isolde had pretty good sense in fashion. The dresses she wore looked fancy, but lacked sweeping trains or hoop bottoms. The black leather and cloth looked less like a dominatrix outfit and more like an old-style business suit. I slipped into one of the outfits, closing the hook and latches, and admired how well it fit. These weren't clothes from someone used to sitting and preening. The Black Queen must have been hands-on, and kicked ass doing it.

I sat down to apply makeup, bypassing "rose shorn" and "pearl dust" in favor of the basics from my purse. As always, my hair refused to obey, fighting the brush strokes and returning to its unruly state. In one of the many drawers, I found a set of bone hair combs, and pinned my hair back on both sides.

I rubbed the dressing mirror, looking at my hair, turning to the side and glancing over my shoulder to make sure the outfit didn't leave my rear showing. As the mirror fogged over again, a chill ran over me. I approached, watching my own outline take dim form, almost certain I'd seen something else, for a moment, looking out at me.

Taking a towel from the tub, I caught my breath, stomped on the butterflies in my stomach, and nearly broke the mirror as I forced the towel down it. I forced my eyes open and almost screamed when I saw eyes looking back.

"Marissa?"

I let out a gasp, and the shaky adrenaline rush began to fade.

Grimm. Just Grimm.

"Why are you wearing that?" His gaze flickered to the top of my head. "Who told you to wear her clothes, her jewelry? What is wrong with you? Have you never seen me before?" The room trembled slightly. Anger. That was anger in his voice.

"The doorman said to wear them. Said I had to dress up for the full court. And I didn't think it was you in the mirror. I saw something." I reached up to take a hairpin out and stopped. "Was it . . . ?"

"She is dead, Marissa." Not anger. Sadness. "Please, my dear, never wear her clothing. If you have any respect for me, you will never do that. When I saw you, for a moment, my dear, I imagined my daughter."

I glanced down at my hand. "You could have told me it was her ring."

"Would you have dared use it if I had?" Grimm dropped his shoulders and let out a breath.

"Never." I had so many things to be angry at Grimm for. All the things he'd never told me, all the secrets he could have shared, but it wasn't in his nature to speak openly. Secrets were his native tongue. "I didn't mean any disrespect. To you. The High Queen sent Ari and I to our rooms." As I spoke, the milky fade at the edges moved in and out, like an oil stain, but it never covered Grimm's face.

"My dear, I believe you. I just wasn't ready to see anyone wearing that outfit. It's what she wore when she went out on assignments with her mother. They were my most trusted agents." I let it go. If Grimm married someone, I figured that trusting them more than me was probably okay. "Arianna would like to speak with you."

A knock at the door nearly gave me a heart attack for the second time in a row. The doorman entered. "Handmaiden, the court is assembled. It is time."

"I have to change." I started to unhook the top.

"Marissa, go. You can dispose of the clothing later. My feelings on the matter shouldn't impact your focus." Grimm faded out, letting the soap cover him.

"Now come," said the doorman.

"Can you carry that box?" I pointed.

"It would be my pleasure. Shall I have it placed in the bag check?" At my nod, he placed his hand on the box, and it shimmered out of view.

As we walked down the abandoned hall, I stopped, wondering about something Grimm said. "Do I look like her? Like the Black Queen?"

The doorman looked at me, squinting. "You both have brown hair and brown eyes, but your queen is more beautiful than words can describe. I will have a painting of her sent to you so you may recognize her face when she comes."

Queens, princesses, and handmaidens lined the plush seats of the amphitheater when we emerged from the hall. The doorman led me down to the front, where the Dian-Xi waited. On one side of her, Queen Mihail stood, dressed in a gray business suit, her makeup flawless. The doorman stepped between us. "Accusers must stand on the left." I walked to the other side, where Ari waited.

Ari wore a simple white dress with long sleeves, and with makeup that hid her freckles and made her lips rich red. I suppressed a giggle at the black sunglasses she wore over her eyes.

"Marissa? What happened to your clothes? You look like a hunter, or barbarian, or something. I love the hair though." Ari stepped to one side, making room for me.

"Let's say my room hasn't had a fashion update for four hundred years—" A whistle from the Dian-Xi silenced the amphitheater.

"Sisters, I gather you to hear charges. Queen Mihail stands accused of assassination attempts on royalty of another family." The Dian-Xi waited until the murmurs died down.

Queen Mihail spoke first. "Who brings these baseless charges?"

"I do." Ari stepped forward, taking off her glasses.

"Nonsense." Queen Mihail gave a presumptuous laugh. "Girl, it is bad form for royalty to act on their own behalf. Not that you seem to know anything about good form."

I stepped forward, wishing I'd brought a stun gun. "That's why I'm here. I charge you with an attempt on Ari's life. You tried to kill her with an apple. You sent the Gray Man to kill her." I kept my voice calm and my gaze fixed on the Dian-Xi as I spoke.

"Doorman, does she speak the truth?" The Dian-Xi turned toward the doorman, and he walked over and took my hand. His ice-cold fingers brushed my palm, sending a shock through me.

"She does." The doorman stepped away.

"Queen Mihail, what have you to say?" The Dian-Xi's tone was neither accusatory nor supportive. Just simple, direct, factual.

"The apple was intended for Marissa Locks, who is no form of royalty. I'm not even convinced she's considered human. Nor does she have standing to act as handmaiden. Her friend there is no queen, and her mother appointed no handmaidens for her." Mihail kept her gaze on the High Queen, but the edges of her mouth turned up in a smile.

"Marissa, young lady, what have you to say?" The Dian-Xi looked back to me.

I made up my mind. Made a decision. This had to end, and it had to end right there. I held up my hand. "I bear the Black Queen's ring."

"Young lady, do you understand the penalty for using a queen's signet without permission?" The doorman stepped forward, his eyes locked on mine. "It is death."

"I too challenge her standing. The Black Queen is dead." Ari's stepmother stood up in the gallery, her hand raised.

"Then how did I get this?" I turned my hand over and pulled the sleeve back, showing the handmaiden's mark. "I have her ring, and her mark. I am the handmaiden, and I dare you to prove otherwise."

The gasps in the crowd grew louder, causing the Dian-Xi

to whistle. "Doorman, is it truly the mark? If it is not, remove it, and the hand."

He stepped up beside me and seized my hand. "I am sorry." With that, a power like a heat lamp and hot tub combined blasted over my hand. When it withdrew, my bare skin lay clean and tan, without a trace of the handmaiden's mark.

I cursed myself for believing Grimm, that he couldn't remove it, and opened my mouth to give voice to the foul thoughts within.

And my skin split open in a long line, tearing as if sliced by something jagged and raw. I think I screamed, as line by line, my skin tore open, until every last line of the mark emerged. I can't really say what I did. I remember Ari tackling the doorman, and I remember feeling like he'd wrenched my arm off at the elbow.

Chaos ruled the court, until I rolled over and found my hand still attached. Ari had the doorman in a hammerlock, doing her best to suffocate him.

"Stop. Stop." I choked out the words, mindless of the tears that dripped down my face. Ari let him go and backed away.

"See?" The doorman rubbed his throat, then pointed. The black lines dripped with blood. "It is real."

Now people actually fled, running for the halls.

"Peace!" The Dian-Xi's order swept like a spell over the amphitheater, locking people in place.

Gwendolyn approached the High Queen. "I maintain my challenge. Mark or no, the Black Queen is dead."

The High Queen looked down at the doorman. "Show me Isolde Faron."

"As you command, Your Highness." He dipped his head, concentrating. The audience gasped, staring past me.

"M, you need to look." Ari put her hand on my shoulder and turned me. The wall behind shone with silver light as it transformed into a mirror. I recognized the grass and sky of Fairy Godmother's realm. Where the thorn tree once stood, a blasted, torn stump remained, shattered into fragments like toothpicks.

Thirty-Four

❧

"I CANNOT FIND her, alive or dead." The doorman hung his head, ashamed, and the view of the field faded, leaving the wall normal.

"Then let it be left to her queen," said Gwendolyn. "Let the matter be between them." Across the amphitheater, faces nodded, voices murmured in agreement.

The High Queen crossed her arms. "So be it. You may remove that ring when your queen takes it from you, hand-maiden."

I clutched at my hand, but no matter how I moved my fingers, it stayed in place, turning loosely, but refusing to slide off. That was going to make removing the engagement ring even harder. Almost as hard as explaining why I was already wearing it.

"Your charges are accepted before the court. For the matter of the apple, an assault on even a commoner is not to be taken lightly. I fine you sixteen ounces of Glitter, Queen Mihail. Consider your actions carefully before acting again." The Dian-Xi nodded to herself, obviously pleased with her punishment.

"I'll have a gift bag sent over." Queen Mihail didn't bother hiding her joy.

"What about the Rip Van Winkle? You sent him for Ari." I tried to shove down the disappointment. The feeling of hopelessness. What had any of this accomplished? At the name of the Gray Man, queens began to giggle, like I'd asked for an honest politician.

Mihail chuckled. "Well, Kingdom be blessed, he obviously didn't find her."

"He found me." I began to count the number of steps separating us. I could have my hands on her throat in three seconds. Maybe less.

"I'm so sorry. I'll send over another pound to make amends."

In the seats, chuckles of laughter began to echo out. The shrewd queen, once again flaunting her riches and power.

"I want my reward for killing him." I glanced to the doorman.

If I thought I had the court's attention before, I didn't know stares or rapt faces.

The High Queen stepped down, walking over to look at me. "The Gray Man is a child's tale. You should depart before you anger your betters."

"He is not." The doorman stepped forward. "Though you are safe within my confines, I have records of all his victims. A blood bounty promise was granted for his head. I concur. The princess killer is dead, by her hand. The bounty is due." He looked to Queen Mihail. "The family Mihail consumed family Lach Connor, taking their power and assuming their debts. It falls to you."

"Fine. Three pounds. Consider this the luckiest day of your miserable life." Mihail shrugged and started to walk away.

The doorman flickered. One moment he was before me, the next he was blocking her exit. "The bounty was one pound, twelve hundred years ago. With interest . . ." He leaned over and whispered the rest to her.

It brought peace to my aching arm, the way she gasped, the curses that erupted from her. "Never. No one has that, not even the High Queen. You could unseal the realms and not have that much magic. I refuse." She attempted to yank her arm free and squealed in pain.

He held on to her like a boat anchor. "It is a blood promise, Your Highness. Backed by your throne. Pay the debt, or I will take it from you in forfeit." I wasn't the only person who felt the mood shift, as people once again fled. This time, the High Queen didn't call them back.

"Irina." The High Queen dared call Mihail by her given name. "Calm down. Marissa, the blood promise cannot be kept. Will you compromise?"

"I'm glad you asked. See, I want something. Mihail made a deal with Malodin. He didn't deliver on that contract, and shouldn't have been allowed to enter a contract with me." I caught Queen Mihail's eye, like looking into the eyes of a rabid panther. "You hold him in contempt of his contract, you can keep all the Glitter. Everyone lives." It was about time we got to something reasonable.

I said reasonable. When she looked back at me, I caught a glimpse into her soul, and while I wasn't always the best judge of character, I felt fairly certain reason hadn't slept in her bed for decades. The look of rage on her face defied words as she twisted in the doorman's grasp. "I am nothing without my word."

"Irina, choose carefully." The Dian-Xi put a hand on her shoulder.

I saw the slap coming, only because I'd gotten the backhand from Ari's mother the same way once before. Queen Mihail sent the High Queen rolling with a backhand. "Never. Let the world burn around you. Let everything die. I promised you rewards beyond anything a fairy could deliver, in return for my son. I would sooner die than grant your request."

She bit her own arm, drawing blood, then spat it. "Demon. I release you from your contract. Keep your payment."

The lights in the court dimmed, like something massive had switched on. The doorman radiated menace, almost darkness, as he bent Queen Mihail's arm until it cracked, forcing her to her knees. "Your throne is forfeit, debt breaker. You have no heir, nor will you. Let any who you have wronged seek you out and find justice as they wish."

Mihail gasped, choking, as the darkness seemed to swirl in about her.

That I didn't mind. When I realized that Ari was hiding behind me, I started to get worried. Grimm always assured me that being a prince or princess was ingrained in your soul.

A process that could never be reversed. Then again, how much of Mihail's soul remained, I couldn't say.

When the doorman threw her backwards, he almost sent her over the first row of chairs. Instead, she caught on the top of one, and flipped over, collapsing to the floor. Not everyone had made it out of the amphitheater, and of those that remained, more than a few sobbed quietly.

"Begone, Irina Mihail. You have no place here." The doorman turned his back.

She rose slowly, one arm hanging at an odd angle, blood smeared down her face. "Wrath. I have promised you wrath, Marissa. Let all the wrath of Inferno fall on you. And you, princess. I will see you dead."

I lunged for her, fueled by blind anger, a rage that welled up from the tips of my toes and colored the world red, but the doorman flickered and appeared before me. I'd run head-on into trucks less solid. With one hand, he gripped my face so tight, my teeth ground.

"Let her go. I will not permit murder in the presence of the High Queen." Only after Mihail limped away did he relax. "Your Highness, the matter is settled. She has forfeited her title."

She sighed. "Hers was a proud line, and a long one, but not the first to come to an end." The High Queen's gaze turned to me. "Let another begin today."

Ari rushed the doorman, swinging her bag at him like a club, pushing him back. "Oh, no you don't. You leave Marissa alone. She's got enough crazy in her life as it is."

Though I'd struggled uselessly against his grip, the doorman dropped me, turning to face Ari. "Young one, this is not up to you. The blood debt has been forfeited to Marissa. I will have the papers drawn up immediately."

I rose to my feet, rubbing my cheek where he'd grabbed me, when Ari grabbed me by the roots of my hair and pulled.

"We're leaving now. I insist." As she spoke she pulled, and because I remained somewhat attached to my hair, I followed.

"This is not settled." The High Queen sat on the edge of the speaker's mound, rubbing gnarled hands on her knees.

Putting my hands on Ari's wrist, I stopped her long enough to look back. "Damn right it isn't. What am I supposed to do with a throne? I don't have room in my apartment. I've barely got room for a couple of cat beds. And the only thing crowns are good for is getting me mugged."

Ari's voice rose to near hysteria. "M, I said we are getting out of here. I meant it. Now." To emphasize, she gave a yank that sent spirals of pain down my neck. "Don't make me spell you."

We limped, almost ran up the aisle, her hand still gripping the short hairs at the back of my neck. At the top of the stairs, she swung me right, then stopped at a white door with brass handles. "Here."

She swung it open, revealing a broom closet, then shoved me inside. A moment later, the door closed behind me as Ari stepped in.

"There's a knob in front of you. Open it."

I felt about, then clicked the door and stumbled out into Ari's bedroom. I flopped on the memory foam mattress I'd bought Ari for her birthday and groaned.

"Grimm. I need you now." Ari stood in her bathroom, her face set in a look of determination like I'd never seen.

"Arianna?" Grimm's voice echoed in the tile. I closed my eyes and listened as Ari relayed the events of the day, becoming more and more frantic.

Finally, she described Mihail's insanity. "They want to give Mihail's title to Marissa. I won't let them. You can't let them do that to her. You have to intervene."

"Ari, come here." I waved to her. "This isn't the worst thing I've been through. So I got a throne today. You want it?"

"Marissa Lambert Locks, sit up and listen to me." Ari spoke with an authority I'd never heard before. I opened my eyes and sat up, feeling the world swirl as the beginnings of a migraine took root.

"I know what you two say about me. Someone walk Ari to college, make sure she's safe. Someone go with Ari, make sure the princes don't creep on her. Someone go bail out Ari; she ran over the postman again." Tears streamed from her eyes as she clenched her fists.

"I won't let them pull you into that world. I won't. You think it's all salons and pink and pretty. I've seen what happens when they elect High Queen. I have friends who were around when the last High Queen was chosen. I visit some of them in therapy. Others, if I want to see them, I have to go to the cemetery. I won't let that happen to you." She put her hands on her hips.

I shook my head and started to rise, but she put a hand on my shoulder. "M, you owe me this. If it's about the money, I'll give you what I earn. If you want pink, I'll buy you a closet full of clothes. Don't get involved with the court."

Grimm appeared in Ari's makeup mirror. "Arianna, calm yourself. Marissa can no more be made a princess than you can be unmade. I don't recall any similar situations, but we'll find a nice young girl who's offended Marissa and make her an offer she can't refuse. I can use a puppet in the Queen's Court."

I flopped back on the bed. "I'm more interested in my three pounds of Glitter. When exactly do I get that? Do I have access to Mihail's bank accounts?"

Grimm laughed. "Hardly. The only thing you actually won was a title that would pass to your children. They would be princes, or princesses, and live with the benefits and drawbacks."

His words chilled me to the core. There wouldn't be any little princes or princesses in my future, assuming there was a future at all.

"I'm sorry, my dear." Grimm's tone sounded of pity, which offended me. "I meant no offense."

"Can I borrow a dress? I need to change into something made in the last century." Ari's stuff would be short on me, but wearable.

"Place the clothes in a pile, Marissa. Call me when you are done." Grimm faded away, not even pretending he'd peek in on me.

Anyone who tells you sneaking around in leather is easy or quiet has never tried it. I squeaked and rippled and finally surrendered, letting Ari peel it off. After I dressed in something sensible, I called Grimm.

"Stand back."

When he spoke, I acted. I knew better than to risk being too close. The pile of leather burst into flame without smoke, glowing white-hot, then collapsing to a pile of gray ash.

I reached up and felt for the hair combs, pulling them out. "I don't think these will burn."

"Do you like them?" Grimm's tone held that same note of sorrow.

"They're beautiful." I handed one to Ari to admire the carving.

"Then consider them yours. I don't believe you had time to grab a matchbook from the restaurant, and it may be your only trip to the court. Liam's flight lands tomorrow morning. You need to get some rest, Marissa. Your healing is not complete."

I hadn't noticed my arms turning to lead, but somehow it happened in the instant my eyes were closed. "Couch. Help."

Ari handed me back the comb. "I've slept enough for a month, M. You can have the bed. Grimm, meet me downstairs. I need to set some wards in case that bitch decides to try something else."

"Michael is standing guard outside. If you would avoid hitting him with lightning or fire, it would help." Grimm's voice began to buzz as I drifted off. Anyone else, passing out on their bed wouldn't have been an option.

Thirty-Five

~❧~

THE DAY OF the apocalypse started a lot like any other day. I woke to a demon sitting in a chair, watching me. "Handmaiden." Malodin looked less and less normal every time I met him. "It is time. The horsemen begin their circle of the city. You owe me a third plague."

"Grimm?" I fumbled for my bracelet.

"Mr. Malodin, consider your message delivered. You'll have your third plague by the time the harbingers are ready." Grimm's voice reassured me. He'd figure something out. He always did.

Malodin rose, his head almost touching the ceiling on spindly legs. With each step, he looked like a spider. "I have waited two eternities. A few hours more don't matter." He hunched and left the room. When the door slammed below, I finally sat up.

"Grimm? What's the plan? You found some secret loophole?"

Black smoke poured from the vent, forming a cloud that solidified into my lawyer. Larry shook his head, causing the cell phone to rattle against his ribs. "No such luck. I haven't slept all night. This contract is well written."

"Looks like garbage to me. Even the translated one." I shook my hair, wondering exactly how that many tangles could creep in overnight.

"Specific language is what makes the contract so clear. Here. Read the part about the apocalypse." Larry broke every rule known to man, shuffling through my purse without permission, and took out my copy of the contract.

"The signer shall call down the demon apocalypse at the appointed time." I shrugged. "I don't get it."

"There isn't much to argue about. It's simple and effective. Unless you can get Malodin to sign the cancellation, it's going to be hell on earth. But we did find a way to buy time." Larry dropped the contract in my hands and drifted back.

"Marissa, in my opinion, you were dangerously close to breach of contract with your first two plagues." Grimm spoke from Ari's makeup mirror. "While I applaud the audacity, your third plague will have to be more traditional. You've hardly unleashed anything that qualifies."

"You answer the door and tell me that. Malodin accepted them as plagues, that's what counts. Going to shower." I hadn't planned to sleep most of the night. Early morning spent fretting over the end of the world, that was the plan.

"Now you are thinking like a lawyer. The key to avoiding more destruction is timing. Which is why I allowed the demon to wake you."

"Get to the point. There's a way to stop all this?"

"No, my dear. But there's a way to prevent the harbingers from joining the destruction. Their arrival is meant to be the culmination of the terror. Section 200, subsection eight, paragraph three states that the harbingers end the plague with their first act."

I shook my head. "Out of the frying pan and into the incinerator."

Grimm clicked his tongue at me in disapproval. "My dear, show some faith. If the plague is already ended by the time they arrive—"

"They can't join the fun." I turned the thought over in my head, seizing at a desperate idea. "I need you to make me reservations."

"I'm staying put in my basement. When the world ends, it will still be safe for me. I'll shelter Arianna there as well, if she so desires." Larry dissolved, drifting back into the vent.

By the time I'd turned my skin lobster red, I knew what my plague had to be. It would tick off Malodin, Grimm, and probably anyone who came into contact with it, but it was the best plan I could come up with. When I got out of the shower, I found a tiny shopping bag filled with clothes from my apartment. Ari really didn't sleep at all, if she had time to fetch me clothes. At least I'd look good for the end of the world

I had two buttons on when the screaming started, three when the window below smashed in, and that's the point where I flew down the stairs.

In the living room, Mikey hulked over, his fur glistening with dew. Beneath him, something mewled like a sick kitten. Mikey looked up at me, his face contorted, his nose long. "Morning, Marissa. Found him halfway up the trellis, peeking into your window." Mikey drew back one claw, flexing points that could carve flesh like butter.

"Please, stop this violence. I came to see Arianna." Wyatt lay crumpled on the carpet.

"Wyatt!" Ari came running from the kitchen, a cook's apron on, a spatula still in hand. She froze, searching for her sunglasses, then gave up in frustration. "Why were you peeking on Marissa?"

"I thought you were her. That is your bedroom." Wyatt tried to stand up, but Mikey kept him pinned to the floor.

"You wanted to peek on me getting dressed?" I couldn't tell if Ari was offended or interested. Offended. Had to be offended.

"No, I wanted to see you. I'm so ashamed of how I acted." Wyatt slowly raised his gaze to match hers, and cringed. "I was afraid."

Larry came from the kitchen, bringing Ari's sunglasses to her. "If you want me to devour his soul, let me know."

Ari raised the spatula like a sword. "Out. All of you, out. I need to talk with Wyatt privately. Marissa, your breakfast is in the kitchen. I made crepes. Mikey, there's a ham in the trunk of Marissa's car for you. Grimm, go anywhere but here. Larry, haunt the attic. Wyatt, you've always said that relationships require communication. So we're going to communicate."

I grabbed Mikey's arm. "I want you to go pick up Beth and have her ready to go. And I'll have you know, you are way better than the plastic ferns." I gave him a mock salute and wandered to the kitchen. While I devoured the best chocolate crepes of my life, and possibly the last ones of it, I called Grimm. "Can't get the ring off."

Grimm showed up in the toaster. "I know. And before you ask, I can't remove it. Magic may not—"

"Magic oppose. I really need this finger though. Can you move it to the other hand?" I didn't mind the silver band. The fact that it would block a gold one, that bugged me.

"You are the one who put it on that finger. I will research ways to change it, but for now you will sport both gold and silver. And don't even think of cutting off your finger. The ring would appear somewhere else."

"Another finger?" I knew a surgeon who could do some fine work with reattaching things.

"Possibly. There are less comfortable places to have a ring attach itself."

"The thorn tree." The memory of that image came back, souring the taste of crepe.

"I know. I visited it as soon as Ari told me. I tell you in confidence that I have enlisted the aid of another fairy." Grimm spoke softly, afraid the walls might hear.

Fairies never asked each other for help. Ever. They couldn't even come near each other. "Why?"

"My daughter's actions are a blind spot for me. Whether it is the love I held for her, or that her power is a fragment of my own, I confess that I cannot determine her whereabouts." Grimm wouldn't look at me.

"So she's alive?"

"The auguries say she is not dead. You would have it be a yes or no, but with that much power, the continuum between alive and dead becomes gray and wide. If she makes a single move on earth, I will know."

I finished my crepe, put my dishes in the sink, and stopped. See, the murmurs, the protests, all of that—gone. I crept to the kitchen door and peeked into the living room. Ari and Wyatt lay locked in an embrace, kissing. Communicate, my ass. Ari was testing the poor boy for tonsillitis, or maybe being tested. Hard to say.

"Marissa," hissed Grimm, "leave them be."

You know what? The end of the world doesn't come every day. Far as I was concerned, they could bump uglies and I'd give Ari a high five for carping the diem.

I'd read most of the business news by the time Ari appeared in the kitchen, her blouse off by one button, her hair wildly messed up.

"I hear you decided to major in communications. Where's your prince?"

Ari poured herself a cup of orange juice. "He's brushing his teeth and washing his hands. Wyatt has," Ari paused, looking for the right word, "issues with contact."

I nodded. "Yeah, looked like it."

"No, really." Ari clenched her fists in frustration. "If we hold hands, he has to go wash afterward. He carries unopened toothbrushes with him, and he buys mouthwash in bulk."

"So you two didn't actually *do* anything."

Ari stomped her foot. "That's enough, Marissa. Wyatt takes physical relationships very seriously. We're moving slow. Giving him time to get used to things." She didn't need to say what those things were.

Grimm reappeared in Ari's toaster. "I've made the arrangements. The baseball stadium is yours."

"Call Mikey, have him meet us there. I want mercenary teams in the parking lots in case my plan goes off the rails. Malodin wants something awful unleashed, I'll give him something awful."

"My dear, I must warn you that violating your contract is not something I can advise. My expertise in these areas is extreme, and thus both the demon and your lawyer agree that I cannot help you subvert it." Grimm almost looked sorry. Almost.

"I can handle this. You make the reservations, handle the small details, I'll take care of plagues and such." I grabbed my purse and my best friend's hand and headed out to finish what I'd started. Namely, the destruction of the world.

*   *   *

FILLED WITH PEOPLE, the baseball stadium is an amazing place. The crowd roars like a single entity every time its team does something largely mediocre. Empty, like the darkest alley of an abandoned ghost town. From outside, the sounds of cars on the freeway and planes on approach to the airport echoed as I stood on home plate.

"Didn't know running the bases was on your bucket list." Ari stood behind me, leaning against the backstop.

"Ms. Locks!" From the dugout behind me came Beth, with Mikey hulking behind her like something from a monster movie. It wasn't the eight-foot wolf man with slobber on his jaws and claws the length of my palm. It was the flock of tiny white poodles surrounding her, each with a pink, blue, or green collar around its neck. And bows.

"Beth, what have you done?" Ari made a run for first base, with a poodle hot on her heels. I'm betting if the princess ever made it to the majors, she could be a hit, given how fast she ran.

"Awww, they're not that bad. Once they stop eating people, the hellfire goes right out of them." Beth knelt on the ground, letting the poodles yip and leap on her until she disappeared into a pile of white fur.

I walked over and reached down into the pile, pulling her up. "Beth, I'm about to unleash a plague of these things. And you're playing with them. How are you going to feel about marching a thousand of them off into the bay?"

"These little ones are my babies. Not like the nasty, bloody ones. I've given them baths, and Mikey bought them bows and let them nibble on him." Beth took out her kazoo and hummed. The flock fell into a formation behind her. "I thought I had a few more weeks until the poodles came."

"Change of plans. We're going to unleash them, corral them, and send them all for a swim in the next hour." I fiddled in my purse, finding the bag of plague sand. If Beth couldn't control the poodles, we'd die. If we couldn't contain them, they'd spread out like a, well, plague, devouring everyone in their path, and getting stronger as they did.

"Teams are ready," said the terse voice on my radio. So the mercenary control line waited, twenty yards out.

"Anything white and fluffy that isn't us, you shoot, unless I say otherwise." I waved to Mikey, and he walked over, each step almost a waddle.

His face was nearly completely transformed, with a long muzzle and ears that twitched and perked as he listened. Close up, he towered almost three feet taller than me.

"Keep Beth safe. She's the key to everything here." I reached up and brushed the fur on his face. "Wow. That's really soft."

"Conditioner." The word sounded gargled, spoken through wolf teeth and wolf tongue. He turned and loped back to Beth, running on hands and feet, almost like an ape.

"Ari?" I looked over to first base.

She'd retrieved a bat from the dugout. "Ready, M."

"Blessing, curse? I need you two." A slight brush of wind, and the shriek Ari let out told me my harakathin were with me. While I couldn't control what they did, the last experience with the fae guards told me it wouldn't be pretty.

Walking to the pitcher's mound, I knelt and dug in the dirt. My previous plagues I scattered to the wind, so that they'd affect the whole city. I took a handful of plague sand and patted it into the hole I'd made, envisioning what must happen.

Then I ran like hell toward Ari, glancing back at the pitcher's mound as I ran. Ari waited for me, her face scrunched in concentration as she prepared some spell.

Nothing moved. Overhead, a jet rumbled, reminding me that Liam's flight would touch down any moment. If the poodle outbreak spread, he'd meet something nastier than a flower-selling freak at the baggage carousel.

One second. Two more. Ten.

The earth erupted.

Thirty-Six

❧

AT FIRST, IT looked like a mole, nosing its way up from the ground. Then the entire mound fell in, as something clawed up through the earth. It shook itself, giving me a clear look at what I'd unleashed, and I gasped.

Burying the plague sand: really bad idea. The thing that scratched itself on centerfield was the size of a delivery truck. That's plenty scary. The worst part, however, was the slurry of heads, tails, and limbs that jutted from it. Each grain of sand had grown into a poodle, and some of them grew at the same time, in the same place.

Tiny heads with glowing eyes snarled at me from the rib cage, like warts on a dog. Tails wagged under its chin where poodle rear ends jutted from the skin, and on its ears, several almost complete poodles hung, squirming, yipping, eager to devour us.

The poodle-puddle stood, shaking its head and growling like construction machinery. I'd killed worse. True, I'd had the army actually running the antitank weaponry at the time, but it could die, and I'd kill it. A flash of white under it stopped my plotting.

First one, then another, then a flood of tiny poodles streamed out of the pit, forming a swirling pool of white around the monster's feet. Their bloodstained muzzles let out the yips of the damned, and their eyes blazed with fresh hellfire. Each dainty paw ended in claws that no doubt had shredded flesh a thousand times before.

"Beth, take the small ones," I shouted, and the sound of my voice suddenly made me stand out. A few thousand tiny eyes turned toward me, and two huge ones that I'd rather have looking anywhere else. The large poodle took a step toward me, growling in a way that made my insides into jelly.

Then a wave of sound came from the stadium speakers. A hum that passed through me, pulling at me, almost commanding me to turn and look at Beth. She stood at home plate, with Mikey over her like some grotesque umpire, a microphone in hand.

Again, she hummed into the mic, and a short whine echoed through the pack of poodles. The white ones rushed forward like a flood, surrounding Beth like a lake, matching with rapt, glowing eyes. The monster, on the other hand, cocked his head to one side, and let out a growl that let me know my plan had a few shortcomings.

Beth tried again, and this time, I took a few steps involuntarily. My feet moved without my control, each step getting easier and easier as I walked her way. "Stop. You're controlling us too."

Beth took out her kazoo and looked at me, fear in her eyes. "I can't control that thing without it."

"Small ones. Get rid of them, we'll handle the big dog," Ari practically screamed, then unleashed a rope of lightning at the monster dog, as she moved toward outfield.

Without the microphone, the hum of Beth's kazoo no longer ripped control of my feet from me. Small problem solved. The big problem, several thousand pounds of it, shrieked like a tiny puppy, then shook off Ari's lightning, and headed for her, bounding across the green grass.

I shot it twice as it ran, my nine millimeter barking in my hand like a good doggy as it spat bullets. What I needed was a ninety millimeter, but those didn't come in pistol sizes. It stopped short, turning to look at me.

"Here, boy!" I waved my arms. I never saw what hit me.

From where I stood, I'd swear the world swung up at me, tackling me at full speed. Then as fast as the weight hit me, it flew off. I looked up and found something ugly enough to reconsider my aversion to cats. The thing that hit me was a poodle. Sort of.

Your average poodle, even a hellfire-driven, bloodthirsty monster one, isn't six feet high and seven hundred pounds. Worse yet, from the gaping maw in the pitcher's mound, five more emerged. With a howl, Mikey bounded after them, tearing into one, then slamming it into another.

The one that hit me squealed as something took a bite out of it, severing a tendon. It snapped at the air, snarling and chasing nothing until it crashed into the ground, shaking. I glanced over at Ari and found her inches from the poodlesaur. Trying to charm it? No. She held up the bat, screaming at it. "Who wants the stick? You want the stick? Go get it."

She hurled it in an arc, pushing it with a bolt of magic so that it sailed over the field, clattering to the ground a few inches from home plate.

Beth stopped humming for an instant. And the poodles converged on her, a storm of white fur and hellfire. I watched my life pass before my eyes twice as the thing loped over me, swallowed the bat, then turned to come after me.

Mikey sprinted past me, a ball of fur and blood, as he leaped on another midsize monster and sank his teeth into its spine.

I ran.

I'm no coward. It's just that facing that thing wasn't going to happen. My best weapon had bullets that were more like flies to it. Ari's heaviest chain lightning only left a singed spot at the end of its nose. I sprinted for the outfield wall, knowing that in three bounds it could cover the distance.

My lungs burned from exertion. My arms shook, but I sprinted as if what was left of my life depended on it. Only when I reached Ari did I glance behind. Something the size of a small truck clung to the poodle-saur's hind leg. Yeller.

Ari's hellhound stood full size, three feet taller than the little ones Mikey fought, but looking like a toy Pomeranian attacking a Great Dane. As the poodle-saur spun, gnashing its teeth, huge slashes opened up on its sides as my harakathin attacked it.

With a crunch, the poodle-saur locked its jaws on Yeller and whipped him from side to side, throwing him off like a rat. Ari let out a soft scream. A cry of pain, shock, and sorrow.

The sky began to boil.

Oh, I'd seen her do magic before. Seen her toss a lightning bolt from time to time. This time, clouds boiled in the sky like a time-lapse video. The doorman had called her "Princess of Clouds." I had a feeling why.

The poodle-saur focused on us, as Ari drew in magic in a way that made the air whistle around her. As if she'd become a storm herself.

It walked toward us, growling in a way that should have felt threatening, if it weren't for the fact that my best friend currently looked like a tesla coil.

"Over here." I screamed at the poodle-saur, leading it off to the side. "Ari, anytime now."

She didn't answer, continuing the spell, as the sky began to hail, first pea sized, then ice the size of cantaloupes. Time. All she needed was time to finish the spell.

So I ran right at it.

Straight for the poodle-saur, sprinting toward it.

It slammed its feet down, trying to adjust, and I slid, feet first, under it. You know those movies where the heroine does some midair move, shooting the bad guy several times in flight? This was exactly nothing like that.

I rolled onto my stomach as the hell beast turned to look at me, so close the stench of its breath washed over me.

The lightning struck it, raining down from the sky onto Ari, reflecting from her into it. The sheer voltage made my muscles convulse as the sizzling of monster flesh filled the air with a smell like a barbecue cook-off in Inferno.

The poodle-saur collapsed, falling halfway into the pit it emerged from. Smoke rose from a dozen cracks in it.

I managed to stagger onto my feet, my hair sticking out like I'd stuck my finger in a light socket. Ari knelt by the out-field wall, and I jogged toward her.

"Can you heal him? Or take him to the vet?" I put one hand on her shoulder.

Her tears answered well enough.

I wanted to comfort her. Really, I did, but right then, it occurred to me that I was missing a wolf, a piper, and at least a thousand little hell spawn. I looked to home plate, expecting to see a crowd of poodles fighting over who got Beth's ears.

The poodles were gone.

So was Beth.

Leaving Ari on the field, I ran across the field fast enough to score a grand slam, then dashed through the stands, and outside. My mercenary teams lay scattered across the parking lot. Dead. On second thought, asleep. All of them. I looked north, where Beth should have been sending all of them for a nice, long swim. The water's edge lapped peacefully.

"She's gone."

I shot Mikey twice before I even realized it was him. He'd changed back to his normal self. Or maybe his abnormal self. I wasn't really clear on which was which.

He waited until his body pushed out the bullets. "Really need to see that gunsmith."

"Where?"

"I'm not telling you, Marissa. She'll take good care of them. Control them. Train them." Mikey put a hand on my shoulder, trying to comfort me. I wasn't terribly comforted.

"That's not how we do this. She leads them off into the water, everyone gets to live another year." Grimm. I could call Grimm, have him find Beth, and send in a flamethrower team to mop up.

"Grimm?" I looked around, finding a stainless steel railing. "I need you to find Beth. She ran off with more poodles than all of Paris."

Grimm appeared, his brow creased. "You have worse problems, Marissa. The harbingers took the wrong bridge and encountered an extremely grumpy troll, but they will arrive at any moment. Also—"

"Handmaiden." I recognized the stench of sulfur without looking behind me.

"Malodin. I gave you your third plague. Poodles."

"Marissa, this guy bothering you? Want me to kill him?" Mikey gave Malodin the same smile Mikey gave a hot dog.

"Down, boy." Malodin strode toward me, a look of rage on his face. "You cannot kill me on this plane. Destroy this form, my essence simply leaks away and reforms more determined. More angry."

"He's telling the truth for once." Grimm spoke softly, trying to calm Mikey. "You cannot kill a demon without containing them."

"I see no pools of blood, I hear no screams of terror. Where is my plague?" Malodin stopped in front of me, resembling a praying mantis in a bowler hat.

"Yeah, about the poodles. They're gone. I summoned them using the plague sand. Unfortunately, they don't build poodles the way they used to." I took the plague sand from my purse and offered it to him.

"Handmaiden, you cannot mock me. The harbingers have arrived. It is time for them to destroy the city, and you to unleash my forces upon your world." Malodin raised a claw, pointing off toward the parking lot.

There, four figures on bicycles raced toward us. I ran down the stairs and out the ticket gates to meet them.

Death looked like always, an elderly Chinese man with legs like a draft horse. War had reverted to his African skin. Pestilence looked like the image of health, having stripped his shirt off. He glistened like some male stripper.

It was Famine that shocked me. He looked like the clerk at the local convenience store more than anything. He pulled up, hopped off, and gave War a high five. "Sorry I'm late. I was getting a really great workout, so we took an extra lap around the city."

"It is time." Malodin practically shrieked as he approached the harbingers. "Destroy the city."

"I think not." I walked a few steps forward to stand even with Malodin. "Contract says that your destruction ends with the third plague. The third plague ended a few minutes ago. I don't think you are allowed to do anything without another third plague. Which would be a fourth plague, and I'm not agreeing to it."

The harbingers conferred, whispering among themselves, while Malodin crackled and creaked with rage.

War stepped forward. "You sent us across the country. Made us ride back. And we don't even get to kill anyone?"

"Sorry." I hope my tone sounded sufficiently insincere.

"This doesn't change anything, Marissa." Death shook his head. "You still have to call down the apocalypse. It means a lot more people die by demons instead."

Malodin turned toward me. "Yes. I demand it. You have robbed me of my plagues, but your world is mine."

"Fine. I'll complete my contract, but not here. We finish this deal where we started it."

"I'll see you at midnight." Malodin erupted into flame, burning away.

I looked at the harbingers. "How do I send you back?"

War shook his head. "I'm sticking around. I'd like to see how this turns out."

"I'm taking a few more laps," said Famine, getting back on his bike.

"Marissa, do you remember what I told you about hate?" Death looked at me with crinkled eyes.

I nodded. "Pins you down. You saying I need to start building up some hate so I can haunt Malodin?"

Death shook his head. "No. You haven't changed anything. But you might." Then he faded out, leaving a perfectly good bicycle.

"You want me to ride that back?" Mikey approached it.

"No. Help Ari with Yeller's body. I'm sure she'll want to bury it." When he'd gone, I sat down on the steps, pulled out my compact, and made a call.

"Grimm?"

He nodded to me. "Well done. Our gambit has paid off. But I question your decision to return to the dealing room. Would you care to enlighten me?"

I hunted down my purse, feeling the bulk of the vial I'd gotten from the angels. "You and Larry study that contract. Find out what happens if I kill Malodin for good."

Thirty-Seven

❧

I WALKED IN the door of my apartment and nearly collapsed. I'd helped Ari bury Yeller in the front yard, violating at least a dozen city codes and standards. I'd dropped off the bag of plague sand at the Agency, where Grimm had it sealed safely in our armament vault. On the way home, I kept wondering what it was I'd forgotten. Having the end of the world on your mind can do that.

"Marissa?" Liam stood in our kitchen, a half-eaten sandwich on the bar.

I sprinted for him. Nearly tackled him. Wrapped my arms around him and buried my head in him, soaking in his warmth. I won't tell you I didn't cry. It was like missing a piece of myself, and then finding it.

After he'd held me.

After I'd kissed him over and over, so frantic at times it felt like fever, after we'd found our way to the bedroom. After the frantic rush and eagerness, and the impatience, I began to settle. With his arms around me, rough and hairy, and his warmth radiating into my back, I finally found words.

"I'm sorry."

He shushed me. "It will be okay."

"No. Tonight I have to end the world." I sat up, not bothering to pull the sheet over me.

"Shopping trip with Ari?" Liam almost sounded amused.

I explained. About the deal. About Ari, and Grimm. About the demons, and the plagues, and wishes, and poodles.

"Being separated for two weeks wasn't supposed to be the end of the world." Liam put his head beside mine, whispering into my ear.

I rolled out of bed and headed for the kitchen. "Let me get your sandwich. We can talk while you eat."

Thing was, the sandwich wasn't on the counter. I looked around, trying to figure out where it had gone.

"It is in the refrigerator. I did not want it to spoil," said a woman's voice. I nearly screamed, then spotted the bombshell blonde on my couch, in a tennis outfit.

Liam came out, a towel wrapped around him. "M, this is Svetlana. She came back to talk with Grimm about my contract."

"Was she here when I walked in?" Part of me screamed that I was stark naked with a strange woman in the house. The other part of me didn't care about the naked, but was carefully calculating a plan of attack on said strange woman.

Liam held his palms out. "Yes. You didn't give me any time to introduce her."

So she'd been sitting on my couch, listening the whole time. "I don't have clothes."

"Take my towel." Liam started to unwind, and I fixed him with a stare.

"In the bedroom. Now." I followed him in, scrambling to find my bra and panties. "What is she doing here?"

"I think we got attacked. Three, four times. Maybe more. They burned down the whole place, nearly made it to the coffin-atorium. So Grimm's contract says I own pretty much everything. And trust me, we don't really want it. The heating bill alone has to be atrocious, there's not a grocery store for fifty miles, and it's dark at three o'clock. So Grimm's going to negotiate a deal. You don't want a vampire kingdom, do you?" Liam came over and overcame my halfhearted effort to push him away.

"Already got one throne I don't have room for. Queen

Mihail—I mean Irina Mihail—got kicked out of the Court of Queens." I meshed our fingers together, squeezing his hand.

Liam froze, his muscles going rigid. He ran his fingers over my ring finger and let go. "Why are you wearing that?"

For a man filled with fire, his tone carried pure ice. He tried to pull it off. Then tried harder, and harder. I'd seen him rip limbs off people as a dragon, but the silver ring on my finger resisted his grasp. Only when I cried out, afraid his pull was going to dislocate my shoulder, did he stop. "Explain."

And I tried.

I told him about the dwarves, and how I felt when I saw the ring, and what it meant to never be burned. Then I told him about the court. About Mihail's insanity. The thorn tree. The High Queen's sentence. "I can't take it off. But I don't want to. I never want to take it off. If the world ends tonight, I want to be wearing it. If the Black Queen comes tomorrow, I want to flaunt it before her."

He drew in a deep breath, his face unreadable. I'd stood in the office of the Adversary and not faced fear like this. I'd fought with demons and not felt such pain. Then he walked over and took my hand, and knelt. "Marissa Locks, will you marry me?"

There is a moment in a woman's heart, when she hears that question, where time stands still. Sudden? Maybe. We'd only known each other a couple of years. But then again, love wasn't known for gently knocking on the door of life, biding its time like an encyclopedia salesman. Love had a habit of backing a delivery truck through the barriers of my heart. That same buzz that filled me when I hit Grimm's beam of light consumed me now.

"Yes." Of course I said yes. My heart had answered before my lips could move. Yes, yes, and more yes. And then we celebrated, until nearly ten o'clock. The next time I left my bedroom, I did so fully clothed.

"We're going out." I pointed to the kitchen. "You can eat anything in there you can eat."

"I must accompany you, if the liege goes." She looked past me, at Liam, in a way that made me want to break a plate over her head.

"We're going to see my best friend. Announce our engagement." I tried not to let her ruin my mood. I didn't have time to get it back before the world ended.

"Let her come. She can ride in back." Liam put his hands on me and ushered me toward the door, and I didn't feel like arguing. The backseat of my car would have been uncomfortable for a toddler, so I took some comfort in that as we drove over.

When I knocked the first time and Ari didn't answer, I started pounding.

"Hold on, M. I can't figure out how to work the peephole." Ari's voice sounded muffled by the heavy door.

"There isn't much point. I already know it's you, I already know you are there. Let me in." I glanced over my shoulder, where Liam and Svetlana exchanged a private joke in whatever guttural language that was.

When Ari finally opened the door, I was surprised to find her wearing sunglasses. "We're engaged!" I held out the ring as if Ari hadn't seen it on my hand every time she'd seen me. After the requisite hugs, Ari invited us in.

"I guess you can come in. Who's the model?" She peered through me to Svetlana.

"Long story." I turned to glance at Svetlana. "You can come inside. It's creepy, but safe."

She gave me a smile that would have melted butter. "It's cozy. Reminds me of home."

That settled it. I wanted nothing to do with wherever she lived.

We bustled into the living room, where the slight hesitation I'd picked up in Ari's invitation made all the sense in the world. On the couch sat Wyatt, his hands folded in his lap.

On the coffee table Ari had a pile of toothbrushes, toothpaste, floss, and mouthwash. Even I could tell exactly how she intended to spend the last hours of her life. "You two communicating?" I watched her face.

Her lips turned down in a pout. "That's all we were doing. Talking."

Liam walked past me and grabbed Wyatt's hand, shaking both it and him. Liam's arms always seemed thicker than fire hydrants, but standing next to Wyatt, Liam looked like Mr. Universe. The two exchanged pleasantries and began to chat.

"My fiancé could snap your boyfriend in half," I whispered to Ari.

"Please, M. I could snap him in half. Grimm called half an hour ago to announce your engagement." Ari nodded her head toward the mirror over her mantel.

"My dear, if I may offer my congratulations, I'd like to." Grimm faded into view.

"You can tell me you found out what happens if I kill Malodin. That's a perfect engagement gift."

At my words, the chatter in the background ceased.

Grimm's face turned down, his eyebrows furrowed. "It isn't clear. I believe ownership of the contract would fall into question, and only the Authority could resolve that. Normally, being demons, it would go to the Adversary, but since he stands to gain the apocalypse, he cannot mediate it."

I nodded. So kill the demon I'd made a contract with, and I'd buy some time.

"However, killing him, particularly in a dealing room, is an act of war. You would unleash the vengeance of Inferno on the world." Grimm shook his head.

Ari came over and put her hand on my shoulder. "Is that better or worse than an apocalypse?"

Grimm nodded side to side, thinking for a moment. "It's hard to say, young lady. The situation hasn't occurred within my memory."

I planned on telling him I'd take *maybe* over *definitely* any day. I planned on taking my fiancé and going to kill a demon. Unfortunately, the front window picked that exact moment to explode in a hurricane of glass.

A snakelike head the size of a trash can poked through the window, looking at each of us, before locking onto Ari. It snapped forward, striking at her, and bounced to one side as she summoned a wall of purple power.

"I don't get why you are so afraid of her." Liam stood up, unbuttoning his shirt.

Ari's body exploded into fire that leaped out from her, lancing through the eye of the snake demon.

"Or maybe I do. Impressive." Liam walked forward, the skin on his chest growing bright red with each step.

"Hellfire won't harm them," said Grimm. A shard of glass had split his mirror, giving us two of him, and an echo.

In answer, Liam put his hand on the snake's jaw, tearing off one side. The head recoiled into the darkness, and Liam ran out the front door after it.

"Preemptive strike?" I glanced back at Grimm.

Grimm shook his head. "Have you been respectful and businesslike in your conversations with Malodin? Or given him reason to hate you?"

I blushed like a schoolkid caught by the principal. "A little."

Svetlana suddenly registered that Liam had slipped out the front door. "Excuse me. I cannot allow harm to my liege." She hopped to the broken window, nimble as a bird, then out of it, disappearing into the darkness.

Outside, cars crunched and glass broke as something else approached. Grimm tilted his head to indicate the window. "They cannot harm Marissa, as signatory to their contract. On the other hand, you two," he looked at Ari and Wyatt, "are under no such protection."

"What about your mirror?" I expected Grimm to at least care about that.

He nodded to me calmly. "Let them try to break the mirror of a fully powerful Fairy Godfather. I am the reason most of the old stories exist. Let them try." His confidence would have warmed me, if not for the fact that his mirror was in my bathroom, in my apartment, where my security deposit was at risk.

"We need to get to Mum's home. It is safe from demons." Wyatt spoke with surprising confidence, considering what he'd seen. And he was right. From outside came a roar I'd heard every time Liam smashed his thumb with a hammer, followed by the sound of more breaking glass.

"You'll never cross the city. I've checked the auguries, and this is more like the opening salvo of a war than a surgical strike. Better to hole up here and defend yourselves. Not even Evangeline could get you from here to Mrs. Pendlebrook's house." Grimm almost sounded unsure.

Evangeline. My mentor. Almost big sister, sometimes friend.

I still kept a set of her knives in my office, though I'd never be her. "Grimm, I need to make a phone call."

He glared at me like I'd demoted him to telephone operator. "Does your cell no longer work? There's a reason I use bracelets."

"I need to call into Kingdom. I have to get ahold of someone at the post office." The stares I got from around the room made it clear how crazy I sounded. I went to Ari's bathroom and placed my call, completely ruining the gnomes' last evening of fun. When I came back, Ari and Larry stood at the broken window, firing bolts into the darkness from time to time.

"Help is on the way." I pulled my gun out of my purse, then put it back. Bullets weren't going to harm these things, and I couldn't waste a drop of sweat on anything less than Malodin, anywhere it wouldn't kill him for good. "You have any holy water?"

Larry smoked, his eyes glowing orange. "Why exactly would I have holy water? Unholy water, sure. Holy water? Do you have any idea what that would do to me?"

"Do you have any mustard?" Ari hated mustard. I'd never find any in her fridge.

Shadows flashed up the stairs, and Liam exploded into the living room. His hair smoked, his skin had scales all over where he used the curse for strength. "They just don't stop. First couple were easy. That last one nearly killed me." He grinned at Svetlana. "I owe you one."

I didn't care for how she smiled at him. It wasn't the double-D chest, or the curve of her hips, or her flawless complexion. It was how she looked at him, like a puppy dog. If she wanted a dog, when I found Beth, I'd get her one all right.

"Our ride will be here any moment." I looked out at the darkness, where all the streetlights went off at once.

"Tell me you didn't call a cab. I seem to have used up most of my dragon juice, or I'd fly you there." Liam's concern almost hurt.

"Not exactly." In the distance, another demon roared. Then another, closer and closer, so loud the glass shards on the floor rattled. Burst of flames lit the night, coming from the—wait. Coming from the headlights. With a crash and a crunch, a monster truck rolled up, destroying what was left of the front fence.

The window rolled down, and a small round face stuck out.

"Petri!" I ran out the front door, heedless of the danger in the dark. "I have a new game for you. My friends need to get to a safe house. Demons are worth points. People aren't. Oh, and the demons will try to kill you along the way."

A second monster truck pulled up behind Petri. I ushered Wyatt and Ari into it, then called Liam.

"I'm staying with you." He put his hands on my cheeks, and I ignored the rough scales.

"They can't harm me. Get Ari and Wyatt to his mother's house. They'll be safe there. Please." I saw the look in his eyes. The protest rising in him. "Please."

Liam climbed up into the cab, pushing Wyatt over and slammed the door. "When they are safe, I'm coming to join you."

The monster truck rolled backwards, squashing a compact car and a station wagon, then roared off into the night, smashing down a demon as it did.

I climbed up into Petri's cab and fastened my seatbelt. "I need a ride to a jewelry store. I need to get there as fast as I can. Any demons that get in our way, feel free to kill."

In answer, Petri revved the accelerator and peeled out, leaving a trail of destruction behind us.

Thirty-Eight

THE SHEER NUMBER of demons that little gnome managed to run over astounded me. Also, the way they meandered down the streets, pulling down the occasional power line, breaking out a window here and there. Like an advance tailgating party, they couldn't wait to start trashing the place.

When we pulled up at the Small Wonders jewelry store, I slapped the hood. "One more thing I need your help with."

With Petri's help, I lashed the winch on his truck to the metal bars. When he hit the accelerator, I was several stores down, expecting the door to fly off. He damn well near took off the front of the building. I strode inside, oblivious to the alarms, and grabbed a mirror from the case. "Grimm, need the code to the safe."

"In your purse, take out the flashing disk inside, attach to the wheel on the door." Grimm spoke rapid fire, expecting me to run, and I did. "Now, get to a safe distance."

"So how does it figure out what the right combination is?" I knelt on the ground, behind a parked truck.

The explosion that rippled out left my ears ringing, and a ball of blue light imprinted on my eyes.

"It's a delicate matter," said Grimm from one of the few unbroken windows.

I grabbed a mirror shard and ran for the elevator, stepping over the molten edges of metal that remained. After Petri's driving, the freefall elevator actually served to refresh me. Like a rollercoaster to hell, in the most literal sense possible.

I ran through the forge, passing a trio of startled dwarves, and crawled down their tunnel. "You with me?" I waited for Grimm's answer.

"Only until you enter the room. I can act as an observer inside, but cannot aid you, my dear." Grimm's eyes were the only thing visible in the fragment of mirror.

"I'm guessing blessing and curse won't be too helpful either."

"If they can enter the room at all, they are forbidden to interfere. Malodin will be under no such restraint."

"I'm going to get him in the summoning circle and kill him with the vial of sweat. Even a demon can't escape there. Whatever comes next, Malodin won't be around to see it or take part in it." I reached into my purse, hefting the vial.

"My dear, before you enter, I want to tell you something. If the apocalypse occurs, I have arranged a safe haven for Rosa and her family. While it is built for eight, it will handle nine. If you desire, I will arrange passage for you." Grimm's tone spoke of defeat.

"And Liam? Ari?"

"I'm sorry, my dear."

"I'd rather die in hell with Liam than live without him. When this goes sideways, you can bet I'll find them." I slipped the mirror into my pocket and walked toward the room, with thirty minutes left until the end of the world.

Honestly, the last thing I expected was an audience. I threw open the door and found the dealing room changed. An outer ring of crystal grew like stalagmites around an inner circle, with the dealing table at the center. Around the outside of the room stood the oddest assortment of observers I'd ever encountered.

Nickolas Scratch lounged against the wall, a copy of the paper rolled up under his arm. "Marissa! So good to see you."

He walked over and patted me on the shoulder. "Came to see my boy perform. It's like a choir performance, only less evil."

Beside him, Eli, archangel of the city, sat. He nodded in my direction, then went back to whispering to Nickolas and laughing.

Next to them stood the harbingers, including Famine, in his grossly overweight form. I walked around the outside to where Death stood. I nodded to him. "Hi."

"Marissa. You don't have much time left for pleasantries." Death remained an asshole, even to the end.

"Good to see you too." I nodded to War and Pestilence and tried to prepare myself for killing Malodin. It wasn't like I hadn't killed before. I'd ventilated more imps than I could count, but normally that was because they were intent on removing my skull.

Even the Gray Man I didn't walk in intending to kill. It wasn't part of who I was.

"You have the look of someone getting ready to kill." War's voice startled me almost as much as his recognition. If it were truly that obvious, my plan wouldn't work.

"I'd rather not."

"You need to get in touch with yourself. Figure out what you are." He patted me on the back, his hands so thick, they thudded against me.

"I'm not a killer." I hoped my voice didn't shake as much as my hands.

"You don't know what you are, lady, until you are forced to find out." I kept my eyes closed until he lumbered away. I reached into my purse, looking for a pack of tissues, and came out with that blasted contract, the large version of which still sat on the dealing table.

"The signer shall call down the demon apocalypse at the appointed time." I crinkled the contract into a ball, cursing myself for ever touching the quill. Just as my lawyer had warned me, every bit of help he gave came with consequences.

I'd unleashed Grimm's power, but that meant the Black Queen grew stronger as well. Ari wound up marked forever as a witch, because she saved me, and pulling her out of a coma had meant bringing in a prince. Liam survived Mihail's assassins, but now his curse was stronger than ever.

At least I could take comfort in making this the lousiest end of the world ever. I'd unleashed sorry excuses for plagues, and not in the manner Malodin intended.

If it turned out to be true, that as the apocalypse bringer, I was immune to the devastation, I'd make my life's mission heading straight to Inferno and bringing down an apocalypse on the demons too.

When the idea hit me, it almost left me seeing stars.

I reached into my purse and pulled out the mirror shard. Grimm appeared, called by my very thought, but I stopped. Too many ears. Too many eyes, and my one slim chance, I couldn't risk. I ran for the door, bolting out as a plume of smoke and a smell like a freezer of rotten meat announced Malodin's arrival.

"Liam." I put my hand on my bracelet, and felt us connect.

"M, they're safe. You won't believe what it's like outside though. Where are you?" Liam sounded out of breath, or maybe out of fire.

I gave him the address of the jewelry store. "But I need you to swing by Ari's house on the way. I need you to bring me something."

"That's not on the way, M. If the world ends, I want to be there with you." I'd hurt him by asking him to waste precious time on a side trip, but if my gambit worked, I could make it up to him for the next fifty years. I tried not to think about what would happen if it didn't.

"I'm coming." He broke the link.

One text message later, I stepped back in the room. Malodin grinned, his eyes wide with glee. "Handmaiden, it is nearly time."

I nodded, checking my phone again. "You'll get your apocalypse, right on schedule. Not one minute early." I paced the outer ring of the dealing room, ignoring the stares of the harbingers as I passed.

"You are wasting time." Malodin walked over to gloat before Nickolas Scratch.

As the minutes passed, my nervous tick grew to an outright tremor. Maybe the lights were out. Maybe traffic made crossing the city, well, normal. Right when I wanted to puke from panic, the oaken door burst open, and Liam stumbled through it. Svetlana held him against her, keeping him upright and earning my ire at the same time.

"Liam!" I shouted, running to him.

He pushed away from Svetlana and collapsed on the ground, coughing and shaking. I cursed myself again for what I'd asked him to do. Black smoke began to ooze from his pores as he gasped and choked, until Larry the Lich floated before me. Larry changed. The gray rags threaded back together into a polyester suit, while plump oozed out to cover the lich's bones. If this was how Larry looked in life, I understood why he preferred the bony look.

"Always dress appropriately for court." Larry looked at Nick Scratch and Eli. "I need a few minutes to confer with my client." He glanced at me. "Give the mirror to your boyfriend, his babe, and have them take a seat."

I pressed the shard into Liam's hand and helped him hobble to the wall, where he slumped, still gasping for breath.

Larry took me by the elbow, leading me to the edge of the circle. "That curse and my possession don't get along. Much longer and he'd have dropped dead on the way."

"I know, but I needed you here. I have an idea . . ." We huddled in the corner as I explained my plan. It wasn't a good plan, but I'll take a bad plan over no plan any day. When my cell phone alarm went off, I broke the huddle and walked forward into the center ring. Behind me, crystals grew from the ground, sealing me inside.

"Give me a moment." Malodin turned around and waved his hand. A new figure shimmered into view seated on the outside of the ring.

Mihail. She'd been there who knows how long.

"She wanted to see this, and I deserve to have a few guests of my own." Malodin waved to her, his crazed grin matching the wild look in her eyes. "I demand that you complete your part of the bargain. Bring forth the apocalypse, handmaiden."

I took a deep breath and closed my eyes. "Fine. I call down the agreed apocalypse. Let it begin."

The earth shook, shuddering like a door the size of a continent swung open somewhere in the depths of hell. Malodin fell to his knees, laughing and thrusting his fists into the air. "At last! At last I have the end."

Nickolas Scratch continued to read his newspaper. "You want to see something evil?" Eli leaned over and the two conversed, then started laughing.

Malodin leaped to the side of the ring, waving for the Adversary's attention. "Bring forth thine armies of destruction, Father. Blacken the skies with demon wing and let the stone catch fire."

Larry flicked the crystal barrier separating him from us, making it ring like a bell. "Might I ask what you are doing?"

Malodin leered at him. "Beginning my dearly earned destruction of the world."

"Not here you aren't." Larry crossed his arms and shook his head.

"Begone, weak spirit of wrath, and I won't send a swarm of hell flies to tear you to shreds."

Larry didn't as much as flinch. "We have a contract, and you'll abide by it. The contract says you may bring about the *demon* apocalypse."

Malodin fell silent for a moment. "I'm a demon. All my armies are demons. Our families are demons. Our pets are little demons."

Larry shrugged. "It clearly says here that you can bring about the demon apocalypse. So go ahead. Go back to Inferno and bring apocalypse down on all the demons there."

"That's not what that means."

"Really? Don't we say 'A plague of locusts'? Wouldn't that mean the right term is *an apocalypse of demons*?"

"That's not what it means." Malodin's voice wavered.

Larry dusted his hands off. "I disagree. I'm going to move to bring this up before the Authority."

"Impossible! She won't convene court until Judgment Day. Not really a point in having an apocalypse if the world has already ended." Malodin managed to both shriek and whine.

"That's not really my client's problem. This contract is on hold until it can be mediated."

Nick folded up his paper. "I think we're done here. Eli, nice seeing you. Marissa, you have my number. Mal, we need to talk later."

"Stop!" Irina Mihail screamed, pulling at her own hair until chunks came out. "I promised you wrath, Marissa. Wrath you *will* receive." Placing her finger in her mouth, she bit until the flesh crunched, then scratched a bloody signature on the crystal. "I offer you a new deal, demon. My soul for her destruction."

A contract scribbled into place in impeccable script, leaving her blood smear perfectly positioned at the signature point.

Liam lunged for the crystal wall, pounding against it with every bit of strength he could muster, but after two weeks, he couldn't even change his hands to claws.

Malodin changed as he advanced on me. His skin glistened black and his eyes became like an insect's, his mouth elongated to allow spider fangs.

"This is the point where you reveal some sort of devious twist." I backed away as I spoke, circling the ring. "Like 'her destruction of old age.' Right?"

"No." His mandibles clicked together as he spoke.

"But I thought demons never did as they were told."

Malodin shivered, and his skin split, freeing wings to spread behind him. "She asked for something simple. Something in line with my nature. Something I *wanted* to do anyway."

I was in trouble. I glanced over to Nick Scratch. "Leash your boy?"

He folded up his paper and sat back down. "You took away his apocalypse; I can sort of understand him not being happy about it." He took something out of his pocket and held it between his hands. It began to shake and steam and then pop. He shook a bag of microwave popcorn and opened it up.

"Eli? Little help? He's going to kill me."

The angel reached over and took some popcorn from the Devil. "Unlawful murderizing, that goes to small claims court. We only handle the important stuff."

"Your contracts are going to be the death of me," I said, dodging a halfhearted blow from Malodin.

"That's sort of the point." Malodin flipped the quill over, raising it like a dagger.

I reached into my purse and brought out the vial. At the sight of it, Malodin recoiled, and both Nickolas and Eli let out howls of laughter. "I'm sick of contracts. How about you and I have a gentleman's agreement? You put down the quill, I'll put down the vial."

"Lady, you make bad deals," said Malodin, "but I'm fine with that."

I carefully placed the vial on the drafting table, not spilling a drop on the copy of that cursed contract. "Your turn."

He swung at me with the quill, missing my chest by an inch.

"We had an agreement." I ran, he advanced, flipping the quill in his hand as he did.

"A gentleman's agreement. I'm not a gentleman." He swelled with each step, lumbering forward.

When he swiped at me the next time, I rolled to the side, kicking his knee so hard it broke. He sagged forward, then rose. The buglike carapace covering his knee popped and crackled as it healed. "I can do this all day."

I charged, leaping onto his back, tearing at the wings, stabbing my thumbs into his eyes, and he twisted. His head swiveled around to look at me. Then the wings I'd leaped on flared out, throwing me toward the crystal floor.

I hit headfirst.

The kick that followed hit my thigh, flipping me over like a rag.

Malodin knelt, grabbed me by the hair, and threw me across the floor, into the drafting table. I grasped at it, hauling myself up. He'd be on me in an instant. I stretched out across the table, reaching for the vial of sweat. Malodin swung the quill overhand, driving it through my hand and snapping it off. I writhed in agony and fell, hanging half crucified from the table.

Malodin grabbed my suit with his claws and lifted me upward. "Any last words? Some sarcastic comment? A witty retort?"

I looked back over my shoulder at the contract. My blood refused to stick to it, dancing to the side to avoid the words. "I accept."

He dropped me like I was made of Cheddar cheese, his hands smoking where he had touched me. "What is this?"

I pulled my hand off the quill. Tremors of agony wracked my body, but I forced myself to my feet and pointed to where he had stabbed the paper. "You canceled the deal. Quill was in your hand. You moved it." As I spoke, the single mark flowed into Malodin's signature. "You have no authority to harm anyone now."

Nick Scratch began to laugh so hard he nearly fell off the bench, and then he stood and clapped his hands softly. "You know, Marissa, that was inspired. Mal, my boy, how did you not see that coming?"

Malodin flexed a clawed hand and reached for me.

"Ahem." I looked back at Nick, who had folded up his paper and put it under his arm. "Mal, you need to decide how we're going to do this. First, you fail to deliver an apocalypse. That I can almost understand. It happens. Canceling your own contract though; that's just plain bad for business. I wouldn't trust you to bring about the end of happy hour at this point. Boys, take Mal to my office."

A swarm of flies rose up and seized Malodin and pulled him down through the crystal into the fire.

The crystal in the floor retracted, and Liam limped over, wrapping my bleeding hand in his shirt.

"Let me see." Grimm sounded angry and happy at the same time, as he looked at the point where the razor tip of the quill pierced my hand. "My dear, you are most fortunate."

The shivering in my body said otherwise, and the thought of disinfectant made me shake. "How about you do the magic thing where everything feels better?"

"Your body will take care of that on its own."

If there was one thing I could count on the Fairy Godfather to do, it was to avoid magic.

Then the screaming started. By the dealing table, Nickolas held Irina Mihail in one hand. With the other claw, he folded her, like a flesh origami, until all that remained of the queen was a cracker-sized square of pulsing flesh. "Maybe she'll taste better with soy sauce. See you later, Marissa." Nickolas nibbled on the edge of the square, causing it to shriek, and walked to the side of the dealing room.

The harbingers stood between me and the door, arms folded. I waved to War. "We're done, right? You guys can go."

Death took a couple of steps forward. "Not exactly. The rest of the contract may be canceled, but we haven't delivered on our end. And we always keep our side of deals."

Thirty-Nine

"WHAT DO YOU want? I'm not going to end the world. Not again." I leaned into Liam, and he responded by picking me up, which, all things considered, I liked.

"Marissa, relax." Larry picked up my crumpled contract from the floor. "Just looking out for you as your lawyer." He unraveled the paper, then pointed to a section I'd skimmed over. "Due, and Gifts." My eyes picked those out pretty well. "You were supposed to receive these when you unleashed the harbingers."

"She didn't give us time." War glared at me. "And after that stunt with the bikes, I wasn't feeling generous."

I kicked my feet in the air, signaling Liam to put me down. He kept his arm around me. "Fine. I've got the head of Rip Van Winkle in a box, a throne I can't use, and Kingdom only knows what else that I don't need. Could you wait and get me something off my wedding registry?"

War approached, exchanging a stare with Liam that I couldn't quite decode. He reached out, and put the palm of one hand on my forehead.

I expected more.

A flash of light, maybe? A rainbow of color? You know,

something to indicate that I'd gotten, well, something. He pulled his hand back, and nodded, almost to himself. "Lady, you gotten your ass kicked from here to Sunday. My gift will fix that."

"I'm not a killer." I wouldn't mind another harakathin, but the idea of him making me into a killing machine, that made me sick at my stomach. When I closed my eyes, a light like a spotlight shone on the inside of my head, like an afterimage. "Take it back."

War chuckled. "When you finally are ready, my gift will be waiting." He stepped back, and nodded to Pestilence.

I swear, the guy could have been an underwear model. The tone of his skin, the ripple of his muscles . . . for the embodiment of disease, he kept it together.

I didn't flinch when he put his hands on my cheeks. When he sneezed, showering me in snot, I flinched. I flinched a lot, as a matter of fact.

"My gift. You'll never catch a cold again." Pestilence bowed his head toward me, while I wiped my face on Liam's shirt.

Famine waddled forward, a diet soda in his greasy hands. "Eat what you want. You'll never grow fat."

Which left only Death. What on earth could Death offer me? More life? Eternal life? His eyes wrinkled as he smiled, and I shook my head. "You don't work that way."

"Do you remember what I told you about hate?" Death's voice sent chills down my spine. More than normal, if there's a normal for conversing with the embodiment of death.

"Yeah, I remember." Hatred could pin my soul. A warning? Love everyone or risk becoming a ghost?

"Then my gift is already given. See you soon, handmaiden." Death turned, as if to walk away, and when I blinked, he was gone.

"On account of your good service to this world, I'm prepared to offer a onetime pass." Eli's voice boomed in the empty chamber. Then I realized his words were to Larry, not me.

In life, Larry Gulberson had all the charm of a walrus wearing a clown mask. After dealing with Larry as a skeleton for so long, he actually looked mildly charming. He nodded to Eli.

"On the other hand, you should consider all your options."

Nickolas Scratch tapped his rolled-up paper in the palm of his hand.

"You don't really want to go with that guy. He's pits of sulfur and fire." Eli glared at Nickolas.

"Women. I've got women. Marilyn, Lizzie. He's got Mother Teresa." Nick winked at me.

"She looks good in a habit." Eli looked over at me. "Get on out of here, Ms. Locks. Gonna get ugly."

Larry walked over and took my hands. "The deed for my house is in Mother's pocket. Make sure Ari gets it." Then he wiped a bead of sweat from his head, smiled, and turned his back. "Let's talk. Eternal damnation. Are we talking one or two eternities here?"

I didn't look back when we left.

"I'M GOING TO miss him." Ari and I sat in the living room of her no-longer-haunted town house. The house felt empty without a spirit of wrath and a hellhound watching over it.

"Yeller, or Larry?" At her dog's name, Ari's face fell further. She'd probably meant both.

"Ladies?" Grimm appeared above the fireplace. "I hate to interrupt, but Arianna has an appointment."

Ari took a pair of sunglasses from her pocket and slipped them on. "Fear therapy for Wyatt. We're making progress. Yesterday he almost looked at me without flinching."

"A man terrified of the woman he's in love with is hardly unique." Grimm spoke with the authority of several thousand years.

"Grimm, any sign of the Black Queen?" I tried to keep the apprehension in my voice under control.

"None. My daughter must gather power, a process that may take decades, or perhaps centuries. Don't waste your life worrying about what may never come." Grimm faded out, off to save the world, or maybe just a prince.

When Liam opened the front door, I was already waiting. Already had my coat and my purse, and the smile that came to my face at the sight of him. Not even the image of Svetlana, following him like a puppy dog, could dampen my joy.

He stood on the step and reached up to take my hand.

"What do you want to do today? We could go to the forge, do some work there. You want to have lunch on the waterfront?"

"I was thinking of looking for wedding bands. I know a jewelry store that's having a great fire sale." I tucked his hand in mine. If anything, I'd learned over the years: Happily ever after may be out there, but it doesn't come to you. So we did what any smart couple would do. We chased it.

TURN THE PAGE FOR A SNEAK PEEK AT THE NEXT
GRIMM AGENCY NOVEL

Wish Bound

COMING SEPTEMBER 2015 FROM ACE BOOKS!

WHEN I WAS a little girl, my mother used to say, "A little birthday party can't hurt anyone." She stopped saying that after my seventh birthday, when the ponies they rented stampeded. Then it was "How bad could a birthday party be?" which lasted until my tenth birthday, when the microwave oven exploded, coating everyone in melted frosting. Then it was "Let's get this over with," followed the year after by "You know, this year let's let Marissa celebrate her own way." Which meant I spent my birthdays reading alone while my parents went out for drinks.

And that's how I planned to spend my twenty-eighth birthday. Which fell on a Monday, which statistically, it does once every seven years. Mondays, in my experience, are lousy, and birthdays are even worse.

I ran to work that Monday, keeping my girlish figure looking slightly more girlish than trash-can-ish, and Liam ran with me. Liam. Almost six feet, built like a barrel, with arms like tree trunks. My fiancé. My other half. The man who'd stood by me through the end of the world. Also, a man in lousy shape.

"Marissa, could we take a break?" Liam limped along a few dozen feet back.

I learned to run earlier in my life. Run to get away from things that wanted to kill me, run to get away from things I couldn't get away from. Technically, these days I could eat the buffet and the table it came on and still not gain a pound, thanks to the gift from a harbinger of the apocalypse, Famine. Being the apocalypse bringer had its benefits, but I wasn't taking chances, so we still ran.

In case you're imagining a romantic run through the city, two lovers getting an endorphin kick to keep us ready for work, stop. We had company. A few feet behind Liam came a bombshell blonde, curvy and pale, with brilliant blue eyes and a figure that stopped hearts.

"You can run on. I will stay with my liege." Svetlana, the aforementioned beautiful disaster, waved to me. I wasn't about to leave her any more than she ever left us. Which was never. It wasn't just devotion to my fiancé, it was a form of contract. Thanks to the machinations of an evil queen and her team of assassins, Liam wound up holding a stake in, well, everything Svetlana's people owned. Given that they were all vegetarian vampires, they objected to stakes of any flavor.

I jogged in place, waiting for Liam to gain his breath.

"This is a lot easier when I have four feet," called a six-foot-eight man with curly brown hair. The head of our shipping department and full-time Big Bad Wolf, Mikey, never passed up a chance to chase people, even if he wasn't allowed to devour them. The crowd parted for him in a way that would have made Old Testament Moses envious. Crowds in the city don't move for anyone, but most folks had a healthy self-preservation instinct. "I'll see you at the office," Mikey shouted. He loped off, nearly sprinting.

We took another forty minutes to arrive, mostly due to my fiancé, partially due to a flower vendor who insisted I wanted a dahlia. What I really wanted was to shove the dahlia somewhere he'd find painful.

For the record, Liam and I had an unremarkable dinner the night before. One without candles, streamers, or balloons, with no mention of "happy birthday" or any of that nonsense. That's exactly how I liked it, exactly how I needed it to be. Parties never worked out well for me. Whether it's the hazmat team having to hose everyone down, the cake catching fire, or the wheel of evil cheese appearing in the office fridge, my birthdays went better without celebration. The end of the world was actually a couple of years ago, and having survived that, I wasn't terribly eager to do anything else to, well, kill everyone. So I didn't plan on attending my own party.

I arrived at the Agency, ran up the stairs for that final calorie-burn burst, and exploded through the front door, ready for a Monday.

Our receptionist, Rosa, hunched over a man, shocking him repeatedly with a stun gun.

I nodded to her. "Morning, Rosa."

She made the sign of the cross with her middle finger, blessing herself and telling me off in one pass, and muttered under her breath.

Since Rosa obviously had the morning crowd under control, I checked the schedule. In my office, a six-by-four mirror pulsed, glowing orange in the darkness. I had the mirror divided into slots for each day and hour, keeping a schedule that Grimm couldn't claim not to see. Monday morning. Liam had an appointment in the sewers, where a group of mud men awaited the "Final Flush." I hoped Svetlana brought her muck boots.

Mikey needed to be down at the docks, where something on a container ship kept eating the night watchmen. If you are what you eat, something had a cholesterol count that might kill it.

I looked at my name and saw the whole day blocked out without explanation.

The column next to mine looked identical.

"Morning, Marissa. Does this outfit make my eyes look more or less yellow?"

I recognized Ari's voice and couldn't help but smile. In the doorway to my office, Arianna Thromson stood, dressed in a yellow tracksuit. The yellow made her red hair look lighter, and it made the diseased, yellow, blind eyes in her head look only mildly diseased and yellow.

Arianna Thromson, my best friend. Also, princess, and witch. Don't hold those last two against her—the first you could blame on her parents, the second on an evil queen who forced Ari to use too much magic at once.

"Looks better." I looked at her dead-on, making sure she

knew that regardless of how she looked, she was still just Ari to me. "You and I have some sort of all-day engagement."

"I'm meeting Wyatt for lunch." Ari narrowed her eyes at me, then looked past me to the board. Despite the fact that her eyes had neither pupils nor irises, she could see perfectly well without them. In fact, if what you were looking for was a spirit, spell, or curse, she saw better than I did.

Ari read the schedule, then put one hand to the bracelet on her wrist. A simple gold bracelet, the key to our communication with the Fairy Godfather. "Bastard Grimm, you come here this instant." Using Grimm's first name was something even I avoided, and I outranked Ari.

The calendar faded from the mirror, and Grimm swirled into view. He adjusted his coat, looking every bit the English butler I always imagined him as. "Ladies, how may I assist you?"

"I was going to have lunch with my prince." Ari crossed her arms and tapped her foot.

Grimm took off the heavy black glasses he wore, revealing eyebrows like a yeti. "Young lady, I'm sorry. We require your assistance. I'll make it up to you. Reservations to anywhere in the city."

"What exactly are we supposed to be doing?" I went around to my desk and opened my ammo drawer.

"Marissa, you always say I never let you travel for business. I think today I'll correct that. You are going to visit another realm." Grimm's calm smile left me worried.

I'd traveled to other realms. Inferno, a few times. It was better than the Department of Licensing. I'd been to a fairy's realm as well, and would rather not go back. "Which one? Avalon? Say Avalon. Or Atlantis."

Grimm looked down. "Nowhere near as extravagant. We've suffered an influx of goblins for the last few weeks, and I would like to check the health of the realm seal."

Of course. The realm seal, if it looked like the others, was a giant ball of lightning that acted as a barrier. Grimm couldn't go himself, but that didn't mean he couldn't send others. "I don't want to go to the Forest. I want to go to Avalon."

"You don't have enough frequent-flier miles built up, but we'll talk about it afterward. Meet me at the portal in fifteen minutes." Grimm faded out.

"You'll get to shoot some goblins, and I'll be that much happier to see Wyatt tonight." That was Ari, always trying to salvage a bad situation.

"There's no point in shooting goblins. They're dumber than the bullets in my gun. As a matter of fact, I'd bet on the bullets—"

Grimm appeared in a burst of light in every reflective surface in my office. He spoke from all of them at once. "Code Mauve, Marissa. I need you immediately in my office. Alone." Grimm kept his tone calm, his eyes fixed on me. Not good.

I ran down the hall, threw open the door, ready for murder, mayhem, or destruction. The air conditioner's hum competed with the murmur of the crowds in the waiting room for loudest noise. "Yes?"

Grimm appeared in his mirror, his regular gray silk suit changed out for black, his look stern. He ignored me, keeping his eyes on the high-back chair, where I noticed two feet in penny loafers.

"Ah, so good of you to come at once." I knew the voice. Knew the man, if you could call him that.

I shut the door behind me. "Nick." Nickolas Scratch. The Adversary. King of demons, ruler of Inferno, and first-order paper pusher.

He rose from his chair, barely as tall as me, with heavy wrinkles around his eyes and a bald spot that could blind a girl. "I hate to bother you, Marissa. I really do, but I have a problem, and your driver's license doesn't expire for another two years." The Adversary's second job, at the Department of Licensing, allowed him to be truly evil.

I chose my words with care. "Anything that's bothering you is way out of my league. I'm trying to pick on things my own size." Refusing the Adversary directly could be bad, but not, in my book, as bad as agreeing to help him.

Nick walked over, putting one hand on my shoulder. "I know. I wouldn't ask, but I don't have anywhere else to turn. There's been a theft."

Grimm disappeared in a flash, leaving me alone. And for once, I didn't feel abandoned. Grimm had mastered the art of foretelling the future in a dozen ways, all of them bloody enough to make me lose my lunch. I was convinced he secretly made no effort to evict the rabbits that infested his home, because they came in handy when a quick fortune needed to be told. Right now, I needed the knowledge he'd gain from slaughtering a few bunnies as much as he did.

"Where?"

"The Vault of Souls." Nick's eyes glowed like fireside embers as he spoke. "Think of it like a bank vault, only instead of your mortgage papers, or some certificates of deposit, I keep valuable things. Mass murderers. Tyrants. Genocidal maniacs."

"Who broke out?" I slipped around the desk and sat down in Grimm's chair.

Nick's hands clenched, turning white, and he trembled with barely contained rage. "There's never been a breakout. Someone broke into Inferno and took three souls from the vault." With each word, the lights in the office flickered, as if each shadow siphoned away the light. I'd stood face-to-face with demons, dealt with the harbingers of the apocalypse, including Death himself, but the Adversary was so far out of my league I didn't even pretend to threaten him.

"The angels did it?" The angels were the only creatures I could imagine being dumb enough to mount an attack on hell itself. Now would be a great time for Grimm to make an appearance. I'd gone toe-to-toe with demons and survived, but the Adversary could squash me like a bug if I said the wrong thing.

He rumbled like a thunderstorm. Anger or laughter, I couldn't tell. "Are you kidding? They want most of the souls in the vault locked up just as much as I do. The two I want back were mine by right. Given to me freely." Blood dripped from Nick's hands as his nails cut into his palms. The blood drops burst into flames that licked the edges of his fingers.

For just a moment, my curiosity got the better of me. "Don't you have armies? You know, the sort that you'd need to bring about the end of the world?"

The Lord of Destruction looked at me over his bifocals, his eyes round. "I can't admit there's been a lapse in security. My own children would rise up against me. So, you are going to retrieve those souls. If they've been lashed into another body, you have my permission to take them apart in any way you find convenient. Death will take care of bringing them back to me at that point."

The friendly grin on Nick's face made my spine tingle. "I'm sorry. I'm your girl if you need a pair of slippers returned, or a library book, but souls? Maybe Fairy Godfather can find them and—" The words got caught and strangled in my throat as Nick began to belch black smoke and sulfur.

"You *will* do it. If I don't get them back, I'm going to start killing random people on the off chance that one of them has a soul I'm looking for. And you won't have to find the two I'm after. They're going to come for you, Marissa. I'd bet on it."

I think his final words scared me more than his threats. "Who?"

For just a moment, Nickolas Scratch looked almost concerned. "An ex-queen and her son. Both of whom have issues with you."

Where two seconds earlier I could have baked bread just by setting it on my desk, now beads of sweat formed on my head and I shivered. I knew who he meant—I had barely survived the last time she tried to kill me. Maybe they hadn't meant to get her. Maybe—

"Marissa, don't kid yourself." The Adversary crossed his arms and shook his head. "That was no accident. There were murderers in that vault a thousand times more deadly; hell, Rip Van Winkle's soul was in a Mason jar two shelves down."

I nearly died at the hands of Rip Van Winkle, Kingdom's own boogeyman. "Who was it that broke in? And who else did they take?" I couldn't have moved from Grimm's seat if I had to, wrapped in a spell of fear as I waited for an answer I dreaded.

"You should probably have that discussion with your Fairy Godfather." He rubbed his hands together, extinguishing the flames. "I'll see myself out, assuming that receptionist of yours doesn't shoot me again. If she ever wants a night job, send her over. She'll fit right in below." Nick put his clipboard under his arm and marched out, leaving scorch marks on the carpet with each step.

I can't tell you how many minutes passed until I felt Grimm's presence in the mirror at my back. I didn't speak. Didn't move. Prince Mihail and his crazy mother were some of the few people who truly deserved their spots in Inferno. The thought of them out and about, watching, waiting—that I couldn't stand.

"Marissa, I listened in on your conversation. You have a special rapport with the Adversary, and I felt it wiser to allow you to deal with him."

"Is he telling the truth?"

"Yes, my dear. I'm afraid he is. I know in the past you've been reluctant to use deadly force, but in this case, I want you to shoot first, reload, and shoot again. Leave the question asking to me." The concern in Grimm's voice only amplified my fear. The Fairy Godfather feared nothing.

"We have to take care of Ari. Prince Mihail might come for her." Mihail had meant to marry Ari. Then murder her.

"His mother won't waste time on Ari or anyone else. I would comfort you, but fear will keep you alert. Alive. I have ordered Jess released from the hospital to accompany Arianna. Anywhere you go in this realm, Liam must remain with you at all times."

The thought of half-djinn Jess roaming the streets of my city worried me almost as much as the Adversary's threats. Jess was violent death given flesh when her bipolar medication wasn't working—or when she wouldn't take it, which was most of the time. Still, nothing and no one would dare come within ten feet of Ari with Jess at her side. Which meant I could spare a moment to worry for myself.

AN URGENT KNOCK on Grimm's door roused me from my worry. Grimm himself had disappeared half an hour before, saying he needed to spend quality time divining the future. There'd be a food bank receiving donations of hasenpfeffer for days.

"Little pig, little pig, let me come in." I recognized Mikey's voice through the oak door.

"Oh, all right." I rose and unlocked the door, looking up to meet his eyes. "What?"

Mikey grabbed my arm, a move that would have earned him a silver bullet two years earlier, and dragged me along. "Emergency in the kitchen. You're in charge." He let go and sprinted off, rounding the corner like he'd just spotted a whitetail deer, or a cheerleader.

I followed him to the kitchen, throwing open the door and marching in, ready to lay down the law.

Darkness engulfed me, absolute darkness, as the door swung shut behind me, and the sounds of shallow breathing made my heart race.

"Surprise!" a hail of voices shouted, and the lights flickered on. A shiver ran from my feet to my ears. In the center of the table sat a cake with "Happy Bar Mitzvah, Joshua" written in pink gel frosting.

"I got it on clearance at the bakery." Mikey reached out and lit a candle on the cake, oblivious to the terror in my eyes.

The kitchen door opened, and Liam shouted, "What idiot brought a cake? Grimm, we need you." He banged on the wall so hard, it shook the door.

I heard the patter of light feet while I clenched my teeth and tried to look away. "It's going to be okay, M." Ari stepped forward. "Everyone out of the building. Move, people." She barked orders while I struggled to contain the wave of nausea that made the world spin when I opened my eyes.

Grimm flashed into the microwave door, glanced around the room, and glowered at Mikey. "What exactly do you think you are doing?"

"Stairs." Ari cupped her hands and shouted. "Only use the stairs. Remember what happened to the elevators last time?"

"Marissa, take a deep breath. Close your eyes." Grimm's voice calmed me, though the panic still swirled in my stomach like a gallon of cheap rum.

Liam snuffed out the candle and threw his jacket over the cake. "It's fine, M. Nothing to see here. We're all going to just go for a walk down the stairs, out onto the street, and take the day off."

In the doorway, Svetlana tossed her blond hair in a contemptuous flip. Up until that moment, I hadn't thought I could detest her more, but that one action said, "This? From her? Again?"

That's when the sprinklers went off.

Then every light in the building went out at once.

A bubbling noise filled my ears, like some monster from the depths reached up out of the sewers, bringing with it the stench of rotten sheep entrails. From the floors above and below, cries of terror and disgust echoed from vents.

"Deep breaths. Eyes closed." Liam put a rough hand on my face and pulled me toward him. "Mikey didn't know."

Mikey didn't know. Didn't know that I avoided every birthday, anniversary, wedding, or funeral for exactly the same reason. They all ended in disaster. If we were unlucky, it required the hazmat squad. If we were lucky, there'd only be a couple of feet of raw sewage flooding the building.

"Grimm, you've got to help me with this." I pushed away from Liam as the emergency lighting came on, flooding the Agency with dull red glow.

"Marissa, everyone has situations in which things do not go well. Little things, where the universe reminds them they have better ways to spend their fleeting days." Grimm spoke like a schoolteacher.

"Do you remember what happened when Ari baked me cupcakes for my birthday?"

Ari tromped back into the room, wearing yellow muck boots and carrying a matching parasol. "Asps. There were no asp eggs in the batter, Grimm. None. Would you like to guess how many cupcakes had asps in them when Marissa cut into them? What does that tell you?"

"It tells me cupcakes are bad for your figure. Now, if you don't mind—" Grimm cut off, his eyes losing focus, then snapping wide open. "Ladies, I need you to check on that realm seal immediately. There isn't a moment to waste."

I followed Ari to the back of the Agency, where Grimm kept portal runes ground into the concrete, having long ago given up any pretense of getting his security deposit returned. This birthday was turning out as bad as the rest.

"Proceed directly along the path to the Seal; contact me when you arrive. Do not waste time shooting goblins." Grimm stood in the full-length mirror, waiting. He looked to Liam. "Sir, I need your assistance as soon as the ladies have departed. We have a minor invasion to deal with."

"You got it." Liam rubbed his hands through his hair, wringing it out.

Svetlana stepped up behind him. "If my liege goes, it is my pleasure to assist."

The portal lit up like a rainbow and solidified, revealing a land that looked like a barren fall landscape.

Grimm waved his hand like a host. "This is your stop. Please keep your hands and feet inside the portal, or a team of surgeons will be required to reattach them. I will reopen the gate once we have inspected the realm seal and understand what is wrong."

Ari stepped through, appearing on the trail visible through the portal. The portal rippled and shook, like it was made of cold, clear water.

"That normal?" I studied Grimm's face.

"Not exactly. Hurry, Marissa. There's a tremor in the fabric of magic itself coming, which might strand Ari." Grimm concentrated, his eyebrows arched.

I dashed forward, ducking down, and stepped across. As I did, the building shook again, and it felt like my insides twisted like a pretzel. Then a grip like iron seized my hand. Ari screamed. Liam cursed, and I disappeared into darkness.

J. C. Nelson is a software developer and ex-beekeeper residing in the Pacific Northwest with family and a few chickens. Visit the author online at authorjcnelson.com.